AVI SIRLIN

Avi Sirlin is a Canadian writer and lawyer who grew up in Toronto. After obtaining a university degree in biology, he attended law school in Kingston, Ontario, then returned to Toronto where he established a practice in immigration and criminal law. Avi now lives on Vancouver Island in British Columbia and is currently at work on a new novel.

www.avisirlin.com

In memory of my father, Harvey Sirlin

THE
EVOLUTIONIST

by

AVI SIRLIN

Published in the UK by Aurora Metro Books in 2014.
67 Grove Avenue, Twickenham TW1 4HX
www.aurorametro.com   info@aurorametro.com

The Evolutionist © copyright 2014 Avi Sirlin
Cover Design: Paul Scott Mulvey and Cheryl Robson © 2014
Editor: Cheryl Robson

Aurora Metro Books would like to thank Neil Gregory, Richard Turk,
Suzanne Mooney, Emma Lee Fitzgerald, Hinesh Pravin, Chantelle
Jagannath and Russell Manning.

Printed in the UK by Berforts Information Press, Fareham, Hants.

ISBN: 978-1-906582-53-1

THE
EVOLUTIONIST

by

AVi SiRLiN

AURORA METRO BOOKS

CHAPTER ONE
Pará (Belém), Brazil July 12, 1852

It was plain to Alfred Wallace that the crew, many of them old salts who'd surely made numerous and sundry South American ports before, had never seen anything quite like it. This despite the opportunities afforded immediately outside the town, where boundless forest stretched to the horizon. Wallace assumed that the men's explorations had been more limited, likely confined to the wharf's nearest taverns, brothels, markets, and perhaps, for some, its churches. So while their captain sorted out another delay – the last-minute arrival of more balsam – several deckhands now gathered for what, to them, was a zoological revelation: Wallace's caged menagerie, arrayed atop the main deck like a shop display.

"Excuse me ignorance, sir," said the sailor with grey side whiskers. He crouched at a distance from the largest cage. "What is it?"

"Its scientific name is *Speothos venaticus*."

The sailor's scarlet nose crinkled and with one knobby thumb he tilted back the brim of his cap, his confusion apparent to all.

"A jungle dog," Wallace explained.

"Ah, right," said the old sailor, nodding as if his supposition had just been confirmed. He then stood aside, allowing others a better glimpse.

"Look at them short legs," said a spindly boy of not more than fifteen, clear blue eyes stark against sun-darkened skin. "And with them little ears and snout, I reckoned him more for a small brown bear."

"Oh, I can assure you that Ollie is most certainly a member of the Canid family."

"Ollie?" said the boy. "That's how you call him, Mr. Wallace?"

"I named him after Oliver Twist."

"Sir?"

"This dog was but a pitiable orphan when I first encountered him. Though wild of nature, he is quite docile and not at all adverse to a gentle hand." Wallace slipped his fingers through the wood slats. The dog raised its muzzle, snuffled, and promptly laid its head back down.

The boy crept closer and cautiously reached into the enclosure. Straining to touch the dense russet fur, he abruptly pulled back. "Them feet is webbed!"

Another deckhand peered in. "Isaac's right."

The rest of the men, semi-circled behind, began murmuring.

"Precisely what makes him of scientific interest," Wallace said. "Ollie's natural forest habitat typically consists of marsh, bogs and streams. In other words, he lives a semi-aquatic existence. The feet are a fine adaptation, wouldn't you say?"

The boy nodded uncertainly.

Ollie allowed a drawn-out yawn. Wallace reached into the cage and rubbed him above the ear.

The dog represented the final addition to what was once a considerable inventory, numbering over one hundred specimens. Through attrition and misfortune, however, his collection was now reduced to five monkeys (one mottle-faced tamarin, a red howler, two capuchins and a collared titi), along with a dozen parrots and parakeets, a macaw, and one imperturbable river tortoise.

"If you don't mind me saying it," said the grey-whiskered sailor, "the way he just lies there, curled up and all, he looks sickly."

"I should think he's in reasonable health," Wallace said. "The first fortnight of captivity he wouldn't remain still – pacing, clawing and chewing at the wood. However, after two months, he has succumbed to boredom."

"I'll wager he takes a shine to England," said the boy. "Then he'll perk up!"

"If you're fixing to bring him home with you," the old sailor said, "then you'd best hope Mr. Roland don't slip up here with his cleaver while the mongrel's unattended. Our good cook ain't so fussed about where he gets his meat."

The men hooted and roared. Then from the quarterdeck the first mate issued orders and it was all business, everyone scattering to their duties.

While the crew made their final preparations, Wallace leaned against the portside rail with its commanding view of Pará's streets. The Brazilian town had undergone significant change in the four years since he and Henry Bates first came ashore in 1848, hardly a missing or broken tile now among the red roofs of the houses. Indeed, fresh white plaster adorned many a wall, and window boxes flourished with brightly-coloured gloxinia, freesias and magnolia. Public areas had also seen extensive maintenance. White-blossomed almond trees and scarlet-flowered silk cottons now canopied newly paved streets serviced by a modern fleet of cabriolets. Squares exuded orderliness, their habitués attending to gossip and dominoes, no longer posing menace to decent citizenry. And at its farthest reaches, residences and roads sprouted where four years ago there had been only jungle; Pará now chafed against its seamless collar of greenery.

Progress? Undoubtedly. Yet having wandered its streets this past week while awaiting his departure, Wallace knew that more than a trace of old Pará lingered. The large shambling market with its sweaty denizens, treacherous peelings under foot and the vultures circling high overhead. The rotting stench that infiltrated surrounding streets, where a legion of plodding bullock carts laden with dubious carcasses clattered beneath clouds of blowflies. And notwithstanding improvements to many local edifices, pockets of neglected properties abounded, weedy pestilent gardens demarcated by rotted or broken wood palings, houses festooned with creepers and filigreed by cracks, entire armies of lizards sunning themselves, ants laying siege to every surface, every unsealed entry-point. For all that, however, Pará's signature characteristic remained the legions of men who, without apparent gainful employment, roamed the town, drunk even at midday, consorting with other morally pliable men and, sad to say, women. All of it needless. For there was no lack of work, at least not for those prepared to bear a little exertion.

How he was sick of it, all of it. How he longed for England.

The additional balsam was finally loaded into the hold, then his animals, too, were stowed. And at last they were underway, the *Helen* slowly nosing into the bay. On the wharf, among the barefoot Indian and Negro children hawking oranges, mangoes and sarsaparilla roots, a young boy of indeterminate heritage waved energetically, wood cross swaying upon his bare chest. Wallace returned the gesture, though unable to muster the same fervour.

Beneath a wide pristine summer sky, the brig steered into the current. They passed a Portuguese schooner at anchor, customs boat fastened alongside. Sandbars and islets slipped past, transmitting their rich alluvial scent, and Pará quickly receded, reduced to a distant corsage of red and white against a profusion of green. The last thing he saw, the final memory he would hold, was on the town's outskirts where he'd wandered the previous day; the plot of land teemed with white crosses.

A mile or so downriver they passed two Indians paddling a canoe filled with oranges destined for town. But there was little else of interest and when the afternoon heat built as usual, his strength drained. He trudged to the cabin and lay down.

Late afternoon he rose refreshed for the rest, enthusiastic even. Despite his usual trepidation for ocean travel, he might relish this voyage. For the first time in months, there would be no foraging through jungle, eyes and ears straining for signs of insect or bird life. No navigation or mapmaking. No supervision of manpower. No equipment repair or specimens waiting to be catalogued. No more perils or physical demands or logistics whatsoever beyond the care of his animals until they reached England in late August, some six weeks hence. Wishing to savour the occasion he went on deck for a final view of the tropics before they commenced the open sea crossing.

The vista, it turned out, was negligible. The nearest shore lay seven or eight miles distant across the yellowish water, the other invisible. At least, he thought in consolation as the mainsails snapped overhead, they were making good speed.

"Good evening, sir."

Wallace was surprised to find Captain Turner at his side. He considered the captain an agreeable sort, but noticed an air of distractedness, as though the man routinely left off amid one task to pursue another, then broke off that activity for a new one, not to return to the original matter except through some random catalyst. Odd someone of his demeanour, let alone ample girth, had come up so silently. Then Wallace caught sight of the wriggling bare toes, and a rather more unsettling vision – the pale skin was sullied with blood-red welts.

The captain followed Wallace's stare. "A ghastly spectacle, I imagine. I purchased new boots from a well-recommended boot-maker in Pará and all day I've suffered. When I went to the cabin to remove the boots, I saw you'd gotten up and thought you might be here. I worried the cabin was not to your satisfaction."

"Very kind of you, Captain, but I find it quite comfortable. I only hope my intrusion into your living quarters isn't too troublesome."

"Not at all. It is a rare pleasure to have on board a gentleman such as yourself for intelligent company. However I do regret we aren't equipped for passengers, or at least able to offer some arrangement that might allow you greater space and privacy."

"Of little concern to me, I can assure you. Expediency is my priority."

"Yes," said Turner, "I imagine in your line of work you've endured far more objectionable conditions than the shared confines of my small cabin."

"Others have known worse than I."

"Be that as it may, we are honoured to have you, sir."

"Captain, in terms of your feet, I have a useful ointment obtained from the Indians on the Rio Negro. I suspect it will furnish greater relief than any chemist's compound."

"Thank you sir, but that is entirely unnecessary. In any event, I must presently attend to the whereabouts of my first mate. I'm afraid my officers sometimes carry on as though I don't exist. However, I needn't bother you with my troubles. You've certainly earned your right to a restful voyage after all your hard work in those savage lands, so I shall leave you in peace."

Turner waddled away one heel to the next like a penguin and Wallace remained at the rail. He intended to make note of the moonrise for his journal. When the crescent finally made its appearance, so too did the young deckhand. He introduced himself as Isaac Plum and, after wishing him a pleasant evening, he enquired as to whether Ollie needed exercise.

Wallace placed his watch in his pocket. "I wouldn't want to inconvenience Captain Turner by depriving him of an able seaman such as yourself."

"Oh, you needn't have no worry, Mr. Wallace. When I've no duties, Captain Turner allows me full liberty. A kinder captain I couldn't ask for."

Wallace took account of those bright eyes and the slender hands worrying the seams of his trousers. A short time later, Ollie was tugging the lead of rope clutched by the boy. Strolling alongside, Wallace too, was well occupied. A white-breasted parrot restlessly shuttled back and forth upon his forearm.

"She's a lively bird, ain't she?" Isaac said.

"Yes, Lily seldom remains still. If I hadn't clipped her flight feathers – something I do with all the birds – I can assure you she'd be performing acrobatics atop the main mast. And she's bolder than any of the monkeys. When I take my meals, I never turn my back for fear that I shall soon find smaller portions, coffee included."

Isaac's laughter was interrupted by a barrage of squawks and Wallace lifted Lily onto his shoulder. From that vantage she dipped her beak to tease out strands of his beard while his forefinger riffled the back of her neck. Their evening ritual.

The boy tenderly rubbed one of Oliver's ears. The bush dog

didn't respond, straining forward, finding exotic scents in the weathered oak planks.

"Sir, what will become of Ollie and the other animals when we get to England?"

"With the exception of Lily, of whom I've grown rather fond, I shall sell them."

"Sell?"

"There's considerable interest in specimens of the Amazon. Through an agent I've engaged in London, some of my insects and bird skins have already been purchased by the British Museum, the Zoological Society and other public institutions, as well as various private individuals, gentlemen naturalists."

Isaac's brow furrowed. "Why would gents pay for them dead things?"

"For some, it is a hobby. But for most, it's a serious matter. At present, I dare say there exists no collection of species that may be called truly comprehensive. The full diversity of the living world – animals, insects, birds, fish, plants – is something we have only started to understand. Its detailed study is likely to yield answers to some of the natural world's most perplexing questions."

"What sort of questions?"

"Well, for instance, why would two different but similar butterfly species be found in neighbouring habitats? And why should such closely allied species exist in the first place? And by what mechanism? These are issues in which I am profoundly interested."

Ollie's paws scrabbled upon the wood as he caught the scent of something ahead.

"Regrettably, I haven't been able to ship anything abroad in three years. Most of the collection I brought aboard was to have preceded me to England, but the Brazilian customs officials had other ideas – Well, now! It appears Ollie has had some luck."

The dog had plunged into a well of coiled rope and when his snout re-materialized it was gnashing at a piece of salted beef.

"That'd be the first time Mr. Roland's grub ever met with such enthusiasm," said Isaac.

Wallace heard himself laughing. How long since he'd last done that? Perhaps the voyage would ease his mind of some of its burdens after all.

The next morning, after feeding and watering his animals, Wallace joined the captain and first mate for breakfast in the captain's dining room. Over coffee and biscuits, he sought to agreeably uphold his end of Captain Turner's discourse – this while Mr. Magnusson hammered his biscuit upon the table until it ceded fragments (which, if not entirely edible, were at least conducive to a varnish of marmalade) then, satisfied with those results, pressed forward with sawing at the unyielding sausage on his plate. A considerable distraction, given that the captain's conversation flitted like a bumblebee among the flower beds.

It began, naturally enough, with commentary about Mr. Roland's cooking (which Wallace now understood to be a regular staple of the crew's mirth) then passed onto the abject quality of Brazilian beef, the comparative cost of English meats, the rapid expansion of international trade routes, the advent of metal-hulled ships, the likely demise of square-rigged brigs in favour of steamers, the Atlantic's prevailing wind patterns, and on that related note, Mr. Wallace's snoring.

This last ricochet caught Wallace off guard – to his knowledge, though a heavy sleeper, he did not snore. But the captain, whose humour strayed on occasion into the realm of playful jest, appeared quite sincere. Wallace wished to enquire further because, truthfully, the nascent origin of his snoring intrigued him, but the subject had already vaulted onwards, in quest of the crew's loudest snorer.

Spoon abandoned upright in his porridge, Magnusson finally weighed into the fray. "Galt," growled the first mate.

Wallace knew the mate referred to the sailor with grey side whiskers.

"That old man," said Magnusson, "snores worse than a braying donkey."

With his appetite lacking sufficient hardiness to allow much progress against his breakfast, and Turner and Magnusson now launched into the comparative merits of English versus Scandinavian crews, Wallace took his leave.

That afternoon he took his sketchbook onto the deck, intent upon capturing the receding contours of the Brazilian coastline as they made open sea. However, when the vessel encountered a steady chop his stomach turned to sand and he retreated to the cabin. He started a letter, but soon the familiar heaviness seeped into his joints. Wallace abandoned his pen and unrolled his mattress. And despite the room's warmth, he pulled a woollen blanket up to his chin when he lay down.

He woke with a start. The oil lamp above the desk was lit. He realized that while he'd slept the Captain must have returned then gone out again. His nightshirt was damp with sweat, so he removed the blanket. He quickly found himself shivering.

The fever broke after three days. A short reprieve. As with his ordeal at São Joaquim a half-year ago, he succumbed again. He took his usual medicines, along with a bitter potion the ship's carpenter attested as efficacious against the most resolute fevers. As expected, none helped. Too weak to leave the cabin for anything but an occasional short foray to the galley, he was grateful that Isaac watered and fed his animals

– without promise of any pay beyond their companionship. The rest of the crew also did their part: they took to depositing Roland's breakfast biscuits with the birds, who then spent the balance of the day chipping away at the bricks. In the case of Ollie, by then unofficial mascot of the *Helen*, the lad gave her regular walks.

No enterprise requiring his own attention, one day melted into the next, the monotony of his confinement wearing on him. He kept up his journal, and for fresh reading, the captain brought him nautical books. But his mind was prone to wander. With all his specimens, botanical samples and indigenous artefacts – an adequate collection, if not everything he had wished for – he anticipated reasonable sales in England. From the notes, journal and sketches he would publish a travel narrative, perhaps replicating the success of Charles Darwin. This in addition to his planned publications on the fishes of the Rios Amazon and Negro, a book on Amazonian palms, and his annotated maps. The combined income from these ventures would permit him to settle down. He imagined a country house with gardens of hardy English ornamental shrubs, mosses and ivies, and a conservatory where he would grow his beloved orchids. There would be a good-sized study, with oak cabinets bearing the finest private collection of Amazonian insect and bird specimens to be found in all of Europe, an attraction drawing distinguished visitors for amiable and lively afternoon discussions. And should there arise times such as these, when he was temporarily felled by illness, there would be the tender ministrations of a wife, for he was almost thirty years old and with his new-found stability, surely the time was ripe.

A few days later, with perhaps a fortnight's sail before they reached England, Wallace was propped on his bedroll late one morning, making a journal entry. His shirt clung damp against his back – the fever had not yet fully abated and the day's heat was already building inside the cabin. He had dipped his pen into the ink bottle when the cabin door flung open. Captain Turner entered, mouth hanging open as if to make an announcement. Wallace lowered his pen, attentive. In the moment before the captain spoke, Wallace heard a distant commotion – men shouting and stamping across the *Helen*'s deck, capering about from the sound of it – and it seemed to him the captain maintained little control aboard his own vessel.

"I shouldn't wish to cause undue alarm, Mr. Wallace," Turner finally said. "But I'm afraid the ship is on fire."

CHAPTER TWO
Mid-Atlantic, August 6, 1852

Wallace struggled into his trousers and boots. The fever had weakened him and he stumbled out of the cabin in pursuit of Captain Turner. On deck, all hands had gathered by the fore hatch, where black smoke curled skyward. The men's voices dropped upon the captain's approach.

"Mr. Magnusson, have we identified the source?"

The broad-shouldered first mate removed the pipe from his lips and pointed at the hatch. "You can smell it real easy, Cap'n. It's the *piassaba*. That extra balsam we stowed must've got it going."

"So why are you lot standing around as if it were a stew pot simmering with your dinner?" Turner exclaimed.

There was some murmuring, but no movement.

The imperturbable Magnusson took a draught from his pipe then he said, "The *piassaba* smokes, ya, but we got no fire – "

"Not yet!" Turner's head swivelled as he stared at his men, signalling his disbelief. "Mr. Magnusson, Mr. Bateman, have the men open the hatch and douse the *piassaba* before we have a conflagration!"

"With respect, Cap'n," said Magnusson. "The main hold, she's jammed tight, so she got pretty near no air. Soon as that air gets used up – *pffffttt*! – no more worry. But we open that hatch, well, then we got a real fire."

The first mate's wisdom appeared sound to Wallace. The flammable balsam resin was susceptible to self-combustion – the very reason its casks were stored in sand – and presently the *piassaba* only smouldered. Depriving the hold of oxygen seemed the best chance to avoid an all-out blaze.

"No, no, no!" Turner roared. "I refuse to enter the annals as a captain who stood idly while his ship burnt to a cinder!"

Most of the crew were soon ferrying pails of water. Two hands prepared the lifeboats, just in case. Isaac, however, slipped away.

"Mr. Plum!" Turner called from the quarterdeck. "What are you doing?"

The boy broke his stride amidships and the mottle-faced tamarind he carried toppled into the side of its cage. "Mr. Wallace's animals might choke down there, Captain!"

The captain glanced in Wallace's direction, rubbed his chin, then nodded. Isaac set the cage down and sprinted after the next one.

In a few minutes thick smoke from the fore hatch constrained the crew from going below. Turner ordered the aft hatch open so the bulkhead between the two holds could be broken and they might resume their firefight. But when the axe blades smashed through, fresh air funnelled in and the *piassaba* sizzled. Ensuing pails of water had no effect. A great crackling was heard.

Wallace foresaw the impending combustion. He tottered below deck, steadying himself against the walls. All the specimens and journals he'd accumulated these past three years were in the aft hold. To that point, with the fire concentrated in the forward hold, his collection likely remained undamaged. Salvageable. Instead, he hobbled towards the cabin.

He entered the room blind, eyes squeezed tight against the smoke. His lungs burned and his throat spluttered. Groping about, he eventually landed his fingers on the tin box at the foot of his bedroll. In it were some shirts, a set of Amazonian drawings, a small notebook, his coin purse and assorted papers. He snatched it up and fumbled his way out. His head, his chest, both screamed for oxygen. He reeled.

Captain Turner was standing over him.

"I say, are you all right?"

Wallace realized he'd dropped onto the quarterdeck, making a most frightful spectacle of himself. "I'm fine, captain, quite fine. I just returned from the cabin and merely need – " He barked to clear his lungs. "I merely need fresh air is all."

"Jolly good, I'm relieved to hear that," Turner said. "And I'm pleased to report we've put the worst behind us. I suspect you shall have the pleasure of your quarters in short order."

Wallace noticed a dense black cloud obscuring the foredeck. Deckhands shuttled among the hatches, their sloshing buckets spilling as much as they dispensed. He did not share the captain's optimism.

Indeed, the men's valiant battle came to an end within the hour. The fire spread to the aft hold; with thirty-four tons of Cuban lumber stowed, there would be no stopping it now. The captain ordered all hands to make ready the lifeboats. The crew rummaged their berths, the stores, carpentry and galley, hauling out various wooden barrels, casks, crates, baskets, duffel bags, burlap sacks, swathes of canvas, oilskins, blankets and coils of rope. All destined for the long-boat on the starboard side and the captain's gig at the transom. Once again however, Isaac seemed bent on his own task.

"Mr. Plum," Captain Turner called out. "I understand your concern. Regrettable as it may be, we have limited space in the boats. The animals will have to fend for themselves and if — Mr. Plum! Stop that!"

Isaac was opening the cage latches. One after another, Wallace watched his parrots and parakeets hop out of their crates and onto the warmed planks, fluttering uselessly with their clipped wings. The collared titi, placid keyhole face giving no impression of panic or haste, briefly paused to pick at something in its thick coat, loped sideways a short distance, then sprang atop the forecastle deck where it made a dash towards the prow. Bent under a heft of cordage, a tall Negro sailor nearly tumbled when the reddish blur streaked past his knees.

No matter the titi and the birds, the remaining monkeys, the somnolent tortoise and Ollie refused to budge from their pens, as though each apprehended the nearby danger. Isaac knelt before the dog's cage and reached inside.

"C'mon, Ollie. It's all right."

The dog yowled and resisted, forelegs rigid as stanchions, hind paws back pedalling.

"Mr. Plum!"

"Captain Turner, please let me bring him. Upon me father's grave, I swear he won't be any bother. I'll feed him from me own rations. There won't be no trouble, you've seen him, he's gentle as a lamb."

The captain lifted his hat and scratched away at his sparsely populated scalp. That instant, perhaps catching the scent of the absconding monkey or simply sensing salvation there, Ollie bolted. Isaac pivoted, ready for pursuit, but the lash in

Turner's voice froze him.

"Mr. Plum, to the stern. Now!"

Isaac complied.

Tin box pressed to his chest, Wallace thought of his specimens below. Thousands collected. Three years of toil.

Turner bellowed, "Everyone to the lifeboats!"

Wallace's chest tightened. But he turned and followed the young deckhand. He arrived alongside Isaac at the stern and with his free hand clenched the rail. He willed himself to peer down. Twenty feet below, the Captain's gig bobbed like an empty rum bottle – one that was rapidly filling.

Lowered only minutes earlier, the boat lay partly submerged, seawater gurgling through its seams. The tall Negro sailor and the carpenter, Appelboom, both frantically bailed with only a pail and a pewter mug between them. Meanwhile, Bateman, the trout-faced second mate, foraged for the boat's rudder amid all the food barrels, ropes, oars and tar sheets, everything hastily strewn before the boat was lowered.

Wallace could not imagine himself in such an unreliable vessel. He was about to say as much to Isaac, but the boy clambered quick as a monkey over the rail and down the rope ladder. Wallace stared after him, immobile. The lifeboat nodded at him drunkenly.

"Mr. Wallace, sir!"

The boy called out for the metal box.

Wallace tossed it down, landing it upon the sail. Then he took hold of the ropes and tried to swing a leg over the rail. His limbs wobbled. He could bring himself to go no further.

He'd never flourished on water. Over the years, he'd learned to sufficiently tolerate streams, rivers, lakes – anywhere he could see shoreline. The Atlantic crossing – an unavoidable aspect of his chosen calling – had been a great strain on his constitution.

AVI SIRLIN

On both the outward bound passage from Liverpool and now from Pará, with or without fever, he'd stayed below as much as possible once they passed out of land's sight. There was solace in that formidable cradle of oak and iron. But as he stood astern and surveyed that unlimited horizon, all that endless water, the lifeboat below looked like a mere plaything. A dubious one, at that.

"It's all right, sir!" called Isaac. "Them leaks you see is from planks that been shrunk in the sun. But she'll be fine and swelled up in no time."

That the boy noticed his timidity mortified him. Wallace again gripped the ropes, his palms sweating, and lifted himself over. The coiled fibre felt warm and smooth as he lowered himself hand over hand. From below, the men's voices washed up and during the lulls, he heard the rumble of the ocean.

He had descended a third of the distance when his left foot slipped. For a moment his boot paddled the air and he remained suspended there a dozen feet above the water line, the tug of gravity not yet exerting itself. Indeed, his right hand almost held him – and it might have were he not so spent by fever – but he couldn't re-establish his foothold fast enough. Momentum wrenched him down. His right hand skidded against the rope, then it released. There was no more friction.

He tumbled through air, head over feet.

In the boat below, the second mate was sloshing his way towards the stern. He had fished out the rudder and, unaware a certain English gentleman plummeted in his direction, Bateman now held the blade skyward.

"Look out!" Isaac shouted.

Neither Wallace nor Bateman was aware of what he should be looking for.

The rudder clipped Wallace's hat and he crashed upon the

canvas sail. Right next to his tin box. No one said anything for a moment or two, then there was a tumult of voices. Wallace gathered himself onto the nearest thwart, sopping wet. His body thrummed. More disconcerting was the alarm he'd registered.

"You all right, sir?" Bateman asked.

Wallace managed a shaky smile. "No, harm. Just a good soaking."

"If that be the case, sir," said Robinson, the Negro, "I'm much appreciating it if I can rest a spell." He extended the pewter mug he'd been using to bail out the tiny rig.

Wallace nodded and took the mug, eager to engage in a task that might deflect attention. It would also distract his focus from the expanse of sea. He plunged the tankard into the water that swirled about his shins. A jolt of pain nearly shocked him off his seat. His right hand burned as if bathed in acid. He glanced at his palm. The skin was shredded, the membrane beneath glistening like raw salmon.

Wallace gingerly wrapped his handkerchief around the wound. With the water still rising and only the five of them to look after the myriad chores there could be no question as to his obligations. He bailed with his uninjured hand. When that arm grew exhausted and tears pocketed his eyes and streamed into his beard, he took a brief turn with the damaged hand, stifling his cries. Perhaps the others apprehended his distress, but each attended his own duty with solemn concentration.

As they went about their work, each man periodically glanced up for signs of Turner. Alone, the captain had remained aboard the *Helen*. Wallace wondered if what he'd presumed as a myth – that captains always went down with their ships – was an inviolable mariner's code. But Turner eventually descended and ordered them to cast off.

They rowed to ship's starboard where the long-boat with first mate Magnusson and the remaining crew awaited them. They lashed the two lifeboats together and Turner conferred with his officers. Meanwhile Appelboom had located some corks and with Robinson, they jammed them into the worst gaps in the hull.

After his caucus, Turner announced, "We shall remain in the *Helen*'s vicinity for as long as she burns. The flames might well attract another ship."

The crew rowed the twinned lifeboats far enough to avoid the collapse of burning shrouds, booms, stays and masts. Then they watched and waited.

The fate of the animals wasn't clear at first. They'd been presumed asphyxiated or incinerated. However when flames erupted on the forecastle and launched halfway up the mast, seven or eight birds materialized on the bowsprit. Among the flock, Wallace saw Lily. Her wings flapped for balance and she stretched her neck, head swivelling, as if sizing up her escape route. From behind the bowsprit, without warning, periodic cinders catapulted through the air, sizzling into the sea.

Wallace chewed his lip as he watched Lily. The past four years, how many birds had he killed? Hundreds, certainly. And his only remorse pertained to those birds that eluded him – to the tune of four pence each. Now, with Lily retreating along the spar, he regretted not only abandoning her upon the *Helen*, but that he'd clipped the feathers that enabled her to fly.

Isaac leapt to his feet. "Ollie! I see Ollie!"

Bateman yanked the boy down by the shoulder, but everyone kept keen watch. The scruff of Ollie's head, and occasionally his forelegs, could just be made out. The dog was struggling to clamber atop one of the bowsprit bitts, apparently seeking to follow the birds.

"Mr. Wallace, you was saying Ollie is semi-aquatic," said Isaac. "Do you not think if we draw up and call out to him, maybe he'll jump into the water and we can rescue him?"

"We'll do no such thing," Turner said. "I will not allow my boats to be placed in peril for a dog. I am sorry, Mr. Plum – and Mr. Wallace." The captain mopped his face. However, his skin remained anointed with the sweat and soot that begrimed them all. Wallace and the crew had shed their jackets, but Turner remained buttoned to the collar, as if it were a sign of office, as though his authority would perish in its absence. Isaac and the other crew glanced at Magnusson, silently appealing to the first mate to plead their case.

"Attempted rescue would be futile in any event," said Turner. "You can hear for yourselves."

The *Helen*'s foresail was muttering. Quickly engulfed, the canvas thrashed, the flames leaping to the higher sails. As the fire whooshed and crumpled, Ollie, now lost from view, had set up a howl. By the time the sails incinerated, Ollie's plaintive call had stopped.

No one spoke. Not when the foremast crashed down. Not even when a muffled explosion aboard the brig launched a fountain of balsam resin forty feet into the air, showering the sea with embers. Bound together, the two boats drifted further astern, none of the oarsmen bothering to prevent their course.

"Away to starboard!" cried Magnusson.

A charred yard arm washed toward the long-boat, threatening to stave it broadside. The men grunted, uttering oaths disproportionate to their modest effort, and the boats veered free.

By then the fire had advanced upon the bowsprit. Three or four of the birds perched there inexplicably hopped directly into the fire. Left upon the tapering spar were a chestnut-crested antbird, a blue parrot and Lily. The antbird called out *wheeu–whew–whew–whew* and dropped among the waves, disappearing. And perhaps it was a wind gust, or build-up of heat, or fatal resignation – whatever the cause, the blue parrot and Lily quickly followed the antbird to the sea.

Wallace balled his injured hand into a fist. The pain came in a rush, flushing through him. Then with his sleeve, he wiped his eyes dry. A few minutes passed with little sound but the crackle of fire and the slap of waves against the hull.

Then Robinson shouted, "I see the bird!"

Beyond the *Helen*'s bow, upon another severed yardarm, lay a white-feathered bundle.

Wallace was astonished to hear his own voice. "That's Lily! We must save her!"

It couldn't be said whether Captain Turner would have ordered otherwise, but before he had a chance, from the long-boat Magnusson added his own voice, "Row, you tars! Row!" The next moment, every blade was pulling. Captain Turner might have wondered whether he had a minor mutiny on his hands. Had he chosen to countermand Magnusson's command he would have learned, but he remained silent.

With the fire snickering and popping, their twinned vessel navigated the waterborne detritus and drew alongside the drifting spar. It was old Galt in the long-boat who scooped Lily up and handed her over. Wallace cradled her carefully.

"Is she alive then, Mr. Wallace?" asked Bateman, peering over his shoulder.

Wallace gently ruffled the tuft above Lily's beak. Her breast was still rising and falling and he saw no visible injuries. He nodded.

"Hurrah!" cheered the men.

"One parrot ought not to be too much inconvenience, I

suppose," said Turner.

For a brief period, the two crews bantered cheerfully and bailing proceeded without so much as a single profanity.

Then without so much as a squawk, Lily died. An internal injury or shock, or both, Wallace suspected.

It would have been uncharacteristic for any of his companions, even Isaac, Wallace imagined, to grieve the loss of a bird. Most of them were hard-travelled men; Bateman, Robinson and Galt had all survived shipwreck, he'd learned. Indeed, every last one had witnessed fatalities at sea. Added to that, a grim night aboard the tiny vessels lay ahead. So Wallace thought the men generous of spirit for the sobriety that settled upon the boat.

They passed the remainder of the afternoon quietly. Despite the fiery spectacle, they seldom glanced at their brig, preferring to search the horizon for sign of approaching vessels and guard against hazardous debris or, in Wallace's case, monitor the water level inside the lifeboat. In early evening, fully engulfed by flames, the *Helen* rolled to starboard. The inferno lit the sky for miles, sometimes flaring high enough to blot out the stars emerging overhead.

The night remained clear. When the flames subsided, Wallace and Isaac identified constellations. For a short time, a pod of perhaps forty dolphins swam abreast their craft and everyone fell silent at the spectacle.

No one slept. The sodden clothing and blankets, the cramped quarters, the dissonant sizzle and crashing of cindered wood a hundred feet distant, the constant chop that snapped a drooping neck off chest or shoulder, the desultory gulp and sploosh of the men who bailed throughout the night – old Galt regularly thumping his tin pot against the gunwale no matter the angry protests – everyone's thoughts gummed in their own uncertainty.

For his own part, Wallace's mind lingered upon the vastness of the black sea, the suspect planking that floated him above those depths, and the likelihood that wind and waves might combine to pitch them all to the abyss. He was a poor one for the water, certainly, but what difference would there be were he some champion swimmer? It was hundreds of miles to the nearest shore, were he even to know which direction to take. The bottom of the sea or even a shark's jaws would surely come sooner. To distract himself he tuned his ears to the metronomic expulsion of water – tiny splashes swallowed by the voracious groan of the deep. He found comfort in the steady rhythms, much as he did with the rustle of trees in the forest. He recalled how, when he and Henry Bates first arrived in Brazil, they would take their evening coffee on the veranda and listen to the wind in the trees. How it sounded nothing like England. A primal life force, a terrestrial lung. The Amazon's warm breathing.

Bates was still back there. In the Amazon. Their plan – their joint plan – had been to stay at least five years. But for himself, four had proven more than enough. As to how long Henry might remain, who was to say? They'd not seen each other for better than two years. Before that, sporadic contact. On this expedition he'd come to realize how, much like the Amazon itself, the bonds of friendship comprised an odd landscape. At a distance, its contours appeared predictable as one benign mass. Yet for all its quotidian days of travel and joyful hours of exploration, its true nature was fraught with, and ultimately defined by, acute moments of revelation. And, he learned, this applied with no less force to the bonds of brotherhood.

CHAPTER THREE
Neath, Wales, March 1845

The door to the Castle Hotel swung open and John Wallace burst in, panting for breath. Strands of dark hair had fallen across his forehead. He swept them back into place as he scanned the room, eyes adjusting to the lobby's low light. Despite the day's chill his coat hung open and from the far corner, undetected as yet, Alfred Wallace observed the heaving barrel chest of his older brother. More than a year since they'd last seen each other, John had grown as sturdy as the houses he helped build. Every bit a man of action. Himself? A schoolmaster's physique, unfortunately. Suffering for lack of exertion. Wallace sighed and hoisted his aching haunches off his plush chair. The jarring overnight coach journey from Leicester that deposited him at the inn a half-hour earlier had drilled the road deep into his bones.

"Alfred! There you are." John came striding over, arms open. "Terribly sorry I'm late."

Wallace feared his burly sibling would embrace him – something their sister Fanny was wont to do, but without the attendant risk of snapping his spine. Instead, John reached round to clap him on the back. They exchanged smiles, but there was no gladness, not in any of it. John's eyes were red.

"As you can tell," John said, "much as I tried, I was unable to pry mother away to come greet you. Herbert also stayed behind, to keep her company."

"Where...?" Wallace searched out John's face.

John nodded. "With William. Mother wishes to remain with him until his interment."

It had been John who'd notified him of their brother's death. Rapid onset of pneumonia. Leicester College granted leave and he caught last night's coach to Neath, the southern Welsh town that served as periodic base for William's surveying business.

With John's hand at his elbow, they left the hotel to join their mother's vigil.

Mother's watch did not end until the next day, in the cemetery. The grass was damp and spongy from morning rain and the blustery sky threatened more. Beards of moss clung to headstones. Wallace shivered against the cold and wind in his black wool coat. His mother stood between John and Herbert, seemingly impervious. She had previously buried four daughters and her husband. Yet she remained rigid, unblinking. Wallace understood what was therefore required of him.

As the cemetery workers lowered the coffin, the rain started. It spattered the box, drumming it into its open grave. Whether it was the rain striking the coffin or sheer exhaustion, his mother closed a gloved hand over her mouth and fell against John's broad shoulder. It was then that Herbert chose to recite a poem, his own composition. The rain fell harder and Wallace heard only snatches of his younger brother's verse. The reedy voice was unfamiliar. Before he'd left home, Herbert had been a modest presence in the household. A born dreamer, their mother called him. Now fifteen, for the past year Herbert had been living in London, riveting brass latches onto steamer trunks. Work for which he was ill-constituted, their sister Fanny had warned in her letters home. Indeed, Wallace observed now how bony ridges and deep-set eyes carved an eternal mournfulness into Herbert's features. It wasn't hard for him to imagine the brief speech their father had made to Herbert preceding that vocational placement. He himself had been the recipient of just such a talk two days after Christmas 1836. Summoned to the front room of the family's cramped quarters, he'd stood in front of his father's upholstered chair. In the fireplace, damp wood hissed and crackled.

A pipe stem protruded from the pocket of his father's smoking jacket and his father tapped it as he spoke. "Alfred, you shall soon be fourteen. An age of manly responsibility."

His mother helped him pack.

A brief stay in London with his brother John, then he found himself travelling the countryside north of the city, acquainting himself with William, fourteen years his senior, who had heard their father's speech regarding manly responsibility when Alfred was but an infant.

Huddled against the rain now, he pictured William. How handsome he had been! Wallace remembered farm houses where his brother had stood with the tenant farmer, the daughters hidden in the next room but staring from the doorway, eyes fixed upon the surveyor, those sharp cheekbones and the squared jaw, eyes and mouth purposeful yet friendly. Sometimes it would be the baker's wife. Or a young woman who shared their coach compartment between towns, face turned to the window, eyes darting sidelong when she believed William unaware. Wallace craved similar glances, but they never fell his way. Those years, many nights he lay in bed imagining the farmer's daughter or the baker's wife or the stagecoach companion staring at him, wanting him. He imagined their hands sliding over his body, caressing him. Then, in silence so as not to awaken William across the room, he stroked himself. And yet, even as pleasure surged, his gratification was doused, undone by the belief it was not deserved.

Hours after the funeral, with mother finally resting in her room, he and John retrieved William's belongings from his boarding house. Back at the inn, they reviewed their brother's business ledgers. The records were meticulous. When they'd finished, John's face was flushed. He got up and paced the room like a stalking bear. "It's a bloody fortune, he's owed."

"What do you suggest?" Wallace replied. "That we resign our salaried positions and pursue William's creditors in the faint hope we can extract payment where he could not?"

"Alfred, do you not read the papers? Everywhere you look, they're building railways. Three thousand miles of new track this year alone. And you know who they need for that, don't you? Surveyors. And builders. Quite the coincidence, don't you think? That description fitting the pair of us to a T. Why not make use of our training?"

Wallace couldn't deny his brother's logic. Against that he weighed his secure teaching income.

"Pardon?"

John had said something.

"Manly responsibility," John repeated. "You recall? Only this wouldn't be an empty speech. We'd be our own masters. Soon as the business is going well and proper, we could get a house. Once Fanny hears of that, I guarantee she'll book her passage home."

"The family under one roof?" Wallace realized that would truly be a marvel. Something their father had been unable, or unwilling, to accomplish. And a Leicester College stipend would never yield such a house.

He resigned his teaching post. In Neath, he and John lodged with a family named Sims. An uncle of Mr. Sims offered the brothers surveying work in Swansea. New contracts followed. By autumn 1846, a year and a half after William's death, the brothers were renting a comfortable stone home on Neath's northern outskirts, one mile from the centre. The valley below carried the scent of autumn apples and revealed a mountain vista. Mother moved in. She helped plan the garden for spring. Herbert was next, happy to be free of the luggage-maker. Finally, Fanny wrote to inform them she would return to Britain next summer.

The family's fortunes had never run so high.

But then the surveying projects began to slow. And Herbert missed London's amusements. Despite assurances that no better fun could be had in the whole vicinity, he declined opportunities to join Wallace in his new hobby, one he'd adopted in Leicester after befriending a young man named Henry Walter Bates.

"You're not serious?" Herbert exclaimed. They stood in the garden, Wallace in straw hat and canvas trousers, burlap sack slung over one shoulder. "You're suggesting I venture out dressed like a mudlark and muck about all day picking up bugs?"

"Beetles, not bugs," Wallace replied. "The mouth parts differ – "

"I'd rather write poetry," Herbert said.

And with that, a gloom settled upon the house. Unable to find a job, Herbert slouched over his journal, went for long walks, and consorted with the town's theatre players. Mother fretted that Herbert shouldn't be prodded too harshly by his brothers lest he flee to London.

By August, when Fanny arrived from America, she encountered a different household than the one described in her brother Alfred's glowing letters. Wallace Brothers Surveying had altogether run out of work. Mother was now contemplating hiring herself out as housekeeper, John was talking of trying his hand at dairy farming, and Herbert found enthusiasm for nothing except sleep: John had found him employment at the local iron works. As for Wallace, he gained solace in but two things: the renewed presence of his doting sister, and the near daily lists of field specimen captures he and Henry Bates traded by mail.

To revive everyone's flagging spirits, Fanny offered to take the family to Paris. The opportunity was not universally embraced. Mother insisted she had no interest in tramping upon foreign soil. Herbert longed to see Paris, but was constrained by employment obligations. The remaining two Wallace brothers? Undeniably at their leisure.

Persistent rains that visited Paris that September made it easier for Wallace to entice John and Fanny into an afternoon at the Natural History Museum. Specimen by specimen, row upon row, display cabinet after display cabinet. Entire rooms devoted to methodical classification of the animal kingdom. Mammals. Birds. Amphibians. Reptiles. Insects segregated from spiders and scorpions, from mites and ticks, from centipedes and millipedes. Flatworms, roundworms, segmented worms, all distinguished. Family, genus, species. For Wallace, everything in its place, plainly identified with nothing missing, a most satisfying feeling instilled him, like sunlight warming bone on a winter's day.

"Surely not more!" Fanny exclaimed.

"Surely not more what?" Wallace asked, genuinely stumped.

They'd just entered another gallery. Glass-faced cabinets ringed the walls and a back-to-back column filled the room's middle. Fanny's slender face pinched tight as she adjusted her shawl. "It's been a rather full afternoon. Perhaps we might now conclude our visit?"

John, standing next to Fanny, suddenly found something on the floor that required his fastidious attention.

"But we've just come to the beetle collection," Wallace said.

"Precisely my point. Look at them," Fanny's hand swept round the gallery. "One might squander days here. Thousands upon thousands, each virtually identical to the other."

Wallace tried to read his sister's expression. No one in his family understood him better than Fanny. Even during her teaching tenure in America, they'd continued to confide in each other, the letters frequently extending to several pages. And yet, time and again, she utterly puzzled him. Certainly she sounded weary now, but at the same time she'd just raised the very issue that augured for a more detailed examination, not less. He could only state the obvious.

"Fanny, we may never again see such a range of specimens from around the globe. Those minute variations which distinguish each – a different mandible, thorax, colouration, antennae, etcetera – only beg the question Why? Are you not curious?"

"Curious? Oh, that I am. The problem is I'm curious to see most everything. And at this rate, we'll know little of the city beyond our hotel, the café next to our hotel, and thousands upon thousand of your creeper crawlers." Fanny paused. When she resumed speaking her voice was gentle. "Alfie, we're in Paris."

Again Wallace looked to his brother, but John merely shrugged. "I acknowledge we're in Paris. Have I not already expressed delight at the tree-lined boulevards and paved promenades? The charming cafés and shops? The numerous parks? I believe I have. All I wished to indicate was that the British Museum's zoological collection pales in comparison, and thus the displays here warrant an additional day."

"A whole day?" Fanny exchanged glances with John. "So I take it that whilst John and I attend both the Notre-Dame Cathedral and the Louvre tomorrow, you wish to resume your visit here unimpeded by our presence?"

There was the shade of a smile on Fanny's face. Almost enough to make him suspect she wished to deliberately confound him. "The Louvre?"

Fanny nodded.

They reached an accommodation. The next day, prior to the three of them convening at the Louvre and while his brother and sister toured the cathedral, Wallace studied beetles. Fanny had been right: there were thousands. He reflected on the dozens of species he and Henry Bates had collected in Leicestershire, and those he'd later added in Neath. It occurred to him that each specimen he presently examined had been captured by someone in the field. Not necessarily a lettered entomologist – perhaps someone not unlike himself or Bates. But these men had been rewarded financially for each capture, deriving an income while in the noble service of public education. How splendid that would be, he thought. And there was the exotic travel, encounters with different cultures, tropical climates, plus flora and fauna unknown in Britain. It brought to mind the exhilarating descriptions of South America by the famous explorer Alexander von Humboldt. And more recently, the

American William Henry Edwards wrote about his expedition along the Amazon. He and Bates had discussed both men's exploits at length.

But what would elevate such travels beyond the realm of high adventure was service in the name of science. Wallace recalled Charles Darwin's *Voyage of the Beagle*. A five-year expedition. However, Darwin was a gentleman naturalist. He had no need for revenue. Wallace imagined what it might be like to earn a living and at the same time accumulate data as did Darwin. Above all, to investigate the mechanism responsible for all these variations. He'd recently read a controversial book about transmutation theory, but it provided no persuasive answer. Work on the subject would have to proceed without any assurance it would yield an answer. But that, Wallace realized, assured a certain purity to the challenge. It demanded of oneself not only time and effort, but faith. Wallace glanced at his pocket watch. It was time for him to go.

He turned his ideas over for a few weeks after his return to England. He then discussed it with the family. The railway boom was over, surveying work had stagnated. Herbert, while miserable at the ironworks, remained the only one among them earning wages. Neath was not so large that employment was readily available. In other words, they would soon once again disperse. Which lent more credibility to his idea.

His affable chum Henry Bates had recently complained of the drudgery in his new clerical position at Allsop & Sons' brewery in Staffordshire. How each evening he climbed aboard a homebound train with ink-stained hands and the odour of fermented malt clinging to his coat. How he longed for something, anything, more worthwhile in the doing.

What Wallace had in mind was not only an opportunity to

build something of a nest egg, but also to make their mark. He wrote Henry immediately.

My Dear Bates,

I recall your visit to Neath when you mentioned how pleasing it might be to collect specimens somewhere unfamiliar. Well, I too begin to feel rather dissatisfied with a mere local collection. I should like to make a more thorough study, principally with a view to the theory of the origin of species. Thus, I have a proposition ...

CHAPTER FOUR

Pará, June 1848

If pressed to describe his first days in the Amazon, Wallace would have confessed to not a little disappointment. After an uneventful passage from Liverpool – uneventful allowing for the panic and nausea that largely confined him to his berth – he and Henry Bates descended onto the quay at Pará anticipating nothing less than a profusion of natural splendour. Why not? Such was the depiction by the renowned explorers Humboldt and Edwards, whose travel chronicles Wallace and Bates had repeatedly feasted upon before setting out. They'd even managed to negotiate a meeting with Mr. Edwards in London shortly before their departure. The gentleman assured them of bountiful wildlife and botanical opportunities. Riches awaited.

The mendacious charlatan!

Initial excursions revealed not a solitary monkey cavorting, snake slithering, parrot preening or single insect worth pinning. Mango trees, yes. And ants in abundance, granted. But how was one to make commerce upon that? As for lizards, they too were plentiful and interesting, but even when they appeared asleep – sunning themselves on a rock or upon a low wall – some singular animalistic faculty informed them of the clod-hopping European intent upon their capture and they shot away, leaving that pale and sweating oaf grasping at air. Maddening.

As for the town? To Wallace's eyes, most of those without respectable businesses in Pará gambled, drank, whored and expended no more energy than would permit them the next day's depravity. Precisely why he arranged with Mr. Daniel Miller, the British consul (for whom Wallace felt great sympathy at such a posting), that Bates and he take possession of a pleasant yet unoccupied country house a mile and a half outside of town. Throughout the vicinity there were similar homes, all owned by Europeans. After a spasm of political violence some dozen years back, Europeans of any means preferred the security of Pará. Well, he and Bates had no wealth to protect and he despised the town, so the choice was rather easy, he thought. Bates played devil's advocate for a brief time, arguing the social advantages of Pará, but really there was no doubt. The house offered a broad veranda with unbroken forest surrounding three sides, including hundreds of miles of walking paths. Finally, they might undertake serious work.

And serious work demanded routine.

Each day at dawn their cook, Isidoro, prepared their coffee while Wallace and Bates assembled their equipment, all of which had been cleaned and, if necessary, repaired the previous night. For each, a shotgun, nets, machete and leather satchel with insect boxes, wrapping papers, skinning and cleaning implements, and numerous other tools of the trade which they added or subtracted as circumstances and experience dictated. By the time all was ready, Isidoro had prepared a hearty breakfast, after which they marched into the forest.

They worked until the hottest part of the day. On their way home they typically stopped for a plunge in a nearby stream. Reclined in the shallows beneath the overarching canopy, each pointed out upon the other's pallid flesh that day's cuts, abrasions and insect or spider bites – along with perhaps some newly acquired leech.

By the time they lay recumbent in fresh clothes upon their hammocks on the back veranda, the blue sky from morning bloomed with swollen black clouds. The wind, recently died, whispered ominous warnings, then rushed among the treetops, bending palm trees against their neighbours. The darkened sky soon rumbled, fracturing with streaks of light. Finally, a brief but terrible downpour ensued, whereafter the air felt considerably refreshed, permitting the evening's specimen preparation to pass more pleasantly.

One morning, as Wallace was on the front veranda sorting various sized insect pins into separate envelopes, a shirtless barefoot boy, about twelve years old, clomped up the wood steps. The boy's dark eyes swept past Wallace and into the house. "*Bom dia, senhor. Onde está Isidoro?*"

Every waif assumed him fluent in Portuguese, the lingua franca outside most towns. As time permitted, he and Bates were learning. "*Isidoro está aqui. Ela …*" How would one say at the cooking shed round the back of the house?

From the yard Isidoro called, "Fernando!"

The boy promptly raced over. They exchanged a few words then the boy ran off across the grass in the direction of town.

Isidoro climbed onto the veranda. As usual he wore a simple clean white cotton shirt against which his black skin stood stark and already glistening with the heat of his morning's labours. He had a raspy voice, and spoke English inflected with creole dialect. "Sorry, Mr. Wallace, he don't know better."

"Who is he?"

"Fernando?" Isidoro broke into a wide smile. "He's my great-grandson. He come with a message from his mother."

"*Great*-grandson? Please forgive my intrusiveness, but might I ask your age?" A frosting of white graced the temples of Isidoro's short-cropped tightly coiled hair, and while deep lines engraved his forehead, he had a lean athletic form and carried out his cooking and cleaning duties with vigour. Wallace had taken him for late forties, perhaps early fifties. Mind, this was the first Negro he'd known – a point not lost on Bates, who'd gently chided him for the clinical manner in which he had apparently studied their cook.

Isidoro licked his lips. "How old? Nobody ever count my years for me, sir. Most my life, I been a slave."

"Portuguese slave owners are a disgrace to all Europeans," Wallace said.

"My master, sir? He was an Englishman, like you and Mr. Bates."

"A Briton owned you?"

"Yes sir. Bought me from my American master and teached me how to cook for English stomachs. Then before he gone home to England, he made me a free man. God bless him."

"Any man who owns another deserves no blessing."

Isidoro lowered his eyes and shifted his feet, then nodded. "Sir, I came to tell you breakfast is ready. Mr. Bates here?"

"Somewhere. We shall dine on the veranda as usual. You may bring the food directly."

Once Isidoro had gone back to the cooking shed, Wallace searched for Bates. He spotted him at a distance, on the grass commons that served as social focal point for the dozen houses in the vicinity. At its far side stood a chapel with a shrine that attracted pilgrims. Bates was speaking with a barefoot young Indian girl in a simple cotton frock. She threw her head back and laughed at something he said and her long black hair shimmered. Wallace wondered what they could possibly be discussing. He carefully folded away his envelopes of specimen pins, rinsed his hands in the basin, then made ready for breakfast.

After settling into their house, he and Bates started venturing deeper and deeper into the forest, and their collections grew rapidly. By August, they'd prepared a shipment to their London sales agent, Samuel Stevens. More than three thousand specimens, predominantly insects and birds, but also over one hundred new butterfly species. Stevens had assured them new species would find an enthusiastic market among collectors.

One evening he and Bates were at work on the veranda. Wallace had relaxed the wings of a lustrous azure blue butterfly and was poised with pin in hand when Bates started to hum. He turned toward him. "My dear fellow."

Bates broke off his tune. "Pardon?"

"The song."

Bates set down a glass jar with its resident spider and cocked his head. "Song?"

"You were humming, I believe."

"And?"

"You are always humming or singing some little ditty."

"I'm afraid I don't take your point."

"My point is that silence would be optimal for work."

"But all day we endure silence. I thought ..."

"I merely raise the topic because we must work together, the two of us, for many months – even years. And my concentration suffers from such distractions."

Bates chewed his thumbnail. Wallace returned to the butterfly.

"Wallace, do you ever ... Do you miss your family?"

Wallace recalled his mother's recent letter. It seemed that Thomas Sims, son of his former landlord in Neath, had begun calling upon Fanny. Meanwhile, John had grown discontented with his failing dairy enterprise, and Herbert talked of returning to London, making use of his theatrical and poetic talents somehow. Were he at home, Wallace would doubtless be party to many interesting discussions. But was that not the point? Here in Brazil, he was doing precisely what captivated him most. And there was no end of it. To Bates he now said, "Truthfully, I find myself quite preoccupied. I would also mention that we've been away from home not four months."

Then he once again set to work on his butterfly. The underside of the hind wings held a thread of satin black that was simply magnificent.

"In England these past many years," Bates resumed, "you've often lived alone, or with one of your brothers. I take it you enjoyed in your domestic life that sort of … simplicity?"

Wallace looked up again. Bates's face bore a look of concentration, as though trying to reach some conclusion about something. "I was always well-occupied whatever my domestic arrangement."

"You see, I've always lived with my family in Leicester," Bates said. "I truly assumed I would remain with them until I married. In addition, I had my evening classes, my glee club, the gardening collective, even the camaraderie of co-workers at that awful brewery. All of which I cherished."

"I really don't understand what you're driving at," Wallace said.

Bates sighed. "Never mind. I shall bother you no more with my music. I have the sudden desire to take some air." He leapt off the veranda onto the lawn. A bright moon outlined his silhouette as it struck towards the chapel. A most curious destination, Wallace thought. He then turned his attention back to his specimen.

Late one morning in early October, Wallace broke off his field work early. Leaving aside an excursion along the Tocantins River, for the past two months he and Bates had collected separately. That had been Henry's idea. He'd suggested their productivity would likely be higher – and he'd been correct. On their own and sometimes with a local boy or two they hired, each had become more adept at distinguishing details and clues that sometimes seemed lost amid the monotony of forest green. Their collections grew more impressive. However, if Bates were ever to ask, Wallace might also admit that working alone in the silent gloom of forest, he'd felt an unexpected solitariness. No matter. He had become a more proficient collector.

Today, however, he could tolerate the slogging and climbing and contorting himself through brush and bog no longer. An hour earlier he'd nudged aside a fallen log to hunt out a skittering wingless black insect, a *triatomine* – the same family of bloodsuckers that so revolted Mr. Darwin whilst he cantered about the pampas of Argentina – and a wasp stung his mouth. Now, the right side of his face throbbed, his lips and cheek swollen. He trudged the final miles home with perspiration soaking his shirt and clayish red mud clotting his boots. He slumped forward with the effort – four birds and a few dozen insects had never weighed so much. He wished only for the house, to splash water upon his face, then gently lower himself upon his hammock.

In hindsight, as he mounted the steps to the veranda some clue might have existed, some indication of what he would find inside – perhaps the crash of a chair or a grunt of exertion –

but he couldn't be sure he hadn't conjured that after the fact. At the time, his state of misery made no allowance for external circumstances. He opened the front door without warning. At the dining table – their table – stood Bates. Or rather, his sweat-slickened backside. Clenched around his thoroughly naked haunches was a pair of slim brown legs. Tawny feet pointed straight at Wallace while Bates's hips thrust like steam-powered pistons.

Bates apparently heard nothing. An ecstatic state, or some such. But on the table, the girl's face – she was no more than sixteen or seventeen years old, black hair framing broad cheekbones and sunken eyes – peered around Bates's gyrations. Following the direction of her gaze, Bates glanced over his shoulder. Face stricken, he broke off intercourse, exposing himself in the most vivid manner conceivable. At that unspeakable sight, Wallace instinctively clamped a hand to his mouth.

"*Owww!*" He'd forgotten his wasp sting.

The Indian girl shrieked, terrified by the sight of the dishevelled lunatic who'd burst into the house with a gun strapped round his shoulder. She scrambled backwards across the table, all dusky elbows and dusky knees, hysterical.

Wallace retreated to the veranda, where he waited. The smoke and crackle of a brush fire drifted over from a neighbour's yard. Otherwise, with the rising heat, there was no sign of activity in the grassy clearing out front. The girl had fled with all her clothes in her arms – not so much as an undergarment to conceal her mysteries. From the yard with the fire, a dog barked. Someone yelled for it to be quiet and achieved quite the opposite effect.

The boards creaked. Bates, now fully clothed, seated himself in the next chair. "Alfred?"

Wallace raised the brim of his hat.

"I wish to offer my most sincere condolences for subjecting you to what must have been … a most unpleasant spectacle."

"She was but a child!"

"Oh, hardly a child!" Bates protested. "You saw her."

"Leaving aside her age," Wallace said, "the point to consider is that we are Englishmen. As members of a civilized nation we must set an example here, not fall in with local ways."

Bates, who in his candid moments, with lower lip plumped out, had the perpetual aspect of one anticipating tragic news, now looked particularly miserable. He folded his arms, but not in a hardened or obstinate manner, rather, as if he were in need of his own embrace. "I am so sorry. It's only that you and I have been working so bloody hard … and the women here are so lovely and unpretentious and they utterly lack the inhibitions that –"

"Stop! I won't hear of it!"

"I'm desperately lonely, dear chap. I yearned for … intimacy."

"Is that what you call it?" Wallace said, louder than intended. "Is it such a sin?"

"Yes, Henry, it is. Whether you call it abuse, or exploitation, it is a sin!"

Wallace felt the right side of his face throbbing. He desperately wished to rinse it with some cool water. He went in, leaving Bates on the veranda. Inside, he averted his gaze from the scene of that indecency and searched for the basin. That was when he realized Bates was standing in the doorway.

Limp and apologetic only moments earlier, Bates's voice now hardened. "I'm not like you! I don't have your cold-blooded detachment, Alfred! I have human feelings!"

The words were not worthy of a retort. Wallace turned and, avoiding his friend, abandoning the idea of freshening up, he made for the hammock on the back porch. There he fell upon it as though he hadn't slept in a week.

CHAPTER FIVE

Pará, July 12, 1849

After he and Henry Bates had their falling out, Wallace petitioned his brother Herbert to join him. Mother expressed unease at the foreign venture, but he saw it as a splendid opportunity. A chance to become a mentor, as William had been to himself. Admittedly, his suggestion to Herbert had come at a time when he was faced with the daunting notion of passing hundreds of evenings alone in this vast indifferent region. But when had Herbert, who remained miserably occupied at the ironworks in Neath, ever held hope for a decent calling? Now the brothers Wallace might strike their fortune, and possibly even fame, together.

Herbert descended from the brig *Britannia* onto Pará's wharf, a brave smile upon his narrow pink face, and his fair hair limp with perspiration. Before Wallace could even enquire after their mother and Fanny, Herbert introduced a tall Englishman he'd met on the voyage, a botanist, Richard Spruce.

Looking quite regal in a herringbone suit and crisp white shirt collar, Spruce's gaze roamed the port as if impatient to investigate all that lay before him. He fixed his eyes upon Wallace and smiled generously. "Sir, I imagine you and Henry Bates have enjoyed many memorable explorations this past year."

Wallace knew his answer would disappoint. He rarely cared what others thought of him but for some odd reason he felt an immediate affinity for Spruce. "I confess I've remained largely within the vicinity of Pará. As for Bates, we agreed several months ago to collect separately. A matter of efficiencies, one might say. However, now that my brother has arrived I anticipate the opportunity to finally delve into the Amazon in a more meaningful way. But shall we first deliver ourselves from the confines of this harbour?"

Wallace summoned four Negro porters. They hoisted the men's trunks onto handcarts. One, in a greying cotton undershirt, displayed an admirable physique. No matter how many trunks he were to lift, Wallace could not imagine amassing such muscle upon his own chest and arms. As they proceeded along the quay, Wallace observed how his brother, now twenty years old but still slight of build, walked with an odd loose-limbed stride. A rolling motion of his narrow hips and shoulder as though still negotiating the deck of his sea-going vessel. Indeed, this day it served him well – Herbert swivelled and gawked at every naked urchin, every scantily clad lady, even the bare torsos of the warehousemen.

At the roadway they said goodbye to Spruce, who had lodgings in town. Wallace hired a bullock cart to the country house he'd been renting not a quarter-mile from the residence he and Bates had formerly shared. When they arrived, to Wallace's surprise, his brother preferred to unpack rather than immediately explore his surroundings. Upon their own arrival, he and Henry Bates had walked until their legs nearly gave out.

The next morning Herbert was slow to rise. Wallace watched

the sunrise alone with his steaming coffee. Finally, he shook his brother awake. "I should have thought a month's confinement at sea would have made you eager for the outdoors."

"Quite eager," Herbert mumbled, one eye cracking open.

"Right then," Wallace said.

The hammock rustled and eventually feet found floorboard, but his brother's sluggish movements belied his professed enthusiasm. When Herbert was finally dressed, Wallace showed him their basic gear. One item after the next was greeted by questions concerning their usage.

"There's little here that won't make greater sense by witnessing its practical application in the field," Wallace said.

Herbert nodded, then lobbed more questions. It almost seemed he wished to do nothing but talk. "I recognize this is your first full day, Herbert, but these are prime working hours,"

His brother's brow furrowed. "If it's not an imposition, Alfred, I prefer my middle name. I find it substantially more lyrical than Herbert and of late I use it exclusively."

Wallace raised an eyebrow. "Fine. Shall we now take our leave, Edward?"

Training could hardly be delayed. Summer would end all too quickly and in the rainy season such lessons as he had to impart would prove impossible. However, it would have been advantageous had Herbert devoted at least an atom of effort to developing his skills before embarking overseas. In the months prior to their own voyage he and Bates both honed their facility at hunting – if that could accurately describe shooting at stones set upon a wall. They also read everything they could get their hands on concerning specimen collection and preservation, and sought out museum experts to supplement that information. Of course, true education came only this past year. Though he'd gleaned some information from the locals, it was mainly through trial and error that he'd learned. No expert by any stretch, at least now he could avow some competence. Which, for Herbert, meant he needn't know the same frustrations borne of self-tutelage.

Wallace confined their initial foray to an easy radius. Even then, his cheeks flushed, Herbert paused regularly to gulp from his canteen, or to remove mud from his boots, or release a caught shirtsleeve. Wallace did his best to keep them moving. An hour's march brought them near a flock of chattering parrots. He signalled Herbert to remain silent. To no avail. At Herbert's crashing approach the birds rose like a giant colourful parasol. When Herbert raised his gun, Wallace grabbed the muzzle and lowered it.

"What's wrong?" Herbert cried.

He controlled his voice. "Edward, if you look about, you will see that the understory precludes any realistic chance of bringing down a bird above the canopy. You may recall, we are looking for passerine species perching amongst the lower branches, possibly a ground-nest."

"I shouldn't wish to question your expertise," Herbert said, "but with all these trees in the way, would it not be preferable to focus on large game? Or at least something on land?"

Wallace stared at his boots. This was quite trying. But he kept in mind that, unlike his own opportunities to ramble the British countryside as William's apprentice, Herbert was much the city lad. "Other than insects, there really aren't a great number of specimens to be had along the ground in this vicinity. So we use our guns almost exclusively for birds."

"That raises a separate matter: aren't most birds awfully small for gunshot?" said Herbert. "I mean, won't they end up as, well, smithereens?"

Removing his spectacles, Wallace mopped his brow. He

AVI SIRLIN

had a better picture now of the enormity of his task. "As I explained before, the gun is double-barrelled. One barrel with number ten shot for small birds, the other, number four for larger ones. Now let's try again, shall we?"

A short time later, Wallace shot a grey-hooded flycatcher. As good a specimen for teaching purposes as any. He placed it on its back, the charcoal-hued wings splayed.

"As you can see, it is quite dead. Were it otherwise, press firmly with your finger and thumb here, just behind the wings. It does the trick quickly."

Lower lip drawn, Herbert nodded.

"The first order of business is to preserve the plumage from stains – blood, usually – otherwise it won't be worth a penny. Now watch carefully."

Wallace pried the bill open and stuffed a bit of cotton into it. Then he separated the breast feathers. "There," he said. "See that?"

Herbert squinted. "That darkish thing?"

"That, Edward, is a shot hole. And there, that's a second one. Remember, each shot contains many pellets and we must be thorough in our examination if we wish our specimen unblemished."

Wallace cleaned the holes with a leaf and plugged them with small amounts of cotton. Then he took the specimen's measurements for his field journal.

"Now we get down to business."

He inserted the tip of his knife blade at the top of the breastbone. "Not too deep, see? We mustn't damage the flesh. Draw downwards, to the vent."

"You mean its arsehole?"

In that lopsided grin that now confronted him, left brow mildly arched and eyes glittering, Wallace saw their father, some preposterous comment about the intellectual delicacy of the Irish or lack of ambition amongst tenant farmers just spilled from that crooked mouth, eagerly awaiting reaction.

"Edward, it's of vital importance to work quickly, given the heat. Try to apply yourself."

A residue of smile still played at the corners of Herbert's lips. "My apologies."

Wallace inserted the knife's blunt end between the skin and underlying flesh, tucking cotton between the two layers as he proceeded. He peeled down towards the rump, then drew upwards along the length of the wings. Next, he severed the bones at the shoulder joints, ensuring he left the tailbone so that the tail feathers would not fall out, and pulled the skin till the skull was laid bare. Finally, he excised the neck vertebra from the head. The whole skin now separated, he wrapped it in paper.

"Quite straight-forward, as you just saw."

Herbert rubbed his chin.

"When we're back at the house, I shall show you how to prepare our specimens for shipment. Make no mistake, it is of equal critical importance to the skinning. If not done properly, the specimen will be rotted or mutilated by insects in little time, and thus utterly valueless when it reaches London. Here," he passed the bird skin to his brother. "Have a look. Lightly now, minding you don't damage the feathers, please."

Early afternoon, Herbert looked a fright. Pale hair plastered to his scalp, a trickle of blood from the bridge of his nose where he'd caught a branch full-stride, and a blister on his left foot that had him not so much limping as dragging one leg the final hour. The clean khaki trousers in which he'd set out that morning – crisp pleats of their mother's iron still visible – were embedded with innumerable burrs and thorns, splatters of mud and a dramatic comet-tail of blood.

For the latter, Wallace blamed himself. He'd brought down an ibis just before noon. A bird large enough for Herbert to have a go at skinning. The work was sloppy – barely salvageable – and Herbert inadvertently wiped a hand upon his trousers. Wallace reminded himself it was only a first effort. Improvement would come.

*

A year later, after they'd already ventured into the fathomless depths of the Amazon, Herbert declared he'd had enough. He would return to England. The news came as something of a relief, Wallace had to admit. Above all, he now wished only to work without hindrance. He understood that his calling demanded it.

They parted ways in Barra. The Amazon's belly, the town offered the only meaningful commercial stores and services for thousands of square miles. They stood outside the post office. A bright summer's afternoon, the final day of August 1850, the distant metallic roofs of the riverside warehouses glinted and the water sparkled.

"If I'd had the remittance I'd hoped to receive from Stevens … and if I didn't have a lengthy expedition to mount …" Wallace could not bring himself to finish. He was only repeating what he'd said a half-dozen times already.

Herbert squinted against the sun, the corners of his mouth shaped into something resembling a smile. "That's all right, Alf. The ten pounds should prove ample till I find work. As you said, it's a bustling town. I should be able to catch on somewhere. Then it won't take long for me to earn my passage to Pará."

"That's right. Home by Christmas, you lucky soul. Now

mind you don't spend the money on frivolous items. Food and shelter, nothing more."

"No need to worry, big brother. While I'm sure Barra has its entertainments – though what they are, I cannot imagine – I'm eager for London. Once there, you shall have your ten pounds quick as a flash. I shan't for a moment forget our loan agreement."

That bit made him squirm. "It's not about the money per se," he'd told Herbert earlier, when his brother prepared to sign the loan paper he'd written out. "It is about taking responsibility for one's actions."

Responsibility. Manly responsibility.

In retrospect, he would concede a certain breeziness regarding the ease with which he'd assumed the proposed itinerary for Herbert's return to England might be consummated. An aspiring young poet in foreign lands. But at the time, he thought mainly of his own ambitions. The sensation he might create in London were he to capture an elusive umbrella-bird. With that in mind, he bid Herbert farewell. Then he journeyed the Rios Negro and Orinoco for better than a year, encountering mixed results generally, but no umbrella-bird specifically.

It was September 1851 when he finally returned to Barra, the town where he'd parted ways with his brother. He envisaged a one-week sojourn, two at the outside. Enough time to dispatch to England his accumulated collection of plants, insects, bird skins, drawings and notes – all his work of the past two years. Then he would make his purchases, hire his labour and strike out on one last expedition, this time to the upper reaches of the Rio Uaupés, rumoured habitat of the white umbrella-bird. Whether or not he succeeded in capturing the legendary, possibly mythical bird, he hoped the venture would at least earn him recognition as an intrepid explorer, that no one might seriously allege Alfred Russel Wallace was merely some avid collector or, worse, a dilettante.

At Barra's post office a bundle of mail awaited him. Letters from his mother, sister Fanny (now Mrs. Thomas Sims) – he marvelled at the name, his London agent, Samuel Stevens (enclosing an accounting of specimen sales to date, along with a correspondingly disappointing bank draft), an Oxford ornithologist seeking specimens of the bristle-tailed manakin, two very keen lepidopterists anxious for his observations of the butterflies along the Rio Negro, and a slim letter from Mr. Daniel Miller, British consul at Pará.

As he slit the wax seal on the consul's letter, Wallace had no dire premonition as to its contents. Why would he? Were it bad news from England – mother's health, to take an example – he would expect the news directly from Fanny. As for Herbert, he would have passed through Pará several months earlier and was likely home right now regaling his circle of poets, actors and musicians with the tribulations his elder brother inflicted upon him in the Brazilian wilds. No, he had no foretelling of calamity. Instead he imagined a benign letter of introduction concerning a Mr. So-and-so, soon to be travelling in his vicinity and wishing the civil company of a fellow Englishman.

His hands, so typically steady, trembled as he reread the single sheet of paper. Mr. Miller reported that Pará lay under plague of yellow fever and, while awaiting passage there to Liverpool, Herbert Edward Wallace had fallen seriously ill. He was not expected to survive. An update would be forthcoming when feasible.

The letter was three months old.

Although several boats had plied the thousand-mile route between the two towns since the letter had been posted, there was no further communiqué. So Wallace shuffled among various offices of administrators, traders and merchants. Hat in hand, he sat in airless vestibules an hour at a time while the clink of rum glasses resounded behind carved doors. He talked to river men and travellers, anyone who might have more recent information. All without result.

The second day of this fruitless endeavour, standing outside the land surveyor's office, he heard his name. Striding across the rutted dirt road, resplendent in tan-coloured jacket, crisp white shirt and twill trousers, was Richard Spruce.

"Not a thread of grey in that beard, my dear Wallace. I should say you've had but a splendid holiday this past year and a half."

Despite his low spirits, Wallace couldn't help but laugh. Those first months after Spruce's arrival in Brazil their paths crossed several times and typically resulted in sterling conversation along with gales of laughter. As ever, his friend appeared none the worse for his own excursions – other than a certain weight loss notable in the sharpened ridges and deepened orbits of his face.

"If ever a beard betrayed a man's idleness," Wallace answered, "I might make a portrait of yours. Trim and tidy as a parson's."

"Ah, that's different," Spruce said. "The enterprising botanist mustn't compromise good grooming upon return to civilization – "

"Or reasonable facsimile thereof." Wallace swept his hand to indicate their surroundings.

"I cannot deny that Barra regrettably lacks refinement," Spruce said. "But one's cleanliness and appearance cannot be sacrificed so long as there exists the possibility of desirable female companionship."

A dray laden with timber trundled towards them along the

AVI SIRLIN

road, dust billowing in its wake. Spruce covered his nose and mouth with his handkerchief and after the cart passed he brushed off as best he could. "Not easy to keep one's lungs clear in this brutish place."

"I take it then," said Wallace, "that notwithstanding some eighteen or twenty months' withdrawal from society, you now miss the forest?"

"The serpents, mosquitoes, monotonous diet, paucity of cultured females, no." A gleam then manifested in Spruce's hollow eyes. "But the *bryophytes*! I found a species of moss with a branch cluster unlike anything I've seen. And the ferns, well … Soon as I hire new men, I'm off again." His eyes narrowed. "Something's wrong, isn't it?"

Wallace told him about Herbert.

"Terrible news." Spruce squeezed Wallace's shoulder. "But something shall turn up. We'll divide the remainder of the names on your list and make quick work of it. Now, where are you staying?"

"My usual lodgings."

"Well then, let us make a start of lifting your spirits immediately. By introduction of Ramsay Newcastle, an acquaintance recently appointed Kew Gardens Assistant Director, I'm in a very well-appointed residence with an abundance of comfortable quarters – and it's unbearably quiet. So none of your usual remonstrations of self-sufficiency. I beg you, please join me."

That evening, after Wallace settled his belongings in his new room, he joined Spruce on the back veranda. They eased into a pair of creaking wicker chairs. Sweet mimosa banished the town's pestilential air and they watched an aerial ballet of fireflies while a servant poured coffee.

Once they were alone, Spruce opened his notebook

and traced a finger down one of the pages. "I have some news. I talked to a local cotton merchant this afternoon. He informed me that not long after Mr. Miller dispatched his letter concerning your brother, a week at most, the consul himself died from an unrelated illness. Fever of the brain, or such."

A lamp stood on the table between them and its glow accentuated the deep orbits around Spruce's eyes. Wallace set his cup and saucer upon the table. In the yard, a solitary frog peeped.

"You face a dilemma, I acknowledge," Spruce said, "but a solution will present itself."

Wallace did not see how. With no ships sailing from Pará for another month or more and now the consul's death, it was highly improbable he would receive word on his brother's condition. Yet if he made the thousand-mile descent to the port town, he would not only expose himself to the plague, but by the time of his arrival Herbert would either very likely be dead or long since recovered and sailed to England. That, and the expense of such a fruitless endeavour would so deplete his coffers he would lack the resources to mount his Rio Uaupés expedition.

"I should never have asked Herbert to come to Brazil. He fancies himself a poet."

"Surely the two pursuits are not incompatible. You know well that Percival is rarely bereft of at least one volume of verse, Tennyson or one of the other greats."

Trust Spruce to gently lighten the mood. Percival was his well-travelled satchel. When instilled with sufficient cognac, Spruce deigned to introduce his bag to those he judged as good-humoured sorts.

"But seriously, Spruce, a poet mucking about the forest and wading through bogs? Skinning birds? Pinning insects?"

"Returning at the end of the day drenched in perspiration, inflicted with a hundred maddening bites, the scratches of a thousand thorns?" Spruce added.

"No evening's amusement," said Wallace, "beyond the sorting of the day's collection and perhaps a cup of cocoa or coffee?"

"Certainly no lovely wife," said Spruce.

They chuckled ruefully.

"You know," Spruce said. "Henry Bates also appreciates good verse."

Wallace folded his arms. "May we not talk of him, please?"

"Still? Well, I leave you to your want. Though I will add – "

"Naturally."

"– that Bates is a thoroughly affable fellow and whatever passed between you two good men can surely be set right."

Wallace stared at the fireflies for several moments. "How long must a desperate naturalist wait before he sets eyes upon your latest collection?"

They spent the rest of the evening in amiable examination of botanical specimens.

The next day and those that followed were not wasted. He'd made his decision. He hired men. He bought provisions, inventorying and packing all he would carry. Then he arranged for shipment to England of all his accumulated specimens and drawings. And with the town's only competent carpenter soused to the gills for the duration, Wallace built his own specimen boxes and packing crates, finding satisfaction in the precise measures, the saw cuts, the assembly – excavation of all those old skills his brother John had imparted long ago. Finally he set off, resolved that he was making the only decision properly available to him under the circumstances, and trying to ignore the guilt that gnawed at him for leaving his brother to his fate.

CHAPTER SIX
Mid-Atlantic, August 7, 1852

Dawn broke beneath a grey-quilted sky, the ocean velvet and iron with flecks of orange on the distant horizon. The lifeboats had stopped leaking. Wallace, in addition to his own relief, sensed a change of mood in the men.

"We'll see another sunset, I'll reckon that much," said Bateman, the second mate.

"Better than that," Captain Turner said, the map, compass and a sextant spread before him, "we are a short distance from the West Indies trade route and enjoy a favourable wind. I daresay we shall sight a ship by day's end, tomorrow at the latest."

"Well then," said Bateman, "Let's get underway, says I."

"Breakfast first, sir," Mr. Roland said.

Roland merely had to point to which barrel contained the salt pork, which held the biscuits, and so on. The men ate heartily and a few attempted a quip or two about how the cook's fare was no worse than usual. In the captain's gig, it was noted more than once that their boat stood the best chance of survival for reason that Roland was in the long-boat. Everyone but Isaac Plum had great appetite. He shared in none of the food or easy conversation. Wallace thought the boy's heavy-lidded eyes a likely product of the sleepless night coupled with the prior day's events.

After breakfast, they untethered the two boats and raised the sails. They were sailors and, though aggrieved over loss of ship, Wallace sensed most embraced the adventure, keenly anticipating their inevitable rescue, the tales that would be told that night or the next day aboard their benefactors' vessel, then amplified and repeated many times over upon reaching safe harbour.

Throughout the day, lest his gaze drift to the open horizon and remind him of the boundless sea, Wallace fastened it upon the only point he could fix, the other lifeboat. The long-boat became his shoreline. The fair wind lasted the day, but that night a gale rose up and pushed them north. Next morning the wind had dropped off altogether.

"Perhaps another day or so," Turner said. "But ships abound in these waters."

On the third night a squall descended. Rain fell, lashing their faces. Combined with the darkness, the chop of sea and the spray that whipped them, Wallace lost sight of the long-boat. Fear ballooned inside his chest. The captain's gig, a flat-bottomed boat intended as small taxi in calm inner harbours, tossed unpredictably. Steep walls of churning seawater lifted then dropped them. Each time, Wallace's heart lurched. He lost count how often he pitched onto his back, he and the men knocking about like ninepins. Every so often a thwart or gunwale punched his ribs, or his shoulder cracked against another's skull – or vice-versa. Seawater spilled over their feet, soon rising to their ankles, to their calves, threatening to swamp them.

"Bail!"

Captain Turner's commands were overtaken by Bateman's imprecations. "Mr. Wallace, use your hat or, if needs be, your blasted hands!"

Wallace scooped out hatfuls of sea water, while sea and sky collapsed together and conspired to drown them. Spasms of pain from his wounded hand flashed white light behind his eyes. He could not imagine they would live to see the sun. But an hour before the eastern sky splintered orange and pink, the wind abated and the swales flattened. With two men still bailing, Wallace and the others were finally able to rest. Slumped forward, elbows on his knees, he fell asleep.

When he woke, his skin was rimed with salt – perspiration or evaporated brine, perhaps both. The ocean was calm, the sky cleansed and bright.

Captain Turner made new calculations.

"It would appear," he said, "we are roughly five hundred miles east of Bermuda."

"Five hundred?" cried Appelboom.

"Bloody hell," Bateman said. "None of us'll be seeing Liverpool no time soon."

There was no more talk of imminent rescue. Turner put them on rations. Barrels of pork, cheese, biscuits and water that had seemed so copious for a short sojourn became community treasure. Everyone rued their failure to catch fresh water during the rains.

The climbing sun grew white and ferocious. Bateman and Robinson jury-rigged a small shelter near the stern and the captain allocated shifts. The day dragged on. Listless boredom was as much their enemy as the sun.

By late afternoon, grumbling wafted over from the long-boat. A litany of complaints and woes. In the gig, talk was rationed more severely than drinking water. Occasionally this one would point out that the other was letting the sail luff. Or there'd be debate over shifting winds. Every so often, one would wistfully describe the first meal he'd enjoy once ashore. And now and then an albatross, petrel or gull would glide overhead, prompting speculation about the nearest land. But generally, having shipped together for months or, in the case of Bateman and Galt (who'd perhaps consciously ended up in different lifeboats), years, each man's stories were known so well to the others that only a few words were necessary to elicit a cry of, "Not that old fairy tale again!"

Thus it came that they entreated the *Helen*'s only paying passenger to relate his accounts of the wondrous Amazon.

Wallace didn't consider himself much of a storyteller. He believed he lacked the proper imagination, the glimmer of feeling as to what keened another man's interest. Besides, what kind of story could he offer? He would be duty-bound to adhere to the facts. With those mundane details and his dull style he would quickly lose his audience. But the men were persistent and, leaving aside the diversion he might create for them, he recognized how recitation of what befell him in the Amazon might draw his own thoughts away from the peril that lurked beyond their vessel, in every direction, for as far as his eyes could see. Seamen, all of them, they had no compass to comprehend how desperate he was to absorb himself in any activity, that the last thing he wanted was more time to ponder the infinite ocean. And so he began to recount his adventures to the eager crew, omitting only that which defied explanation.

*

Four months after he departed Barra, Wallace lay motionless upon his hammock, entombed in a wretched hovel. It was the

29th of January, 1852. For the past sixty days already, in ebbs and flows, he'd been dying. And there was nothing to be done for it, not in this place. São Joaquim. A thieving village of twenty, or perhaps one hundred and twenty, Wallace couldn't say; the inhabitants disappeared into the surrounding trees and watercourses for days or weeks at a time. Whatever their number, they'd made plain their belief he would not regain his health. They were stealing his supplies – those few not already stolen.

The Indians he'd hired downriver had been first to take advantage of his infirmity. When he arrived at the village in late November, sweat-soaked and bone-chilled, he traded two machetes for use of a small shack, then fell unconscious upon his hammock. That night, his men pilfered everything they could carry, absconding before sunrise.

By contrast, the local thieves had grown so emboldened by his deteriorating condition they stole at hours more convenient to them, even as he watched plaintive and wide-eyed from across the room. More and more, it looked as though he was at his end. On this, what was to be his final Amazonian expedition. Final, indeed.

If he bore with equanimity his fate it was not on account of the supposed glory of having his name added to that era's prolific annals of valiant adventurers who'd met their untimely demise; rather, he saw in it a certain poetic nature. Odd, how eager he'd been such a short time ago for his ambition to be given dominion. His zeal for the uncharted Uaupés had now vanished. All seemed lost. His medicines had utterly failed. Despite the stifling heat, he shivered. Loss of appetite left him struggling to consume more than a handful of cashews or a half-papaya daily. He withered like a melon rotting in the fields.

Unable to work, unable to do anything productive, his

drawn-out struggle had resulted in a lingering embattled state with no end in sight. What he wanted – what he *needed* – was an end to this prolonged siege upon his body. Stripped of all care, he surrendered his will to fate, conscious that only recently he'd also turned away from Herbert's struggle for life. He could see now he'd been wrong, his decisions motivated by self-interest – greed and vanity, under cloak of reason. Wallace tried to imagine how his brother must have suffered. The feverish chills compounded by a grinding backache. Skin and eyes jaundiced, black vomit crusting his mouth and crimson blood at his nether orifice. Then his organs failing one by one. Picturing this, Wallace wept until eventually drifting into fitful sleep.

He dreamt his mother visited him in the room he rented in Neath after William's funeral. And though it was a wintry day and cold draughts swam between every stone of the old house, the room sweltered. Cheeks flushed, mother's upper lip beaded perspiration as she bent over the small table where he sat. She implored him to finish the pie she'd baked. It was his childhood favourite, quince, but he pushed it aside after a few bites. No more.

A dream of Herbert followed. Herbert's sandy hair plastered upon his forehead, eyes and lips dark-rimmed, expressionless, waving to him from the wharf in Pará. Wallace stood on board a schooner. The ship weighed anchor and Herbert receded. Within seconds, he lost sight not only of his brother but the town itself.

Finally, he dreamt of an old Indian. Bare-chested, the Indian prowled his hut in São Joaquim, surveying its meagre contents, but not showing any inclination to steal. The Indian came and stood over him. Black eagle feathers hung from his greyed head, a sombre well-lined face peered intently at his own.

After signalling someone outside the door, the Indian uttered a strange incantation. The room filled with a strong loamy odour, overpowering Wallace's own fetor. The Indian's face bent close, speaking in a whisper. Sensing importance in the old man's words, he tried to explain his inability to catch what was said, and would he kindly repeat himself? But no speech escaped, Wallace's voice box rendered mute, perhaps by the incantation. The force that produced his speechlessness then spread through him like a wave, weakness sweeping his body, pulling him under some blanketing influence that smothered his resistance until, unable to do otherwise, his head fell back, his muscles slackened, and his eyes closed.

A loamy stench – the one he'd dreamt – now infiltrated his nose. Bitter liquid presently coated his mouth.

"Drink it all down, old man. It's medicinal."

His senses misled him, surely. Eyes prying open, he found Richard Spruce pressing a cup to his lips. The tarry liquid at the back of his throat had the pungency of both earth and beast. Wallace felt the first convulsion bring up the contents of his stomach. Someone holding his head now leaned him over. A basin appeared. He spewed until he was dry, until all that remained was the bilious aftertaste. Then the same powerful force that had earlier pulled him under tugged at his eyelids.

At first, there was only darkness. Then he saw a shimmering phosphorescence made of fluid and light. A spectral ribbon, it glowed green at its edges and blue and indigo at its core. The vision swayed upon air, touching nothing in the darkened space. Its energy was calm and expansive, enveloping him. When the spectre floated towards the doorway, Wallace raised his head so that he might follow its progress. At the threshold the shimmering green transformed to gold, a warm incandescence, the glow of contentedness. It was then that a recognition pierced him, one that bore no clear explanation, yet remained unequivocal – logic, for once in his life, displaced by inchoate perception, by feeling. As the glimmering light spilled outside, it reverted to green and dissolved. Wallace wanted to pursue it, find its residue upon the soil before it bled into the ground, but he could not move; he slowly and inexorably sank back into his hammock.

He was awake. Richard Spruce was speaking to him.

"Pardon?"

"He is a *kumu*," Spruce said. "A shaman, of sorts." He referred to the old Indian who lay in the far corner of the hut, curled beneath a blanket, sleeping.

"A jungle doctor? You had a jungle doctor treat me when I don't trust even our own doctors?"

"My dear Wallace, our medical men know nothing of the ague, its causes or its treatment. Yet the Indians have been living with it since the start of time. A *kumu* receives the cumulative knowledge of all his predecessors, millennia of training passed down. And the medicines are botanical, grown in the region where the illness arises, which makes perfect sense."

"So says the botanist."

"Think of it: our natural world exists with a certain amount of symmetry and balance. Earth and sky. Fire and water. Growth and decay. Whatever the cause of ague, it is only logical that its cure would exist nearby in the natural world, not the chemist's shop."

"Where did you find him?"

"Last year I happened upon his village while exploring tributaries of the upper Rio Negro. From where I'm currently staying, São Gabriel, it was only two days' travel."

"Richard Spruce! Two days' journey on my behalf? I trust you involved no one else."

"Only myself and Percival." Spruce's smile vanished as quickly as it had appeared and his fingers twined together. "When I received your letter, your handwriting alone forewarned me of your condition's severity. What else was I to do? You were dying, old man."

Wallace swallowed hard and turned his head. He only spoke again when confident his voice wouldn't break. "I … I vaguely recall the *kumu* standing over me, speaking words I couldn't hear clearly. Neither English nor Portuguese, I'm fairly certain. How do you communicate?"

"We speak in his language, Tukanoan. I spent some weeks in his village the past year and picked up a bit of the vocabulary."

Ah, Spruce. Were he interested in the study of animals, given a few weeks in their company, he would surely be able to trade limericks with monkeys or even crocodiles.

"I recall a cup of vile liquid. You tried to get me to drink, but I vomited."

"I gave you two cups. You emptied your stomach only after the second. And though it's unlikely to offer any solace, our tired friend," he indicated the old Indian, now snoring lightly, "also imbibed two servings."

"Horrible. Is it a purgative?"

"It's made from a liana, *Banisteriopsis caapi*. The Indians call it the vine of the soul, or *ayahuasca*. The bark is scraped off, then boiled until thick."

"I assume you've drunk it yourself then?"

"I'd hoped to, but … "

"You mean you've never tried it yourself?"

"I made one attempt, but quite frankly it made me nauseous."

"Imagine that."

Spruce's eyes narrowed. "Bear in mind, I wasn't ill. I was merely curious from a scientific standpoint. Had I been ill like

71

yourself, rest assured I would have consumed it in its entirety."

"What happened to me after I drank it? I ... I saw something, perhaps in a dream."

"According to the *kumu*, you and he travelled to the spirit world. He guided you. He claims the spirits revealed the cause of your illness and how best to treat it. He then made a medicinal compound which you ingested."

Wallace blinked. A fog of memory receded, leaving flickering images.

Spruce leaned near. "Did you see something? A vision?"

The images continued to flicker, nothing clear and indelible. An iridescence, a sinewy shape gliding through the room, towards the doorway.

"So memorable it strikes you silent?" Spruce raised an eyebrow. "Well, I remain fascinated. From the anecdotal information of the Tukanos and the hearsay of others, I suspect this *ayahuasca* might offer healthful benefits once we better understand its properties. In Barra this past September, I sent off a sample of the vine to Ramsay Newcastle at Kew Gardens. A brilliant naturalist and part of Charles Darwin's inner circle, I'm fortunate to have his acquaintance and asked him to make an analysis."

Ayahuasca or not, that evening, Wallace's appetite returned. Soon he was sitting up. And within two days, by aid of walking sticks, he was able to get down to the river and bathe. Spruce stayed long enough to be assured of his recovery. Then he had to take the *kumu* back to his village.

Wallace walked them down to the riverbank. He intended to watch until the canoe glided out of view, but his bones went brittle and he feared that should he not make his way to his hammock right then, he would be compelled to crawl on all fours to conquer the incline.

Within a week however, he was able to clamber into his canoe. Once again he was intent upon the far end of the Uaupés that some benefit should derive from all this suffering. But first he went downriver, to São Gabriel.

He and Spruce sat together on the front porch of the small house Spruce shared with a family of five or six or seven – as with São Joaquim, the number of inhabitants in São Gabriel was in flux. From inside, smoke carried the roasted aroma of the fish Wallace had brought. He and Spruce watched a pair of small naked boys chase each other back and forth in an apparent game of tag. When Spruce called their names they broke off their pursuit and approached, each one stifling giggles. He addressed them in their own language and after a brief exchange the boys set off again, hooting with pleasure.

"I owe you my life."

"Oh, please," said Spruce. "It was the *kumu*."

"No protest or modesty permitted."

"All right then," Spruce said, doffing his straw hat. "I accept responsibility for the imminent return to the wilds of the nemesis to umbrella-birds everywhere, Alfred Russel Wallace." He tapped the hat back into place, brim angled jauntily.

"You may feel uncomfortable with praise but I remain indebted."

"*P'shaw!*"

"Rest assured I do not take the matter lightly. While dearly hoping the circumstances where I might reciprocate never arise – "

"I'm afraid I'd have to be a good deal more unconscious than you were in order to swallow that vile brew!"

"Yes, yes, I mustn't forget that unpleasant business."

"Diminishes the good deed, wouldn't you say?" said Spruce. "In any event, I now offer you a chance to repay your imaginary debt. All information I've received suggests that the *ayahuasca* is a remarkable vine. Yet evidence concerning its effect is often second-hand and, needless to say, never from a fellow Englishman. If you would so kindly describe for me the details of your experience we might consider that to be your *quid quo pro*." He took out his notebook and pencil.

Wallace described what he saw, what he tasted, felt, heard and smelled, all that he remembered. Most especially the pulsing green form that, while having no distinct human features – no face, no arms or legs, indeed no substance – evoked for him a human aspect, one that drifted out of memory's haze: his brother Herbert, moving in his peculiar rolling manner. Surely that memory hadn't been invented in São Joaquim. This was observation. This was fact. And what then of that pulsing green silhouette he'd known while in his feverish state? Was that not observation? Was that not fact? Describing now to Richard Spruce the luminous green vision he'd seen, the feeling that gave root to his earlier belief – that there was something undeniably sentient in that distinctive form and movement – was now supplanted by cognition. Certainty in both name and consequence. The floating spectre he'd witnessed at São Joaquim could only have been Herbert. And what it meant, above all else, was that his younger brother was dead.

CHAPTER SEVEN
Mid-Atlantic, August 8, 1852

Wallace awoke amid darkness and a howling wind. The lifeboat had plunged into a steep black swell, walls of foaming water towering on all sides. His backside lost its purchase and he scrabbled for something to hold onto, but it was too late. He pitched onto someone's chest.

"Bloody hell!"

"My apologies, Mr. Appelboom."

"Sorry, sir," Appelboom said. "Y'z caught me unexpected, is all."

Wallace tried to lift himself off the groaning seaman but found himself entangled in a rope. The next instant, Appelboom tumbled out from beneath him, joining men and gear spilling forward. But Wallace held fast – he'd copied Bateman who slept each night with his ankle lashed to a seat post. "If she goes to Davey's locker," the second mate said, "I'd just as soon go with her."

They reached the bottom of the pocket and the boat began to climb. A wooden object toppled across Wallace's back. He didn't look to see what it was. The crew scrambled, Turner and Bateman shouting orders back and forth. Wallace lay rigid, eyes fixed on the looming mountain of water. The boat climbed and climbed. Sea water slashed his face. Then the boat crested the wave and his stomach fell.

Up and down they rolled, the waves twenty, twenty-five feet. Lightning soon shattered the black sky, followed by a rumble Wallace felt in his bones. When the rain came, it fell in swaths so heavy it flattened them. Wallace saw no sign of the long-boat, the lightning flashes revealing nothing but curtains of rain and roiling waves. Water pooled, swirling round their calves. One of the kegs – the last of the salted pork – came unmoored and, despite Isaac and Mr. Appelboom's noble effort, washed overboard.

"Mr. Wallace," the captain shouted, "we need all hands to preserve our stores."

Wallace latched onto the water cask and held tight, then he closed his eyes.

The boat rose and fell, rose and fell. But the storm receded as quickly as it struck. Soon the crew took to setting everything as it had been before and there was also water to be emptied from the boat. They all bent to the task, Turner included.

"I've had meself baths in less water than this," Bateman grumbled.

"Bloody surprise to me," said Appelboom, "y'z even known a bath."

Everyone, Turner included, joined in the laughter. Eventually each one eased into his most comfortable position, never mind the odd puddle and all of them soaked through and through. Sleep came quickly.

When Wallace's eyes pried open, the sky was fair and the wind light. The sun had already climbed high. All the others were stirring, except Isaac. He'd bailed longer than anyone, Bateman finally wresting the pewter mug from his hand. Wallace searched out the long-boat. A mile to starboard, Magnusson signalled that all were accounted for.

When the heat of day dissipated, they ate an especially light supper. Only Bateman and Robinson finished their ration. The mug of drinking water had just passed the rounds when Isaac said, "Mr. Wallace? I dreamt I had a fever like the one that laid you low in the jungle. Maybe it was the heat and me dozing in them wet clothes and all. I was wondering, sir, if you doesn't mind me asking, the sickness on the *Helen*, was it the same one you had in the jungle?"

"I suspect so," Wallace said. "The fever continues to recur sporadically, though with less severity now. I should like to think that one day it will never return."

"After you met Mr. Spruce that last time, did you carry on up that river?"

"Yeah, and did you find your black umbrella-bird?" asked Bateman.

"White umbrella-bird," Captain Turner interjected. "Am I right, Mr. Wallace?"

Wallace could not help but bask in the attention. In recounting his journey, he'd done his best to describe that which interested less the scientist and more the common man, albeit without acute personal details that would only have made the men, and himself, quite uncomfortable, his *ayahuasca* vision especially. Still, the eagerness on the men's faces was gratifying. He wished for them, as well as himself, good diversion in his story, that their fate should not weigh so heavily.

"To answer your question first, Isaac," he said, "yes, I went on with my expedition. Indeed, when I look back upon it now, I might say that I was rather determined."

*

He'd intended to follow the Rio Uaupés to the Colombian border. There he would remain two or three weeks, collecting what he could. Despite the imminent change of seasons, in mid-February, a mere six months prior to what had now become his fateful voyage aboard the *Helen*, he procured a thirty-foot canoe, planked with *jatobá* and a deck of stonewood. He hired seven Indians: a coxswain who stood to stern, and six who paddled from a raised platform above the bow deck. Beneath the platform Wallace stowed his supplies and the currency with which he expected to pay for services: tools, cooking pots, utensils, baskets, blankets, hammocks, boxes of coarse cotton and calico, needles and thread, buttons, beads, flints, candles, mirrors, fish hooks, arrowheads, axes and machetes.

Each day began at dawn, the oars dipping into calm shadowed water in measured tempo. By the time the ruffled black silhouette of jungle revealed itself as a rampaging clamour of green, the men's backs glistened. The Indians sang while they pulled against the current. Wallace's ears struggled to find melody in their folk tunes. He picked out familiar words such as parrot, toucan and cassava and from these he tried to deduce the stories. Evenings, when bird chatter percolated and great pans of fish sizzled in butter, in stuttering Portuguese, which always amused the men for it was not their first language either, and it struck them as odd that a white man should be more defective in it than themselves, Wallace enquired about the songs. To their puzzlement, he wrote in his journal the verses that pleased him. And to their great delight, he demonstrably blushed at lyrics he found ribald.

On the water, he took bearings for every island and every point. He sketched the fissured granite banks and copied the carved pictograms on boulders. He drew waterfalls and cascades and measured off each portage. From local inhabitants he solicited information about villages, notable landmarks, water and food sources, local animals and vegetation. At noon each day he took a plumb-line of the sun to calculate latitude while at night he captured the reflection of the southern star to measure the meridian. Should any man wish to navigate the Uaupés in the future, he would have the benefit of the finest map of which Alfred Russel Wallace was capable, with his name affixed as pledge.

After a week or so, his hat no longer served for shade, but to shed water – the dry season was over. Through a mix of fair weather and light rains they had paddled one hundred and thirty miles of flat water to arrive at São Jeronymo. One mile upriver the first falls awaited. They would now need to ascend more than forty rapids and a dozen waterfalls to reach his destination.

At the first cascades they simply lifted the canoe over a rocky shelf. But then came waterfalls where the canoe had to be hauled up by rope. More violent rapids forced them to portage, and this required tedious unloading then reloading of the canoe. When they didn't confront white water or portages, the river confounded. It took unexpected twists and bends, narrowed to but a hundred yards, split into tributaries, launched drowned trees like battering rams, and ambushed them with submerged rocks. Every day they arrested progress in order to repair damage to the hull.

Rain routinely doused the sacks of food, trading goods and his hammock, thwarting the possibility of a decent night's sleep. And each time he trudged through sopping unbroken forest, he fastened his eyes upon the mud-splattered heels of the man ahead of him and tried to keep pace. Invariably, with his muscles atrophied from weeks of disuse in São Joaquim, the man steadily widened the gap between them, always while shouldering a much heavier load. Did the Indians even notice the misery? Was there some adaptation they'd made and he had not? He stopped swatting the legions of insects that beset him. It was futile. Black flies inflicted welts upon his face and neck. Buffalo-flies harvested his hands and feet. Worse still, Chigoe fleas burrowed around his toenails, festooning them with purplish ulcers that soon felt like shards of glass beneath the skin. Yet for all the trials, not once did he think of resigning. The opportunity remained considerable. *Terra incognita.* The stuff of Humboldt, and others who no doubt endured as bad or worse.

In early March – he'd grown so exhausted that somewhere along the way he'd foolishly forgotten to mark off the days in his journal and lost track of the precise date – at a village of mud-walled huts, he bought a dugout canoe that proved more manoeuvrable, if less stable. Still, the upriver battle wore on him and exhausted the men. Some abandoned him, slipping away at night to who knew where. He sent emissaries to recruit assistance from the nearest village, paying with axes, machetes, fish-hooks and beads. New men typically paddled only to the next rapids or falls. He'd heard of Portuguese traders and landowners who recruited at the end of a gun, enslaving their labourers. He had his own guns, of course, and the fierce desire to attain his ends. But to stoop to such barbarism?

A few days more paddling and one morning a clearing came into view. Several wood houses, animal sheds, gardens and an orchard.

"*Mucúra*," said his senior man. Three more crew declared they'd travel no more.

Wallace had been hobbling on bandaged feet for nearly

a week. And for infinitely longer he'd seemingly eaten little more than farina meal. And he could no longer recall the last solid sleep he'd enjoyed. With still a week's travel to the Devil's Cataract, final whitewater along the Uaupés, he elected to rest.

For the price of a small knife and a mirror he obtained shared lodging. Which meant that, by evening, he was encircled by an audience amounting to thirty or more, with a score of children darting among all the legs. Wallace observed how the villagers' complexions shone quite pleasingly, like polished filberts. And their flawless white smiles would arouse envy in any Englishman. Moreover, their centre-parted hair fell straight, framing shimmering black eyes. A most attractive race, he decided.

In turn, his own physical features did not escape attention. The blue eyes spurred debate which, he later learned, was settled under the assumption he suffered from a birth defect that prompted his tribe to cast him out. Fingers tugged at his beard and stroked the hair upon his arms. Performed by women, the latter intimacy produced not an insignificant stimulation – but for a strip of bark that hung from a twine belt and covered their most private region, the women were naked. However, he had little opportunity to dwell upon the women's most natural state. Hands regularly grabbed at his wire spectacles, hat, shirt and boots. For several anxious minutes his pocket watch passed from one to another, often out of sight. Then the William Harris sextant followed suit, the same model he'd owned since he began his surveying apprenticeship at fourteen, its brass nicked and scuffed from use and cherished all the more for it. Wallace soon longed for the solitude that would come with night. Above all, he longed for precious sleep.

When the house eventually fell dark and silent, despite

exhaustion and a fastidious habituation to self-denial, Wallace lay infuriatingly awake. His mind's eye buzzed with the memory of the women who had touched him. In particular, there was one girl of about twenty whose full lips parted slightly to reveal the tip of her pink tongue as she caressed his arm. He remembered the Indian girl he'd witnessed copulating with Bates, her bare legs spread and sheened with sweat. These past years he'd tried to banish the image only to find his mind's eye lured back again and again. Now, in the dark silence, he once again surrendered to it, every molecule in him stirring with the sensation of warm fingers gently kneading his skin as he imagined himself in Bates's place. This time there were full lips and a pink tongue, its glistening tip entering his own mouth, tasting him. Finally, gratefully, he gained his relief. Then came sleep.

The next day, a villager who spoke fragments of Portuguese and Spanish turned up. He had twice paddled the Devil's Cataract. He described how, at a distance of two miles, the sheer blasting roar of it made all spoken communication impossible. How the furious rapids crashed through a quarter-mile long canyon, shattering upon jagged boulders and spike-shaped rocks. How white fountains of water punched the air and rained back down in a blinding curtain. How eddies and whirlpools lurked invisibly, swallowing everything in reach. How for the length of the canyon, no landing was possible except such as conferred by submersion or destruction.

That evening, as rain thrummed the palm-thatch roof and the house filled with the grassy scent of intermingling bodies and close air, Wallace had a premonition. He'd not been given to such phenomena before. But this occurred in an instant, right after he'd capped his ink bottle and put his journal away. Amid all the jovial chatter, and cocooned against the elements, he experienced a glimpse of future events. He envisioned himself and his men in their ascent of the final cataract, crashing against the canyon's granite walls. It caused him to take stock of his situation. Six weeks ago, his death seemed, if not imminent, then reasonably certain. Thus he was fortunate to be in Mucúra. Conflicting reports of the white umbrella-bird troubled him, thus proceeding to the Devil's Cataract promised no further return and only held significant risk. Meanwhile, the immediate vicinity promised a bounty. Local hunters were eager to work for small payment. Detached appraisal of all the circumstances augured in favour of a reasoned decision. Facts and logic. He would go no further.

He remained intrigued by his hosts. They were true savages, untainted by European dogma. They conversed easily and often, regardless of age or gender. And they regularly touched each other without apparent sexual implications, plainly comfortable in the altogether. Was this not the more admirable state of man in his natural surroundings? Vivid contrast to the reticence of his own countrymen. He pondered his own capacity to 'go native', as some called it. The many practical advantages in terms of comfort, savings in resources and even hygiene certainly appealed. However, try as he might, he could not imagine himself gadding about shirtless.

An immutable product of Mother England.

Three families occupied the house in which he slept. They lived in a most communal spirit, sharing meals. He found the diet quite agreeable. In addition to cassava, sweet potato and peppers, there were several varieties of fruit, some entirely unknown to him. For meat, the villagers hunted monkey with bow and arrow, birds with blowpipe and in the river they speared fish. They also found plentiful nutrition in the abundant ant and worm populations. The ants, when salted, he liked well enough, the worms less so.

At night, they congregated for stories, reminding him of his own childhood. When he was very young his family lived at the grand house in Usk. This of course, was prior to the financial troubles. Each night they gathered in the back parlour where he would race for his spot on the oval rug by the blazing hearth. He remembered his father reading *Gulliver's Travels* and how the shortest interruptions proved unendurable. "Quickly, John, quickly!" he urged while his brother sprang up to prepare the pipe for which his father had laid down the book. Fanny stroked his hair, seeking to calm him, mother insensible, never looked up from her knitting. After his father broke off for the night, he would lie in bed, wondering what might happen next in the story. Those suspended moments – the Houyhnhms and Yahoos planted in his mind like magnificent gourds, each passing minute threatening to uproot them from the soil and dash them into shards – were as delicious as they were painful.

A fortnight in Mucúra and it was time to go. Wallace rued his illness at São Joaquim and the delay it occasioned. The rains had meant a paucity of wildlife. All he had to show for this excursion were four monkeys, two dozen parrots and smaller birds, two boxes of insect, bird and fish specimens, and several boxes of clothing, headdresses, necklaces, spears and arrows purchased from the villagers. He took solace that his previous collection, left at Barra for shipment had surely arrived in England by now.

Indeed, those earlier acquisitions occupied much of his current thoughts. Questions nagged him. Questions predicated upon the sheer diversity of what he'd discovered. Why so many variations of the same organism in such a small geographic range? It begged in the strongest terms the question of speciation. How might one reasonably believe such variation had been created in a single act? That some godly entity had made creatures with distinct and minute differences conferring no discernible advantage? Certain theories of organic change by transmutation seemed more credible in the result, but not persuasive in the process. Assuming some process was responsible for all this variety, how and for what purpose did it operate? Upon his return to England he would investigate the matter more seriously.

To navigate their descent, he hired a local pilot. However, it turned out whitewater terrified the fellow. From one village to the next, men departed and others were taken on. On several occasions he bought more birds. At an inlet where they'd put in to make breakfast one day, an elderly Indian paddled over to exchange greetings. A net hung off the stern and before Wallace had sat down to his farina porridge he was the owner of a river turtle. Near the end of their journey, at a squalid village run like a fiefdom by a Portuguese priest, he found a jungle dog that had been recently captured and now seemed partly domesticated.

The feeding and maintenance of his menagerie was time-consuming. Several of his captive birds died when he could not find food to their liking. A monkey and toucan were lost when their cages fell overboard as they descended a set of rapids. It appeared that would be the extent of his losses until the draught of a twelve-foot waterfall caught them before they could reach the bank and portage. They were swept over. Five birds and a basket of farina were lost, the canoe heavily damaged. Two of his men, both bruised and one with a particularly bloody gash above his left eye, quit on the spot. For his own part, each sputtering cough he affected to clear his lungs of water suggested a cracked rib or two.

He finally arrived in São Gabriel amid a driving rain. They dragged the canoe ashore then hauled the boxes, baskets and fifty-two surviving animals up the muddy trail into the clearing.

Upon the worn porch of the same hut where Wallace had last seen him, Richard Spruce stood without a jacket, hands on hips, offering a wide grin. A bare-breasted woman at Spruce's side drifted into the house.

"Good Lord, Wallace! Is it not possible to find one decent barber on all of the Rio Uaupés prior to presenting oneself for supper?"

"Mr. Spruce, I see those whiskers of yours have finally achieved an unruliness equal to your surroundings."

"Touché!"

"May I enquire what day it is?"

Spruce chuckled. "April 28th, of the year 1852, I might add, in case all those contusions indicate total loss of memory."

Wallace instinctively raised a hand to his right cheekbone. "I'm fine, really."

"Then come in out of the rain already. I cannot wait to learn of your adventures."

Upon reaching the porch Wallace searched Spruce's eyes. "I don't suppose … ?"

Spruce clamped a hand upon Wallace's shoulder. "Sorry, old man. No reports of Herbert, I'm afraid. A priest from Santarém passed through recently and said no ships have sailed upriver from Pará these past five months."

Wallace nodded. Drops of rain rolled off the brim of his hat.

"Sometimes the absence of any news is good news," Spruce said. "I retain hope this is one such occasion." He rubbed his hands together. "Right then, you must be famished. I suspect you might wish something other than the farina that has undoubtedly sustained you for much of the time. Let us see whether, as a consequence of your esteemed presence, we might persuade our cook to prepare an appropriate feast."

That evening, Wallace talked more than he had the entire

preceding week. How he'd missed intelligent conversation! Not merely the informed and considered intercourse concerning flora and fauna – in English, no less – but land ownership, workers' rights, colonialism, international trade, abolition and, of course, literature. However, there was no question of staying beyond the one night.

The next morning, cindered knuckly clouds filled the sky. Along the riverbank, between the scattered grey-pink rocks, rain had kindled growth of a bristly weed that smelled of mint. The fragrance carried to where he and Spruce stood.

They shook hands.

"I daresay we'll see each other again in England before too long," Wallace said.

"Not until I've completed my collection of ferns and bryophytes."

"Think of the museums, libraries, country walks, family visits – "

"And I confess to a growing fascination with the native medicinal practices," Spruce said.

"– lectures by forward-thinkers and perhaps a collaborative paper for publication."

Spruce re-seated the straw hat, pushing it back from his eyes. A pink indentation circumscribed his forehead. A broad smile broke out. "Yes, all that and more."

"Goodbye, my friend," said Wallace, climbing into his boat.

The canoe slipped into the current and when it neared the river's bend, Wallace glanced back. Spruce had retreated to the highest point in the clearing. Encircled by several children tugging enthusiastically at his trousers, he waved. Wallace raised his own hand and waved back. Then the canoe swung round the bend and his friend was lost from sight.

CHAPTER EIGHT
Mid-Atlantic, August 13, 1852

Seated upon the forward thwart, Bateman shaded his brow from the sun. "Where's Mr. Spruce now?"

"In Pará I spoke with an English merchant," Wallace said. "He informed me of a rumour that the British government has engaged Spruce for some botanical work in the remotest areas."

"If it'd been me," said the second mate, "I'd've stayed in that village with the naked Indian women and been Lord and Master."

Appelboom and Robinson guffawed, but Turner's stubbled face turned sour and they quietened. The captain was burnt scarlet. Wallace had pleaded for him to take his turn beneath their makeshift shelter (the other men made no such appeal), but Turner declined. He seemed intent upon his own code of conduct and made no complaint over his sun-ravaged condition.

Not that any of them escaped. It had been a full week now in the open boat. They wrapped shirts, towels, even undergarments, over their burnt faces, necks and hands. Yet Wallace saw blistered skin and cracked lips on every man. He imagined each endured a similar misery of headaches, muscle cramps, listlessness and above all else, thirst. The captain had rationed them to six ounces of water daily. When the order was given two days earlier, Bateman, crouching beneath the tarp, mimicked the captain's order *sotto voce*.

"Mr. Bateman!" Turner jabbed a finger in the second mate's direction. "Do not mock me, sir! I remain your captain!"

Wallace had waited with the others to see what punishment the captain would impose and how Bateman would react to it, but that was the extent of the confrontation.

Wallace now shifted his weight. It was no use. His bony bottom craved reprieve from all that sitting. The only sound was the boat's creaking wood. The crew remained silent – Isaac in particular had been quiet of late. Even last evening, when Wallace resumed his Amazonian tale, the boy withdrew.

He had been relating his final journey downriver towards Pará. The men launched question after question: Did any of them Indians rob you? Any cannibals lurking thereabouts? What about crocodiles? When you was tired of farina, did you catch some fish? Why not eat some of them animals you bought? Only the boy remained silent. He tried to draw him out, describing Lily's antics, Ollie's voracious appetite – how one afternoon he'd released the turtle so that he might make a sketch of its mottled shell and Ollie hurtled at the poor creature, jaws agape, only to drop well short of his target, painfully reminded of the rope round his throat – but Isaac only set his chin upon his palm and gazed into the dark.

As for the men's questions, he answered all of them. The mind was an unpredictable repository: was there an absolute truth in any of it? Certain recollections remained rich in minutiae while others retained little but one striking fact. Sometimes a simple question shook loose surprising shards of information, true gifts of memory, yet other facts remained unremittingly fastened to bedrock, and still more, irrespective of volition, desire or aversion, slipped away.

*

On July 2, 1852 he arrived in Pará seeking passage for England. At his lodgings he found waiting for him a mouldered envelope. A one year-old letter. Its author, of all people, was Henry Bates.

June 9, 1851

My Dear Wallace,

It is with considerable sadness that I write you at this time. I bear in mind we have neither spoken nor written for more than one year & I ask you to pardon the abruptness of this communication, not least for reason that it delivers terrible news. By the time you read this you might already have heard what I am about to describe.

I arrived at Pará just over one month ago to find the town under epidemic of yellow fever. With so many victims, all medical men were fully occupied. Visitors were left much to their own devices. It is with this background (& I beg your pardon for my long-winded manner in arriving to this point) that I learnt your brother Edward arrived at Pará on May 18th to find passage to England. He was soon stricken with the fever.

His abode was of poor standards and at a distance from town so I insisted he join me at Mr. Phillips's residence (you undoubtedly recall our acquaintance, Andrew Phillips, the English gentleman recently established in the trade of vegetable oils & by-products). Edward shivered much, suffered great weakness & informed me of aching in all his bones. He took several blankets & assured me they helped warm him. The doctor I summoned gave the diagnosis of yellow fever and administered ameliorative plasters. I supplemented this regimen with a tea of bitter herb, a leguminous plant known by Indians to alleviate fever symptoms. Mr. Phillips and I took cheer the next day when he proclaimed himself feeling better.

However I very much regret to say the fever returned, its symptoms magnified. Poor Edward began to bleed. I shall not indulge in the unpleasant details here. Suffice to say that early on the morning of June 8th, we expected the worst. Edward wished to convey to your mother certain matters that were then on his mind and begged that I write her.

I am most profoundly saddened to say that at half-past six that evening, Edward drew his last breath. I held his hand throughout & notwithstanding his youthful age, he entered those final moments with as much dignity as could be had in the circumstances. Mrs. Wallace, Frances, John and yourself were very much on his mind at this time, I assure you.

Having already purchased his passage to Liverpool, Edward had little more than the clothes he wore. With his remaining funds supplemented by my own, a casket was purchased. Edward was interred earlier today in the grounds south of town where, by order of the presiding Health Officer, all victims of the fever must be buried. I shall fulfill my pledge to Edward and compose a letter bearing news to your mother forthwith. Not knowing precisely when, but being nonetheless certain you would pass through Pará again, I wished also to inform you directly and entrusted this letter to Mr. Phillips.

Having my own plans to explore the region surrounding Santarém, I suspect it may well be several more years before you and I shall meet again (given my great fondness for Brazil, I have no immediate plans to return to England). I would therefore be remiss were I not to mention how it remains my greatest wish we might set aside our past strife. For my part, I can only once again offer my sincerest apology and reiterate that, notwithstanding my zealous scientific ambitions & commitment thereto, on occasion, I have been overwhelmed by bouts of loneliness. It surely is a mark of weakness & I have much admiration for someone such as yourself who has the strength to endure in what can, at times, be very solitary work.

I am grateful for your example.

> Best regards, as always,
> Very faithfully,

> H.W. Bates

From Phillips, Wallace learned more. They stood on Pará's wharf where the burly trader awaited with his labourers for the arrival of a barge laden with *piassaba*. The England-bound brig *Helen* had berthed and Phillips consulted his watch, anxious to get his harvest aboard. Phillips described how Bates had initially come to Pará with the intention of returning to England.

"His servant had robbed him of all his funds and belongings – shoes included. Reduced to a pauper's state, he believed his career as naturalist was simply not viable. However, before he could secure a berth on an outward bound vessel he was stricken by fever, the same plague that afflicted the town. All looked quite grim for Bates then, I'm afraid."

Phillips checked the horizon for signs of his barge and shook his head. "But your friend displayed a stout constitution. Why, he rose from his sickbed ready to resume his travel plans within forty-eight hours – the same time as mail arrived from your man, Stevens. Bates received not only a fair-sized remittance, but news that several of his writings had found publication. Like a new man, he commenced an extended expedition to central Brazil. Your friend Bates is quite the doer, is he not?"

"Indeed, sir," Wallace mumbled, picturing his brother's deathbed, blankets heaped, the pestilential air of the shuttered room, the hand of Henry Bates mopping Herbert's brow.

"I certainly admire that working spirit," Phillips said. "Quite commendable."

Wallace realized that Bates and Spruce continued to prove their mettle. He, on the other hand, wished only to safely flee these parts for the calm and civility of England.

The day before his sailing, he went to the burial grounds on Pará's southern outskirts, a weedy hump of land away from the rest of town. A lopsided white gate provided ingress. He found no logical arrangement, just summer-scorched tussock and randomly dispersed plots. The grave markers were rotted and sun-bleached and in disarray, lacking any chronological or alphabetical sequence. He backtracked to the entrance and began again. Hundreds of plots, most prepared in obvious haste, something he found detestable notwithstanding the exigencies. The land itself had been selected and prepared in similar spirit. With no understanding of the contagion or its means of communication, medical officers had declared Pará's cemetery off limits. With the stacks of bodies rotting in an abandoned warehouse, this hummock was cleared and ground broken. Quarantined even after death.

Three-quarters of an hour brought him to an unpainted cross canted in the direction of the river. Wallace traced his fingers along the lettering, nothing but crude furrows soon to be eroded by wind and rain, the marker itself slapdash, meant to be forgotten. Such was the public commemoration of his brother's life. Wallace would soon be aboard the *Helen*. After, who would take notice? Thousands of miles from a home and loved ones he should never have left – should never have been persuaded to leave. He wished he'd brought some token to place upon the marker, so that others might know there lay someone who was missed. But he had nothing.

Wallace removed his hat and knelt upon the grass. He intended to summon memories that would revive Herbert's words, his face, thoughts that would honour his brother's life. But little more than distant echoes and hazy images resulted and his mind wandered. In the end, there was only the engraving: 'H E Wallace, age 22, d. June 8, 1851'. He gave his moist eyes a passing wipe and got to his feet, the long grass where he'd knelt now flattened. He looked about the cemetery. Other than the whirring cicadas and a shirtless Indian moored to a distant spot with his scythe stationary, he'd had the grounds to himself the entire visit.

The next morning two wagons took his unwieldy collection to the harbour. The shipment to Stevens which he'd arranged in Barra last September had been held up by customs. It not only meant there'd been no money waiting for him, but it cost him dearly to pay officials for release of his boxes. Now he travelled with a burdensome number of boxes, cases, trunks and cages. More than ten thousand bird skins alone. Another several thousand animal, insect, fish and plant specimens. All this, along with his thirty-four surviving animals and his compiled journals, maps and sketches.

*

The lifeboat rose and fell on the waves. Wallace rubbed his thumb over the dressing on his injured hand and a tremor ran through him. He lifted his head and resumed his story. "It was thus an extraordinary relief when I finally had my entire collection aboard the *Helen*," he said to his fellow sunburnt survivors. "And I concede a not inconsiderable disappointment at witnessing its demise. Yes, indeed. Not inconsiderable."

It was the second mate who finally broke the silence. "I wouldn't feel none too bad about them bugs and birds, Mr. Wallace. Them kinds of things ain't nearly so dear as what we lost aboard the brig. All that timber would've fetched a pretty price in England."

"I'm afraid you've missed his point, Mr. Bateman," said Turner. The captain faced them from the fore thwart, the sun at his back and the last two casks of water at his feet. Even as he spoke, the men's spidered eyes fixed upon the sloshing casks. "Timber can be replaced. His own collection was unique, and he'd expended great energy and taken enormous risk."

Turner tipped his hat at Wallace. "I congratulate you upon your remarkable achievement, sir."

"Thank you, Captain. That's very kind."

Wallace noticed that Turner had recently been courting his favour, as if he were the key to reducing the rising tension in their small boat. But if the captain believed he had sway over the men he was certainly mistaken. He remained an interloper, at best. A mere guest who offered some light entertainment and therefore incurred no resentment.

"Beggin' your pardon, Mr. Wallace," said Isaac Plum. The boy had been nibbling at his biscuit ration and now set it aside – despite Wallace's regular coaxing and prodding, he barely ate. "But it ain't the insects and whatnot that's the biggest loss, is it now?"

"No, Isaac, you're right."

Isaac nodded. "I lost me Pa more'n three years back."

"You're hardly putting the gentleman at ease," said Turner. "We must maintain spirits."

"Spirits?" Bateman squinted out of one eye, the other crusted shut. "Ten days we been bobbin like a cork, broiled in our own skin and eating rations that ain't fit for a dog. You said one day, no more'n two, and we'd be saved, but we still ain't seen a ship! Nobody's got reason to be maintaining spirits."

In the eternal interval during which the slack-jawed captain readied his reply, Wallace glimpsed Turner's swollen tongue, dry as a stale loaf – like his own. Finally, the captain said, "Mr. Bateman, I am your superior officer."

A plea more than a declaration, it convinced no one.

Turner tried to lock eyes with Wallace, but he wished no part of it. Instead, he worked his way to the stern, away from the conflict, so that he might scan the horizon for the long-boat, apprehensive lest it be lost from view. He spotted the boat's

sails to the northeast, perhaps two miles distant, sailing close-
reefed. A stiff westerly had been in their faces much of the
day. For the next few hours Wallace kept surveillance. Then
in late afternoon something queer happened on the horizon:
the long-boat's masts swung round, inexplicably tacking. At
first, he didn't know how to interpret the manoeuvre – the
direction would take them away from the trade route – but
then Bateman shouted for all to hear.

"Sail ho!"

That evening they climbed aboard the England-bound
merchant ship *Jordeson*. And though they were saved, and their
sunburn would heal, and their stomachs would eventually know
better fare than the coarse biscuits, wormy pork and weak tea
with which their saviours plied them and which soon had the
men fondly conjuring memories of Mr. Roland's questionable
talents, it was not without further toll. The *Jordeson* lurched and
reeled through a succession of storms before finally reaching
the Channel on a blustery late September night. Despite the
smothering cloud and a wind that shrieked outside a cabin he
once again shared with Captain Turner of the demised *Helen*,
Wallace supposed themselves safe now that they were within
sight of English shores. That night, however, the old tub rolled
hard to portside. The cabin listed, books tumbled from their
shelf.

"Nothing to worry ourselves over," Wallace said. "Am I
right, Captain Turner?"

The captain failed to answer him.

The next moment the floor tilted at the heavens. A chair
crashed and the coat stand toppled. Wallace latched onto
the writing desk. His heart pounded and his eyes circled the
upturned cabin. He heard distant urgent voices on deck. Then
a booming thud. The cabin plunged into darkness and sea

water crashed through the skylight. Icy water drenched him.

A flash of lightning revealed Captain Turner on the floor laid out flat as a domino.

"We're done, we're done!" shouted Turner. "She's fallen on her beam ends!"

Wallace staggered towards the captain. He stumbled over volumes of Drake, Cook, Nelson, Parker and Hood scattered upon the floor. He slipped and landed hard at the foot of the chart table. Just then the whole world groaned with the sound of one hundred thousand nails, bolts and clamps screaming for release. Another flash of lightning revealed Turner, glistening tears rolling down his cheeks, hands clasped upon his chest. Wallace took hold of Turner's arm, but it was no use, the captain wished only to remain where he was. There was a deep shudder from below, as though the ship itself had shrugged in resignation. Wallace sank to the floor alongside Turner. He would accept the outcome, whatever form it took. Another deep shudder, like the human body's death rattle, followed. But this time it was the opposite – it brought life. The *Jordeson* gradually lurched back from the waterline. Turner, still on his back, seized Wallace's hand. The whites of the captain's eyes finally revealed as they blinked open.

"The Lord has severely tested us," Turner gasped. "But my prayers have been answered."

"I should hardly think it a necessary test," Wallace said.

With four feet of water in the hold, on October 1, 1852, two days after the storm, the *Jordeson* reached Deal, England. Despite the ordeal, Wallace was the only survivor of the *Helen* to immediately trade the narrow sinister streets of Deal for a coach to London. Not even young Plum could be persuaded.

"'Tis a very kind offer, Mr. Wallace," Isaac said.

They stood to one side of the pier, the rest of the *Helen*'s crew streaming past, collars turned up against the cold greasy rain. On the wet sand below lay a shattered buoy, the tattered rope trailing twenty feet to where it wrapped around a dead dog. Isaac closed the drawstrings of his bag then hoisted it upon his shoulder. "But even if you was to give me the coach fare, I can't be going home to me ma without the pay that's owed. And for that, Captain Turner says I got to wait. Paperwork and insurance and such."

So with legs woozy after nearly three months at sea and the *Helen*'s crew one family again, Wallace went his separate way, the interloper once more.

CHAPTER NINE
London, October 7, 1852

Wallace recovered in the comfortable Kensington home of Augusta Stevens, his agent's mother. For nearly a full week he was off his feet. How glad he was for Mrs. Stevens's fine cooking. It made the hollows at his cheeks less prominent for his mother's visit.

The butler ushered Mrs. Mary Anne Wallace to the drawing room. At the threshold, she faltered, lips pressed tight as if everything within her would fall apart. Wallace helped her to the settee, suggesting she lie down. On the wall overhead, Godfrey Stevens, Samuel's father, gazed benevolently from his gilded frame, rouged cheeks raised in mirth, while mother dabbed her eyes. Slowly she regained composure.

"Perhaps, mother, you would be more comfortable were you to remove your bonnet."

She did not respond. Instead, she reached for his hand, the one he'd seared while falling into the lifeboat. Her fingers skimmed the pink new flesh. By contrast, his mother's hand was coarse and pale by dint of her daily work. Proper measure, perhaps, of the Wallace men's financial inadequacies. Ever gently, she enfolded his hand in her own. Wallace noticed the creases to either side of his mother's mouth had deepened, and that there was the slightest quiver of her lips when she spoke.

"With John off in California now, you're the only son I have left, so I'm afraid my emotions are high. But let us talk of only good things, that our time today should be pleasant."

They spoke at length of the tremendous hospitality shown him by Samuel Stevens: clothing purchases that allowed a man with little more than the shirt on his back and pennies to his name to once again venture in all decency among society, great wisdom concerning matters of insurance, promises of introductions into scientific spheres, and the generosity and comforts of Mrs. Stevens' home. Mother told him of Fanny's excitement that, once Wallace's insurance proceeds arrived, they should soon be living together in London. She spoke of wonderful new novels he'd missed these past few years, particularly one by an American woman, a Mrs. Harriet Beecher Stowe that he simply must begin immediately. And she rhapsodized over the Great Exhibition that stood the previous year in Hyde Park – the glorious Crystal Palace that, with its vaulted glass plate roof enclosed walkways, full-size trees, statuary and pink crystal fountain twenty-seven feet high rendered, for Mrs. Wallace, as mere backdrop all the magnificent art objects and scientific displays.

Once or twice during their conversation he thought to raise the topic of Herbert's death. But there was a vulnerability in her eyes, a form of bewilderment, as if his safe return had wrought for her an unforeseen reconfiguration of the family puzzle, with its pieces strewn and missing. He realized that with Herbert's passing, she'd had no one to bury, her son's remains destined to lie beyond an ocean she would never cross.

That evening, from under the iron bedstead in Mrs. Stevens' guest room, he took out the tin box he'd saved from the *Helen*. He opened the clasp and removed a bundle of papers. They included miscellaneous receipts, letters of introduction and a sheaf of old correspondence. Atop the packet, crimped at the corners, was a page torn from the back of his field journal. The string that bound it left a faintly braided impression when he untied it: two intersecting lines forming a cross. He traced his finger along the vertical score and passed through several lines of handwriting to the place where the final writing appeared: Herbert's signature. The loan had been intended to mark a transaction, but he'd also told his brother it stood for something more. Responsibility, he'd said. He now tore the paper to shreds.

Those early days, when the giddiness of survival – not merely reaching solid ground, but the amenities of London, the ready comforts of Mrs. Stevens' fine home and her delicious fare, the pleasant surprise over the insurance proceeds – when all of that began to wane, he took careful stock. Aboard the lifeboat, bobbing amid thousands of square miles of open sea, his losses hardly seemed real. In the ten days that followed the sinking of the *Helen*, all that mattered, all that counted, was there in the captain's gig. His losses, to the extent he considered them, were like the very waters in which he and the other men wallowed: for all their peril and ubiquity, they remained abstract in their unactivated affect. The specimens, the animals, the drawings, the sketches. His notes and journals. The prestige and income that ought to have attended him. All that for which he had endured numerous privations and hardships.

And there was the other loss, evoked in the mist and fogs of London, when a lantern threw spectral light upon a moving shadow. Of this one loss, and of his role in it, he would not readily speak; it apprehended him like a gloved hand round the throat. But pain thwarted action; that much he knew. In the forests, an injured animal, unable to heal, withered and succumbed. He recognized Herbert's death would have to be placed behind him. And if this loss, this terrible wound, could be set in the past, then he resolved that the material losses, no matter their toll, must never be counted.

Mother asked him but once to describe the cemetery and Herbert's plot. He took pains to capture for her a pastoral setting, the view of the grand river, the swaying grass, the sheltering palm trees, even planting for her an English willow mere steps from Herbert's grave until he caught on her lips the emergence of a wistful smile. She patted his hand, thanking him. From that time, she asked no more questions about her youngest son and never again spoke aloud her longings.

It was Fanny who spoke unprompted about Herbert. "I miss Bertie," she would say apropos of nothing but her poached egg on toast. Then she'd sip her tea while he and mother found means to avoid each other's eyes.

One wanly lit morning early November, Wallace escorted his sister to Regent's Park. He led her to a bench where he did his best to remove the beads of overnight rain. Then he laid out his handkerchief for her so they might sit. On a beech tree a red squirrel perched, tail switching back and forth, regarding them with what seemed to Wallace particular interest.

"*Sciurus spadiceus.*"

"Pardon?" said Fanny.

"The southern Amazon red squirrel," he said, pointing. "A most vigilant creature. I had a dreadful time capturing them in Brazil."

"Undoubtedly," she said.

The English cousin of that elusive creature tired of them

and raced up the tree out of view.

"Something is on your mind, Alfie. I can tell."

He had no idea how to ease into the subject. Moreover, this was his sister and he saw no need for anything but direct talk. So he described his experience in São Joaquim – the terrible fever, the shaman, his consumption of the vine concoction – everything but Richard Spruce's involvement lest she become critical of his friend's role. When he told her about the shimmering green image, the manner of its movement, how it crossed the threshold of his hut and changed colour, she burst into tears, palms pressed into that narrow face as if to prevent her misery from seeping out. A nursemaid pushing a pram gave him a scolding look for the terrible mischief he'd caused his lady friend.

Fanny finally wiped her tears then adjusted her bonnet. "Herbert."

He nodded.

"He was letting you know he's all right. That you should not follow him, but rather that your place was here, in this world."

"I ... I don't know that," he said. "How does one interpret such – ?"

"Some things aren't intended to be parsed for interpretation, Alfie. They simply exist and you recognize their truth."

Recalling the rolling stride of the luminous vision, how in a fraction of a second that motion left him in no doubt, he nodded.

"I've had dreams about him since you returned," she said. "Sitting across from him at the table while he buttered his bread right to the edges – the same as I've seen you do, except he'd spread the butter too thick at one edge or say, the middle. Yours was always uniform. Perfect." She brushed the tears pooling in her eyes, chuckling. "I dreamt one time that I crept up behind him on a London street. He was looking at a playbill for the Haymarket. He was gazing it with this look of … I think it was awe."

"The world he wished to join."

"Exactly." She stared into her lap.

For the first time Wallace noticed on Fanny the emergence of wrinkles, even jowls. His older sister had aged more than he'd expected these years he'd been away.

Sniffling, she said, "There were other dreams, equally mundane. I've spent considerable time thinking about them, but really it's quite futile, isn't it? I mean, what are we to learn of something that emanates from within? You, on the other hand, experienced something quite different. A communication. That is what I would most dearly want."

They walked down to the water. She'd brought some stale bread that wouldn't be missed, and he stood watching while she fed a family of tufted ducks, allocating the morsels quite fairly. He noticed the ducklings' coarse grey bristles lacked the oily sheen of the adult feathers, particularly the majestic male resplendent in his elegant black cape and white vest. When the food was depleted the ducks paddled off.

Fanny dusted her gloves and glanced at him sideways. Then she gazed out over the pond. "Women are always reminded that nothing exceeds the importance of family. That family equates with love. But what of a woman unable to bear children? What is she to do? There is no natural outlet for all the love stored inside her. It remains bottled up, searching for a channel. The result is that she grows attuned to certain rhythms of life, she even cultivates it, so that seemingly unremarkable events, phenomena well outside the normal course and lacking meaning to others less sensitive in such matters, to her have clear import."

He could not recall having ever been privy before to such intimate thoughts. He said nothing at first, then mentioned what a shame it was that such ideal weather should be contaminated by the stench of all that coal particulate. Fanny sniffled – the precise side effect of such disagreeable air, he thought – and said she agreed entirely.

A week before Christmas, when Fanny and Thomas were out for the afternoon – having had his interest piqued by a display at the Great Exhibition, Thomas had become intrigued by the new medium of photography and they'd gone over to Adam Street for a Royal Society of Arts exhibition – Wallace raised the topic of Herbert's death with his mother one last time.

"You must wonder why I was not with him at his time of need."

She shook her head, her eyes glistening. "There's nothing to be said. We're here together now, that's what counts. A new beginning."

A new beginning. He accepted that.

When he'd first arrived in London, haggard and wobbly on his swollen feet and ankles, Samuel Stevens revealed he'd taken out insurance on his collection aboard the *Helen*. Two hundred pounds. While the funds represented less than half of what he might have realized had his collection survived, it allowed for a modest rental in Camden Town. Perhaps not an ideal neighbourhood in the social sense, it was nonetheless close to Regent's Park and within walking distance of both the Zoological Society and British Museum. Sufficient space for Mother, Fanny and Thomas to join him. At the time, he even allowed himself to dream that once he settled into something remunerative, he would seek a roomier home, one with space enough for a family of his own. But better than two months after his re-entry into civilization, he'd made few strides in establishing himself. Enquiries at the city's various scientific institutions and museums had proven fruitless. None were hiring. The Royal Geographic, Linnean, Zoological, Entomological, Geological, the Anthropological – none of the venerable societies had need for his services, even at the most modest stipend.

Come the new year of 1853 Wallace steered between the crammed bookshelves and teetering boxes that encircled the desk of Samuel Stevens. His agent relieved an armchair of its impressive mound of catalogues, manuals and field guides so that he might offer a seat. Stevens appeared to momentarily consider excavating a second chair, but elected instead to shove aside the microscope and glass slides occupying one corner of his desk. Obtaining sufficient aperture, he perched there, legs crossed, one shoe tapping the air. Over his shoulder, dust motes caught the light.

"Truthfully, all I desire is some stability," Wallace said. "From my father, I've seen the pitfalls associated with lack of gainful work. We moved homes a half-dozen times before I'd turned thirteen. Constantly uprooting, family torn asunder, it takes a toll upon one's health."

Stevens scratched his left ear. "Without credentials, the scientific establishment tends to be starchly resistant to newcomers."

"Newcomer? I've expended the past four years in the name of science."

"True, but before you ventured off to the Amazon there was little to distinguish you from a thousand other avid scientific collectors. Indeed, you even lacked the sort of friendly relations which so often confers an advantage. And while your explorations have attracted considerable interest, those with whom I have acquaintance – curators, educators, private collectors, etcetera – appear reluctant to see you as, how shall I put this … ?"

"Directly as possible, please."

Stevens spent a moment studying the carpet, a highly decorative Persian affair of golden lotuses, red peacocks and diamonds. "If only you would write more – like your friend, Bates. From South America he continues to transmit reports and has had great success in publication. I suspect this will greatly assist him in securing a position upon his return. You may wish to consider presenting a paper or two at one of our scientific organizations. I've been a member of the Entomological Society for fifteen years. Its President, Edward Newman, is a friend. I suspect there may be a place for you on one of their agendas should you prepare a suitable topic." A shadow crossed the office window as, outside on Bloomsbury Street, a hansom clopped past. "Speaking of writing, how is your book coming along?"

Wallace shook his head. "Slowly."

He'd been at it steadily. The scant records from his tin box had been supplemented with modest materials from his first year's shipments to Stevens. Specimens, sketches, artefacts, even an essay he'd entirely forgotten. To that he added his old letters such as could be retrieved from family and friends. How glad those creased and oil-stained pages made him! His compunction for exacting description, setting out precisely the scene he wished his reader to envision, now served to flush from memory further images, odours, sounds, textures. He also beset the British Museum, Kew Herbarium and scientific libraries, hunting out books, journals, diaries, drawings, maps and exhibits. The by-products of other intrepid explorers.

But if fashioning a travel narrative was akin to stitching myriad cloths of fact into an elaborate quilt, his rags of memory and threadbare details certainly made for a difficult business. He had good recall – excellent, he liked to think – yet how might he recreate the plumage, wingspan, bill shape and nesting habits for a wading bird he'd once seen fishing on a misty morning in the upper reaches of the Uaupés? Or the geological composition and precise location of a landmark hill he'd climbed one December day in 1850? And what about the precise ornamentation of a thorny flowering vine on which he'd snagged his sleeve three years earlier near the Orinoco? None of these materials were available for his quilt. His publisher, however, insisted that verisimilitude could also be acquired through careful and selective embroidery – quite distinct, he emphasized, from anything so vulgar and disreputable as deliberate deceit.

Wallace took that advice under consideration.

*

The door to the Entomological Society's meeting room stood open and, as he neared it, Alfred Wallace heard the buzz. He shared the audience's enthusiasm: the evening's agenda for February 10, 1853 promised John Westwood's keenly anticipated talk on a wingless insect species of *Coccus*. Inside, Wallace prowled the wainscoted room, every seat apparently spoken for. Eventually he secured a chair near the back, next to a grim-faced gentleman, hair fairly varnished in apple pomade and a wool blanket covering his lap. To the other side sat a man partly concealed by a great muffler. Taking the cue, Wallace did not remove his coat. Still, the damp winter chill permeated and not a dozen minutes into the meeting he'd begun to shiver.

Fever continued to afflict him. At his mother's insistence he'd seen two doctors. One advised a poultice and daily doses of fish oil, the other wished to shutter him in a dark room for three months – neither prescription had any scientific basis. Time and money squandered, he complained. If he'd survived São Joaquim, he could tolerate a moderate chill.

Penultimate to the Westwood talk, a paper on *Hesperiidae* was delivered by Richard Spruce's acquaintance, Ramsay Newcastle of Kew Gardens. Newcastle addressed the audience while pacing the front of the room, offering the audience a fine view of his aquiline nose. Rarely so much as glancing at his notes upon the lectern, the gentleman even managed to nod his acknowledgement to this one or that without so much as slowing a word. Wallace thought if only he himself were capable of such ripping good oratory. Citing Belgian and Italian studies in support of his own observations, Newcastle posited that the majority of *Hesperiidae* reposed with forewings vertical and hindwings horizontal.

After the applause subsided and Newcastle took his seat, Burton Salmon leaned upon his silver-handled cane. "Had I the vitality of a young man such as Mr. Newcastle," Salmon said, "I might have authored a similar report. For I have summered in the Scottish glens better than fifteen years and observed the very same phenomena."

A kindly gentleman produced an elbow and Mr. Salmon re-seated himself amid a smattering of applause. At the front table, Edward Newman cast about the room for further comments. In the first row, Westwood cleared his throat and released the hasp on his insect box.

Wallace raised his hand. Newcastle's thesis caused him concern.

"Does the visitor wish to add a remark?"

He stood and introduced himself. "In Brazil, I examined more than two hundred specimens of the *Hesperiidae* family. The vast majority rested with both sets of wings either vertical or horizontal, rather than one drawn and the other deflexed. I might therefore suggest that universal extrapolations from the resting posture observed in European localities be exercised with restraint."

In the first row, Newcastle launched to his feet. "Do you have empirical evidence, sir?"

"Mr. Newcastle, point of order, please," said Newman.

"To answer the question," said Wallace, "Yes, or at least – "

"Speak up!" someone called out.

Wallace heard the hesitation in his own voice. "You see, I captured each specimen. However, my collection was lost at sea prior to my return to England."

"Lost at sea?" said Newcastle. "A Robinson Crusoe tale!"

That remark provoked a good deal of laughter, awakening several gentlemen in the back row, members who came mainly for the social tea that followed the meeting.

Wallace felt his face redden.

"Please, Mr. Newcastle," Newman said, "we mustn't allow our comments to stray from the scientific.

Newcastle folded his arms, nostrils flaring, but said nothing further. Were it himself, thought Wallace, he would have been grateful for the new information. He stayed for the social part of the evening and scarcely had a quiet moment to himself. Several members came forward, prompting him for stories of the Amazon, his ship's fire and rescue, and information about Henry Bates's adventures. In regard to the latter, he told them that he did not wish to deprive Mr. Bates of the privilege which he himself currently enjoyed, relating his tales first-hand.

"It most certainly makes for the best stories," someone piped up. "No one to contradict you." And they all had a hearty laugh.

A handsome well-turned out man not much older than

Wallace was staring. A mischievous grin broke out on his sunburnt face and he strode over. "At long last I have the good fortune of meeting another intrepid adventurer!" said James Brooke by way of greeting. The other gentlemen immediately announced commitments elsewhere and drifted away. Remarkable coincidence, thought Wallace. However, in what seemed only seconds, he and Brooke were immersed in discussion of Robert Owen's theory of a new universal morality.

Three-quarters of an hour later they had moved onto Sir Charles Lyell's contention that old land-bridges had acted as highways for species distribution among what were now islands. The custodian notified them he wished to lock the doors. Making their way out, Wallace expressed his hope to see Brooke at the next Society gathering.

"I shall be sailing for Singapore by then, dear fellow," Brooke said. "I reside in Borneo – perhaps a destination for your next expedition?"

"I'm afraid there shall be no next expedition," Wallace replied.

They stood in the corridor outside the meeting room. "I am dreadfully sorry to hear that, sir. You clearly have a facility for such work."

Wallace detected a noble, even honorable quality in Brooke. A man of action and ideas, but not without his sympathies. A man with whom he could be frank. "I'm currently seeking a steady position in London, one that might allow me to remain with family. Perhaps marry."

"Ah yes, family and marriage," Brooke said. "Strong instincts, these. Well, should you change your mind, I can assure you Borneo provides fertile grounds for investigation of all manner of species. As governor, I would do all within my power to ensure your needs are met."

"As governor … ?"

Brooke's eyes gleamed and he laughed. "Truly, you didn't know? Well, dear sir, I like you all the more then."

Only later that evening did Wallace learn of James Brooke's knighthood, and of the explosive scandal then pursuing him. "Oh, Alfie!" Fanny cried out. "Do you even read the news unrelated to bugs and your other creepy-crawlies?"

The charges raised in the House of Commons – which Wallace learned Brooke had forcefully and candidly answered upon his return to England in 1851 – were presently awaiting adjudication by Royal Commission in Singapore. To Wallace's mind, only political connivance could explain the preposterous notion that Sir James would have acted in ruthless blood-lust while suppressing the pirates and insurrectionists who wished to destablize and plunder Borneo.

Having made the acquaintance of Brooke and other good men that evening, Wallace believed all boded well for his advancement within scientific circles. Offers would materialize. In the meanwhile, he would devote himself to his writing. The house's location was highly conducive for the task, granting him both the space for work and proximity to several fine institutions for research. Which was not to say he found all with his new address to be favourable.

Among even the most seemingly innocent crowds, pickpockets skulked and wild unattended children scampered – the impish nippers most often being the culprits of all that thievery: his purse was stolen twice that winter. And at the end of a long day the most respectable resident returned home steeped in odours of coal dust, manure, rotting vegetables and unwashed bodies. Nor did matters improve at night. Trolling cab drivers called "Halloa!" no matter what the hour, animalistic sounds emanated from doorways where whores tucked away, and street musicians – organ grinders in particular, but also players of banjos, drums, cymbals, accordions, fiddles and mouth harps – made up for lack of both melody and technique with a most unrestrained carnivalistic reverie.

His sleep was much disturbed.

"Common criminals," Fanny complained. "Transport the lot of them, I say, and you'll shortly find a new London." There'd been another fracas below their windows last night. Whilst Fanny's views had been offered to Thomas and mother, neither challenged her antiquated notions.

Wallace set down his pen. "Offered a decent chance at the right age, those criminals are just as likely to contribute to society as anyone else. Transportation does not address – "

"The underlying issue," said Fanny. "Yes, Alf, I've heard you go on before about land ownership and labour exploitation and how difficult it is for criminals – "

"People, Fanny," said Wallace. "They're people."

"Well, some of those people stole your silver last week and giving them a plot of land won't put the jingle back in your pocket, now will it?"

So they went back at it all over again. He felt his sister's intelligence augured for a breakthrough in her thinking one of these days. Mother, as always, remained neutral on these subjects – the peacemaker – happy merely to be among her children.

CHAPTER TEN
London, April 1853

The next time Wallace appeared at the Entomological Society, his own paper was on the agenda. A topic wholly original and of the provocative fashion Ramsay Newcastle presented with much success. He felt confident of a rapt audience. The room wasn't but half-full, which proved a disappointment, but the mild spring weather had likely posed a distraction.

Mr. Newman's introduction more than did him justice. When he described how he'd rallied from his fever at São Joaquim – ignorant, naturally, as to the particulars of his medicinal course of treatment – and thereafter charted the better portion of the upper Rio Uaupés, a few of the good gentlemen were heard to utter 'Well done!'. Then Mr. Newman announced the title of his paper, 'On the Insects Used for Food by the Indians of the Amazon'. Silence fell upon the room. Wallace imagined his audience's intrigue as he stepped to the podium.

During the early portion of his presentation he heard some garbled remarks and he wished the members would quell their enthusiasm until afforded proper opportunity to make comment. But as he entered into the various meal preparations made from nematodes the reaction grew more ill-mannered. He endured, however, and finally arrived at his favourite part. "I should now describe for you good gentlemen how the great red-headed ant is consumed. The Indian will hold it alive by its head then bite off the abdomen much like an Englishman holds a strawberry by its stalk and – "

An uncivil outburst of voices ensued.

"Rubbish!"

"Enough already."

"What vulgar nonsense."

"Twaddle!"

Then Wallace heard the whispers.

Hobbyist. Newcastle. Field collector. Debacle.

"Gentlemen, please!" Mr. Newman instructed the Secretary to strike from the minutes the most intemperate comments. But the free-for-all did not cease until Newman conceded a motion on standards for presentation by non-members would be formally tabled at the next session.

On this occasion, Wallace did not linger for the social tea.

A steady rain lashed his face as he tramped back to Camden. He realized how little had changed since he'd left Neath to pursue his scientific career. He couldn't rely upon others for help. But a short time later an exchange of correspondence with far-flung Richard Spruce brought a heartening opportunity. Spruce provided a letter of recommendation to one of the last men Wallace would have considered approaching: Ramsay Newcastle, member of Darwin's inner circle and assistant director of that most venerable scientific institution, Kew Gardens.

At the outset of his appointment, Wallace presented Spruce's letter. While he waited for Newcastle to complete his perusal, he discreetly looked about. Atop the credenza there was an aquatic vivarium. Shimmering paradise fish attested to the new fish-keeping craze inspired by the world's first public aquarium, opening next month at the London Zoo. However, for a botanist's office, it was curiously devoid of living plants. Indeed, the only terrestrial plants were a series of dried flowers framed and mounted on the wall.

"Mr. Spruce heaps high praise in your direction, very high praise indeed," Newcastle glanced up from the letter and followed Wallace's gaze. "A fancier of orchids, are we?"

"It's delightful – the Lady's Slipper, I mean."

Newcastle turned his chair to better admire the pink flower. Wallace noticed a dash of something feminine in the man – he could not be certain, perhaps the high cut of his cheekbones or the chisel tip to his nose. Newcastle said, "Ah, yes. The little shoe of Venus. *Cypripedium calceolus*. I collected this one amid the limestone dales of Yorkshire."

"Regrettably, with the sheer number of enthusiasts collecting them, I would venture that they shall become rare, if not extinct, in the near future."

Like shadows on the wall, those nostrils flared. "I assure you this orchid remains plentiful."

"I speak, of course, of hobbyists," Wallace sputtered. "In no way do I mean to disparage the collections of Kew Gardens! They fulfill a most valuable function in terms of public education and preservation of botanical specimens."

"You certainly speak your mind, Mr. Wallace. I am reminded of your remarks before the Entomological Society in regards my paper."

There ensued a brief silence, and Wallace knew not what to say. Newcastle's eyes were latched onto his, catlike, waiting. For what? He tried to recall how his comments at the Entomological

Society meeting in February bore upon their conversation now, months later. His comments had been limited to butterfly wing deflexion. An entirely different matter.

"Let us in any event move forward, shall we?" said Newcastle. "I greatly admire our mutual friend. Dr. Hooker predicts that Richard Spruce shall one day be regarded as one of our most renowned botanists. And Mr. Spruce wishes to recommend you for any suitable position that might fit – and here I quote – 'your immense talents.'"

Wallace couldn't help but bask in the compliment. How grand to have such a generous friend. A shame that Spruce hadn't written to Dr. Hooker directly.

"I gather, however, that Mr. Spruce speaks of your field work," said Newcastle. "No doubt you are an exceptional explorer and collector. I would also add that I find you an amusing narrator on a vast number of topics. While I wasn't there for its presentation, I certainly heard about your colourful account of the barbaric dietary habits maintained by jungle savages." Newcastle smiled, but Wallace most assuredly thought he did not appear amused.

"Given your scant scientific background, Mr. Wallace, I believe you may not be familiar with what is transpiring in London. We have entered upon an unparalled epoch in scientific theory. Our institutions have long promulgated dogma that not only stagnates knowledge of the natural world, but undermines it." Newcastle leaned forward upon his elbows, the space between them now as intimate as a tent. "If science is to emerge as the authoritative voice concerning the workings of our natural world, then we must battle scepticism in both the public realm and the scientific. Battle! You understand? And in that conflict there are only two sides. Success depends upon accretion of reliable evidence. Anyone who professes to be in our camp but does not adhere to this protocol is an obfuscator. At best, that renders him a harmless meddler. At worst, he imperils our objectives."

"If you are referring to the loss of my collection at sea, I can assure you that each item was meticulously documented."

Newcastle raised his hand, signalling quiet. "A theory without empirical data has no more value than superstition."

Wallace contemplated how the chasm between himself and Newcastle might yet be bridged, an opportunity still salvaged instead of demolished. And perhaps that might have been so, had Newcastle cited some other example – any other example – in what he next said.

"Need I emphasize," Newcastle said, "that we must conduct ourselves as English scientists, not jungle shamans?"

Wallace tried not to betray his irritation. "Surely our knowledge ought not to be defined by what is visible and what is invisible."

Newcastle smirked. "Am I to presume that when you refer to the invisible you mean spirits? An afterlife?"

"Not necessarily. But where an anecdotal history is repeated amongst different peoples and where there exists no reason to impugn their credibility, we must not close our minds. Shamanic beliefs remain worthy of our close attention. I would not close my mind to the possibility of an afterlife."

Newcastle blinked rapidly. It was then Wallace noticed Newcastle's long lashes, their sensual upward sweep. Quite feminine, indeed. Newcastle rose from behind his desk. "I regret, sir, that we are not of the same outlook in terms of the great cause of science. However I shall, on account of my good acquaintance with Mr. Spruce, continue to be mindful of your circumstances. Perhaps there may yet emerge a position for which you shall prove suitable."

Wallace caught a final glimpse of Newcastle leaning back in his chair, staring up at the Lady's Slipper. Then the door closed.

"Thank'ee, sir," said the conductor. "Mind yer step, now!"

Wallace tipped his hat and alighted onto Albany Street. The omnibus rattled off. From behind a voice barked, "Move off, ya idjit!" Wallace wheeled around. A wagon bulging with sacks rumbled straight at him, its driver shaking his fist. Wallace leapt aside. The wagon thundered past and the driver twisted atop his seat. He shouted something Wallace couldn't decipher, but the man's sneer betrayed its gist. When he set off again, one of his boots lifted with mucky resistance. He glanced down and sighed, then scraped off the manure as best he could. Plodding home, he mulled over the half-year since his return to England. Oh, the ideas he'd had! How he would circulate among the leading men of natural science. His research and writing would gain attention. From one of his admirers would come an offer of employment to which he would apply himself in the most dedicated manner. And in this fashion, he would gain a foothold and become the pillar to his family. None of it had happened.

Not long after Easter, a footman pulled upon the Wallaces' door bell. Lewis Leslie's servant. Through Samuel Stevens, Wallace had been introduced to a circle of gentlemen who enjoyed a good game of chess. Typically, they met Tuesdays and Thursdays at a social club. Early on, Mr. Leslie, a widower, told Wallace he'd taken a liking to his bold style of play, something not all the gentlemen of the club shared – Leslie thought them on the whole a rather cautious lot. And in contrast to the others, Leslie didn't mind in the least an amiable discussion during play. Now he'd extended an invitation for Wallace to make a social call. Wallace bade the footman wait while he dashed off his acceptance.

Leslie lived with his children in a three-storey brick house on a fashionable street in Campden Hill, west of Hyde Park. On the appointed Sunday, Wallace attended with fresh-cut tulips and a pound of candied ginger. After presenting his calling card to the butler, he was led upstairs to a sunlit drawing room. Leslie strode across the carpet to shake hands. The proprietor of Leslie & Son Auctioneers was a small rosy-cheeked man extraordinarily fond of the word splendid.

"Mr. Wallace, you look splendid!"

Introductions were made to a sombre young man who turned out to be Leslie's son, John. Leslie removed three cut-glass tumblers from a row atop the mantle and poured out healthy measures of gin. Young Mr. Leslie, in what appeared a practised routine between the two, retrieved a crystal water pitcher from the sideboard. After toasting each other's health, they sank into leather arm chairs and chatted of Wallace's re-adaptation to English life – London in particular, with all its entertainments. Then Leslie spoke of business. He glanced at his son and raised his glass. "To auctioneering. A most splendid business."

To Wallace's eye, Leslie enjoyed an awfully generous tipple. The young man, his unsmiling face already flush from drink, followed suit.

When they took their coffee, Leslie's two daughters joined them. The youngest, sixteen-year-old Harriet, shared the same fair hair as her father and brother. Her artistic skills were on display upon the room's walls. The Chiltern Hills under broken cloud, a reedy pond at what appeared Hampstead Heath, a still-life of gleaming apples alongside a crusty loaf of bread, and some half-dozen renderings of the same chestnut mare. Her pictures reminded Wallace of when he was twelve or thirteen in Hertford. His family had moved into an old house they shared with the Silk family and he and Georgie Silk would often sit upon the stone bridge near the old mill and sketch for hours. It was not apparent when and how he'd learned of those sketches, but one evening the Anglican minister with whom father was on such cordial terms visited the house. He remarked upon Wallace's artistic talent and told his father there might be a considerable future in it. Father replied that William and John had every bit as much artistic talent and did just fine in proper trades. It was more important for a man to make a living wage than engage in a fanciful pastime that might just as readily be pursued as hobby. The matter was then dropped from conversation.

Wallace felt Harriet's keen eyes upon him. Each time he glanced over, she appeared to study her slippers, hands folded in her lap. In contrast, when not directly involved in conversation, her sister Marion gazed out the tall Palladian windows that gave onto the residential street. Beyond the slate rooftops, a few renegade clouds skirted the azure spring sky. Marion's blue eyes appeared captivated by that horizon, Wallace thought. Perhaps she imagined the idyllic lands outside the city. She wore a crinoline dress of robin's egg blue with white lace collar, and over this collar spilled a few stray coils of hair – hair as black as the Rio Negro. Perhaps it was the contrast with her blue eyes that created such a distraction – he would later have great difficulty recalling much of that afternoon beyond the loosened strands upon Marion's collar and those eyes.

"Are you all right, love?" his mother asked after supper that evening.

"Alfie's smitten," said Fanny. She knitted on the sofa next to Thomas who, notwithstanding the book opened on his lap, appeared asleep.

Wallace glanced at his sister, then picked up his pencil, attending to his notes.

"See, mother?" Fanny exclaimed. "He does not deny the fact."

"All that travel and adventure hasn't altered his constitution," his mother said. "He would never deceive anyone." She cleared her throat. "So, Alfred dear, we don't mean to pry, but … "

"Yes," Fanny said earnestly, though her eyes betrayed amusement, "Not to pry, Alfie, but when do we meet the young lady?"

His lips barely moving, and to all other appearances still in mid-slumber, Thomas said, "Dearest, leave the poor man alone."

Fanny waved him off. "Oh, my. Look mother! Your son is blushing."

Wallace shielded his face with his notebook, but could not block out the sound of Fanny's giggles.

Late May, he received an invitation for a dinner party at the Leslies. It was a lavish feast, the mahogany table weighted with salvers of roasted beef, saddle of mutton, jugged hare and stuffed duck, all accompanied by various sauces and an array of mashed and boiled vegetables. Even before the decline in his own family's fortune, the Wallaces never dined in such excessive manner. Judging by the restraint Marion displayed – Wallace recalled she'd barely eaten a crumb his prior visit as well – it seemed she shared his discernment. She sat demure but radiant in a ruby red dress over which she wrapped a shawl dark as her raven hair. How he admired her refined and delicate architecture! Again, she seemed insensible to his presence, but with all the lively banter it was a convivial evening.

Another dinner party followed a fortnight later. Over the ensuing weeks, Wallace became a regular caller. At Lewis Leslie's instigation – greatly worried over his daughter's pallor – Wallace and Marion took some air together. That summer they frequented various parks and gardens. Side by side, his shoulders straightened – her sizable bouffant and persistent rectitude granted him no more than a modest allowance in height – he attempted to draw her out of her shell. He sought her impression of the flowers, shrubs and ornamental climbers he couldn't help but stop to admire. Marion offered only a modest appreciation for the most common garden blossoms. She shared her younger sister's fondness for horses, that much he learned, but little more. Her reticence was disappointing, but he was not uncomfortable with her silences. Indeed he came to view it as an admirable economy with words. Much better to afford a companionable silence than devise some burdensome small talk. Perhaps it was her quiet manner that had miraculously kept other suitors away from such a beauty. And no matter the muteness of her company, his other senses heightened in her presence. He had acquired a considerable depth of feeling. Of that, he was certain.

Wallace spoke to his mother of his intentions and she was pleased. He'd just turned one and thirty and while not everything had settled into place as he'd hoped, mother told him he made a fine catch. He made an appointment to see Lewis Leslie the next day.

Mr. Leslie welcomed him into his study with a hearty handshake and thump on the back. He directed Wallace to a chair. The shelves were crammed with knick-knacks, curios and tobacco pipes. Were it his study, Wallace would be sure to have more books.

He explained his intentions. Leslie's face turned grave. "Let us be candid, if you please."

"Why, of course," Wallace replied.

"Please don't take this as criticism, old fellow, but as Marion's father, I have a duty to ensure her future is secure. From our recent acquaintance and our mutual friend, Mr. Stevens, I am well aware of your conscientious and hard-working nature. Nothing like the privations of a foreign land to test a man's mettle, I must say. However, were your prospects to materialize – and at present there is little positive evidence, you'll grant – it would most likely place you in some low-paid curator role or teacher's position."

Seated on the verge of his chair, Wallace's stomach coiled tight and his throat went dry.

Leslie smoothed the lapels of his jacket. "And again, speaking most candidly, after grooming him for my business these past several years, my son John, to wit, the son amid Leslie & Son Auctioneers, recently declared his comprehensive distaste for the splendid world of auctioneering. Seems he would rather sally about the law courts in wig and gown than remain a part of my illustrious firm." Leslie rubbed his thighs then exhaled. "I now have no one trustworthy to share the burden of my enterprise. You, as coincidence would have it, have some familiarity with the sale of artefacts and specimens, are of industrious nature, and could do with a steady income. Indeed, I would surely expect my future son-in-law to be nothing less than financially sound."

So there it was. He had never conceived of himself as an auctioneer. However, with nothing opening up for him in London's scientific community, at least he might enjoy a pleasantly comfortable lifestyle. And while he had dreamt of raising his children in the English countryside, living in the city he might still avail himself of the museums and botanical gardens. Most of all, there was Marion. He could think of little else these past months.

In a matter of weeks they were engaged, the wedding scheduled for early in the new year.

CHAPTER ELEVEN
Camden Town, December 1853

Mid-December, Marion declined an invitation to join mother, Fanny, Thomas and himself for luncheon. Her note explained how that month was often a poor one for her, the dreary cold dampness seeping into her bones, exhausting her. He was disappointed, but she was his darling. The wedding invitations had been sent out and his mother informed him that for many young ladies that precipitated malaise. There had been other cancellations: the illness of a cousin and, later, one of her dear uncles, the foul London air, her brother's moods, disturbed digestion and, on one occasion, a migraine brought on by the tightness of her corset. Poor dear! Once they were married he would ensure a dietary regimen based on healthful cookery and long daily walks. That and marital bliss would be certain to restore her vigour.

One bright morning in early January, when there was still a sufficient chill that horses' nostrils steamed the air, he was pulling on his boots, intent upon the library, when the front bell resounded. The Leslies' footman. Wallace took the letter.

A single glance at the handwriting and his blood stirred. Since their engagement he had regularly written Marion, professing his admiration and respect. Her reciprocation was wholly unnecessary, for love was unconditional or it was not pure (he believed Keats had written such sentiment – perhaps not, but it hardly mattered for it rang true). So there had been no disappointment when she'd failed to reply. There was only her Christmas letter wishing him glad tidings (which, truthfully, might have bothered him for the banality of the expression had it not been her hand that penned it). He attributed her restrained communications to a quiet nature and reconciled it with the laws of nature. As with the animal kingdom, he was the male and in pursuit he would make his display.

He carried the letter up the stairs two at a time. At his desk he carefully opened the paper sleeve. The single page, dyed pale blue, consisted of two paragraphs. The first proclaimed that she held him in high esteem and predicted good things for him in the world of science or auctioneering or wherever he decided to devote himself. The second broke off the engagement. No elaboration except to say she could not imagine herself his wife.

He set upon the Leslies' house.

Neither the footman nor the butler could be cajoled. He was left with no choice. He attended Lewis Leslie's business office.

"Very sorry, my dear fellow," Leslie said with a hand upon his shoulder.

"Surely I'm entitled to some explanation?"

He hadn't intended to sound so pitiful. There was a furtive look, some uncertainty then Leslie circled the desk and settled into his chair.

"What I wish to say at the outset is that I firmly disapprove of it, but she's a headstrong woman." Leslie offered an apologetic shrug. "What am I to do? She places herself ahead of everyone else, including her own family. Always has."

This was almost too much to hear. He respected Leslie – the man was to become his father-in-law, his employer, his friend – but he could not stand to listen to him speak of his beloved that way.

"I can see from the painful expression on your face, Alfred" – following the engagement, Leslie had taken to calling him by his Christian name, a sign of their closeness – "that the truth might be unpleasant and I shall gladly spare you unnecessary details …" He arched his eyebrows in invitation, but when no response was elicited, he wrapped his fingers around a snifter that stood hidden behind his desk clock. There was an amber residue in the glass which he proceeded to swirl. "You are a fine young man. Someone I trust. And you are, or rather were – bloody hell, I'm sorry – Marion's fiancée. I am therefore prepared to reveal the full circumstances, but only on the condition you give your word that you shall never speak of this to anyone. It would tarnish not only Marion, but my family, likely my business. Are we agreed?"

It was thus he learned there had been another beau. The young man was a tailor who had aspirations of becoming a theatre costume designer. "Neither a sober nor respectable individual," Leslie said. He bemoaned his children's affinity for the arts, a fixation for which he blamed his late wife. "Naturally I forbade Marion to see him as soon as I learned."

"But she hasn't? Stopped seeing him, I mean?" Again, Wallace lamented his pitiable tone.

"I learned as much only one week ago and demanded she put a stop to it. Said I would disown her." Leslie sneered. "Need I say that despite all I have done for my two eldest children, each is sorely lacking in character. Had they been compelled to fend for themselves – in the manner which you have so admirably done, I might add – I suspect they would not suffer such deficiencies. In this instance, having no confidence in Marion's resolve, I have decided to send her to Paris. She will remain there while she regains her composure and learns a little French. To achieve a clean slate, as it were, at Marion's behest I agreed the wedding should be cancelled and the engagement broken."

They were walking towards the outer door. Wallace could not recall leaving the office or entering the corridor. Leslie again had a hand on his shoulder. "It's deeply personal for her, Alfred. And a potential scandal for me. I ask that you respect her wish not to continue contact. And I remind you of our bargain that you mention this to no one."

He wished to reply. But to her. To express his love. To shout his devotion. To describe the distress that now rendered him incapable of eating, sleeping, working. He needed to see her, to hear from her own lips. From her mouth. *Her mouth*. But he remained soundless. The hand on the shoulder. Then his feet on the blunt edges of the paving stones as he laboured home.

That evening in the parlour, while mother and Fanny discussed some frock pattern, and with Thomas away visiting his parents, Wallace stared at a recent essay on the zoology of paramecia unable to read a word. He'd played a fool – that much was clear. He found no fault with Marion, notwithstanding that he would have wished she'd been candid with him about her feelings. No, Marion was not to blame. Surely Leslie had orchestrated matters against his daughter's wishes. He imagined how he'd procured her consent to their relationship: her sullied reputation, a suitor without prospects, and a hard-working man dedicated to building the family's prosperity? In one stroke he might insulate his daughter from scandal and salvage his business.

He wrote Marion to explain that he understood all, that he absolved her of blame for injury to his feelings, that he only wished a splendid future for her. The next day he regretted very much the expression employed – that he'd "absolved" her. How arrogant! He certainly hadn't intended to strike such a tone nor suggest she'd done anything wrong. He maintained a very great respect for her.

All this he wrote in a new letter. When he received no immediate reply, he wrote again to offer a profuse apology for his thoughtless language. He explained that, while it could not excuse his behaviour in any way, he felt a certain amount of strain from the loss of her affection. Finally, while he knew she could not reciprocate the sentiment, he still loved her. Should she ever change her mind and reconsider the matter, he wished her to know that there could be no embarrassment between them. That he would accept her with open and uncritical arms.

He wrote eleven letters. Far too many, he despaired. But he wasn't good for anything else. He could not work. He could not read. He did not enjoy his daily walk. How could he, when hardly a moment passed without an arrow emblazoned Marion crossing his mind? Reminding him of the life they were to build together? Of how she should have been there with him right then as they completed their wedding arrangements? Instead he was mired in the woeful land of what ifs? He'd never known anything like this and saw not a semblance of imminent recovery.

There was no indication Marion received, let alone read, any of his words. As best he could tell (he'd been discreetly monitoring the house, paying a flower-monger in the Leslies' neighbourhood to keep him informed should he witness the young lady depart with her luggage), Marion remained in

London. He would desist immediately, if only he had direct word from her that this was her wish!

He was in a poor position. Very poor.

One more letter, in which he imprudently mentioned the coster's surveillance, earned a sharply worded missive on Lewis Leslie's business stationary advising him that he was acting dishonorably. Himself dishonorable? Oh, the pot calling the kettle black, indeed. Moreover, how mortifying that Leslie had read his personal thoughts. He needed to distance himself from this debacle.

Yet he had no options. His Amazonian travel narrative had finally received its publication, but it sold poorly. Reputable academics, naturalists and critics issued lukewarm praise or, citing his lack of data, mixed reviews. Certainly nothing that might have opened the doors to a funded position or at least stimulated greater interest in his services.

Insufficient embroidery, his publisher lamented.

And his vision of heading a unified family dissolved. Thomas became intent upon a foray into the photography business. Acceding to her husband's plan to open a studio, Fanny announced their intention to return to Neath. His mother did not immediately declare her decision to follow, but Wallace deemed it a likely scenario.

February 1854 arrived. For two days, Camden enjoyed a light blanket of snow. Ash-grey within hours of its arrival, the snow nonetheless hid the sight and smell of peelings, manure, and decaying vermin. Then the rains arrived, a steady wash that lasted better than a week. It had now been a full month since he'd received Marion's letter. He could barely string his thoughts together. Though it served no purpose to dwell on Marion, she scratched away at his mind. Every endeavour fell to tatters. Work? Impossible. He could not sleep. He did eat –

his mother claimed he ate more heartily now than she'd ever recalled – but food gave him no pleasure. The bricks of his life's ambitions lay in a heap and he was clueless on to how to pick up and re-build. His inability all the more abject for the fact he'd never known anything like it before. When his mother ushered him out of the house for his own well-being, he took long walks. The city streets, the parks, sometimes the museums.

And it was at the British Museum that a new future was revealed. It began with a lone figure he spotted in the insect room. For the better part of an hour, Wallace lurked in the room's margins, trailing the hunched figure as he dawdled one display cabinet to the next. The man paused in his studies now and then only to uncrook his shoulders or rest on one of the benches. Winter rain pattered the skylight and a few other visitors wandered about, but the room remained churchly silent – Wallace had no trouble hearing the man's tremulous sighs. Indeed, when the gentlemen brought his prominent forehead to within inches of a *Trichopteryx polycommata* in order that he might examine it, Wallace feared that were it not pinned down, the moth might fairly flutter away beneath the vigorous exhalation bearing upon it.

Feeling like a common stalker, Wallace tried to turn his attention back to the magnificent freckled wings of the August Thorn mounted in the drawer before him. He imagined that papery tan camouflage amid the dry summer heath, wings drawn, a mere wisp of foliage to even the most astute predator. But it was no use. He slid the drawer shut and, summoning his resolve, strode over.

"I beg your pardon, sir. If it's not inconvenient, may I introduce myself?"

Blue-grey eyes clamped upon Wallace. Confident eyes, set amid a ruddy countenance that belied his seemingly frail form. Most of the hairs atop the man's head appeared to have migrated south, reconstituting themselves as a pair of greying side whiskers that now churned side to side. Wallace soon found his hand within the soft damp grip of Charles Robert Darwin.

"You do look familiar," Darwin said. "Perhaps the Linnean Society?"

"I've attended a number of scientific meetings in London. But not the Linnean, I confess."

"Are you not then a member of any of our associations?"

Thinking of the societies' prohibitive membership costs, Wallace ran his hands into his pockets. "No, sir. I have mainly enjoyed the libraries and reading rooms whilst preparing some writings concerning the Amazon. Last year, I presented at the Entomological Society."

"Wallace? Yes, of course. A colleague referred me to your recently published travels." Again, Darwin worked his jaw, but the eyes sparkled with a smile. "On the whole, a rather eventful and entertaining volume."

A flush of pride infused Wallace. "I found much inspiration in the travels of Mr. Humboldt, of whom I understand you are also an admirer ..." He dearly hoped he wasn't overstepping their acquaintance. However, Darwin nodded encouragingly. "Your own experiences too, I would add, proved something of a model." Now the great man looked confused. His own fault, surely. He hadn't been specific. "Your journals from the Beagle?"

"Yes, yes, I understood. Please take no offence, Mr. Wallace. I do not wish you to believe I found your field work without merit. However, I held official appointment within a scientific surveying expedition. We returned with extensive data to promote further research and analysis."

"I did not mean to compare my work with yours, sir, and please accept my apology if that was the conclusion I forced upon you." Wallace's spectacles slipped and he pressed them back into place, wishing the conversation could be as easily restored. "Naturally I had hoped to produce more empirical evidence, but ... Well, most of my work was lost at sea."

"Yes, I imagine that loss was rather disheartening," Darwin said. "I have little doubt that the quality of your discourse stood to benefit but for that unfortunate episode."

"Precisely! Why, if I had been able to return with all my specimens, I feel confident that ... What I mean to say is, notwithstanding the commercial aspect of my endeavours, I also harboured a scholarly intent. Foremost, I wished to consider the origin of species."

Darwin raised an eyebrow. "The origin of species? A rather profound issue."

"I could not agree more."

"I should like to think then, that it merits deeper examination than, shall we say, a dietary indulgence in red-headed ants."

Wallace felt his blood swimming, his face reddening. "I concede I have much to learn ..."

"If men of reason are to succeed in our most embattled areas of knowledge, Mr. Wallace, the key is a fearlessly thorough and proper assay of our natural world order. That requires scientific purpose and scientific rigour. It is what distinguishes the competent naturalist from the intrepid collector. To quote my friend, John Lindley: 'Method, zeal and perseverance.'"

"Yes, yes, exactly." Wallace bobbed his head in agreement. "I've read Mr. Lindley's *Elements of Botany* and wholeheartedly embrace his maxim. However, I have experienced a ... recent disappointment. My work – or my ability to work – has abruptly faltered."

Darwin studied him, a penetrating gaze beneath which Wallace felt compelled to eventually lower his eyes.

"I take it this disappointment was of a close personal nature?"

Marion spilled forward in myriad images and Wallace felt his throat tighten. He could raise neither eyes nor voice. He nodded.

"*Mm-hmm*," Darwin murmured. "Then there is but one solution, sir. Work. Nothing but work. It mends the soul and heals the heart. Commend yourself into the service of science, my good man. Dedicate your efforts. The natural world requires as much industry as we can afford, and if there shall be no other reward in the deed, then at least there shall be honour."

"I certainly intend another expedition. And this time, my travel narrative shall encompass all aspects of the natural sciences. A truly thorough assay, as you've just said." Wallace took a sharp breath, stunned by what he'd just told Darwin. He'd made no such plans. Yet even to his own ears, his voice brimmed with resolve. Indeed, as of that moment, he felt fully committed to the undertaking. In terms of his life's current purpose, it was as though Darwin's directive to work had appeared on a previously empty horizon, and much like the *Jordeson*'s sails eighteen months earlier, he now found himself headed to shore.

Darwin gave a slight nod of approval. "What is your destination? Not the Amazon again, I trust. What with Bates and Spruce performing stellar work there."

"I have not yet decided …"

"Might I then make a recommendation? The Malay Archipelago has been long neglected. A veritable lacuna, despite its potential scientific wealth. But this is merely my suggestion." Darwin glanced at his pocketwatch. "Now kindly excuse me, but I come into the city rather infrequently these days. It leaves me with little time and a busy schedule."

"Certainly – I mean to say, thank you for the indulgence."

Darwin did not immediately take his leave. For a few moments, jaw working, he appeared to study the floor. "Mr. Wallace, please understand I am always receptive to serious discussion on the question of speciation. Should you one day delve into it in commensurate fashion and wish to share your insights, I extend an invitation for you to write me at Down."

"Thank you, sir," he said. "Thank you very much. I shall do so. You shall hear from me."

Wallace watched the celebrated scientist shuffle away, observing that Darwin looked substantially older than his forty-five years. Surely, in another fourteen years when he himself reached that age he would not be reduced to such frailty.

He glanced around. None of the other visitors in the room appeared to have taken notice of what that had just taken place: he and Charles Darwin had spoken as colleagues. Darwin welcomed him as correspondent. Never mind the recent disappointments – oh, glorious day!

That evening after supper, to ensure their attention, Wallace directed everyone into the front parlour. With mother in the armchair and Fanny and Thomas upon the sofa, he narrated his encounter with the famous scientist. Then in the midst of describing their meeting, he bit down on his lip and sunk his head into his hands.

"Dear Lord, what's wrong, Alfred?" his mother asked. "Have you fallen ill again?"

"Really, mother, I'm fine."

"Almost one and a half years removed from those infernal tropics and I see little improvement in your health."

His sister nodded. "Thin as a fence-post."

"I can only attribute those gaunt cheeks to dyspepsia," his mother said.

"Truly, there is nothing wrong with my digestion," Wallace said.

"Then it was the food. Was it so displeasing?"

"I assure you mother, the mutton, the potatoes – everything – was delicious. The meal caused me no upset whatsoever."

"It's Marion then, isn't it?" said Fanny. "You mustn't let that distress you, Alfie."

But he would not talk of it and quickly steered back to his meeting that afternoon. Still, even as he described Darwin's sartorial elegance, Wallace's mind marked the singular opportunity he'd squandered, a chance to draw Darwin into a more substantive discussion, to demonstrate that despite his modest background and the commercial aspects of his earlier endeavours, their interests accorded in a field of study dear to both their hearts.

Beetles. He'd omitted their mutual affection for beetles.

Another loss.

CHAPTER TWELVE

Simunjon Coal Works, Sarawak (Borneo),

June 21, 1855

If he'd known disappointment these past years then, as Charles Darwin predicted, at least he'd found solace in his work. As was his routine, he began the day at half-past five. Believing his weak eyes benefited from the rigour, and also so as not to create a disturbance, Wallace did not light the bedroom lamp. Instead, he inched his way alongside the cot, arms extended mid-air like a somnambulist. Soon as his fingertips tapped the wood crates stacked against the wall, he side-stepped left, found the door, then passed into the front room.

A smoky char lingered this morning. He'd roasted his coffee the night before, the beans still atop the stove, cooled right in the skillet. He lit the kindling, ensured it was well underway, then carried the skillet over to the table. He tumbled the beans into the brass hopper of his Kenrick and while he cranked the handle, his mind sifted through the pending chores: gear that required mending, items to be sorted and labelled, and the weeding that had been neglected in the garden.

As Sir James Brooke commended, Borneo, an island which formed part of the Malay Archipelago, proved an inspired location. Its profusion of species had kept him going. That and Nellie. He dared not admit how the little one's presence appreciably improved his mood. Ludicrous, of course, to call it fatherhood – there was no biological connection (other than in the most remote sense, one might argue) – nonetheless the infant inspired a paternal instinct he'd never known. Most mornings he attended to her before his coffee. But this day there'd been no cries from the direction of her crib. Delighted to let her sleep, he would check on her before breakfast.

He slid out the cast iron drawer on the coffee mill, pleased it glided so easily from the oil he'd applied yesterday, and emptied the grounds into the coffee-pot. Then he added water from the basin and set the vessel atop the stove to boil. Voices outside. A pair of miners trudging past, start of the morning shift at the Coal Works. By the time he lit the lamp and opened his journal, the eastern horizon revealed an aubergine sky. In London this day would be deliciously long, but close to the equator the days remained more or less the same. He had no complaint – dull uniformity made for better routine. And routine adhered the body and mind through healthful productivity.

He and his young assistant Charles Allen had settled in at mid-March. The nearest town, Sarawak City, was twenty miles distant. The house afforded a base for short forays. No need for the burdensome packing and unpacking that wore him down so much in the Amazon. Situated alongside two dozen workers' cottages on the lower flank of the very hill that was the source of the coal, he now stored his belongings without worry over weather or thieves or misplacement. For the first time in his travels, everything had a regular place. Scientific

138

instruments, books, maps, medicines, chemical cleaners and preservatives, nets and collection boxes, jars, casks, corks, carpentry tools, oil skins, utensils, guns and ammunition, camp bed, mosquito netting and clothing, each had its assigned location. Highly gratifying.

In the garden, he'd planted tomatoes, onion, peppers, garlic, pumpkin and several herbs. For eggs and meat, he purchased several chickens and the fussiest pig with which he'd ever been acquainted. Most importantly, the area provided an abundance of insect life. A railway would eventually shuttle between the coal mine and the Sadong River two miles distant. But for now, the surrounding forest remained pristine.

The coffee was ready. He brought a steaming mug to the table and sipped while jotting down his thoughts. The writing proceeded slowly that morning. Sunlight had already fallen across the table when he finally heard the scuffle of feet in the bedroom. He set his pen aside.

"You up and about now, Charlie?"

No immediate response, only more of a rumpus. Then those half-peeled eyes, the left one getting a lackadaisical rub, finally made their appearance.

"Aye, sir. Shall I get the breakfast underway then?"

"Please." More than a dozen weeks in the same location with the same unvaried routine, his assistant's duties as plain as a pikestaff, but still he asked.

Charles nodded and, pawing at the mat of hair on one side of his head, drifted towards the stove. Granted the boy was only sixteen, but surely he ought to look more refreshed after ten hours' sleep. Only the dead remained insensible that long. The bedraggled waif. Pip. But no, that couldn't be, for it would be nominating himself as Magwitch. At the very notion, that he was capable of such corruption, he couldn't help but smile.

He carried that smile over to the corner of the room where Nellie persisted in her uncustomary silence. She was awake, sitting up in the crib he'd improvised, brown button eyes upon him.

"Are you hungry, my little one?"

She smacked her lips. Then she gave the top of her head a vigorous rub-down and, finding something in that russet fur, squeezed it between thumb and forefinger and popped it into her toothless mouth.

"Clearly so. We shall have something ready in the blink of an eye, little ducky. Charlie!" Wallace called out. "Would you fix a bottle of water and rice milk for Nell?"

The boy turned from the stove. "After we've taken our breakfast, sir?"

"Before, please. Don't look so sullen, Charlie. She's an infant and quite helpless. We need to have a little sensitivity and compassion."

She was whimpering now. He bent over the crib. Her feet churned at the calico blanket he'd folded at the bottom. Seeing his face, her noises remitted, mouth agape.

"I see you've soiled your blanket, young miss. I shall find you fresh linens."

Soon as he had his back turned, the whimpering set up again. He crossed the room to fetch the blanket. On his way, he passed Nellie's mother – or her remnants, to be more precise. Her skin was preserved in a cask of arrack and, like all his other orangutan specimens, the sterilized bones were stored separately in one of the crates in the bedroom.

Five weeks earlier, he and Charlie had been toiling in a section of bog a mile and a half east of the house. Several Dayak men emerged from the trail. With glistening brown torsos and soot-covered trousers, Wallace assumed they were

140

mine workers finished their shift. They'd tracked him down to relate news. They'd spotted an orangutan.

He and Charlie followed the men upon the ramin trees that lay end-to-end to form their walkway across the swamp. Though the boles ran straight – sometimes as long as a hundred and twenty feet – and the rust-coloured bark admitted some traction, leather boots were no match for the men's barefoot grip. Wallace paid great heed to his footing. The surrounding peat swamps never lacked for moisture and several times these past months he'd toppled into the black morass. Misfortune that had him squelching and reeking of compost until the end of the day. So although the men indicated urgency, he picked his way along as fast as prudence permitted.

The orangutan had moved only a short distance from where it was first sighted. It crouched ninety feet up a durian tree across a narrow swamp. A docile contentment animated its face as it snacked upon fruit it gently picked apart. He considered orangutans remarkably human-like: intelligent, nurturing, playful. He once watched two juveniles high in the canopy chase each other in a friendly game of tag. Despite the disparate length of their limbs and torso – their arms fifty percent longer than their bodies – they moved through the trees with both speed and grace. And in stark contrast to man, they did not employ their considerable strength for a violent purpose unless provoked or attacked. Small wonder the interest from museums and private collectors was so immense. To which end he'd thus far killed thirteen.

The workers squatted on their haunches, watching keenly as he loaded his double-barrelled gun. They'd already earned their finders' fee and were now interested in the spectacle. He didn't mind the audience. He was a good shot and the creature seemed unconcerned for their presence.

The first blast caught the ape on its left side, near the hip. It dropped its fruit and fell forward upon the branch, lying quite still. Wallace wondered if he might have to dispatch one of the men to climb the tree in order to bring it down. But soon the furry mass stirred, attempting to drag itself forward. Presumably trying for cover. He reloaded. The next shot caught the nearest shoulder. The beast put up a horrid wail, rolled onto its side, then plummeted. It struck the ground face down.

He and Charlie waded into the bog. Thigh deep in some sections, progress was slow. When they reached the body Wallace saw it was a mature female. The angle of her hips and legs suggested her back had broken, but she remained alive, emitting a low plaintive murmur. Charlie finished her off with his handgun, one shot to the heart.

Fourteen.

For another small fee, the Dayaks cut down a ficus branch, lashed the orangutan then lifted the load onto their shoulders. "Bound for home," Wallace joked to Charlie. "Aye sir," replied the humourless lad. They'd marched but a few steps when a mysterious whine rose up behind them. Wallace took out his machete. "Stay here," he instructed Charles. He re-entered the swamp and the shrill cry immediately stopped. He picked his way across, black water moving in thick ripples around his trousers, the ground spongy under his boots. A short distance from where his specimen had landed he spotted a cart-wheel sized fern. Then a tuft of fur.

Wallace guessed her no more than a month old. She removed her fingers from her mouth upon seeing him, then she reached out. When he leaned closer she caught hold of his beard. An infant of not more than three pounds, her grip was formidable. She continued to cling tight as they journeyed home through the forest.

"You seem terribly fond of those whiskers, young miss."

"What's that, sir?"

"Nothing, Charlie."

"Sir, were you talking to the monkey?"

"She's an ape, Charlie."

Charles mopped his forehead on his sleeve. "It's what I meant to say. I just forgot the right word."

"To answer your question, yes, I was speaking to her."

Her toothless mouth opened. Hungry, he presumed. He could offer only his forefinger. She sucked it with vigour, but unappeased she refused to release his beard. His face thus held close to hers, they studied each other. It was a most amiable, guileless face, he had to admit. Bright wide eyes, lips puckering affectionately. A gentle soul.

Nellie's household presence became his blessing. After each evening's work, he settled down with his night-time reading and Nellie curled on his lap. She burrowed into him and he could not but stroke that darling head. No matter the dryness of his scientific material, he read aloud to her, confident she gained something in those words. Before bed, he would install her in her crib with a lullaby, then coax her to release his whiskers with a kiss on the forehead. He imagined the day he would return with her to England, Nell then perhaps two or three years old. How they would saunter into a stuffy gathering of the Zoological Society. Oh, the shouts of astonishment! A brisk learner, by then she would know the meaning of any number of phrases and a brief demonstration would highlight her undoubted intellect. He would then defy anyone to look into those eyes and try to refute the conspicuous ancestry therein! He returned now to her crib with a fresh blanket and removed the soiled sheet. It was specked with blood.

Nellie lay listless in her crib all through the day. That evening he found more blood.

He altered her diet. Next day, however, she developed a fever. He could guess its cause. She was undersized and weak for lack of mother's milk these past five weeks. He'd tried his best, prepared to pay dearly for human milk. But while the Dayaks in the region all knew of him and were happy to help in most every other way, in that they'd resisted. Orangutans feasted on unripened fruit. Durian, mangosteen, banana – just as the fruit showed promise of sugaring, villagers would encounter the broken rinds upon the forest floor. He'd been encouraged to shoot as many as possible.

One day to the next, the little one showed no appetite. She even lost interest in his beard. Four days after the fever first manifested, Nellie succumbed. Wallace lifted her out of the crib – now just a specimen box again – and carried her outside. She was not much heavier than when he'd found her, a weightlessness that burdened him. He laid her on the saw-tooth grass beyond the veranda. Charles had offered to carry out the essential duties, but that was unthinkable.

Wallace spread his oil cloth alongside her small body. Then he set out his instruments, tape measure and field journal. Nellie's mother was his last entry, pertinently identified as *Simia satyrus*, adult female and marked with her specimen number, date of death and vital statistics. He picked up his knife and spread the fur to reveal the epidermis, took a long breath and, sure enough, his trembling stopped. Then he inserted the blade just above the clavicle.

Number fifteen.

Next morning he insisted on an early start. They'd gone about a half-mile when Charles said, "Sir, are we in a special hurry?" Wallace's only reply was to hasten some more.

"Have I done something wrong?" Charles called out.

Wallace answered with nothing more than a view of his back. Sometimes the boy could be irritating beyond measure. Could he not see that he wanted only to work? Routine. He needed routine.

By mid-afternoon they'd covered half as much again as their usual terrain and his bag held a copious assortment. Eight new species of beetle, possibly nine – he would know better after consulting his field book. Turning home, heedless of exhaustion, he'd resumed his long swinging stride. Charles quickly lagged. In his sweat-soaked rankness, Wallace felt insulated. Shoulder bag jouncing against right hip, leaves crunching under his boots, he heard only the hot chuffing of his breath. For once, the forest was blessedly expunged, wholly blotted out. Next thing he knew he was on the ground, pain exploding from his ankle.

His left foot had caught a divot. A woody stem had punched through the skin just above his boot. He carried antiseptic and clean bandages, but he told Charles the house was near enough. He preferred to tend to the injury there. He'd hurt himself worse. He could endure.

Within two days, infection set in. The thick abscess and angry inflammation prevented him from bearing weight. The tropics, he admonished himself. What else should he have expected for being neglectful?

He was house-bound. Denied his outdoor work, denied his exertion, denied his natural splendours. Charles pottered about alone in the forest, wasting gunshot, botching everything he laid hands on. He, on the other hand, remained trapped with his thoughts, trapped amid the gloom that infiltrated every corner. Memories of Nellie, whose skin now rested with her mother's. Memories of Marion, surely now with her tailor. Summertime, they likely availed themselves of London's gardens, strolling arm in arm until they found themselves behind the screen of a willow tree where, perhaps, he would kiss her smooth white neck. What did it matter? Marion would never be his own. He knew he needed to push aside memories of the personal. Nellie, Marion, the disintegration of his family, rejection by London's scientific men – all of it no better than a lump of coal in his mug.

He sat at his table and demanded of himself that he write. Write his daring ideas and send them out to be mocked. He cared not a whit. He'd begun a separate journal on speciation, sorting out some ideas, a progression really. Concepts rooted in the Amazon, now cultivated and augmented by a rich supply of new observations that impelled him to extend his theories one branch of thought to the next in a seamless sure-footed journey. He already envisioned the series of articles. Oh, the furore they would incite! An unflinching debate would burst forth, the very discussion others, the reputable men of science, seemed presently reluctant to embark upon, perhaps concerned over their standing – like Robert Chambers, publishing his controversial work on transmutation anonymously. He, Alfred Russel Wallace, a mere collector, had no standing, nothing to be torn down. Nor would he care otherwise. He would publish under his own name.

Method, zeal and perseverance. It would deliver him his answer, unravelling that greatest of mysteries: the engine of organic change, how and why species came to differ. Then he would write a book on the subject.

Since his arrival in the archipelago he'd assiduously followed Samuel Stevens' encouragement to publish what he could. Not simply to gain a foothold inside reputable circles, but to generate ideas that mattered, ideas that changed the way other men would interpret facts, interpret history. A few months earlier he'd written a paper entitled 'On the Law Which Has Regulated the Introduction of New Species'. It argued that over vast geologic spans of time species emerged organically, through gradual modification of a common predecessor or anti-type. The fact each species came into existence coincident both in space and time with a pre-existing closely-allied species – observations he'd first made in Brazil and witnessed again among thousands of specimens he'd collected in the archipelago to date – described how similar yet varied organisms were found in one general locale. Modification of the common ancestor progressed in a non-linear fashion, one species diverging from the previous in a never-ending series of branches. Thus a schematic representation of the fossil records and current distribution of species resembled a sort of tree. The tree of organic change.

He knew the theory was novel and a provocation to creationists. Yet where was the reasoned rebuttal? The open and scholarly debate? Why the ensuing silence? Mr. Darwin closeted at Down head bent low, Sir Charles Lyell still an inveterate Believer, and Newcastle, well, the man was elitist, preferring his evidence from an approved cadre, refusing to air significant public issues precisely where they belonged: in the public realm. If only he might have his idea thrashed out more fully by these great men, he felt certain his argument would distil into something greater. Then the mechanism by which new species were created would inevitably come into focus. After that, there would be no forestalling him. His planned book would lay waste to the conventional. Among scientific breakthroughs he could imagine none more important. It would secure his place in the pantheon of science. Homage to the idea, not the man, though offers of employment would inevitably pour forth.

But the idea, the mechanism, continued to elude him. Much like some fantastic recipe missing its one key ingredient. And from all those great cooks of science he could entice no one to make a suggestion. Well, if that was the case, he would give the pot a good stir and see its effect.

He had the perfect subject: the *Orang Utan* – Man of the Forest in the Malay language. Existing research revealed few white men had been privileged to see them in their natural environment. So little was known of the orangutan that there wasn't even agreement on the number of species. With the number of orangutans he'd now killed and dissected, there was no one – certainly no scientist – better placed to furnish the data for his current theory.

His thesis started with indisputable statistics. Body dimensions, weight, colour, bone structure, internal organs. The data demonstrated only two species of orangutans – not three or four as some had argued. The Bornean species, he explained, foraged only lowland marshes and swamps where a dense canopy existed. The boggy terrain deterred predators, most notably man, and the high overlapping canopy permitted them both food and travel without ever descending to the soil. Indeed only once in his four months of observation had he seen an orangutan on the ground (other than when they fell from his gunshot, of course).

But these observations were only a build-up, fortification for the cannon shot he launched in a separate essay he penned in the following days. Among the incendiary facts he offered were the incisors he'd witnessed in all his orangutan specimens, including young Nellie. Yet when he sliced open those pink stomach linings and ferreted through the contents, what had he found? No evidence of anything other than a strict vegetarian diet. Precisely what he'd observed in the field. Thus it begged the question: why would a peaceful fruit-eating creature without any natural predators need incisors? The inescapable conclusion, he wrote, was that incisors were vestigial dentition from a closely-allied species. And if that species was to be discovered in the fossil record it would surely reveal a form and structure more or less human.

No one had dared to publish such a public assertion. With the audacious contention that orangutans and humans had descended from a common ancestor, he believed the preceding silence he'd encountered would most assuredly be broken.

Until such time as Charlie would post the mail in Sarawak City, Wallace put his articles in his strongbox. The strongbox he placed inside his trunk. Closing the lid, he noticed how time had worn the black paint on his trunk to grey – not unlike some of the whiskers emerging in his beard. What else should he have expected? He was thirty-two years old, a point in his life when he'd believed he would be married with a family and a stable respectable profession; his name on the office door, an umbrella stand and coat rack, and a window box for his plants. Sunday strolls through Hyde Park with a picnic hamper, parasol and blanket, the children skipping ahead, he and his wife chatting gaily. Pointing out to his children the grey cracked bark of the plane tree or the red bill and whiskers of a mandarin duck, while he and his wife exchanged one of those intimate glances he'd witnessed between couples. It seemed the normal course.

His own course, however, would clearly be a far different one.

CHAPTER THIRTEEN
Simunjon Coal Works, Sarawak,
August 28, 1855

His body had rebelled. Or so it seemed. Two months, yet his festering ankle refused to heal. With little to occupy him during the day, he found himself waking earlier than usual. Perhaps he simply needed less rest. Or maybe his mind was too agitated – for it wasn't merely his leg that festered, his mood had suffered.

He generally considered himself of a pliable nature. Not lately, though. He'd had enough of the waiting, enough of the disappointment, enough uncertainty. He wanted to move forward. Above all, he wanted his answer to the origin of species. The elusive mechanism.

He'd captured tens of thousands of specimens – thousands of beetles alone – and many exhibited only the slightest variation one from the other, so that the line between species and varieties was blurred. Why all these modifications without obvious utility? And how had they come about? If he knew that much, then the rest of it he would gladly suffer.

At the unholy hours in which he now woke there was no bird chatter. Only the steady huff-huff-huff that emanated from Charlie's cot. A veritable steam engine, that one. In the dark, Wallace would hobble to the front room, the wood crutch clomping horribly. Thrice he'd stumbled and fallen. The first occasion, his crutch struck the stack of boxes by the door (said stack thereafter relocated to the space formerly occupied by Nellie's crib). Next time, a misstep hurtled him directly into the door frame for a resounding crack above the right ear. And two mornings ago, he'd somehow pinned the tail of his nightshirt against the mattress, a most peculiar happenstance that spun him backward off the cot and onto the floor. On not one of these occasions did Charles awaken.

Remarkable.

In the front room he lit a lamp and hung it over the table. Haloed beneath the glow he would sit there until first light, his pen scratching upon paper. Then, for the balance of the day, when he wasn't writing or re-examining his specimens, he parsed his field notes, his hoard of scientific journals, and tried to jog loose facts that would bring him closer to solving his mystery.

Typically, Charlie returned mid-afternoon with the day's collection. It was now the apprentice who performed all the skinning and skeletal preservation. All he could do was provide occasional helpful guidance.

"What was that, sir?"

"I said nothing."

Wallace sat on the front steps to the house. A few feet away, Charles knelt on the grass working on a partly-skinned squirrel. The boy put his knife down, then mopped his forehead with his sleeve.

"With all respect, sir, when I know you're watching it makes me twitchy."

"Twitchy?" Wallace asked. The boy had a way with words.

"*Mmm-hmm.*" Charles picked the knife up again.

Wallace levered himself up with the crutch. Even though the boy did his best to shield the specimen from his view, he could see the carcass had been butchered, its skin perfectly useless. Yet it was apparently his fault for making the boy twitchy. He hobbled onto the veranda, from where he might more discreetly resume observation of the ongoing massacre. For over a year he'd explained again and again that the trade in specimens – from which Charlie's apprentice salary was drawn – required both volume and quality.

It was, of course, the desire for volume that led Wallace to hire the boy in the first place. His loving sister's idea. "Think about it, Alf," Fanny said one morning amid those frenzied weeks prior to his departure. "In order to turn a profit, you need to sell as many specimens as possible. Take a young lad and show him how it's done, then pretty soon he's not only earning his keep, he's paying dividends. And a second set of eyes means more's the chance for something special in your collection." He could not deny the logic. He also recognized that to study the question of speciation he needed quantity – the means for comparison. Fanny went a step further. She put forward a candidate. The fifteen-year old son of a carpenter acquaintance in Neath. Good with his hands, Wallace was assured.

More than a year later, Wallace now wondered who his sister had wished to favour by the arrangement. He tried to teach Charles care and precision so he might one day earn a decent living. And while the boy could shoot a gun, he faltered with almost every other task. Why? Inattentiveness, clumsiness, occasional laziness. The time spent hunting and skinning thus incompensable.

Not that he was unsympathetic to a working class boy. The lad was thousands of miles from family and familiar society without complaint of homesickness. And while he'd recently been so bold as to criticize the monotony of their diet (and prevalence of biting insects), he travelled intrepidly, displaying admirable curiosity for the people and their culture. He was a decent lad, if nothing more. Fanny had undertaken to find a replacement, but Wallace held out little hope. She was a fine one for the business logic of hiring, but he suspected her acumen less acute in assessing aptitude.

It was early November before his leg bore weight again, four months without real work. Four months of little but rumination and suppuration. A lifetime. He was in need of both physical and spiritual sustenance. He packed his shoulder bag and one box. Then he instructed Charles to concentrate on ants and other insects – specimens on which the boy could do the least damage while he was away.

He would go inland.

In a fourteen-foot dugout canoe, with a Dayak-speaking guide recommended by the coal works' foreman, he chose a small branch of the Simunjan. They left mid-morning and for a while the stream ran straight southeast, the swift black water spangled with sunlight. Then the banks twisted and tapered, pinching closer as they wended. Upon each embankment a brawling green profusion crowded to the very limit of the land, allowing no ingress.

He and the guide slept that first night on the boat. At twilight, a colony of fruit bats, thousands upon thousands, had flown past. He'd wondered where they would find the food necessary to sustain such a large number. Mosquitoes. The air pulsed and whined. Wallace wrapped every inch of skin against intrusion. A handkerchief covered his face, its corners tucked into his ears. Wedged amid his gear and the confining walls of the canoe, trapped inside his clothing, sweat streamed over every fold and cleft of skin. Rarely did more than fifteen or twenty minutes pass when he wasn't compelled to remove his handkerchief and gulp some air. He did not sleep. He only yearned for dawn so that they might once again be on the move.

The next morning they paddled beneath a tunnel of interlaced tree branches. Nipa palms and screw-pines arced so low he had to curl into his lap to pass beneath them. Dangling shawls of liana brushed his hat and shoulders. The fern and creeper-covered banks on either side narrowed close enough for him to reach with his paddle. How he had missed exploration and discovery! The embanked walls of greenery revealed variety at every turn. Bright red seed pods hung from kalumpang trees. Purple and scarlet macaws shrieked and fluttered at their approach then settled back into somnolent repose after they had passed. Long-nosed monkeys cavorted through the underbrush and howlers gorged on jackfruit and mangosteen, showering their canoe with rinds and derisive hoots.

Late afternoon they landed at a silt and rock-strewn slope. Looking at the worn trail that climbed the embankment, Wallace wondered if this was where he would at last find some answers. Much to his satisfaction, the several men who greeted their arrival wore nothing beyond the single coloured fabric strip strategically hung to preserve only ultimate modesty. It boosted his hope that the villagers hadn't yet encountered any missionaries; he admired the fair-minded autocratic rule of his friend, the Rajah, Sir James, but differed from him on the need for proselytization.

As the villagers exchanged words with his guide, Wallace removed his spectacles to give his brow a passing wipe. Each of the round faces encircling him went silent. Recalling his experiences among the natives of the Amazon, he resigned himself to the inevitable and passed the spectacles forward. Each man then gauged for himself the lenses' effect, not with the schoolboy giggles he expected, but rather with an air of reverence he found touching.

His guide finished conversing with the men and announced, "We can stay."

"How much do they want for payment?" Wallace asked.

"No payment."

"Do they wish some gift? Anything?"

The guide shook his head. "You is a guest."

"Extraordinary."

A pair of men were already lifting his box out of the canoe. Others beckoned him to follow them up the path.

"Did they indicate how long I might stay with them?"

The guide tendered a puzzled look. "You is the guest. You decide."

They paraded single file into a clearing dominated by a lone building. Elevated on pilings, its length rivalled all but the longest English pier. Together with surrounding animal enclosures and gardens, it apparently constituted the village. Ushered up the ladder and inside, he discovered a long hall, one side partitioned into separated family quarters and the opposite a communal area with several stone fireplaces. The split-bamboo floor, polished smooth and dark as cinder by wear and fire smoke, provided a delightful spring under foot. He was directed through the communal area to a woven mat onto which he settled. Around the room, he noticed bamboo baskets, drinking cups, food containers, utensils, bird cages and fish traps. He wondered whether the versatile wood might grow in England.

More of the building's occupants returned throughout the afternoon and once again he became the centre of attention. All this he tolerated reasonably well, mainly because the residents were utterly respectful, seeking his assent before stroking his beard or fingering his garments. By the time darkness infiltrated the clearing, cooking fires blazed in the hearths and the oaty scent of the room was displaced by a sweet, almost nutty fragrance. He was served a bowl of steamed fish and rice, the grain cooked to an unusual sticky texture he found undesirable, but deliciously flavoured by coconut and nutmeg. Once he'd emptied his bowl, he was presented with a folded square of banana leaf. Upon it lay a yellowish oblong appendage which, even at arm's length, issued a repulsive sulphuric stench. This was the durian fruit he'd been desperately avoiding. He knew, however, that on this occasion there would be no escape. Mustering an expression of what he hoped resembled gratitude, he lifted the fruit to his lips, and braced himself.

The texture astonished him, reminding him of a lush custard. But the flavour? It combined honey, almond and melon with an almost floral taste. Sublime. He ate his portion and gladly accepted a second. An elderly woman pointed her spoon at him and everyone laughed. He joined in the merriment and someone kindly brought to his attention that he had durian in his beard, which made him laugh only harder. For the balance of his stay, he indulged not only in more fresh durian, but durian stew, durian porridge, durian rice, durian pudding and durian cake.

Early each morning, he set out with one of the hunting

parties. He marvelled at the men's skill with bow and arrow, and their instincts. One day, a path split into two. They forked right and carried on for the better part of an hour. Then a shout came from the front of the line and the men spun on their heels. Returning to the fork, they pursued the left track this time. He was informed that a hornbill had flown from right to left across the path of the lead man. The bird acted as agent for a benevolent spirit and had directed them to where they would enjoy better hunting. Wallace thought of Newcastle: how easy to dismiss such a claim as nonsense when a truly open mind recognized that these people were no more inclined to waste their energies than Englishmen. Accordingly, there might be an empirical basis to their assertion.

For eleven days he participated in village life and collected specimens. He felt, if not at home, then at ease. More so than in London. He recognized the benefit of his hosts' generous nature, how harmonious a community might be when it lived in balance with its surroundings. Had he not his own ambitions, his personal quest, he would not have disturbed this status quo for anything. But he needed his answers. And to that end, he finally approached the shaman.

Wallace had his doubts about the man. This was no wizened elder – indeed, the man appeared younger than himself – and he constantly blinked as if irritated by smoke. There were also the missing front teeth that suggested the losing end of a tavern brawl. Nonetheless, with guide in tow he approached the shaman and made his request. As the guide translated, the shaman twisted the beads garlanded round his neck. Then he released the strands and mumbled something. This began a rapid exchange.

"Well?"

"He say he know," replied the guide. "You is the guest.

Everything is good."

"Good …?"

"Tonight."

"Tonight?" Wallace searched his guide's face for signs of misapprehension. "Just like that? He doesn't need more time? Or – "

The guide was staring at him out of one eye as though he were a simpleton.

"Fine. Never mind. Tell him thank you."

"You is – "

"His guest," said Wallace. "Yes, I know: there is no thanking."

The guide nodded.

He tried not to betray his anxiety. The impetus for his request could not be traced to any one event – it had welled within him from the earliest juncture of the expedition. In May 1854, not two months after leaving England, he and Charlie arrived in Singapore. At the post office he found waiting letters from Samuel Stevens, Sir Roderick Murchison of the Royal Geographic Society, his friend George Silk, a certain Professor Cargill at Cambridge, and one envelope with a distinctively feminine hand. For the briefest moment, his heart pitched, then he recognized the writing as his sister's.

He carried his mail into the reading room and spread the letters before him like a series of moths he wished to compare. A pair of cheap tallow candles emitting a noxious acrid odour provided the room's only illumination. At the far end of the trestle table a Malay merchant, the only other patron, seemed equally preoccupied with a letter he composed and some shred of pork or such he wished to dislodge from between his teeth by prying his pencil tip and utilizing a good loud suctioning.

Wallace opened Stevens' letter first, then his sister's. Penned in early April, Fanny wrote that she felt obliged, having regard to their conversation about her dreams of Herbert and his own experience in São Joaquim, to inform him she'd just returned from London where she'd attended her first séance. The result was unclear, she said. She'd been nervous and distracted and the knocks upon the table had startled her greatly so that she had little time to consider their import, but she believed it was a path she needed to pursue. She intended to enquire of a certain well-known spiritualist and would write him of the outcome.

Since that first letter, he'd heard from Fanny twice more. Several more séances had proven gratifying. Living in Neath however, she found herself isolated from spiritualist pursuits. She was trying to persuade Thomas to return to London. Knowing he was engaged in his own explorations, she encouraged her brother to open himself to the world beyond the visible.

That evening, the earthy-sweet fragrance of agarwood incense filled the longhouse. From a roof beam hung two lengths of rattan, free ends brought together to form a saddle a few feet above the floor. A sort of swing, upon which he presently sat. Except for the young men drumming in the corner, the villagers pressed round him. A public spectacle, he'd become. And whether it was lack of worry that anyone of his acquaintance would learn, or the knowledge he would never see the villagers again, or simply that he'd come to feel comfortable in their presence, the public aspect caused Wallace no concern. Not that his mind was at ease; no matter how personal, this remained science.

The shaman parted the crowd. Affixed to his head was a set of deer horns and he carried a wood tablet bearing bowls of blackened fish, cooked pumpkin and rice. He began a passionate speech, or plea. Not a word was translated – prior to the ceremony Wallace's guide had been banished – so while the audience murmured or nodded their heads at intervals, for Wallace the significance was left to be decoded. The shaman broke off abruptly and pointed to the food. Then he swept his arms wide to encompass the hall and all its inhabitants and chanted. The crowd repeated the words like an incantation. The shaman lifted the wood aloft, signalled for Wallace to rise and, with everyone singing, the lot of them filed out of the building.

They descended to the riverbank. The shaman knelt and, reciting a few words, slipped the tablet into the water. The crowd watched silently as the wood drifted slowly at first, then turned in the current and floated out of sight. A swell of congratulatory remarks and smiles immediately rose all around and soon everyone returned to the longhouse for a wonderful feast.

That was all of it. No vile liquid to force down. No nausea. Nothing.

"You much happy now," commented his guide when they met after the meal.

"I am?"

"Yes, I see in the eyes. What they do with you?"

Wallace combed a hand through his beard. "I can't be entirely certain, but it would appear that, using an offer of food, the shaman drew into a piece of wood my bad spirits, then floated them downriver."

The guide shrugged. "Black magic jungle people."

*

Wallace returned to the coal works late November. The specimens Charles captured during his absence were, on the whole, reasonably preserved. He wondered if there could have been something to Charlie's earlier complaint, that his constant observation made the boy nervous. Little matter, the rainy season was due to begin and there'd be no collecting now. He told Charles to help him pack.

They travelled to Sarawak City where Wallace intended to retrieve his mail, ship specimens to Samuel Stevens, enjoy a visit with his friend Sir James Brooke and prepare for travels to the Spice Islands. Previously, he'd been inclined to dismiss Charlie upon arrival in town, but the lad's recent work had changed his mind.

Which was why Charles's announcement caught him off his guard.

"But … but are you absolutely sure about this decision?" Wallace asked.

They were standing upon the wooden walkway that spanned the front of the bank, a healthy remittance from Stevens presently filling his purse. In the street a swallow dipped low over the roadway, where a man cursed and flogged his recalcitrant donkey. "I reckon I just need something more of a Christian calling right now, sir. But I'm going to stay on in the tropics, maybe in Singapore. A man can live by his wits in these territories. And an Englishman gets a certain amount of respect no matter his station, if you know what I mean."

Wallace nodded, though he wasn't sure of the assertion's truth. How utterly frustrating that all the training of the past year and a half had just started to pay off. But truthfully there'd be a not inconsiderable relief at being disencumbered.

"Have you thought of how you'll manage? At home you have your family, your father."

"Britain's a mongrel's life for me if I was to go back. No work. No room for another mouth at the table. Here, there's opportunity."

"But you are a little young to remain on your own. Sixteen?"

"Seventeen now, sir."

Wallace remembered how, when they'd made their initial acquaintance back in Neath almost two years earlier, Charles's father, in what was likely his only suit, prodded his son forward. "Shake hands with your new master, lad. Go on." A pale hand, small and leafy, had grasped his own. Now, as he clapped the boy upon the shoulders, beneath the jacket he felt muscle. Durability. Borne, perhaps, out of the tropics.

From the funds Stevens had remitted, he paid Charlie out. "You are a pleasant young man, Charlie. I wish you all the best." They shook hands a final time, the young man's grip now quite assured. He then watched as Charles marched in the direction of the harbour, towards a future he would shape in his own fashion.

Meanwhile he had his own future to marshal. There was a shipment of specimens to prepare and new facts and experiences to reflect upon. Of all this, he felt eager. Joyous, even.

His renaissance, he knew, could have been entirely self-generated, a sense of well-being that was no more than the rational product of several independent salutary influences: his leg had fully healed and he once again enjoyed the healthful benefit of physical exertion; there was the successful collection he'd amassed to date; and the resumption of sound sleep; finally, there was the convivial aspect of communal living he'd recently enjoyed among the Dayak people – a most amiable people notwithstanding their headhunting antecedents. So his renewed outlook was almost certainly attributable to a coincidence of environment and timing, rather than the ambivalent evidence concerning the shaman's exorcism. He would not, however, rule out any possibility.

It had been ages since he felt so clear in his thoughts and purpose, and so wonderfully free.

CHAPTER FOURTEEN
Sarawak City, December 1855

As often seemed to happen, the happiest events conspired to occur after he'd manufactured the circumstances, whether by design or inadvertence, to ascend from his personal nadir. In Sarawak City, Wallace received a particularly notable piece of mail. Upon reading, then re-reading it, he instantly composed in his imagination the news he would send to his mother, Fanny and Richard Spruce: he'd received a most collegial letter from none other than Charles Darwin. Despite the fleeting nature of their meeting at the British Museum, he had clearly made an impression.

Mr. Darwin wrote that he was undertaking a comparative collection of waterfowl, a study that was to find a place within a larger compendium simultaneously underway. He would be grateful therefore to receive such specimens from the archipelago as might be arranged. The letter said nothing of reading Wallace's 'On the Law Which Has Regulated the Introduction of New Species', the essay on closely-allied species he'd penned in Sarawak. Wallace knew however, that Darwin was a busy man (indeed, he'd addressed the letter to 'Russell Wallace', a minor oversight so typical of one preoccupied with great matters). Thus it was understandable that in his appeal for assistance, albeit a trifle disappointing, he might avoid other topics. Besides, the essay had received publication only a few months earlier, appearing in the September 1855 volume of *Annals and Magazine of Natural History*. Darwin would most certainly wish time to digest the ramifications. Little doubt, however, that once Darwin considered the matter and weighed in with his own thoughts, it would greatly advance Wallace's quest for the origin of species. Buoyed by these thoughts, he bore down upon the task of preparing his shipment.

He sent Stevens five orangutan hides, sixteen orangutan skulls, two complete skeletons, fifteen hundred moths, over five thousand beetles, and an assortment of other insects, animals, reptiles, and botanical specimens. Worth a good amount, Wallace noted with satisfaction. This work completed, he finally allowed himself some leisure.

In Borneo, the very height of the social sphere was an invitation for dinner at the Rajah's palace. Wallace counted himself fortunate to have the friendship of the region's most powerful, yet gracious, man. And the Rajah had invited him to a party in the week before Christmas.

The evening of the party Wallace stood on the road before a square wooden bungalow. The locals referred to Sir James Brooke's residence as the Palace. A most amusing description, Wallace thought. Scarcely forty feet wide with a thatched roof, the house had been elevated on posts of nibong palm in the local fashion. From the road Wallace crossed over a weedy ditch, passed through a wood palisade, then navigated a dirt yard checker-boarded with pens emitting the collective noise and gases of cows, sheep, goats, chickens, ducks, geese, pigeons, monkeys, cats and dogs – any of which Wallace suspected might find their way onto the table that evening.

Entry to the house was gained by ladder. A pair of Malay boys not more than ten years old stood at the base of the ladder. To assist the ladies, Wallace presumed. The boys smartly saluted and he made a show of straightening his linens, fixing each with magisterial regard, then returning their salutes with great solemnity. Climbing the rungs, he left the pair in a fit of laughter.

Wallace arrived at a central hall. About fourteen or fifteen people were spread about the room with the largest cluster at the far end, surrounding Brooke. The walls were adorned with a handsome collection of muskets, pistols and gleaming cutlasses, suitable to any discriminating brigand. To his left a sideboard held several porcelain vases of pink and white orchids. He was on his way to examine the orchids when he was intercepted by a dashing young man.

"Mr. Wallace? I am Spenser St. John, Sir James's secretary."

St. John's warm hand pillowed his own, the air between them now steeped in patchouli.

"A pleasure," said Wallace. "Thank you for the kind invitation."

St. John tucked his chin into his collar and dropped his voice to a conspiratorial whisper. "We are truly delighted to have you join us, sir. Sir James has been eager for some enlightened conversation." St. John's eyes rounded and he pressed his fingers to his lips. "Oh, my. Please, please, do not repeat that. It was quite … impolitic. I really must be more careful. However …" Again with the conspiratorial smile, he lifted an imaginary glass to his lips.

Without further ado, St. John took Wallace's elbow in a most intimate manner that Wallace might have thought inappropriate were this not the tropics, and escorted him towards Brooke and his coterie. They started, however, in quite the opposite direction. St. John took him past a copiously-coiffed Spanish-looking woman and a starched English couple (Wallace recognized them as missionaries recently returned to town), arced past the peninsula of sofa and end table then trod a determined path across the elaborate Indian carpet with its motif of tigers and elephants. There St. John intercepted a young servant circulating a tray of *hors d'oeuvre*s. In a gesture that seemed to Wallace perhaps overly familiar – undoubtedly abetted by St. John's apparent intoxication, but stemming from an unusual playfulness – St. John affectionately patted the boy on the cheek, then picked off a fried scallop. The fringe of the secretary's moustache glistened with butter when they finally stood before Sir James.

Brooke was expounding on the advent of iron-hulled ships to the Bishop, the Bishop's wife and a Chinese merchant. Wallace saw the Rajah's handsome physical appearance had conspicuously declined since they'd last met two years earlier in London, his face now pitted by the unmistakable devastation of small-pox. Yet no matter that he no longer looked invincible, Sir James maintained his same air of confidence and charm.

As St. John insinuated them into the small circle, the Rajah discreetly signalled to his secretary that some attention was warranted in the direction of his upper lip. Wallace thought that a considerate gesture for a man of such stature, and yet another counterpoint to the man's undeservedly maligned reputation. A sponsor of maurauders and headhunters? Hardly. He'd stamped out piracy and brought peace among his subjects. Regrettably, that could not have come about without some bloodshed. The Singapore Commission had cleared him of all charges. Full exoneration had been denied him simply as a mattter of political vendetta. It chagrined Wallace no end that the corridors of power were filled with dishonorable peevish men who, because they'd never once lifted a finger to improve the lives of others as his friend Sir James had done, resented his achievements.

Sir James received him like a learned dignitary, magnifying his accomplishments and acumen to their assembly of guests. They chatted most congenially until summoned for dinner.

There were seventeen at the table and St. John delicately inserted him between Bishop Crofter and Senora Alvares, the Latin woman with the rather sizable hair.

"Gallant sir," St. John said, "you are the only other Portuguese speaker present. Mrs. Alvares's husband has abandoned his beautiful wife among us English and Malay speakers."

There was some muffled comment by Linus Atwell, the rattan trader, but St. John instantly shushed him.

The Bishop's range of conversation met Wallace's expectation for a clergyman. Thus he found himself engaging Senora Alvares as the evening wore on. He knew of her husband, the Portuguese botanist Jose Alvares. She apparently shared none of Senor Alvares's enthusiasm for plants, nor for any of the local attractions.

"He told me we would live in Singapore," she said. "Four months after we arrive, he tells me it's impossible to work there and he brings me here. He called it the 'Paris of Sarawak.'" She snorted.

"It is the finest town in the region," Wallace said.

"In damned Borneo!"

They were speaking in Portuguese. Still, her candour was surprising, if not alarming. Mr. Chiu, seated across, briefly lifted his eyes from his roast duck, then resumed its meticulous dismemberment. Everyone else pretended not to notice.

Senor Alvares was currently in Celebes, Wallace learned. Or Flores, perhaps. She said she didn't care. Better without him than having him present and paying more attention to his plants than to her.

"You are not married, Mr. Wallace?" Senora Alvares asked.

She patted a corner of the napkin to her pretty mouth – at least he thought it pretty (Mrs. Alvares had a heavy hand with cosmetics).

"No?" she repeated after his reply, then her upper lip curled. "Well I am certain that if you were, you would not drag your wife to such a dung heap and discard her like … No, of course you would not. You are a gentleman. My husband? A sonofabitch!"

At that moment the bishop knocked over his wine glass. Wallace allowed that the clergyman perhaps understood some Portuguese after all.

Following the meal, Wallace stood at the sideboard examining the petals of a bright yellow dillenia when Mrs. Alvares sidled next to him.

"Senor Brooke tells me that you will be famous one day," she said.

"The Rajah is quite kind. His goodwill tends to exaggerate – "

"And you are tall," she said, inching closer. "I wish my husband was tall. A tiny grasshopper is what he is. He would come no higher than here on you."

Her fingertips pressed firmly against the breast of his waistcoat. She gazed up at him, eyes wide and a sly smile, a trace of red lipstick at the corner of her mouth smudged. "And *he* will never be famous."

He didn't wish to presume ill of anyone, but the senora appeared to express something beyond professional admiration. A married woman. The wife of a respectable botanist, no less.

Wallace desperately looked about, but Sir James could offer no assistance – he was demonstrating for the Chinese banker and his wife the loading action on a prized musket. In the distant corner however, with an impish smile, the Rajah's secretary hoisted a glass of sherry in his direction. Then he tilted it back in one swallow.

Mrs. Alvares was speaking, still intently gazing up at him. "I believe a man who is strong, with true character and strong ambition, understands women better than one who chases after plants like a tiny rabbit. Do you not think so, Senor Wallace?"

Her lips parted ever so slightly. One hand traced the curve of her bosom, lingering there as if to draw his attention to that endowment. Notwithstanding his disinclination towards Mrs. Alvares's temperament, Wallace felt his chest rising and falling like a bird's. Considerably more disturbing, he throbbed further below, feeling an aching need he hadn't felt in ages. For much of the preceding year and a half he'd suppressed all other longing outside of Marion. There'd been an idea that, were he to successfully explore the Malay Archipelago and return to England as an acclaimed naturalist – the next Darwin, Huxley or Hooker, Marion might change her mind. But he recently acknowledged that her decision had nothing to do with his vocation or wealth or fame. She'd chosen a tailor. So perhaps it was his personality – that he was at his liveliest when engaged about nature. Or his looks – he had nothing of the flamboyant in him, like someone of Sir James Brooke's distinction. Either way, it was inalterable. Dull and dull-looking, he would never gain her love. Yet she still had his – a matter beyond his volition. Which was how he finally came to comprehend how Marion's own feelings must have been.

"What do you think, Senor Wallace?"

Mrs. Alvares pressed closer, an almost imperceptible

movement, but one that had the effect of extinguishing all air between them. The cloying scent of her flowery perfume filled the void. If he were to step forward now, just the slightest, they would be touching, his chest to her bosom. And should that occur, Wallace believed that with everything he had walled up inside him, he might very well burst.

Mateu Orfila's treatise on poisons lay in Wallace's hands when Sir James peered into his own library from the doorway. "So this is where you've been hiding." Sir James put on a look of mock disapproval and entered. When he saw the book Wallace was holding he could not suppress a grin. He dove into an anecdote about a recent case – Brooke presided as Sarawak's lone judge – concerning two rival rattan traders engaged in a vicious campaign against each other. When one was found dead from suspected arsenic poisoning, the other was charged with murder despite no evidence beyond motive.

They were debating the availability of antidotes to arsenic poisoning when St. John entered and announced, "No need to concern yourself, Mr. Wallace. It is now safe. All our other guests – including any whom you may wish to have avoided – have departed."

Sir James folded his arms across his chest. "What have you done, Spenser?"

A coy smile. "Nothing so terrible."

"Out with it."

"You are well aware of Mrs. Alvares's social isolation."

"Who isn't?"

"Our esteemed Mr. Wallace has just returned from an extended sojourn in the forest and appears – if I may be pardoned for saying so, for I do not mean it unsympathetically – to be quite capable of benefitting from companionship."

"Spenser!" Sir James shook his head. "Mr. Wallace, I am so sorry."

"No bother," replied Wallace. "My desire for some solitude led me to your wonderful library. Nowhere in my travels have I seen a finer sanctuary."

Sir James admirably deflected the compliment, claiming the marvellous collection of Lord Radcliffe was vastly superior to his own and a short time later they exchanged good nights. The two young boys who'd greeted Wallace upon arrival were asleep on the veranda. He tried to descend noiselessly so as not to disturb them, but the ladder sighed terribly under his weight. Neither boy stirred. Recalling the young age of all the various household servants, Wallace thought it typical of Sir James's kindness that he gave employment to so many young orphans.

Small puffs of dirt lingered in his wake as he made his way to the palisade. But for some snuffling among the animal pens, the yard was still. When Wallace glanced back at the house he saw above its roof a thin filament of cloud bisecting the crescent moon. In the doorway Brooke and St. John stood silhouetted by lamplight. They waved in unison and called goodnight again. He waved back then crossed onto the dark road.

Two days after dinner at the Rajah's, Wallace was navigating through the Chinese bazaar. He was provisioning himself to depart next month for the Spice Islands. A Malay trader he'd recently encountered informed him he could find much of what he sought in those islands. Rain clouds hung low over the crowded tin roofs of the bazaar. Birds darted to drink among the wheel ruts and craters that littered the roadway. Fruit, vegetables, dry-goods, meats, knives, candles and lanterns, bolts of fabric, woven mats, fishing supplies and cooking vessels burgeoned beneath canvas awnings. Inside the darkened shops vendors sullenly waited amid shelves and crates, barrels and baskets. Amid this inconspicuous setting he found himself being trailed by a dark-skinned shirtless boy perhaps twelve years old. It was not uncommon that beggar children pursued him all the way to the front door of his guest house.

"Great Sir," the boy beseeched in Malay. "I am Ali. A better worker you will never know."

All the street urchins were in need of a good meal and this one was no different. A societal problem for which he bore no responsibility. Sad to say, England had its own share of malnourished children. "I have no need of assistance at this time, thank you kindly," Wallace answered in English. He'd learned that the language barrier quickly discouraged many.

"I work for you tomorrow?" the boy said in clipped yet comprehensible English.

He stopped and turned round. "Where did you learn English?"

"Much before, I work in shop for selling the foodstuffs. Many Englishman come to buy. I talks English to them and do small work when they ask." The lad pointed at the cuffs of Wallace's trousers. "I clean good."

"Thank you, but I have no need for a laundry boy."

"You need boy to shoot bird? Shoot many animal? I shoot very good."

No random stalker, the young fellow had done his research. "Right now I have no greater need than the purchase of some oil cloths. I would suggest you seek me out in another month before I leave Sarawak. Perhaps I might then reconsider."

"Oil cloths? I help you. Please."

"I admire your persistence, young man. However I am perfectly competent to make purchases on my own. I've been doing so for quite a long time."

"You go Chun Fat store?"

Wallace must have betrayed his surprise because he hadn't yet replied when the boy tapped a forefinger to his temple. "The Chinaman very smart. He give you bad price because you Englishman. I help you bargain best price."

Wherever he'd travelled honesty had been on short supply, Wallace learned. Thus it was axiomatic a healthy amount of cynicism be retained. Yet in the boy's boast he detected a note of genuine pride. "All right, you can come along. Mind you, if I should learn you are receiving some commission from the proprietor – and I make no allegation of the kind, I simply warn you I am a sceptical man – then I shall refer the matter for appropriate discipline. I am a good friend of the Rajah." No doubt many words had eluded the youngster's vocabulary, but Wallace felt confident that the import was not lost. "Right then. Off we go."

Out the corner of his eye, he saw his prospective assistant retrieve a comb from the pocket of his breeches and attempt to bring his hair into some kind of order. Well now, thought Wallace, perhaps he would indeed receive a better price.

Which he most surely did. After the transaction, as they stood outside the store, he studied the boy. "How old are you?"

"Fourteen, sir. Almost fifteen years. Very strong, see?" The boy flexed one arm.

"I will need your father's consent before I am prepared to take you on."

"No father, sir."

"Your mother, then. Or an uncle."

"I do not know the word in English, sir. *Anak yatim*."

"Orphan?" Wallace asked.

The boy nodded.

"Well then, I shall need to speak with the proprietor of your orphanage – the house where you reside."

"No house. I live on street."

The lad's intelligence and agreeableness was self-evident. Still, he had doubts about the putative orphanhood. The last thing he wished was to deprive a family of its son – even a runaway – by taking him a thousand miles distant against their wishes. He considered how he might authenticate the boy's claim.

A short time later, he presented Ali to the very source of authority in the region.

"You have come to precisely the right man, Mr. Wallace."

Standing in the Rajah's common hall, Spenser St. John conducted a thorough and, by appearances, approving inspection of the young boy. "I agree he does appear younger than his stated age and this raises concerns. While the Rajah would normally be pleased to be of service, he is currently adjudicating a land dispute. So leave this to me and I shall investigate the boy."

St. John's enthusiasm for the task was a comfort.

Ali on the other hand, appeared ill at ease under the gentleman's gaze. Perhaps he had something to hide after all, thought Wallace. How fortunate to have the Rajah as a friend. And though St. John was a peculiar sort, his smile like that of a curled cat upon a sunny porch, the personal secretary to the Rajah was undoubtedly capable. Indeed it would gravely insult Sir James to think otherwise.

"Very well, then …"

"Leave the young man with me and rest assured tomorrow I shall furnish you with all the pertinent facts, Mr. Wallace."

Ali's eyes fixed upon his own in a mute plea, a reluctance that only fortified him in his suspicions. Wallace invoked a stern look of reproval. He needed his conscience clear on this point. "Tomorrow, then," he said and thereupon took his leave, believing his association with the young waif likely at an end.

The next day he was both surprised and gratified when the secretary assured him the boy's story had been verified. St. John patted Ali's head and said, "He shall make a fine servant. I can see that already."

The boy said nothing, eyes downcast. It was only after they'd departed Sarawak that the lad seemed to regain his old disposition. And it was only over the ensuing months, as they made their way to the Spice Islands, that Wallace began to get a true measure of his new assistant.

CHAPTER FIFTEEN
Lombok, June 1856

Wallace hunched forward, shotgun clasped tight to his body, and did his best not to veer off the path. Invariably, however, a few more steps and another thorn would pierce his trousers. Or his shirtsleeve would suffer another rip, his hands another cut, his beard another burr, or his spectacles would be torn from his face and leave him momentarily blind as a mole. How was he to carry on, let alone capture a bird in such a dense thicket of brambles and vines?

"Sir, you must be smallest," Ali said over his shoulder. He crouched ten feet ahead, in a small clearing, the sunlight gleaming on his uncovered brow. Skin and clothing unblemished.

"I am attempting to make myself as compact as possible," Wallace answered, perhaps a little gruffly. Were his assistant perhaps another foot taller and seventy pounds heavier, he might understand the hazards that presently inconvenienced himself. Wallace readjusted the satchel slung over his shoulder, then crept forward some more. When he glanced up again, the boy had vanished.

"Ali?"

He caught up to him several minutes later, the boy again on his haunches, one hand cupped behind his ear.

"Why did you keep racing off?"

Ali pointed out another burr. Wallace plucked it from his beard and studied the boy. "Don't look so miserable. Just tell me what it is. I prefer truth in all circumstances."

Ali scratched a fingernail into the dirt. "I cannot catch nothing sir, because you make much noises."

A valid complaint, Wallace knew. With each step, the black volcanic soil crunched beneath his boots. Birds fell silent at his every approach. Wildlife fled. They'd been out the whole morning with nothing to show for it.

Worse still, no creature proved more adept at evasion than the very specimen he sought most desperately. The Elegant Pitta. A cunning, even diabolical little bird. How else to explain why it selected this inhospitable habitat for its foraging? At the slightest disturbance, it vanished into the thick underbrush before a muzzle could so much as be lifted, let alone aimed. Yet it was too splendorous to forego. A black head with colourful accents, a straw-coloured breast, and on its back, soft green plumage bearing silvery blue bands. No less of a prize could explain why he presently endured such damage to his clothing and to his person: blood trickling from a dozen small nicks and abrasions, each one sharply alive with the sweat that soaked his skin.

That he would be in such a state amid Lombok's vegetation at all would have surprised him only a week ago. That was when he and Ali crossed the twenty-mile strait from Bali. There, they'd spent a mere two days – not that he'd minded Bali in the least. With its fertile, rolling plains, it reminded him of Europe, which was also to say it was highly cultivated.

Thus it was poor for wildlife. Given the two islands' proximity, volcanic origins and similar size, he expected nothing different upon their arrival in Lombok. Just a brief sojourn, then they would sail eastward to the Spice Islands.

To his surprise, however, Lombok teemed with wildlife. He and Ali became so preoccupied, he'd missed his intended sailing for the Spice Islands. Which meant they now had two more months on Lombok.

Wallace drank from his canteen then passed it to Ali. He waited for him to quench his thirst. "How am I to avoid making 'much noises'? We must travel by foot and on this ground, silence is impossible."

"You are always walking, walking, sir. You use eyes for finding everything. But in jungle, so much trees, eyes cannot find. You must be walking, then stop so all is quiet. You wait like this, then animal come." Ali cupped a hand behind his ear, and swivelled in all directions. "Also good to use this." Ali tapped his nose. "Much animal smells in jungle. If no hear and no smells, then you be walking again."

Wallace could hardly dispute the futility of his own efforts to that point. He did as Ali suggested and one hour later, he shot his first Elegant Pitta. They took it to a nearby clearing and skinned the bird. Ali stood over his shoulder to observe and learn.

"Where did you learn to track birds and animals?" Wallace asked.

"My father tells me – "

Wallace lowered his knife. "Your father?" It was the first time the boy had mentioned either of his parents. He had assumed the lad had been abandoned at birth.

Ali's eyes rounded, the whites bulging. "I say wrong way. I mean, this is before, when father is alive. I am much small when he die."

Wallace considered that for a moment. "My apologies. I sometimes expect a precision with your English which I ought not, given that for you it is a new language. And I am sorry for the loss of your father … for the loss of both your parents."

Ali smiled sadly, and nodded his acknowledgement. "Before the city, Malay people live in forest. My father teaches me this life."

Wallace resumed his incision. "Your father certainly taught you wisely."

By the time he and Ali left Lombok in late August, Wallace had amassed a considerable body of specimens. Much of it was the boy's doing. He merely had to be provided a description of desirable specimens, pointed in a direction and instructed to return at such-and-such a time. At the appointed hour his young assistant's bag of specimens often rivalled his own. King-crows, flower-peckers, cuckoos, even a waterfowl Wallace felt certain would satisfy Charles Darwin's request. While the competence of his assistant was certainly a wonderful revelation, the greatest surprise occurred when Wallace compared fauna from Bali and Lombok. For two similar neighbouring islands, the wildlife was vastly different. Bali's resembled the fauna found in Asia, while just a short distance away in Lombok the animals were typical of the Australian continent. No one had ever noticed this dichotomy before. A discovery that warranted a letter to Samuel Stevens, and the promise of a future paper on the subject.

Wallace realized something else too, something of a more personal significance. He recalled how he originally planned to investigate neither Bali nor Lombok. However, in Singapore he'd missed that season's final direct sailing to the Spice Islands.

Then in Lombok he'd been compelled to extend his stay. But for those two events, originally perceived as misfortune, his discovery of regional dichotomy in wildlife would not have occurred. In hindsight, it was as if by design. And this was not the first occasion when he'd benefited from what at first blush seemed bad luck. He only had to think how, throughout much of his apprenticeship, his brother William's surveying business struggled. That provided the pockets of free time which allowed him to wander meadows and forests – from whence sprung his passion for the natural world. Could such fundamental turns in life merely be the result of chance? If one discerned a pattern, did that not refute an assertion of mere coincidence?

Wallace had various goals in mind as he sailed for the Spice Islands. In terms of specimens, the most coveted was the fabled bird of paradise. European ladies of sophistication prized the bird's feathers as fashion accoutrements. A single bird of paradise might fetch a sufficient price in London to subsidize weeks of research into the origin of species. He learned the birds could most readily be found in the easternmost Aru Islands, close to New Guinea. He was warned, however, that the surrounding waters were patrolled by pirates and the islands themselves were inhabited by ferocious savages.

On his thirty-fourth birthday, January 8, 1857, Wallace and Ali arrived at Dobbo, the main village in the Aru Islands. They immediately travelled inland. To that date, no European had seen the bird of paradise in its natural habitat, let alone captured one.

He and Ali shot them by the bagful.

Early specimens disappointed. They were of the more common species, albeit the adjective wholly unsuitable for such an exceptional creature. But Ali soon took down the King Bird of Paradise. Its plumage was of the softest texture Wallace had encountered, and arrayed brilliantly. Scarlet dorsal feathers richly contrasted with the snowy breast. Throat and shoulders shone metallic green while the legs and feet were of a sky blue. Its greatest radiance, however, emerged at the crown where red feathers melded into orange then tapered at the bill to pale yellow. A veritable sunrise. While capturing the legendary bird was a feat perhaps insufficient to earn the fame Sir James had warranted to his dinner party guests, Wallace imagined accolades would unquestionably flow. Among England's discriminating scientific auspices, the resplendent plumage would be welcomed as nothing less than a national treasure.

Its flesh, on the other hand, tasted not so different from partridge.

Hours after its capture, small cutlets of *Paradisea regia* swam in a curried gravy with onions. He and Ali accompanied the meal with celebratory bamboo cups of the local brew. And as they toasted their success, their salutations were echoed, in a fashion, by avid spectators. Crouched at spitting distance – truly, a stream of betel juice splashed nearby each time its originator overshot the gap in the floor that was its intended target – eleven sets of eyes trained on their actions.

In this settlement, comprised of a single palm-roofed platform perched above a grim bog cross-hatched by trails of black mud and mosquito-infested streams, he had rented the only available space for lodging: a five-by-ten foot allotment shared with the home owner and his family. There he and Ali hunkered on their bedrolls (the low roof permitting no standing), trapped between the perilously stacked supplies (there being no walls and thus everything, including an unwary sleeper, risking danger should they come too close to the edge) and a semi-circle of sarong-clad onlookers.

Wallace raised his cup in Ali's direction. The beverage smelled of wood resin and boiled cabbage, but tasted even worse. "Here is to your outstanding marksmanship." Eleven hands then raised their own cups and eleven sets of vocal chords roared, *"Rearist yer standink maxim ship!"*

After several toasts, the householders were well in their cups. Wallace's smallest gestures and most benign words elicited peals of laughter that shook the platform. It would not be an early night. Yet that remained far from his only cause of discomfort. Soon as he and Ali had landed upon the beach at the main town of Dobbo, squadrons of sand-flies bore down on him. When he travelled the interior, whether on jungle trail or mid-stream, mosquitoes stippled the air, piercing all exposed flesh. But from these at least he had respite when he finally sat at night by the smoking fire. From one scourge there was no escape.

Ants.

The shiny black *Formica quadriceps* populated leaves, stems, trunks, vines, roots, rotting debris and soil – which was to say, they were everywhere. Disturbed by passing hand or boot they glommed on with remarkable determination such that a casual swipe proved insufficient to dislodge them. The ferocity of those terrorists were, however, but a trifle compared with the trap-jawed ants. Those mandibles snapped tight with distressing alacrity and disengaged only by the violence of tweezers or open flame. Nor did the assaults desist upon attaining the threshold of their accommodations. Anything not isolated in water was soon crawling with red or yellow house ants: his hosts slept upon bed-stands steeped in cocoa-nut shells of water. He and Ali lay down upon cotton bed rolls flat against the floor. Their mosquito netting seemed only to challenge the ants' enterprising nature. Many mornings – following a night of regular agitation accompanied by grunts of pain – that he awoke to find his body festooned with ants. Upon brushing them off there would be a series of angry red welts demarcating their overnight travel, showing not the slightest respect for the sensitivity of his most anterior regions.

After a fortnight, his wounds had grown intolerable. The sores begged for relief, yet at the slightest touch they ulcerated. Given that their lodgings left something to be desired, Wallace hoped the siege was specific to their northern island location. They boated south.

On the next island he found communal accommodation among a half-dozen families. Utter savages, all of them, he was pleased to note (indeed, if the world were truly demarcated between the civilised and the savages, the former characterized foremost by adherence to religious dogma, he was predisposed to savagery himself). Happily, he'd found not a jot of religion anywhere in the interior, though much like the ants that always seemed to find him, he harboured little doubt enterprising missionaries would eventually contaminate the inhabitants.

Their new lodging was raised seven feet above the soil with waist-high walls, lofty gabled roof and proper floor. But for the occasional scorpion, snake and poisonous spider, he thought it a veritable fortress.

It mattered not. His sores would not heal. Nocturnal itching, humidity and poor sanitary conditions ensured infection set in. Feet, ankles, wrists and hands bore ranks of crimson-encircled black lesions. At his direction, Ali lanced them daily, squeezing out the poison in a painful ritual that his hosts turned into spectator sport, inviting the neighbours, everyone with opinions on what needed closest attention, where the application of greater force was required and, with every wince and stifled cry, nods of approval. His feet suffered most. The skin of his ankles and feet resembled a volcanic landscape. He crawled on all fours in order to perform his ablutions.

Ali on the other hand, was not nearly so afflicted. Whether it was his Malay blood, spry youthfulness or lack of anything so much as an extra ounce of meat on that diminutive dark frame, mosquitoes, flies, mites and all other manner of annoying insect veered around the servant in favour of his master. As for ants, the boy slept each night cocooned amid blankets such it was a wonder he failed to suffocate. But thank goodness at least one of them could continue working. Each day Ali returned with nothing less than what Wallace imagined he himself capable of having captured. Three weeks of inactivity, however, and Wallace was ravenous for new reading material. It was April 1857 and he'd had no mail since December. He dispatched Ali to Dobbo.

Four days later Ali brought him a magnificent bundle. The boy unravelled its string then carefully rewound it, inserting the coil into the ligature compartment of Wallace's collection bag. When the manila paper was finally peeled away, there lay a trove of six scientific journals, accompanied by stationary bearing Sir James's hand:

My Dear Wallace,

That one intelligent set of eyes would derive further use of the enclosed volumes gratifies me immensely. I would be remiss, however, were I not to mention a certain essay in the February 1857 Annals. Its author thinly veils as legitimate scientific critique a truly intemperate personal attack upon your good name. As your friend & an admirer of your considerable talents, I respectfully urge you not to take this assault lightly, dear Wallace. Reputation & Honour are cardinal (who should know better than I? You undoubtedly chuckle at that remark but, alas, it is quite true). One must not bend before such brutes! Only a thorough & public castigation of this cretin will remove the stain!

Yours very humbly,
Sir James Brooke, Rajah of Sarawak

The cretin to whom Sir James referred was Ramsay Newcastle. Wallace had nearly given up hope that his articles would attract debate. Henry Bates had written a flattering review in which he'd referred to his paper on closely allied species as 'The Sarawak Law,' calling it a leap forward in man's understanding of species' development. Mending fences, he believed. However, Wallace's ideas had garnered little attention elsewhere. From Darwin and Lyell, only silence. Now Newcastle weighed in with an essay entitled, 'Nothing New Under the Tropical Sun'. Wallace read it carefully, focusing upon Newcastle's key points:

The so-called Sarawak Law is merely a restatement of the general principles previously formulated and published by our nation's most eminent naturalist, Charles Darwin. As if to make amends for this redundancy, Mr. Wallace authors a series of tracts ostensibly concerning the orangutans of Borneo. The series culminates with his claim that man and primate are commonly descended from an unknown progenitor. Thus our redoubtable collector has swiftly ventured from the previously formulated to the unsupportable. An ambitious, even courageous collector is no substitute for the cool intellectual reasoning of our best-trained minds. While important scientific issues unquestionably remain to be answered in this modern era, we must stand vigilant against the cursory and spurious in our rush to progress.

Wallace noted Newcastle's argument cited no errors. Nor did it present contrary evidence. Thus a sensible man could only dismiss the criticism as baseless. So, notwithstanding

Brooke's warning he saw little reason for concern. He instead turned his attention to the many worthwhile articles and ideas for which he was starved.

At mid-afternoon, he lay upon his bed working on his notebook. The tropical air pulsed with the pounding of sago into flour, concussions that wafted from the clearing into the shelter, finding life in his throbbing sores. Unable to concentrate, he set aside his notebook and lifted the muslin cloth that protected his outstretched feet just as Ali arrived from the day's excursion.

"I come back, sir."

"*Ahh*, very good." Wallace replaced the cloth and opened his notebook again.

Ali lowered his collection bag alongside the bed. The bag smelled of wet canvas and spilled blood.

"You read your ideas again?"

"Sorry? Yes, yes, my ideas." Wallace reached for the bag, curious to see the day's results.

"Why?" Ali was shirtless, skin glistening and specked with bits of leaf, grass and grit. The boy hiked the dense bush half-naked yet somehow avoided all those pernicious insects that had been so devastating to himself.

"Why what?"

"Why you read your ideas more? You write these things, so you must know already. Why read what you know?"

"I review my ideas in concert with articles I've recently read – "

The boy furrowed his brow, so Wallace tried again. "I still have much to figure out. There is one question in particular. The answer seems to circulate so tantalizingly close that I catch glimpses of it. Yet I struggle …"

"Maybe you ask a friend to give help?"

"A very good suggestion, however it is not so simple. In fact, my request for assistance has provoked an angry reaction in certain quarters."

"Sir? Maybe you tell to me? I know some things."

One more thing he liked about the boy. An unquenchable thirst for knowledge and an appetite for discussion. Charles? Quenchable thirst, minimal appetite. "I certainly appreciate your offer, Ali. You mean well, of that I have no doubt, but it is a rather difficult question."

"Maybe you tell the question and I will start to think for the answer."

A yellow house ant had climbed Wallace's sleeve and he gave it a slap, then brushed away its corpse. "Very well. The question is: how did we as humans get to be who we are today? And how did every animal and every fish and every insect and every plant come to be where they are and in the form they have taken?"

Ali sunk upon his haunches and rubbed his chin.

Wallace watched a red grasshawk dragonfly hovering near the rafters. Its mottled scarlet wings captured the light like miniature stained glass windows. Infirm as he was, should it have lingered another moment he would not have been able to resist an ill-advised effort to capture it. But it droned in the direction of the eaves then disappeared.

"I think," Ali finally said, "maybe Allah makes everything like this."

"That is certainly what some suggest." Wallace had noticed that Mohamedans seemed to place at least as much faith in their Holy Book as the average Christian.

"You think different?" asked Ali.

"If every species was specially created and put in specific places on earth by God or Allah, then why are similar species found on the very same island? Even the same vicinity? And why are dramatically different species found on Lombok than on Bali, an island physically comparable and only twenty miles distant? For me, all evidence points to the conclusion that new species come about proximate in space and time to older similar species. But then why? And how is that achieved?"

Ali was tracing the paper margin of the notebook.

"There, I've done it. I've killed your interest."

"No sir, but so many questions.'"

"Let me try it this way: what reason might we have for both the yellow and the red ants that torment me? Other than their colour, they appear identical in size, characteristics, habits and location."

Ali scratched at his knee. "Maybe one time they are one family, all same colour. Then one day there is a big argument. Some ants go away and start a different family. Now they must fight for food with old family. How can they fight if all look the same? So they make their own colour. Now no mistake if they fight."

"A Malthusian argument, if ever I've heard one."

"Sir?"

"It is an interesting idea. I shall give it more thought. Now, let us see what specimens you've brought me today."

While they picked through one lifeless item after another, Ali beaming as he described a shot he'd made, or the fine detective work involved in turning over a particular rotting bit of plant material, Wallace couldn't help but ponder his circumstances. No matter his efforts, his reputation as a scientific essayist had yet to grow in the least. Worse, he was presently reduced to a sedentary role. He needed change. Soon as he could manage it, they would flee the insects and vermin of Aru for another region of the Spice Islands, the comparatively civil surrounds of Ternate. There he would resume what, at least from a collector's perspective, was a successful expedition.

That settled, he dedicated his attention to what had obviously been a splendid catch that day. He offered his compliments to Ali. He examined each specimen for damage, assessing memory's catalogue for similar specimens, and estimated the payment he might expect. Doing so, he found himself amazed yet again at the audacious variety of creation encountered – all in one day's outing! A seemingly boundless series of variations in any one given species, yet by unknown agency and for no obvious purpose. The confounded beautiful mystery of it all. Somehow, he could not help but believe the answers he sought were near, and his spirits soared.

CHAPTER SIXTEEN

Macassar, Celebes (Sulawesi), July 1857

From Aru's main settlement, Dobbo, Wallace and Ali gained passage to Celebes. They sailed amid a flotilla of fifteen praus banded together to deter pirates. But with better than one thousand miles of open ocean to Celebes, Wallace remained more anxious about the sea. Indeed, provided they didn't imperil his collection or notebooks or cause him physical harm, an encounter with the sea marauders – rumoured to have robbed at least a half-dozen crafts and plundered an equal number of villages these past months – would not be entirely unwelcome, thought Wallace. Nothing approaching the pitched clashes for which the Rajah was famed, but just enough excitement for a delightful dash of romance in his future book on the region. Contents for that book, along with the volume on speciation, were both developing apace.

Storm winds at their back propelled them to Macassar in little more than nine days, not a pirate ship in sight. Wallace wished to immediately sail onwards to the Spice Islands of Ternate and Gilolo. There he planned some investigations that had been on his mind since Borneo. However, Ali was felled by fever. At the local hospital, Wallace retained the services of a German doctor, a skeletal figure whose spectacles perched at the end of a flute-like nose.

"He shall pull through, am I right?" Wallace asked.

They stood in the corridor outside the ward. The doctor lit a cigarette. "I will give him the best treatment, no different than if he is European. But will he survive …?" The doctor blew a stream of smoke at the ceiling, as though the answer resided in those vapours.

Wallace gritted his teeth. "Please, do your utmost."

"I understand. A good servant is not so easy to find."

Wallace said nothing. He pulled out his billfold and counted the money into the doctor's hand before his anger got the best of him. Then he left. In the courtyard outside, sunken-eyed patients meandered the gravel paths beneath the shade of fig trees, their hospital whites shadowed purplish-blue. Wallace hastened past, scattering gravel into the grass. In his wake, a servant in coolie hat scurried about, raking the small stones back onto the pathways.

Early next morning, golden light slanted into Ali's ward from the doorway. The door closed behind Wallace and gloom descended. The windows were shuttered closed. When his eyes adjusted, Wallace made out patches of unpainted plaster upon the walls. However the room was clean. A few heads lifted off their pillows as he made his way to Ali's bed. Wallace nodded a greeting to a Malay family gathered at the bedside of an elderly patriarch.

Ali was still asleep. Wallace placed on the window ledge the fruit basket he'd brought. Bananas, oranges, sapodillas, rambutans, mango and tamarinds. For a few minutes he stood there, hands folded, but Ali slept on. Wallace quietly retreated the way he came.

That afternoon when he returned, a pair of paraffin lamps hung from the ceiling. Tolerable illumination. How much better, Wallace thought, were the staff to unseal the shutters. Around the world, doctors had a predilection for confining inmates to their own fetor amid darkness, which common sense dictated insalubrious.

He was pleased to see Ali awake. The fruit was well-depleted.

"Quite fond of the tamarinds, I'd say."

Ali managed a smile. "At my house, my mother give tamarind when I am sick. It make me better."

Wallace couldn't help but raise an eyebrow. "Your mother? When was this?" Ali's smile fell away. No doubt an emotionally-charged subject.

"This is before I am orphan."

"Yes, I understand. But was your mother – ?"

"Sir? Sorry for the interrupt but I am very thirsty." Ali clutched his throat for emphasis.

He would like to have pursued the point, but well recalled his own bouts of fever – the aches, chills, disorientation, the utter exhaustion – how one would say 'yes' to almost anything in order to avoid the effort of a more comprehensive reply.

"Some water? Certainly, my lad."

He fetched the water and was surprised to find Ali asleep again. The scourge of fever, he supposed. He did not linger.

At his rental quarters, Wallace set straight to work. Despite his infirmity on the Aru Islands, better than nine thousand specimens awaited shipment. The paradise birds alone would fetch quite a nice sum. Sufficient for his intended journey to Ternate and New Guinea. Waiting for Ali to convalesce allowed him the time to elaborate on his findings from Bali and Lombok. He'd supplemented those findings with additional data this past year. The pattern was clear. The animal species collected in the tropical forests of Celebes bore close similarity to those of Australia, a land of great deserts. Yet the animals in Borneo – the nearest large land mass west of Celebes and quite similar in terms of landscape and climate – more closely resembled Asiatic fauna. This was the same phenomenon he'd observed with Bali and Lombok. Plainly, there were two distinct zoogeographical zones.

When he traced a line upon the map, dividing the two regions along a southwest to northeast axis, he instantly recognized its significance. Islands west of the line – Java, Bali and Celebes – must have once been contiguous with Asia, while to the east, Lombok, Borneo, the Arus and New Guinea long ago formed part of the Australian continent. Over eons, the land masses had separated from the two continents and land-bridges subsided to form separate islands. Correspondingly, there would have been climatic changes and these led to extinctions. But they also led to new species closely allied with the earlier ones – his very own Sarawak Law applied. In this fashion, over vast periods of time, species differed more and more from the original. Thus the Biblical explanation offered by men such as Sir Charles Lyell – that species were both immutable and given their own unique habitats – had been utterly refuted!

The work had him hunched over his table until the cook brought his evening coffee. He took the cup onto the veranda. Moths flicked against the lamp, but there were no other sounds. How extraordinarily quiet these evenings were without Ali's presence. Wallace recalled how, during their first months together, he'd tended to work or he'd written letters until it was time for bed. For Ali, there was little to do, secluded as they were in the middle of forest or in the isolated villages where they sojourned. One night he heard his assistant softly humming.

"Is that a song?"

"It is old Malay story."

"Are there words to the song?"

The boy seemed unsure.

"In England, there are many stories one sings."

"Sir?"

Wallace did not consider himself musical, but he supposed his voice serviceable. He drew a breath and sang:

"She's all my fancy painted her.
She's lovely, she's divine,
But her heart it is another's,
It never can be mine;
O few have loved as I have loved,
My love cannot decay,
O my heart, my heart is breaking,
For the love of Alice Gray."

Wallace glanced at Ali. "Are you familiar with this song?"

"Sir? I am Malay boy. I never be in England."

"Quite right," said Wallace. "Well then, you shall learn. It will be excellent practice for your English, and jolly good fun."

How many hundreds of nights had their voices convened since? Ali could now sing not only Alice Gray, but a dozen other songs. And he in turn had learned a pair of Malay children's songs. No doubt the boy's English had come along much quicker for it. But its main advantage, he had to say, resided in the sheer pleasure. Wallace suspected that were Ali not in hospital right then, the veranda would have resounded with verse. His company that evening instead came in the form of his accumulated mail. A letter from Charles Darwin dated May 1, 1857 expressed gratitude for the Lombok duck Wallace had shipped. More significantly, Darwin finally commented on the Sarawak Law. Wallace slowed his reading, pulse racing. He wished to absorb every word of Darwin's tribute.

By your letter & even still more by your paper in The Annals a year or more ago, I can plainly see that we have thought much alike & to a certain extent have come to similar conclusions. I agree to the truth of almost every word of your paper & I daresay that you will agree with me that it is very rare to find oneself agreeing closely with any theoretical paper; for it is lamentable how each man draws his own different conclusions from the very same fact. I should mention that this summer will make the 20th year (!) since I began notes on the question of how & in what way do species & varieties differ from each other. I am now preparing my work for publication, but I find the subject so very large that I do not suppose I shall go to press for several years.

One of the subjects which I have been considering at length is the means of distribution of all organic beings found on oceanic islands; & any facts on this subject would be most gratefully received: Land molluscs are a great perplexity to me.

I regret that I have written a very dull letter, but I am a good deal out of health & am writing this, not from my home, but from a water-cure establishment.

With most sincere good wishes for your success in every way,
I remain, My dear Sir,
Yours sincerely,
Ch. Darwin

Wallace read it through a second time. Almost two years to elicit reasoned response concerning his essay and all Darwin could muster was that they had reached the same conclusions? And which paper, pray tell, had Mr. Darwin published setting out similar conclusions? None, that he could recall. Wallace slapped the letter down.

After several deep breaths, he admonished himself.

He had expected too much. Darwin suffered from poor health. He was also at work on that comprehensive assay of which he'd intimated during their encounter at the British Museum. Quite a marvel. Twenty years on his compendium and still unfinished? He supposed the great man had no pressing need for income. Were it himself, he would be in the poor house.

His own theorizing proceeded blazingly. He saw it approaching a critical juncture, the notebook on speciation growing daily. Once settled at Ternate he anticipated even greater progress. How stupendous were he to have Darwin's data, too. Given that his own work examined not only fauna, but the different races of man and their distribution, he wondered whether Darwin's compendium would include the human species. In writing his reply, he posed that very question.

The next letter he opened was a two-month old letter of Fanny's. A nice thick sheaf written in her striding hand, letters bent against the wind. He settled back in his chair to enjoy. She wrote of everyone's health (good), their fondest wishes (that he return safely at the first instance), the success of Thomas's photography studio in Neath (questionable) and the prevalence of crime in England (unbridled). Had he been aware that their much beloved writer Douglas Jerrold recently died? Mr. Dickens held a public reading of *A Christmas Carol* at St Martin's Hall to benefit the writer's family. How tragic Mr. Jerrold's premature demise and how sorry that, as an ardent admirer off chasing bugs half-way round the world, he could not attend those readings. Did he have any occasion to partake of cultural diversions whilst in the jungle?

Ah, Fanny. Her hobby-horse at full gallop.

She counted off the sugary ripeness of the local strawberries, the myriad flowers in bloom and the new science museum in South Kensington. Queen Victoria herself had opened it, so Fanny discovered during her stay in London. Fanny's recent visit to London, mentioned in a manner most casual, was coincident to a stay in that city by the world-renowned American medium, Miss Fitzgerald. Fanny had followed the publicity attending the medium's arrival with great interest and thought a personal investigation well worth the time.

In published notices, Miss Fitzgerald challenges even the most ardent sceptic to attend her séances and remain unpersuaded. Given that she offers a vital channel of communication for the bereaved, I found her fee quite reasonable. Yet you would have thought she was robbing graves from the storm of adverse criticism amongst some of our leading citizens. We are such a prudish hidebound society, Alfie! If I learned nothing else during my teaching tenure in America, this much became evident. Someone of your unrecognized yet immense talents would, I suspect, be so much better received in America, where, unsurprisingly, Spiritualism happens to originate and have a great and respected following.

Fanny reported that all who attended the séance, including one gentleman in a most ostentatious silk jacket – most certainly a sceptic, she surmised – received messages from the beyond.

The words were inscribed upon a small slate Miss Fitzgerald retrieved periodically from behind a heavy drape hung to one side of the darkened room. To an outsider the messages might have sounded quite general (they included no names). Fortunately Miss Fitzgerald prepared us for that eventuality explaining that the public nature of the séance precluded more intimate communication. The departed and the beloved suitably understood each other however, and the recognizable hand of the departed loved one provided such assurance that each intended recipient was able to gain the full meaning. Even the sceptic confirmed his faith in the proceedings.

Miss Fitzgerald, Fanny explained, had already informed attendees that brevity of communications was essential due to the tremendous energy expended in the effort.

As for my own personalized message, it was indisputably father's handwriting. I nearly fainted at the sight of it. It read: *everyone is fine* What could have been clearer? Father let us know he has reached the afterlife and that our beloved brothers and sisters are with him and untroubled. I cannot state the sense of relief and gratitude I feel, Alfie. I understand that all of your heart's wounds may not be mended by this knowledge, but my fondest wish is that this message brings you a measure of the same comfort I achieved. Family provides solace where distance cannot, dearest brother. Time to come home.

All my love,
Francis

~

Wallace reached for his coffee and found he'd already finished it, only the coarse grounds remaining. Like a fortune teller, he stared at that residue. An odd coincidence, he thought, mulling over the letters from Darwin and Fanny. Each pertained to a mystery he presently sought to solve. Not unsurprising in respect of Mr. Darwin. It was Fanny's letter that gave him pause. Besides the exhortation to return home, he detected in her description of the séance an incitement to investigate with her the spiritual realm. The possibility of a spiritual world had remained with him since his brush with death in São Joaquim. However, his limited investigations had always been strictly from a personal perspective. He'd viewed the spiritual as entirely separate from the scientific. But with the two letters at hand, for the first time he saw a connection. The questions of speciation and the existence of an afterlife both concerned life changes. One looked at man's origin, the other, his ultimate state. He had embarked upon simultaneous exploration at opposite ends of the same tunnel.

Ali mended slowly. When he was well enough to leave the hospital, Wallace instructed the cook to lavish as much fattening food upon the boy as he could withstand – the jut of his ribs was disconcerting. While his recovery was underway, Wallace added to his notebook and finished preparations for the next excursion, one that promised to be like no other he'd known.

His examination of the origin of species had proceeded by collecting and analyzing data to substantiate empirical-based conclusions. Scientific inquiry into the spiritual realm also required data. To date, he had limited evidence. Beyond his own experience in the Amazon, he only had various anecdotes of archipelago natives who regaled him with their spiritual experiences or introduced him to shamans or mentioned medicinal substances intended to facilitate insight (as when, in Sarawak City, a Malay trader had told him stories that powerful visions could result from a tincture of nutmeg). None of it scientifically authenticated, all hearsay. But since when did that mandate disbelief? Indeed, since when did it not dictate that failure to investigate was an abdication of duty to seek the truth?

Ali knelt on the veranda cleaning the guns. He pulled the cleaning rod from the shotgun barrel and laid it on an oilcloth, next to a canvas rag blackened by carbon.

"Looking splendid, Ali."

"Thank you, sir."

He'd told the boy to wait until peak health before resuming work, but Ali had insisted. He had a sensibility to him, Wallace noticed, a maturity beyond his years that bestowed upon him a credibility rarely seen in men thrice his age. Yet of the lad's views on spiritual matters, he knew nothing.

"Sir?" Ali stared up expectedly.

Wallace rubbed the back of his neck. "I confess to a certain curiosity about your beliefs."

"Yes, sir?"

"When we go into the forest to collect specimens … outside of ourselves, and the animals, birds and insects, do you ever feel ... What I mean is, do you ever sense the presence of ... well, other life?"

Ali stared out into the yard. A macadamia tree grew at its centre and it cast an afternoon shadow that reached the foot of the veranda. "When I am walking in jungle, for me, everything is life. The tree, all flowers, the water, even the rock."

"You mean they communicate − er, they talk to you?"

Ali laughed. "No, sir. They not talking. They not doing anything. They just be."

"They just be," Wallace repeated. A foolish question he'd posed. Talking trees, indeed. A practical lad, Ali had tactfully reminded him how everything merely comprised parts of a unified whole, separate entities within the same intricate design.

"Well, I shall leave you to finish the guns," Wallace said. With that, he returned inside.

It was weeks before Ali was well enough to voyage again, the fever gone but a lingering weakness prevailing. By the time they sailed, Wallace was most eager to resume his investigations. Questions concerning both the origin of species and the existence of a spirit world remained unsettled.

They arrived on Ternate, mid-January, 1858. Wallace found a suitable, albeit run-down house and instructed Ali concerning repairs, food to be planted and specimens for collection on the island. Then he packed a single trunk and hired a crew to sail him across the strait that separated Ternate from Gilolo, the larger neighbouring island to the east. Where no European had ever collected specimens, so he informed everyone.

And where the nutmeg grew.

CHAPTER SEVENTEEN
Gilolo (Halmahera), Spice Islands,
February 1858

Wallace's sleep was broken by gossamer feet skimming his chest. The bed creaked when he reached for his spectacles then slipped them on. A knuckle-sized spider. Head, abdomen and legs in bands of black and sienna, while the thorax revealed a lovely variegated orange. It was prepared to traverse his left clavicle, aiming for the hollow of his throat, but now, one leg crooked mid-air, it gauged the disturbance he'd created. An unfamiliar species, he had neither the strength nor the inclination to capture it. He was, however, curious and didn't judge it poisonous. Thus he struck a bargain with the arachnid: as host, he would permit his visitor continued exploration of all anatomical terrain, save and except face and other unmentionable sensitive regions (with naught but the sarong across his hips, he remained vulnerable in that regard). In consideration for which, said visitor would permit the host all manner of discreet observation without complaint and, most specifically, without resort to violence. That understanding achieved, the observer adjusted his pillow for better surveillance.

The spider remained arrested. As per his end of the bargain, he too, stayed motionless. However his mind's eye refused to follow suit. Images continued to flicker from his interrupted dream. He'd been drowning – not in the Atlantic, but a fast-flowing river. His canoe had struck a submerged boulder and the furious jolt tumbled him over the gunwale. He spun slow-motion towards the river bottom, choking water, arms fluttering uselessly. Overhead, he could still make out the boat and beyond that, his brother. John's face floated just above the waterline, his nose and mouth distorted, bulging frog-like, staring down. He reached up, arms extended as far as possible, fingers stretching towards the surface. Save me, John!

An old dream. As much as he suppressed his fear of water, it never went away. But the location was unfamiliar. Uaupés? Sadang? Orinoco?

His visitor flatly refused to budge. The spider seemed to be investigating those twin streams of warm air from its host, working out whether it was under threat. Mistrust. Entirely inconsistent with their mutual understanding. It made him wonder whether he was as safe as he'd imagined.

Mistrust on both sides, then.

Outside, palm fronds raked the walls. The wind was up. From inside there was no way to know whether a storm was coming; semi-dark forest pressed up against the window keeping the hut in perpetual dusk. He guessed it was afternoon – but of which day? Away from civilization it was hard enough to track the passage of time under normal circumstances; the problem compounded now that he'd left off his diary. Days had passed, maybe a week. Late February was all he could be certain of.

His notebook lay on the chair by the door, but he had no memory of putting it there. Or of moving the chair from the table. And it was uncharacteristic of him to leave his notebook out at all, let alone open. Across the room he could see what appeared to be a drawing. He propped an elbow up to give himself better vantage. Then he remembered – the spider!

Small but vehement fangs clamped onto his skin. The pain was white hot, yet distant, his senses clouded with fatigue and other aches. He grabbed his hat from beneath the bed – why he'd put it there and how he'd known to reach for that precise spot also defied explanation – and with the brim he swept the intruder off his chest. It landed upon the floor, righted itself, then skittered into a crevice between the stones.

No welt yet, but he knew the swelling would come, skin already throbbing. He found his way onto his feet. His innards fluttered, so he went outside to use the latrine. A short time later he found his way back to the hut, lamenting another futile effort. Bad enough that he was losing time from his collecting, this was intolerable. He would give this experiment one more day, no longer.

The wind was still blowing hard, clouds hurtled over the swaying kauri trees. But on this side of his hut, in the enclave of flowering red hibiscus, frangipani, ixora and pavetta, all remained still. He'd nearly reached his hut when the sky suddenly tilted. Wallace tasted acid in his throat and his breath came hard. He stumbled for the door, grabbing hold like a common drunkard until his senses revived, then he lurched inside. At the basin he rinsed his face and hands, then he dried his fingers, combing them through his hair and beard. Everything would be all right, he just needed a little more time.

Catching sight of the notebook again, he picked it up, searching for clues. On one page, an arcing line terminated in a series of overlapping whorls. He had no memory and tried to puzzle out its significance. A crude rendering of a palm tree? Opposite was a similar sketch except the whorls were replaced by dozens of wildly segmented branches. He leafed over to find another set of doodles. Scarecrow figures, disembodied eyes, serpents and spiders floated against a cross-hatched background.

He remembered now. Spiders. Thousands upon thousands. They'd been inside the hut. They leapt and pranced through space, defying gravity, filling every inch of the place.

Madness.

He inspected the premises – just the one room and a few sticks of furniture – and found nothing out of the ordinary. He even had a look at the crevice where he'd last seen his little orange and black visitor and it revealed only a narrow black void.

So the spiders he remembered, but what to make of the scarecrows, the serpents, the floating sets of eyes? Nightmarish bogeymen, dragons and spirits? Nonsense. Base superstitions. Not what he'd come for.

He'd come to Gilolo for its seclusion. His self-imposed isolation offered an opportunity to collect not merely specimens, but a specific experience. Yet the cost was mounting – nausea, constipation, vertigo, headaches, black-outs. He accepted illness and incapacitation as an intrinsic risk, an inherent part of his work, but self-infliction was another matter. Meanwhile he forfeited time.

He would take one more dose, no more.

He prepared the tincture precisely as before. Next to the basin he mixed two tablespoons of the oil into six ounces of water, stirred well then swallowed. He lay down to await the effect. He'd been warned that the onset often took as long as four hours, sometimes as much as six, and could not be accelerated. Fortunately, amid his first effort, while lying on the bed he heard a *chik-chik*, *chik-chik* overhead. He soon identified several brown-speckled reptilian bodies in the thatched roof. A gecko family. Until the tincture took effect, they became his focus. He marked each of their locations, monitored their travels, parsed their communications. Spotting a mosquito or moth or cockroach, he mentally willed the adults in its direction, urging them to secure nutrition for their little ones. And under his watchful eyes the mama and papa demonstrated their dedication, darting and pouncing upon prey tirelessly so that, by the time the dose finally took effect, he lay contented. This was repeated on each subsequent trial. Then on the fourth or fifth day, the reptiles vanished. Perhaps a rat or squirrel had made its way in. In any event, he no longer had his distraction. Time now shackled him.

How he missed his gecko family! From his perspective, there'd grown something akin to admiration and (dared he say it?) affection. Not that it was always easy. The papa's unflinching adherence to a single strand of thatch – nothing more than the swivel of eyes for an hour at a time – failed as even the most modest diversion. Nonetheless, he admired how against adversity of predation, human encroachment, climatic uncertainties and limited food supply, the small family appeared to thrive. Unburdened by the human mind with its lists of past disappointments and future aspirations, they had formed an enduring union, a family compact. What a noble and pure achievement to establish balance with one's natural environment. How contented they must have been! He wished to believe the gecko family had merely relocated. That they'd heard the call of a relative, trilling about the plentiful food to be had elsewhere. That they had now found themselves better hunting grounds. He wouldn't begrudge them that. Not at all.

Wallace shifted upon the bed. Nothing yet beyond mild headache. He turned his gaze towards the floor, the wall opposite, the open door, the window sill upon which lay blackened bananas and a cluster of spiny rambutans. Anywhere but the lifeless ceiling of thatch.

Eventually his thoughts curlicued back to the house on Ternate, only ten miles distant. A comfortable domicile, now occupied only by Ali and the servants. He allowed himself the hope they had not slackened in their labours. The house held great potential as a long-term base once repairs were completed. He began cataloguing the work awaiting completion, then reminded himself to rest both body and mind. The effect would come. Patience. After all, he could crouch inert for an hour or longer amid the most oppressive heat and malevolent insects and never consider the time wasted, even when unsuccessful. He reminded himself that what he did now, too, was work.

The drug had taken effect. He wasn't sure how long he'd lain there before this awareness crept in, but his fingertips were now tingling. His breath sat trapped at the top of his chest. He needed to stand. He hoisted himself off the bed and air slowly penetrated his lungs. He needed more, enough to feel its cleansing flow right through his soles. He went outside, into the small clearing and breathed deeply. Beneath a star-drenched sky the crowns of the great kauri trees gently rocked. The night breeze smelled of the sea and it cooled his skin.

Skin.

He remembered: his fingers, they'd been tingling.

He examined his hands, turning them over and over. No discolouration, nor any indication of insect or vermin intrusion. The flesh, however, visibly palpitated.

Curious, that.

Somewhere beyond the darkened trees there were voices. Shouts and laughter. Fishermen at the harbour, he supposed. The wind picked up and the voices dissolved. Then, amid the mob of vegetation, he caught movement. Not the flutter or sway of foliage, nor the night prowl of animal or man, but something else. Something fluid, something tidal.

He edged closer, bare feet treading leaves that glinted a moonlit silver on the black ground. Again a glimpse of something stirring. He squinted against the darkness. In the lee of a breadfruit tree, a shrub – a pavetta judging by its leaves and radiating petals – had just shifted. Of that he was certain. He stole forward, staying on the balls of his feet, ready for – for what?

Then he saw it. The shrub hadn't moved, it grew, or rather continued growing, enlarging before his very eyes. He watched as stalks thickened, leaves spread into spatulas, blossoms widened into bowls, stamens burgeoned into batons. The engorged foliage shouldered into surrounding space, filling the interstices between its neighbours, one plant jostling the next, until there were no more empty pockets. Then the bush heaved a breath – of that he was no less certain than were it his own lungs that expelled their air – and slowly contracted until it assumed its original dimensions. A brief pause, then it repeated its performance.

He stumbled back a step. This, this process, expansion and contraction, was happening all around. The great elongated barrel of the kauri swelled and collapsed, huffing like an old dog, a sago tree bent with quivering fronds then, by degrees, straightened to draw a breath, hibiscus flowers trembled, then dilated into cymbals before tapering again.

Thoughts percolated unbidden, swimming about in

uncalculated directions. He needed to channel his observations, navigate by what he knew. A scientific explanation existed for every phenomenon. He'd read von Mayer. He knew plant respiration took place through the leaves, and the rate increased at night. However, even if an identical respiratory process occurred in trunks and stems and flowers it would not look like this. There had to be a reason. What was it?

The only answer came from the ground. It swelled skyward, tilting the soil and spinning the forest until his skull received its swift and violent reproach.

All he knew was that he lay face down on the grass, the night air cool on his back and on his legs. Cool everywhere – not a stitch of clothing, it seemed. The weight of the air pressed him into the earth. His head wouldn't obey his commands, wouldn't so much as lift an inch. He glimpsed over his shoulder that he was in the clearing not far from the house, but then he caught sight of a most unnatural scene.

Spiders, the night air blurred with them. Orange, red and black, they sailed across the clearing towards the house. He'd foolishly left the door open – the hut would be stuffed with them. What should he do? There would be too many spiders to eradicate. Yet if he could not go in, he would have to figure out where he would spend the night. Despite his nakedness, remaining outside probably entailed no harm beyond that which nocturnal creatures might inflict. The alternative was to try to get onto his feet and make his way the two miles or so to the village. Among the twenty-odd households scattered around the bay, someone might accommodate him. Since it was unthinkable to enter the hut and retrieve his sarong, he would have to uproot suitable vegetation – a pair of ferns, perhaps, one fore and one aft – to attain even the slightest shred of decency. And heaven help him should anyone ask the precise cause of his eviction. His reputation would be cemented. The Mad Englishman.

Wallace planted his elbows and pushed himself into a kneeling position. When he attempted to stand his ribs clenched. Convulsions shook his chest and he sank to the ground, retching hard, spasm after spasm, until he was empty. Exhausted, he crawled to the wall of the hut. The stone still radiated the day's heat and he placed his back against it for warmth.

He woke to find himself on his side. The heavens brimmed with stars, but the wind had died, a stillness and quiet punctured by intermittent birdsong. A bilious film lined his mouth, recalling for him the circumstances precedent to his slumber. He righted himself and again settled back against the stone, now cool to the touch. Various irritations led him to identify several trespassers upon his person. He picked them off one by one until, finally, there was only the night air whispering his skin, turning it to gooseflesh. He rose and shambled towards the door. Inside he found only the usual allotment of invaders: ants, beetles, ear wigs, cockroaches and a few common spiders, each thankfully adhering to surfaces in the conventional manner. With trembling hands he lit a candle. Upon the table he arranged several sheets of writing paper, his ink bottle and a pen. Then he eased himself onto the chair and picked up the pen. Something like a brick pressed against the back of his eyes. He sighed and blew out the candle.

Sleep came fitfully. In the hazy terrain between memory and dream-world a green shimmering light dissolved, draining into the soil as he watched helplessly, immobilized by grief and guilt. Then a sago tree appeared, bowing in the wind, in danger of splintering.

He was awake. He recalled how, before he'd lost consciousness, all the natural world had bristled with energy. Each plant pulsed with vitality, straining for growth, crowding its neighbours as it made its bid for life. None more than the ancient kauri tree, with its fissures and creaking limbs heaving and suffering. Struggling for its very existence.

His mind bolted.

He remembered how, years earlier on a cold winter's evening in Leicester, wool shawl pulled tight round his neck to ward off the draught, he'd read a small book that had been famous through the early part of the century. Thomas Malthus's 'Essay on the Principle of Population'. It was Malthus who coined the expression 'the struggle for existence'. He argued that humans, like plants and animals, produced more offspring than were capable of survival. The human population had thus always been subject to a culling effect by famine, disease and war – events that acted to control growth, and always took their greatest toll upon the weak and poor. Wallace recognized its truth. Even as he sat in his armchair with the book in his hands, the economic recession of the early 1840s was emptying the English countryside into the crowded slums of London. Newspapers reported daily on disease, poverty and children dying on the streets for want of food. A few years later, he was made to recall Malthus again when the potato blight struck. Britain's population had exploded during the first half-century, yet a hopelessly impoverished underclass relied upon the potato for their nourishment. By the time he and Bates left for the Amazon more than one million Irish had perished. The struggle manifested, exactly as Malthus predicted.

Now, ten years later, as he lay upon his cot in a small hut on the island of Gilolo, his blood still infiltrated with nutmeg, what had just been revealed was that the struggle for survival was not limited to humans – it extended to all organisms. Every living entity contended with pressures of food supply, drought, disease and infertility. Life was an ongoing competition for scarce resources and reproduction.

And those that best adapted, survived.

How obvious. In the course of his expeditions he'd amassed tens of thousands of specimens, many differentiated by only the slightest variation. Colouring, size, wing design, antennae length, bill shape, defensive scales, on and on, the list was endless. Yet one seemingly inconspicuous variation might bestow an advantage in survival. Those best suited to secure resources and reproduce eked out an existence; the remainder, over many successive generations, found extinction.

A cycle carried on in perpetuity.

Thus it became clear: the progressive change he'd postulated in his Sarawak Law – an original anti-type ceaselessly diverging until it gave rise to a new species – had its cause in the varietal modifications that promoted the greatest chance for survival. It was an explanation that seemed almost too simple. Yet it made sense that such a fundamental and transparent natural law would have its origin in something so straightforward.

Spine angry and brittle, he hobbled to the table and opened his ink bottle. As the wind rustled the trees and a column of ants trooped around his right heel he began to write. He did not lay down his pen for hours.

Days later he felt sufficiently well to make the voyage back to Ternate. He hired a fishing dory from the village and had his trunk hauled aboard. The boat's owner, a dark thick-set man of mixed blood, said in Malay, "You catch animals?" Wallace had never met the man before, but he wasn't surprised that he'd been the topic of some discussion. The man from whom he rented the hut had regarded him with a suspicion that was only partly veiled.

"Some," he replied.

"You catch snakes?"

Wallace shook his head.

"Too many snakes," said the man. "You come again, next time kill snakes."

"I most assuredly shall do that, if I come again."

The man grunted, then called to his crewmen to make sail. Not an hour later, Ternate loomed over the bow, rising out of sapphire waters like a colossal blue pyramid, its peak shrouded by a tissue of cloud. Wallace felt a keen eagerness for the small island.

At the harbour he hired a buffalo cart. They set off on a road parallel to the beach. Against the sea's murmur and the cart's creaking, they passed a serried line of barringtonia, canarium and galala trees that granted Wallace glimpses of town – a flickering succession of low white stone walls behind which he heard barking dogs.

Beyond the town centre they turned inland. The road sloped gently, but insistently; the island comprised naught but a narrow coastline fringing a single volcanic cone: the blue snout of Mount Gamalama. He saw heaps of shattered wood and all manner of rubble to either side, reminder of the deadly earthquake of 1840. They trundled past the Chinese cemetery – the Malays, Christian descendents of Portuguese colonists and Arabs preferring separate burial grounds – then skirted round the dry moat that surrounded the old Dutch fort. Beyond the fort the road crossed an empty field of coarse tall grass before entering forest. After the bright sunshine, the thick gloom of trees was more than welcome. The cart creaked and rolled at a walking pace, which suited him fine.

As the tracks emerged into the glade that fronted the house,

AVI SIRLIN

the right cartwheel caught a deep rut. The driver shouted some imprecation and lashed his stick against the beast's hindquarters. The creature bellowed and strained forward, the cords in its neck bulging as the yoke took the tension. They listed to starboard, the entire enterprise threatening to capsize. Wallace clutched the bench board with one hand and his hat with the other. Behind him, his trunk skidded and thumped the rail. He envisioned how the next moment, he and his belongings would be flung to the ground, the heavy cart then toppling to crush him. But instead, the buffalo groaned, and with a lurch they finally righted themselves. By which time the house had materialized at the top of the rise.

The cook and groundskeeper must have heard the atrocious rattle of the contraption for they sprang out the front door. They hefted his trunk towards the house and he followed. After a month's absence, Wallace anticipated the place would be in disarray. Instead, the thatch in the roof and walls had been mended and the yard tidied. Climbing the front steps, boards no longer sagged and, upon the decluttered veranda, crevices of all dimension had been closed with aromatic wood. Inside, the stucco floor had been overlaid with a new coat of parging and all the rooms had been organized. Ali had yet again exceeded expectations. How glad it made him that he'd selected the house with not merely work in mind. At the back of the house, the vista revealed Mount Gamalama's southwest flank. Its shadow descended over barren cone and black boulders to cloak the forest at the northern reach of the property. However, as the ground levelled and approached the house, a sizable orchard basked in sunlight.

"We have tamarind tree?" Ali had asked the day of their arrival.

"As many tamarinds as you can eat. And mangosteen,

214

durian, rambutan, guava, papaya, lime, orange, banana, lansat, cocoa-nut ... shall I go on?"

Ali didn't reply. To the contrary, he covered his mouth. But he couldn't suppress his laughter. Wallace too, soon erupted. He laughed so hard he had to brace himself against his knees to keep from falling down.

Now, upon his return, he again felt that buoyant spirit. For the first time in his travels he would have a workplace that truly felt like home. A dedicated kitchen and eating area, separate specimen room and bedroom. A freshwater well. A residence that wouldn't derogate from his calling. He could immediately devote himself to the most important work of his life.

His essay on the origin of species was only twelve pages long, but it proposed a law as fundamental to life as oxygen. He'd re-read it several times and not a word of it would he change. Yet what to do with it required carefully calculated judgment. Wallace recalled Newcastle's criticism of his Sarawak Law and, later, his theory of common descent. The newly discovered mechanism for organic change now underpinned all his work. Underpinned the work of others, as well. Were he to build his case, only to learn of some crack in its foundation, he would do a disservice to all naturalists. He needed to think upon his next step. If only Spruce or Bates were there to discuss the matter.

He reached a decision a week later. The mail steamer from Singapore brought a letter dated December 22, 1857 from Charles Darwin.

My dear Sir,

You say you have been surprised at no notice having been taken of your Sarawak Law, but you must not suppose that your paper has not been attended to: Sir Charles Lyell has specially called my attention to it. Though agreeing with you on your conclusions in that paper, I believe I go much further than you; but it is too long a subject to enter on my speculative notions.

You ask whether I shall discuss "man" in my forthcoming book. I think I shall avoid the whole subject as it is so surrounded with prejudices, though I fully admit that it is the highest & most interesting problem for the naturalist. My work, on which I have now been labouring more or less for twenty years, will not fix or settle anything; but I hope it will aid by giving a large collection of facts with one definite end. I get on very slowly, partly from ill-health, partly from being a very slow worker. I have got it about half written. I have now been three whole months on one chapter on Hybridism! I infinitely admire & honour your zeal & courage in the good cause of Natural Science; & you have my very sincere & cordial good wishes for success of all kinds.

Pray believe me, my dear Sir,
Yours very sincerely,
C. Darwin

Not that he cared for personal tributes when the cause of science was itself sufficient reward, but what gratifying praise. And a considerable relief that Darwin's search for the origin of species would result in a compendium of facts, but no strong answer. It left the realm for him to fill. A golden burden. One oddity was that for the second time now, Darwin reminded him he'd been trained upon his current task for some twenty years. The poor man's health was likely the culprit for poor memory, he supposed. And it must surely aggravate his condition that after twenty years of toil his extensive volume would not settle any outstanding question. Yet were it Darwin who proposed the explanation for the origin of species, his reputation would almost certainly better promote the theory's acceptance. At least through Mr. Darwin's consideration of his Sarawak Law Wallace now had the acquaintance of Sir Charles Lyell.

Thus the solution of what to do with his origin of species paper.

Given Sir Charles Lyell's approval of his Sarawak Law and Darwin's slowness to grasp same, Lyell was the ideal man to evaluate his essay. Trouble was that men of their standing placed so much weight upon protocol. Best to follow form – something for which mother and Fanny regularly admonished his lack of attention – and ask Darwin to review his paper and, if he deemed it sufficiently worthy, forward the essay to Sir Charles. In all probability, come five or six months, he would receive Lyell's comments (favourable ones, one might presume). Then he would set to work on a proper treatise upon the topic. And with Sir Charles Lyell's endorsement this work would not languish. No mere travel narrative, the book would find its place in any respectable library alongside *Principles of Geology*, even *Newton's Principia*.

As for how the revelation regarding organic change came to him, he recalled Newcastle's reaction to his mention of shamans. Wallace only imagined the inflamed prejudice his enquiry into the spiritual world was bound to stir. Nutmeg and apparitions had no bearing upon the merits of his theory. Furthermore, his own interest in the spiritual realm remained uncertain. Unsettled really. He needed to pursue additional evidence before reaching any final conclusions on the spiritual realm. And with the eventual publication of his ground-breaking conclusions certain to elevate his reputation and provide an unprecedented level of scrutiny, such further investigation was something best left off until he was back within the borders of his own homeland. That would come about soon enough.

CHAPTER EIGHTEEN
Waigiou, New Guinea (Waigeo, Irian Jaya),
July 1860

More than two years after he'd mailed his essay on the organic change in species to Darwin, rather than returning to England and basking in the glory of his grand discovery, Wallace had ventured into the destitute northwest tip of New Guinea. From various traders and hunters he'd learned certain species of birds of paradise unknown to any European collections abounded. To date, the *Paradisaeidae* he'd shipped to England had yielded over a thousand pounds, a small fortune. So long as he and Ali retained their health, he was confident they should do very well indeed. And leaving aside some arrangements still in the making with Sir Charles Lyell, there was little else for him but to add to his collection. England remained years away. Years. His plans had been thwarted.

He did not understand Mr. Darwin. Not at all.

In September 1858 he'd received letters at his residence on Ternate from each of Messrs Darwin, Lyell and Newcastle.

He learned of a special meeting of the Linnean Society held in London on July first. Newcastle and Lyell had presented Wallace's twelve-page essay, along with certain materials composed by Charles Darwin some years earlier. Those materials — a letter and a short abstract — bore similar conclusions to Wallace's essay.

He and Darwin had independently arrived at the same theory.

Credit for the discovery now belonged to both he and Darwin, or so he was informed. Their works would be published together in the Society's August journal. Of course, by the time he received the letters, they *had* been published — the news already old. A *fait accompli*.

Darwin also revealed he intended to abridge his work in progress. He would publish a book within a year's time. On the origin of species.

Fine for Mr. Darwin.

But what of his own work? A notebook crammed with elaborate proofs, painstaking observations, carefully wrought ideas. Foundation for Wallace's landmark treatise! There was no longer originality in any of it. To think, had he submitted his essay directly to a journal, or utilized the auspices of his agent, as was his normal course, the discovery would have been hailed as his alone — no matter Darwin's prior musings.

Plainly, he'd misconstrued Darwin's earlier intimations concerning his twenty years' work on the subject. Why, oh why, would Darwin, having long ago deduced the idea, the elusive mechanism itself, refrain from publishing all these years? How utterly heedless of others! Had Darwin put the proposition into print when it first occurred to him, he would not only have obviated hundreds — no, thousands — of hours he himself (and who knows how many other naturalists) had devoted to the topic, but Darwin would have also promoted wider scientific progress. Who might say what further advances, what other ideas might have been stimulated in the intervening years?

Nor could he claim to understand the odd bit of triangulation that occurred in order that their work might be presented together. Rather queer that all three letters sounded rather apologetic about the circumstances. Darwin insisted he'd had no direct involvement, that he'd merely acted as conduit, forwarding Wallace's own essay onto Sir Charles as per his request.

No direct involvement? Given how his own two items – years in the cupboard, as they were – went forward as well, what should he make of that? Merely a staggering coincidence? And that, of all people, Newcastle should be involved, a man hardly well-disposed towards himself? Quite confounding, no less so for having learned of it months after the fact.

For several days after the news he could not work. He dispatched Ali to another island, ostensibly to collect while he pursued his writing in peace. Meanwhile, the very idea of opening his notebook sent a squall through his most vital organs. Yet his mind would not move on – if it were a book, he felt condemned to review the same chapter. Again and again, what intruded upon his thoughts was his lost foothold in London's scientific community. It was that from which all else would spring – a permanent position, a wife and family, the country home. Lost foothold? No, perhaps that might have been an apt description for the losses incurred by the *Helen*'s fire. Publication on the origin of species would have catapulted him far higher – the highest echelons. The difference was incalculably more significant.

Wallace took long walks through Ternate's forests, seeing nothing of interest, collecting nothing, returning to the house exhausted. For hours at a time he stood like a piece of statuary at the harbour, watching the fishermen rig their dories or mend their nets or haul in their catch. He had no appetite, yet in the course of four days he consumed an entire basket of durians. He oiled his shotguns, but gave them no use. Eventually, caught upon a future untold, he compelled himself to do what the scientist must – he re-examined his most fundamental assumption: if he had published first, what then?

Certainly the credit would have been his alone. But it was Darwin who had first conceived the idea. And it was Darwin whose proof was most advanced. Moreover, his own essay had been mailed without expectation of publication, yet the Linnean Society's journal had laid his name alongside Darwin's for the course of history. That and he'd gained the fellowship of three of the most eminent men in science. Could he thus complain? Was he not the favoured party?

To all three gentlemen he conveyed his delight at their news. Then, with work to be done, he and Ali went off collecting. It was some time before his letters elicited any response." Sir Charles Lyell was first to answer, insisting he could not imagine a more honourable response to such a delicate situation. Should the occasion arise, he would gladly extend such favour as might be within his influence to affect.

Then, in September 1859, Wallace finally received a reply from Darwin. His letter stated that he would soon go to press on his "small volume of about 500 pages or so". That bit of news out of the way, he added:

I see by Natural History notices that you are doing great work in the Archipelago; & most heartily do I sympathize with you. For God sake take care of your health. There have been few such noble labourers in the cause of Natural Science as you are.

Farewell, with every good wish,
Yours sincerely,
C. Darwin

P.S. You cannot tell how I admire your spirit, and the manner in which you have taken all that was done about publishing our papers. I had actually written a letter to you, stating that I would not publish anything before you had published. I had not yet posted that letter when I received one from Lyell & Newcastle, urging me to send some materials on natural selection to them & allow them to act as they thought fair & honourably to both of us. & I did so.

Mr. Darwin's sympathies and admiration were endearing. Peculiar, however, that he should have mentioned that letter of his, the one he'd composed, but not mailed. It seemed somewhat like telling a hungry man of a meal prepared for him, then thrown away. Whom did that benefit?

Months later, *On the Origin of Species by Means of Natural Selection* arrived on Ternate. Wallace found it an admirable treatise, albeit with the glaring omission concerning man's own origin. Darwin preferred not to provoke the creationists on this thorniest of topics. A tack that seemed to Wallace unnecessary in its caution. How might one claim a meticulously researched and uncompromising truth when the dominant and most advanced organism on the planet is spared examination? It reminded him once more of his own unrealized treatise. But with the cloth of Darwin's book cradled in his hands, one fact penetrated irreversibly. His notebook on speciation was finally, and forever, redundant.

Rendered extinct.

In answer to Sir Charles Lyell's kind enquiry concerning his own plans for publication, he replied: "Why should the world wait another year, or two, or three, for me to articulate the theory, when Darwin has done it greater justice at an earlier date? It is in the public's interest to air ideas sooner rather than later. And the more profound the implications, the greater the imperative. I have now instead turned my attention to the elucidation of certain zoogeographical issues and to collecting birds of paradise, both of which promise to keep me well-occupied."

Thus, contrary to the assertion in Fanny's recent letter that he was simply running away, he was not hiding from failure. He'd simply determined a new scenario for himself, adapted to the circumstances, as the human species was wont to do. As mother had once put it in respect of a very different loss, it would be a new beginning. His future now consisted of New Guinea's imminent bounty, a rousing written chronicle of his travels and a further volume on the engrossing topic of species distribution. Upon his eventual return to England in several years' time, he would avail himself of his newly made acquaintances. A salaried position at a reputable scientific organization was considerable solace.

New Guinea was a place of abject poverty with but one exception. Birds of paradise. Arriving in early July, he discovered a new species, a red bird of paradise. He hired local hunters who shot several red beauties and he imagined a considerable inventory in short order. But by mid-August fever struck the village where they stayed. One of his helpers perished. He too was briefly brought down. Ali, however, became gravely ill. No hospital, no doctors, Wallace could only ply him with a herbal tea concoction urged by the local medicine man.

Time fell away.

Ali lay upon his mat in the stifling hut, large flies circling over his head. Gulping some air, he said, "I think I die here, sir."

The boy's hair was slick upon his scalp and a small pool of moisture collected in the gully of his throat. Wallace daubed it with the hand towel. "You will be fine. I insist as much. Without you, I would be … lost. You now handle the specimens more deftly than myself."

"I do my job, sir. You pay me."

"That's not the point." Wallace realized he'd spoken more brusquely than he'd intended. He gazed down at his assistant, his only companion amid thousands of square miles of foreign soil and foreign sea. "What I mean to say is I am a rather demanding employer. When my mind often homes in on a task, I see quite clearly the approach to be taken and I have difficulty appreciating a different course or different result than what I expect. My former assistant Charles and my late brother Herbert learned as much and …" A pill of memory stuck in his throat. "Were I capable of changing, I would. But the leopard does not change his spots."

"Leopard, sir?"

Wallace was staring at his hands, begrimed, riddled with insect bites, the nails ragged. But he was seeing his heart, focusing upon it as if it were an amber insect held to sunlight. The fellowship he felt for the boy extended beyond his role as employer. It was akin to a familial bond. He could acknowledge that, if silently.

And if life exacted its toll by losses suffered, the only antidote was love, and more of it. He knew, however, that love would not befall him for his sheer desire of it any more than a prize *Lepidoptera* would descend upon his net were he to merely hold it steady. What was required was a delicate yet determined pursuit. And such pursuit must surely – could only – take place among the heaths and glades of England.

This single thought prompted his emergence from the dark cave that was science. He began to anticipate some of the simple pleasures of home. Cool crisp linens upon his bed. *The Times*. Marmalade and buttered bread with his coffee. The smell of a freshly baked pie, and of autumn apples. An English garden, with its dew-drenched emerald lawn. The elongated shadows of a mid-summer evening and the languorous affair of drawn-out sunset. A calamity of longings.

"Soon as you are well, we shall start westward. It is time. Time to go home."

Ali's eyes were closed. He said nothing.

He stroked the boy's head and felt the heat in his palm. "I've told you before that I had plans for you. I can't say all of it is worked out quite yet, mind you, but there will be time. The main thing is – are you listening?"

An almost imperceptible nod.

"Good. This is important." Outside, Wallace heard the sough of wings, a large bird of prey, he would hazard, perhaps a sea eagle. Suddenly, it pained him to think that the boy had yet to know the pleasure of a comfortable armchair at a proper library, its air imbued with aromas of leather and paper, the susurration of contented readers and distant ring of footwear upon lattice-steel floors. Had Ali received proper education and training at the right age what might have been his achievements? Thankfully, mankind retained the unique ability among species to self-direct, to consciously determine outcome.

"You shall return with me to England. For someone with your abilities there will be opportunities. Mark that you might find the country's climate somewhat disagreeable, but you will never again have to suffer a diet of sago. My mother, I can assure you, bakes a most delicious quince pie."

Ali's eyes squeezed tight, face wrenched. A spasm of pain, Wallace imagined. But then he saw tears streaming over the bony ridges of his cheeks.

"Then it's settled. You shall recover – you are stronger than

I am, and I have recovered. You cannot leave me in the lurch. You are …" His mind fumbled, grasping first for one word, then another, that might describe this Malay orphan, his employee, his companion, a product of the great unpredictable dispersal of life upon this planet – seeds scattered to the wind. "Hear this, my dear boy," he said finally, "you are irreplaceable."

Happily, as if he'd taken those words to heart, Ali rallied. In two days he was on his feet. The voyages west were slow, but Wallace returned to Ternate and packed up the house. Then he and Ali gradually wended their way. All the while, Wallace anxiously exchanged letters with Sir Charles.

In January 1862 they arrived in Singapore where Wallace finally received the good news. Few men in England were better positioned socially or politically to undertake such a Herculean feat than Sir Charles, yet that hardly made it any less astonishing. He had persuaded London's Royal Polytechnic Institution to accept for placement the following school year an uneducated Malay boy of unknown pedigree. His way of making amends, said Lyell.

Wallace had withheld his plans from Ali until receipt of Lyell's letter, so as not to raise false hope. Now, swollen with pride, he divulged how the grand future would unfold and awaited the boy's euphoric reaction.

"Please sir, I cannot accept this most kind offer."

"What do you mean, you cannot accept?"

They were crossing the footbridge that vaulted the Singapore River, the placid waters below clotted with skiffs. Behind them was the Post Office where he'd taken delivery of the excellent news, while ahead on the other side lay Singapore's Commercial Square – Raffles Square, as they'd taken to calling it – with its bevy of merchants' offices, shops, banks and trading companies; the Far East remade in evocation of a

European city, the inescapable encroachment of modern life under colonial rule.

"Surely you have not understood," Wallace said. "This is an immense opportunity. Think of your future, your prospects."

"Too generous, sir," Ali protested.

Wallace placed his hand upon the boy's slender shoulder, cognizant that, except for ministrations during illnesses and the congratulatory handshake incumbent upon capture of a prized specimen, they'd seldom shared physical contact.

"Science is changing the world, Ali, and good men – men of curiosity, intelligence and diligence – will forge the direction in which these changes shall occur. Such men are few and far between. The Institution offers all the modern facilities to train you for precisely just such a role. Had my own family been better situated, I should have wished for just such an opportunity as a young man. You most certainly must accept and say nothing more of it."

They proceeded to Commercial Square where Wallace purchased for Ali a handsome ready-made suit from a Chinese tailor – if the jacket was a little loose now, then some English meat pies would remedy that. Then he acquired for the lad his first proper haircut. In this ready state, they pressed towards a destination where this stupendous occasion would be commemorated.

"Please, sir," said the proprietor of Lawson's Photography, his head materializing from beneath the black canvas of his camera bellows. "Kindly have the young man remain stationary."

Across the studio, perched on a stool in front of a whitewashed wall, the lad stared apprehensively at the camera and fidgeted against the constraint of his very first shirt collar.

"Ali …?"

The boy straightened.

"Mr. Lawson and I both thank you. Now where was I in our little talk?"

"Family," Ali replied. "You say it is important."

"Precisely! There is no more crucial pillar to a man's life than his family. Their love provides the spiritual sustenance every man needs. Without that, there is no tranquility."

"The man will be without peace?"

"Quite so. But once you are in England, you shall be an orphan no longer. You will be embraced without hesitation. Mother, Francis and Thomas all eagerly await your presence."

Ali remained silent, waiting for the homily to finish. Wallace, too, said no more on the subject, cherishing the moment as prologue to a new story he was fashioning.

Later, they wandered amid the forest of sailing masts in the harbour. Everywhere, crews clambered and shouted, winches cranked and grated, hammer blows echoed and coolies paraded gangplanks under all manner of loads. The pervasive carbolic tar stench and all the clamour made Wallace eager for their hotel. Nonetheless he sought out the vessel that would bear them to Bombay, relieved to find it a fine iron-hulled steamship. He spent the balance of the afternoon instructing the ship's steward on arrangements for his collection. They were scheduled to embark the next morning and the logistical complexity had grown.

The previous day a Malay trader had arrived in port with two live birds of paradise. Wallace rushed to make the purchase. Should he be able to deliver the birds to London alive, he would sell them at a healthy profit. But tropical birds required careful handling over the seven-week long journey and the steward, in turn, required very specific instructions. When all those logistics were arranged he and Ali retreated to the hotel.

In the lobby, Wallace's mind hurtled towards the following

dawn. Upon embarkation, he would be free of all responsibility except the birds and the boy.

"Sir, I may tell you something now?"

"Must we talk here, Ali? Can it not wait until we are in our room? Room seventeen, please." The desk clerk, an elderly Chinaman, placed a woven tassel between the pages of his book, laid the book on the desk, and shuffled to the far end of the desk with its cubby hole stand.

"I think it is better to talk now, sir."

Wallace noticed Ali's tunic could use a good wash, but there was no time for that now. The metallic tinkle alerted him that the clerk now held the key out to him.

"Thank you." Wallace placed the key in his pocket and directed Ali to the wicker furniture by the front plate glass window. There he dropped onto the sofa cushions with a deep sigh. "You needn't remain standing, Ali, or I should think it's bad news of some sort."

Ali made no move.

"Oh dear."

Ali bit his lip then he said, "I am not an orphan. I have father and mother."

Wallace felt dizzy. "You have family, alive?"

"My father, he have a shop in Sarawak City."

"Why did you – ?"

"Six brothers, sir. I am the youngest. I am good at speaking the languages and sometime the foreigner hire me for small job. Then I find you … You need helper …"

"But I took you to the Rajah's house when I was suspicious of your story. The Rajah's secretary assured me they investigated your claim and that you indeed were an orphan."

Ali made no answer at first – a large party of Germans had entered the lobby, their voices booming. They proceeded up the staircase.

"The Rajah's man did not ask about my family."

"But, but … he …" Wallace stammered. "You remained there overnight … and …"

The boy stared unblinking at a fruit palm in a ceramic planter. "Well – ?"

"This man say he can help me, but I must first … This part I cannot say."

Then Wallace remembered. The soirée at the Rajah's palace. The young boys. The unscrupulous air of Spenser St. John. He felt a hot tremor of pain. All the more so that he himself had entrusted Ali to that man. He wished to enfold Ali, offer him his condolences. But it was too late for that. Far too late.

"So for the past six years you haven't seen your family?"

"When I start my work, you say we will go six months, maybe one year."

"Yes, quite frankly, I had no idea how indispensable you'd be. Nor how long I would remain in the region. But you could have left at any time."

"If I leave, you will have no good helper for the work. So I stay and give you help and learn many things. Now the work finish. Now I can make home and I can have wife."

"A wife? You're just a boy."

Ali grinned. "When you hire me, your beard is dark. That time, I am a boy. Now your beard is getting much white."

"I'm at a loss for words. It is a profound shock."

"I am sorry to shock you, sir. But with the money you pay me, my father can make a good bride price. Then I will make my own family. Like you say before, I then have peace."

A boulder had lodged on Wallace's chest. The heaviness suffocated him, wearying him beyond his years. But he had no right to stand in the young man's path. Particularly, after his years of loyal work and generous companionship.

The next morning he gave Ali all the collecting equipment, guns and utilities. He had no need for them again. Their liquidation would yield a considerable sum.

"A good bride price, I think," Ali said.

"I should hope so."

"Thank you, sir. I am sorry not to visit England."

"I'm sorry too… more than I can say."

He and Ali shook hands and Wallace picked up his bag and ascended the gangway, resisting the urge to look back. Upon reaching the deck he went straight to his cabin and lay down. He did not rise again until the following morning, when they were well out at sea, the shoreline nowhere in sight.

CHAPTER NINETEEN
London, April 1, 1862

Wallace combed his hair and beard then he brushed the lint off the lapels of his coat. His train was pulling into London and he intended to be ready for any of the press who might be there. At Paris, his railway carriage had been greeted by several news correspondents and a magazine illustrator. That was the doing of the London Zoological Society. They'd agreed to purchase both his birds of paradise. And to promote the first paradise birds ever seen in Europe they began a publicity campaign once their safe arrival in Marseille had been confirmed. He was caught unaware, standing on the train platform with his travelling clothes rumpled, his beard ragged.

This time, his boots were polished, his clothes crisp and his collar straight. He adjusted his top hat and descended from the carriage. Two newspapermen awaited – and no illustrators. Nonetheless, the men knew much about his travels and exhibited great inquisitiveness. He patiently answered all questions before summoning porters to help with his cases and trunks.

Outside the station, though only mid-afternoon, the darkened sky resembled dusk and a thin rain fell. His hired driver was lashing the final trunk atop the carriage roof when the gentleman from the *Times*, a small man with white moustache bearing the amber tinge of a tobacco-user, approached.

"Mr. Wallace, one final question, if I might. Concerning your natural selection theory – "

"Darwinism, sir. Therefore hardly my theory."

The reporter shifted his feet. "Fine, but as co-originator of Darwinism, are you discouraged that many religious leaders, while accepting its application to plant life and animals, maintain the theory does not apply to humans? And that Darwin, having omitted treatment of the issue in *The Origin of Species*, remains silent in the face of this opposition?"

Wallace shook his head. "Clergymen resist natural selection because they are afraid. The duty of scientists is to call upon the facts and dispel fear and misconception. I remain confident that Mr. Darwin shall duly clarify how humans are no more exempt from natural law than higher animals, lowly insects or, dare I say,"– Wallace pointed to the cobblestones below the horse's hindquarters – "the microscopic organisms that crawl upon that dung heap."

"Oh my," said the reporter and he reached for his notebook and pencil.

Wallace climbed aboard the carriage. "Notting Hill," he instructed the driver.

*

Wallace had left the door to his room open, trying to relieve the garret of its musty smell, the by-product of all his books, crates and boxes, many just out of storage after these past years with Samuel Stevens. Fanny entered unannounced. As it was his sister and her husband Thomas's house, he could hardly object to her wandering in, no matter that she knew he wished to work. He needed to complete the organization of his collection. Samuel Stevens had urged him to capitalize on his current fame. Three weeks had passed since his arrival: the birds of paradise continued to attract thousands daily to the new aviary at the Zoological Gardens in Regent's Park. Meanwhile, field scientists sought out his advice, the best scientific societies solicited his membership and he was being petitioned to present papers.

"Please, Alf, won't you reconsider?" Fanny said. "I do wish you would accompany me."

She leaned upon the end of his work table, slippers skating back and forth upon the floorboards as she awaited his answer. He set down his magnifying glass. "What makes you believe my attendance at this séance would have any benefit? Or that I have any interest?"

"Your letters, silly."

He'd written her about the Dayak ceremony in Sarawak and his experimentation with nutmeg on Gilolo. She also knew there'd been a pair of failed attempts with a shaman in New Guinea. Fanny picked up his forceps and absent-mindedly tugged the cuff of her dress with it. He tapped her wrist.

"Oh dear," she said, handing him the instrument. "Sorry …"

"Truthfully, I hardly see the point. I've made my efforts and the only success I've achieved coincided with a bout of severe fever, when I was susceptible to hallucination. Perhaps it's like the mesmerism I experimented with as a boy, whereby some people are simply more susceptible to these encounters."

"I am surprised at you, Alfred," Fanny said. "You've always been keen to learn. You now have an opportunity to assess matters for yourself without consuming any of your jungle potions or suffering any physical discomfort or language barrier. Nor will you be alone – you will find yourself amongst like-minded individuals and a gifted medium who wishes only to facilitate communication with the after-world. If mother is right and there is something crooked in all this, then I shall be grateful should you find it. You have the sharpest mind of anyone I know."

"Perhaps. But as you know, I've hardly left the house these past weeks, what with my health and all my obligations. Thus I can hardly see expending what little time I might now have in order to attend such an activity."

"But you won't rule it out in the future?"

"A man must keep an open mind. Now, please ..." His hand indicated the many boxes awaiting attention and Fanny nodded, then slipped out.

Wallace returned to his moth collection. He tried not to dwell on the social and professional events he currently forfeited – but for the delicate state of his innards and recurring bouts of fever, he could well be guest of honour at a different dinner party every week of his choosing. The one odd bit, so far as he was concerned, was the extent to which certain colleagues still dwelled upon events of four years past. Discovery of natural selection theory. Darwin, Huxley, Lyell, Hooker and Newcastle lavished praise not on his essay per se, but his handling of the aftermath. His equanimity and aplomb. All rather perplexing that he should gain this admiration when, truthfully, he'd done nothing.

Over the next few months, intent upon his collection, he rarely left home. He even turned down the honour of a visit with Darwin at Down House. Mid-summer, however, he accepted an invitation for luncheon with Sir Charles Lyell.

On an afternoon that reminded Wallace of those pleasant days on Ternate when the rains had drained the sky of its humidity and the world sparkled, he found himself seated beneath a grape arbour in the garden of Sir Charles's summer home. Luscious red-black globes dangled over his head, sunlight dappled the white linen table and wafts of jasmine perfumed the air. Waiting for the ladies to join them, his host bantered lightly. He, in turn, did his best to respond in appropriate fashion. But how grateful he was when a Clouded Yellow alighted upon the buddleia near the trellis. Sir Charles commented upon the butterfly's colouration.

"Wait until the wings deflex," Wallace said. "I trust you shall find the colour even more intense." He and Sir Charles then sat in what Wallace regarded as amiable silence until those gold wings with dark borders revealed themselves.

"Very pleasing," Sir Charles said.

"If you'd like, I shall be quite happy to pin it for your collection."

"Very kind of you, Mr. Wallace, but I'm afraid I must decline the offer. Lady Lyell strictly forbids all additions to any but my geological and archaeological collections. She fears we shall otherwise have to engage a full-time curator."

In their ensuing laughter, Wallace felt all his awkwardness and nerves vanish. It was as companionable an interlude as he'd enjoyed with a fellow scientist since his last visit with Spruce in Brazil. Eventually, Lady Lyell and Lyell's secretary, Arabella Buckley, emerged from the house. They were followed by a train of four domestics guiding wheeled serving carts. Fortunately, the luncheon was not as protracted as appearances made out and, in any case, Sir Charles and Miss Buckley greatly assisted the flow of conversation.

After the meal, Wallace and his host retreated inside. Sir

Charles's library stood no poor comparison to a well-stocked bookshop, each of the several hundred spines neatly aligned and dust-free. Few literary works, but the breadth of scientific material was impressive. Forgetting his mother's admonition that one should never peruse a gentleman's library uninvited, Wallace teased off the shelf Kepler's *Astronomia Nova*. The pages appeared well-studied.

"I admire your temperance when it comes to small talk, Mr. Wallace."

Wallace slid the book back into its slot. "My apologies. Several months' re-immersion among English society and I should be much further along in my socialisation."

"I cannot imagine for myself such abstinence from regular social intercourse as you've endured. The cultural isolation of the tropics." Lyell rubbed his jaw in thoughtful manner. "I gather your young servant was ill-equipped for worthy conversation?"

Wallace summoned to mind Ali's face. Despite six years tramping through forest, enduring interminable voyages, and enjoying countless quiet evenings together, the image that lingered was the one immortalized in the daguerreotype taken at Singapore. It had turned out well-executed but for Ali's disinclination to smile – a public school boy about to leave home, not quite petulant, but not lacking in apprehension. The portrait remained much admired by his mother, Fanny, Thomas and himself and was prominently displayed on their console in the salon, notwithstanding that his letters to the lad had gone unanswered. Should he one day be so privileged as to have his own children, he could not but imagine Ali's photograph arrayed proudly alongside those of his offspring.

"My assistant? One might say he lacked British refinement …"

"Unsurprising."

"True. And he was uneducated ..."

"Ah, there's the trouble."

"However, Ali remained infinitely curious about the natural world. We had many talks and, I must say, they never grew tiresome."

"How unfortunate, then," Sir Charles said, his eyes betraying no malevolence, "that he chose to turn his back on the opportunity afforded him, especially after all our trouble. But perhaps for the best. I suspect a young man incapable of recognizing such a charitable gesture to uplift him from his primitive surroundings was unlikely to improve himself."

Given Lyell's amicability, Wallace felt he could speak candidly. "I've given that matter considerable thought in the interval since I left the Far East. Though I was terribly sorry for Ali's decision, with the benefit of time and reflection, I believe he made the right choice. Perhaps improvement may be measured in different ways."

Sir Charles breathed sharply, as if to answer, but remained silent. He reached for his cigar case, an exquisite tortoise-shell affair, Wallace noticed. Inlaid mother-of-pearl in a floral arrangement, silver threads delineating the petals and leaves. Sir Charles offered him a cigar and he politely declined. Sir Charles nodded and, as he prepared his cigar, offered free reign among his titles.

Once the spicy tobacco fragrance began to waft, Sir Charles prompted him for some stories of the Archipelago. Wallace then described various geological formations whilst, from the arm chair by the bay window, illuminated by a broad swath of afternoon light, cigar smoke discharged from Sir Charles in remarkable imitation of an East Javanese fumarole.

"How I envy your journeys," Lyell eventually said. "Nonetheless, I imagine that in such exotic, distant lands you must have felt quite removed from all news. For instance, after sending your splendid essay on natural selection theory, several months would have passed before you learned of our presentation before the Linnean Society. That is, I should say, consequent to your remote location, you learned *ex post facto*."

Wallace followed Lyell's point, or at least thought he had, but he wondered if there was something else behind it.

Sir Charles edged forward in his chair. "Might I inquire? When you learned of that presentation, were you troubled by our actions?"

"My main objective in sending the essay to Mr. Darwin was to elicit your views. Geological time, as described in your treatise, played a critical role in my thinking. And you'd previously apprehended the implications of my Sarawak Law paper. Yet your opinion on the immutability of species was renowned. I could therefore imagine no more vociferous nor estimable critic. When I learned you and Mr. Newcastle made a joint presentation of my paper together with Mr. Darwin's work, it implied your approval and Mr. Darwin's synchronous thinking. I saw no cause for complaint."

Lyell tugged the fold of skin beneath his jaw and that rugged chin instantly transformed into a reptilian pouch. Wallace found it a spellbinding sight.

"You do realize," Sir Charles said, "that Darwin had no publishable material at the time. Newcastle and I had previously both counselled him to publish and when your essay arrived – the chickens home to roost, as they say – he lamented not following our advice and desperately urged our guidance again. It was a dreadful period for him, with his children and wife seriously ill, and he himself of poor health. Added to that, he saw the pinnacle achievement of his career slipping away. We pressed him to bring forward some of his earlier writings –

anything, really – on the subject. All he had was a short abstract and an old letter in which he'd further summarized his theory. Hardly adequate before such an august scientific organization. Typically, at least."

Lyell rubbed his jaw again. He remembered his cigar and looked of a mind to put it out. Instead, he drew on it and exhaled a hazy cloud that obscured him. "So I utilized my influence. Together with Newcastle, we ensured Darwin's writings were placed on the agenda along with your essay and presented chronologically. Though few at the time paid much attention, I'm certain you can appreciate how these machinations unfolded. In that regard, I only wish to say that I never intended to deprive you of due credit for your remarkable achievements."

Lyell now sank back as though exhausted by all that explication. Wallace pondered Lyell's admission. How he'd previously indicated his efforts on behalf of Ali's educational placement was his way of making amends. All his hand-wringing, all his smoke, but for what? For the past. Meanwhile today, well, today was lovely.

"To my thinking, sir," Wallace said, "You and Mr. Newcastle nobly brought Mr. Darwin's theory to light and allowed me to share in that illumination."

Lyell stamped out his cigar and came forward to extend his hand. "I must say, Mr. Wallace, your conduct in this matter is well beyond civil. Were history to be a fair commentator, she could only rank yours as one of the most magnanimous gestures in the annals of science."

Utter hyperbole, thought Wallace. Nevertheless, he took pleasure in the words.

*

Among Wallace's several new acquaintances was the ornithologist Alfred Newton. He'd been among the first to openly subscribe to natural selection theory, writing to Wallace in the archipelago most enthusiastically about it. Subsequently Newton consulted him on any number of scientific issues. In December 1862, as Newton's guest, Wallace attended the British Association for the Advancement of Science meeting in Cambridge. An annual gathering of the most esteemed minds from across the various scientific disciplines. To Wallace's surprise, outside the staid business of various lectures and workshops there existed a delightful social whorl. At the inn where Newton's clique gathered, fifteen jovial fellows elbowed together at one table. Hearth blazing in the corner and the windows steaming, they imbibed no small amount of wine and beer. It was then Wallace learned of their hidden talents for story-telling, in verse and song, even play-acting. No longer haughty men of science, but naughty children.

With Newton and others egging him on for a tale from the exotic Far East, Wallace recounted an episode from New Guinea. He'd had a small prau built in May 1860 so that he might sail among the Papuan islands according to his own schedule. However, news of murderous ways on the islands made the hiring of crew difficult and the majority of his men deserted him at their first destination.

"Dreadful cowards," Geoffrey Chalmers commented.

Round the table, scowling faces nodded their concurrence.

"Gale force winds bludgeoned our undermanned prau and powerful currents wrenched us out to sea. It was only after four days' battle that we put into the lee of a small island. Two of my men, a Papuan and a Malay, swam ashore with hatchets. They were to return with vines so that the craft might be securely moored. While awaiting their return, the anchor slipped. We dropped the spare anchor. It too slipped. "

Gasps and groans from his colleagues.

"Desperate, we rowed, but remember, we'd been in rough waters four days and nights and thus had hardly eaten or slept. It was to no avail. My two men came racing onto the island's beach – " Here he affected considerable leaping about and wild howls which had the gentlemen pealing with laughter "– just as the vessel was swept into deep waters. Seeing no choice for it, we put up our sails. The wind chose this most inopportune time to utterly drop off."

"Odious tropics," muttered Chalmers.

"Having no choice for it, exhausted though we were, we rowed. An hour passed, then two. It was growing dark. Finally, another island appeared. If we failed to safely anchor there, nothing but open sea awaited."

"And?"

"We caught the westernmost point," Wallace declared.

"Good show!" Newton shouted, caught up in the moment even though he'd heard the tale before. The others applauded.

With all those shining eyes upon him, cheeks flushed with excitement, and not a bit of drink, Wallace described the happy ending: how after several more days they reached a town and hired a small boat and crew to rescue the two deserted men.

"Bloody hell, you did!" cried Chalmers, pounding the table. "I would have sought out the nearest public house and not got myself sober for weeks!"

"There is the English sense of duty and fair play!"

"Unlikely those savages would do as much for two of their own!"

Wallace took a hearty drink of ale and enjoyed the shower of compliments. Even those who believed he'd conspicuously embellished his account enjoyed it immensely all the same.

He protested that, in the spirit of the gathering, he'd merely added a spoonful of melodrama. Upon the insistent plea of several members he repeated the comical voices he'd affected in the voices of the two abandoned crew and basked anew in their amusement.

The final result was unanimous. Full admission into the fraternity of Red Lions.

An informal club within the Association, the Red Lions' coat of arms depicted a lion with pipe in one paw and glass of beer in the other and an inscription that read: feeding hour of the carnivore, six o'clock precisely. So far as Wallace could tell, the club's main activities consisted of light-hearted parodies of presentations by their contemporaries in the Association – known as 'Asses' – and celebration of their own achievements, even their failures. All accompanied by copious food and drink. Proper British lions, they expressed approval by roaring and wagging of their coat-tails. A favourite target was Newcastle. At a recent event, Wallace learned, a glass of ink had been substituted for Newcastle's supper wine. A gentleman's pen being immersed in the goblet, to the disappointment of several, he was forewarned.

As pleasurable as it was to gain new friends, even more gratifying was the renewal of friendships. Wallace eagerly anticipated Richard Spruce's return. And after corresponding throughout his sojourn in the archipelago with Henry Bates, they'd finally resumed cordial relations. So it was that Wallace declared it time to visit with Sir James Brooke.

The former governor of thousands of square miles, Sir James Brooke had settled on a small estate in Devonshire, his failing health and one too many rebellions having finally driven him from his beloved Sarawak. He led Wallace through the estate's narrow glen and a thick copse of beech to a small waterfall that was the limit of his property. Shafts of light glittered in the mist of the crashing water. They sat together upon the cool granite rock and talked of Borneo.

Finally, Wallace broached a subject on his mind since his last days in the archipelago, when he'd parted ways with Ali. He asked about his secretary's proclivities. The Rajah slammed his walking stick against the rock. "You wish to malign a good man based on allegations by a Malay? A boy you admit deceived you for six years?"

Wallace replied by walking away. It was the last time he saw Sir James Brooke.

CHAPTER TWENTY
London, March 1, 1864

Wallace imagined it only a matter of time until a worthy scientific position materialized. Since his return, he'd published papers on everything from bird taxonomy to physical geography to the distribution of animals to ethnographical profiles. The writing certainly heightened his status in the hope of attracting a benefactor, but there was also another reason impelling him.

As he'd travelled through the Malay Archipelago he'd ascertained solutions to puzzles that flummoxed other scientific minds. Flatly stated, he had an unerring talent for reasoning. Yet in 1858, when deciding what to do with his essay on organic change, he'd sought a second opinion, asking Mr. Darwin to forward his essay to Sir Charles Lyell. Thus he'd resorted to the back channels of insiders, a route at which he was not adept. He thrived in the open plains of debate, in the boisterous dusty skirmishes by which ideas were publicly tested and either heralded, or found wanting. And not without coincidence, where ideas had the greatest chance of affecting change. Had he not stumbled in affecting notice of his idea through the auspices of Charles Darwin, this lesson would not have taken hold. Which it most certainly did. Another apparent disappointment which, in hindsight, emerged as unexpected benefit.

And in an era when natural selection was hotly debated less for its application to plants and animals, but to humans, he sensed an opportunity to put his lesson to use. That evening, the meeting room of the Anthropological Society pulsed with kinetic energy. Even goose-faced Francis Bacon seemed ready to burst from his oil canvas upon the front wall and shake his fist at the gathering. Humidity and hair grease imbued the dark-panelled room with a primordial ambience that suited the circumstances

Dr. James Hunt, President of the Society, swept to the front of the assembly. There was a smattering of applause, but most kept their counsel. Wallace suspected they, like himself, were well aware of Hunt's views from his recently published pamphlet 'The Negro's Place in Nature'.

Hunt's youthfulness surprised Wallace. He observed the bloom of a newly-minted missionary in his chiselled features. Hunt cleared his throat. "I remind you gentlemen that this evening's topic, the origin of our human races, is a scientific one. Do not let bald theorizing take the place of hard fact. We would do well to remember that by whatever means the Negro acquired his present physical, mental and moral character – whether he has risen from an ape or descended from a perfect man – the races of Europe have much in their mental and moral nature which the races of Africa have not. Now to this evening's speaker. For most of you, our guest needs little introduction. But for the uninitiated, from 1854 to 1862, by boat and on foot, Mr. Alfred Wallace famously covered some fourteen thousand miles of the Malay Archipelago. He traversed inhospitable lands and encountered barbaric peoples that in some cases had never known a civilized countenance."

A pair of latecomers cracked open the door and with murmurs of apology scurried to find seats. The President waited until their rustling subsided before resuming.

"During his travels, Mr. Wallace amassed more than one hundred and twenty-five thousand scientific specimens. These included more than one thousand previously unknown species. All that, in addition to his now-famous essays on the orangutans, birds of paradise, geographic distribution of the region's flora and fauna, and his role in the public revelation of organic change in species."

A most flattering introduction, thought Wallace during the ensuing applause. But he wasn't fooled. He had an inkling as to what kind of reception awaited him after his presentation.

"This evening," said Hunt, "Mr. Wallace shall present his paper entitled 'The Origin of Human Races and the Antiquity of Man Deduced from the Theory of Natural Selection'." Hunt offered a corner-mouth smile and bow of the head in Wallace's direction. "Sir?"

Wallace set his notes atop the podium. He made his case with what he considered irrefutable logic. Through the process of natural selection, man reached a rudimentary bipedal form much earlier than previously believed, and most likely in tropical Africa, from whence he dispersed. Accordingly the races now prevalent with their varied stages of development had their ancient ancestry in one species. The key point, he said, was that while natural selection had ceased to operate upon man's physical appearance, through social development it continued to exact changes on the mental and moral realms.

As he outlined his thesis, Wallace noticed Dr. Hunt at the side of the room, arms folded, fingers drumming. Whenever

Hunt noticed him looking over, that lopsided smile emerged. Nothing to be done for it but plow through and await the attack.

"The inevitable result," Wallace concluded, "is that with man's perpetual development, one day the world shall once again be inhabited by a single homogeneous human race. That race, while retaining physical differences, will be indistinguishable in terms of moral and mental ability. Thank you for your attention, gentlemen. I will be pleased to hear and answer your comments."

Luke Burke, editor of the Ethnological Society was first. He made a convoluted critique. Wallace listened to that garbled voice carefully, but it carried on nearly as long as the presentation. He found it difficult to pay attention. And it wasn't just him, because when Mr. Burke finally returned to his seat, the ensuing speakers attacked both his paper and Burke's seemingly random collection of thoughts.

All this created considerable confusion before Dr. Hunt silenced the gathering.

"There is no doubt that hypotheses like Mr. Darwin's and the one brought forward this evening have a very great charm because they attempt to easily explain so much. However, does Mr. Wallace found his theory on any known facts? If so, then he failed to give them, leaving a strong impression that he has no facts to bring forward."

"We have the evidence here at home," said Wallace. "Our own geological evidence shows that human races are not immutable. When the Romans conquered England they found our ancestors not far above the savage. We Britons once tinted out skins blue and partook in human sacrifices."

"You mock us, sir!" said Hunt. "Those anecdotal records of Caesar have been repudiated."

Wallace's blood was surging. He felt it in the warmth of his ears, and on his cheeks and forehead, he felt its tingling in his fingertips as he clasped his lapels, and he felt it in his lungs as he laboured to enunciate carefully, so the men might hear him well. "Sir, you have requested facts which I accordingly furnished. You merely prefer your own interpretation to those facts. You wish to believe that Europeans have always been and always will be superior to other races and seek to establish this on a biological basis. As convenience would have it, such interpretation so happens to support anti-abolitionism. How much easier it must be to justify slavery where a man is not of one's own species."

One audience member stamped his boot and several others raised their voices, but he was undeterred.

"At Dr. Hunt's behest, I now offer less controversial facts for your consideration, gentlemen. Ponder, if you will, the incursions to our land over the centuries. Romans, Norsemen, Gauls, Basques, etcetera, etcetera. Each invading empire introduced social and moral institutions that were of decidedly foreign origin. Thus the current state of civilization, which Dr. Hunt holds as model of racial superiority, has been hastened not by racial isolation,"– here Wallace allowed himself a smile – "but racial intermixture."

Oh, the howls of indignation and protest!

He could not have been more pleased.

*

"Your attitude has attracted some unfavourable attention, old man."

"Say again, Spruce?"

The Anthropological Society meeting of two months ago was far from Wallace's mind. He and Richard Spruce, along with thousands of others, were taking in the early summer splendour of Hyde Park on a Sunday afternoon. Or at least, that was what Wallace thought as their purpose that day. So far, at Spruce's request, they'd cleaved to Rotten Row, with its incessant pageant of equestrians and little to offer by way of botanical interest. Very queer that on this day an exuberant contingent of dandies milled about. A symptom of the times, perhaps – the fortunate few wishing to flaunt their wealth under the guise of nature appreciation. However, this was where Spruce wished to take some air and he indulged his friend – at least it offered a modicum of exercise for the poor fellow, freshly returned to England and yet to regain his health. His final years in South America had been spent in the high Andes, where the India Office had commissioned him to harvest specimen seeds and plants capable of quinine drug production. To Wallace's mind, the economic value of Spruce's labours was worth millions, yet his friend returned to England both an invalid and a pauper. If it had been himself, he could only imagine a store of bitterness at his government's indifference. Spruce, however, remained uncomplaining, speaking of his travails with a romantic glint in his eyes.

"I was saying," Spruce repeated, "that reports of your demeanour these past several months has attracted some unfavourable attention. The Anthropological Society meeting. The Ethnological Society. The Geography Section of the Association. Need I go on?"

"I utterly fail to see how my demeanour – "

Spruce signalled for him to hold his thought. A cry of alarm had gone up and the dandies now stampeded towards the roadway. The mob pressed against the rail, gawking at something. Spruce hobbled in pursuit.

Wallace strained to understand. It seemed nothing but the

usual preening assortment of riders. But the spectators' heads had swivelled as one, fixed upon a dun-coloured horse that came at a most leisurely trot. A lady with blue fluttering ribbon trailing her hat sat side-saddle upon the horse. Wallace could not but notice her dark riding habit appeared altogether far too confining to allow a pleasurable ride. The woman's eyes brazenly skimmed over the bystanders. Spruce and the other men doffed their hats, turning like a school of fish when she passed. For several moments, no one moved. Once she had ridden considerably past the gallery a swell of high-spirited voices erupted as though a trance had been broken. Then, slowly, the crowd dispersed.

A broad smile creased Spruce's face. "Quite comely, isn't she?"

"I am surprised at you, Spruce. A prostitute?"

"Skittles is a courtesan, old fellow."

"Skittles?"

"Miss Catherine Walters, if you prefer." Spruce chuckled, the hollows beneath his eyes momentarily padded. "Rumour has it that, on occasion, a gentleman catches her eye. Later a messenger discreetly delivers a note to the fortunate fellow providing directions for a rendezvous."

"You continue to astonish me, Spruce. Despite the apparent widespread popularity of this ... lady, I'm hearing of her for the first time from a fellow but one month removed from fifteen years of jungle isolation."

"A man in my condition needs his distractions."

"Perhaps you're not as ill as you let on."

"Perhaps, dear Wallace, I require a different type of medicine than that which doctors prescribe."

Wallace squinted, trying to measure the expression in his friend's eyes. "As you know, I have little enthusiasm for traditional medicine, but I share none of your passion in regard to Miss Skittles. You ought to get married, old chum. A wife and children would be just the tonic – "

"For what ails me? Does it occur to you that perhaps we suffer different ailments? Look at me, Wallace. I cannot stand straight, I have difficulty walking, let alone any stronger exertion. I suffer chronic diarrhoea. And …" Spruce's impish grin revealed several blackened teeth, "I am impoverished. No proper Englishwoman would wish a husband with my infirmities. Nor would I wish a proper Englishwoman. But as I recall from earlier discussions, it is you who seeks the traditional cure. How goes that?"

He gave no reply.

"Wallace?"

A dozen years had passed since they'd seen each other. Notwithstanding his closeness to Fanny, and the many friendships he now enjoyed, both new and old, it occurred to Wallace that with his brother John now permanently settled in California, the closest kinship he felt was with Richard Spruce. Perhaps that explained how his friend managed to elicit information no one else could.

"A few introductions have been made on my behalf. None offer encouragement. I cannot seem to acquire the depth of feeling I once knew."

"I believe that speaks to the trouble." Despite his smile, Spruce's eyes betrayed no levity. "I suspect that so long as you search for a new love who stands to your old measure, you shall never find her. My suggestion, if I may be so bold?"

"I would be grateful, dear fellow."

"Rather than seeking revival of the old frisson you knew in Miss Leslie's presence, try to open yourself to feelings that may take some time to build. Does that seem logical?"

"I shall give it full consideration."

"Good. Then let's walk some more, shall we?"

Wallace confined himself to such pace as Spruce could manage and they meandered toward the Serpentine. At an unoccupied bench near the riverbank, rasping for air, Spruce brushed aside some ashy residue and eased himself down.

For several minutes they didn't speak.

"Might I now acquire some particulars of the behaviour which has brought me – how did you express it?" asked Wallace.

"Unfavourable attention?"

"Yes."

"Shall I summarize?"

"Facts, Spruce. I'm entitled to facts."

"Fine. At a recent luncheon at Kew Gardens to mark my return, there were comments. Among them, Mr. Newcastle said you've entered into the habit of circulating your personal views rather freely."

"As though that is a terrible deed!"

"You know what he means."

"No," he replied. "I do not."

"To cite one example, your paper on how to civilize savages."

"Quite a lively discussion that produced, I don't mind saying."

"I'm afraid you miss the point," Spruce said.

"No, *they* miss the point. Instead of deploying outdated modes of imperialism, the Dutch civilized entire communities by cultivating coffee plantations under direction of local chiefs and headmen."

"It was the political dimension – "

"I see," Wallace said, "The apologists for our private businessmen take umbrage that local families should share in the plantation's profits."

"It breeds socialism, they say."

"Conjures visions of Robert Owen does it?" Wallace shook his head. "How terrible, that! Better to throw local industries open to whomever might produce commodities at the lowest cost until all indigenous self-esteem is shattered and the rule of law is the crack of the European's whip. As with India."

"Another example, then. Your critique of colonial rule."

"Are you aware, dear Spruce, that in Australia, colonialists – I shall not call them men – have been known to prove the quality of a rifle by shooting the native blacks?"

"Where have you heard this?"

"No less reliable a source than – "

A couple, the gentleman in a three-piece suit that seemed the latest style, strolled past. When they were sufficiently distant, Wallace said, "You were the one who told me of the Brazilian friar who boasted of having saved the government the expense of a war with an Indian tribe by arranging for clothing infected with the smallpox to be gifted to them, thus nearly exterminating the population."

They fell into silence. Two geese waddled onto shore, pecking at the grass. The fallen leaves of the nearby willow seemed of particular interest. Wallace noticed that the pair grazed without communication but in perfect compatibility, never competing.

"Do you disagree with anything I have written?" Wallace said.

"We are scientists."

"Where is the line, Spruce?"

"Line?"

"Yes. I presume you believe there must be a sharp separation between the scientific and non-scientific worlds. I, on the other hand, see no such distinction."

"The point," said Spruce, "is that Newcastle thinks a man of your station – "

"Station?"

"Someone without good relations – a man without children to bear the stain of his rash comments, who bears no risk – need not fear the price of his haughtiness."

"He made no attack upon my theses?"

"None. So far as I know, I believe he thinks them excellent."

"So does the man dislike me for personal reasons then?"

"I cannot venture to know with certainty. He is a first-rate botanist and in our limited dealings, he's always been a most courteous chap, if a bit irascible. However ..."

"Yes?"

"You surely know that he, along with Huxley and Lyell, are Darwin's closest advisors. And given the controversy concerning your natural selection essay – "

"I consider there to be no controversy."

"I am aware of that." Spruce's lips tucked into a grim smile. "In light of that incident, Newcastle, Huxley and Lyell – not to mention Darwin himself – appear to accord you a certain amount of deference."

"Balderdash!"

"And it seems Newcastle now believes you are taking liberties."

Wallace folded his arms and muttered into his beard, "If I'd heard this from anyone else ..."

"I suspect no one else would tell you."

Wallace thought about that. He had his collegial social circle, the Red Lions. A fraternal sort, but with them it was all frivolity. And though he could now proudly claim acquaintance with Darwin and Lyell, there remained a respectful distance. Even his rejuvenated relationship with Henry Bates was moderated by a certain caution, inflected by their falling out and Bates's adherence to convention. Indeed, who else would have this discussion with him?

He placed a hand on Spruce's shoulder. "Quite right, as you so often are, old chum. I am grateful for your candour – and fortunate for your friendship."

Spruce broke into a wide grin. "I worry that when I leave London our visits will become all too rare and your education shall fall off considerably. Who else might edify you on matters such as the lovely manifestation of Skittles?"

Wallace turned sombre. "I truly wish it weren't necessary for you to leave London."

"It will take at least one year, perhaps two, for William Mitten to classify the collection of mosses from my travels. So it makes perfect sense that I should take my lodgings near his home. In any event, my lungs cannot tolerate this damned city air."

"Quite logical," said Wallace. "Except that it leaves behind another old friend who has waited these ten years for the fellowship of a kindred soul, one to whom he owes his very life."

Spruce gently squeezed Wallace's arm. "That was a long time ago, old man. You owe me nothing. Perhaps I can entice you to visit – it is only West Sussex, after all. And in view of your confessed desire for marriage, perhaps you might wish an introduction to one of Mr. Mitten's daughters."

"You cad!" Wallace said with mock indignation. "I shall make every effort to visit, of course, but I have no expectation in regard to the man's daughters."

CHAPTER TWENTY-ONE
Hurstpierpoint, West Sussex, June 1865

When William Mitten, England's most illustrious bryophyte expert, suggested his eldest daughter Annie escort their visitor Mr. Wallace into the garden so he might see for himself some of the mosses and plants they'd been discussing, Wallace's first reaction had been reluctance. He and Richard Spruce were enjoying a very pleasant conversation with their host. He glanced over at Spruce for assistance, but his silver-tongued friend seemed absorbed in detailed examination of a patterned lampshade. He couldn't recall him ever having expressed the slightest interest in household furnishings before. Truly, the man had an unsurpassed range of interests.

A short time later, Wallace and Miss Mitten strolled amid her father's garden, the soil pliant underfoot from the morning rain. He estimated the young lady as twenty years his junior. She'd elected not to wear a bonnet, her dark hair pinned back in a very handsome fashion. From her sober manner and plain style of dress, he adjudged her a highly practical young woman.

AVI SIRLIN

She seemed unhurried and Wallace fought to suppress his impatience. Not that her company was anything but pleasant, but he imagined that in his absence Spruce had launched upon another dramatic tale of snow blizzards, frostbite, avalanches and altitude sickness. Or how he'd stumbled into the thick of a tribal war and had been suspected of a spy, negotiating his freedom at the point of a bow and arrow. Or perhaps, a discreet description of the *ayahuasca*. And no matter the intrigue or peril, his friend always related with detailed eye the natural surroundings and native life.

No matter. Wallace took solace in that he was outdoors, in a botanical haven.

As befitted the property of a well-respected botanist, the Mittens' lawns were studded with a wide variety of trees, shrubs, grasses, ferns, mosses and flowers. At Miss Mitten's pleasure, she would indicate a specimen that struck her interest and he identified it then described its range of habitat and key characteristics. Eventually a cluster of green worm-like liverworts at the base of a western hemlock dumbfounded him. Her eyes rounded. "The much-travelled, oft-published naturalist fails to recognize *Bazzania trilobata* from its incubous leaf arrangement? Oh, my goodness. To whom can a poor country girl turn for reliable botanical guidance?" He chafed, but her eyes were shimmering, and the gloved hand with which she masked her lips failed to conceal their crescent corners.

Wallace could not have guessed at the breezy confidence William Mitten had instilled in his daughter. That evening, bidding Spruce good night prior to embarking on his rail journey back to London, he confided that he found Miss Mitten somewhat bewildering.

"You mean she does not conform to your ideal of the English rose?" Spruce said.

258

"A rose, yes, insofar as one emerges from her company mauled by thorns."

"Truly? You were so injured?"

Wallace sighed. "I grant her botanical knowledge is impressive for a woman …"

"Ah, so we arrive at the source of your discomfort – beg pardon, your injury. This young woman of modest background is sufficiently well-versed in plant classification that it causes you some nervousness."

Wallace believed his friend had missed the crux of his complaint – no, not so much a complaint as an observation. "I might put it that on any given point she does not hesitate to challenge. The slightest pause in one's answer and she leaps into the void, brandishing the solution."

Spruce's eyes crinkled in what Wallace took for amusement. The next instant his chest shuddered and he coughed at some length. Wallace seized his friend's shoulder, fearful he might collapse, but was waved off. Spruce recovered, and a smile played upon his lips. "Given your description of Miss Mitten, I cannot help wonder how it is that she is so much different from yourself, old chap?"

Wallace drew a breath to protest, but Spruce added, "I ask, is that such a terrible thing?"

Wallace furrowed his brow. "I shall give it some thought."

*

That summer, Wallace's opinions and ideas were much in demand. The previous year he'd delivered a paper that further expounded on his theory concerning the two distinct zoogeographical zones of the Malay Archipelago, the one associated with Asia, the other Australia. Darwin and others hailed it a significant discovery. Thomas Huxley declared the theory the beginning of a new scientific discipline, and named the boundary between the two zones the Wallace Line.

On a blistering afternoon when London's tanneries, cow sheds, slaughterhouses and roadways collectively radiated a deep fungal stench, Wallace had escaped his garret for the comparative freshness of Kew Gardens. Returning home to Notting Hill he stopped at a flower monger to purchase lilies for his mother. Tucking the paper-wrapped bouquet under his arm, he glanced up the street and caught sight of a man holding the hand of a young boy. The man had his back to Wallace, but fair hair escaped from beneath a foppish hat, suggesting something familiar. When the man half-turned to speak to the boy, his narrow face conveyed a dream-like expression. He said something that prompted the boy to laugh. The man seemed satisfied with the response and led the boy around the corner, disappearing from sight with a swaying gait.

Wallace froze where he stood, the flowers dropping to the pavement. He told himself it was nothing but mere resemblance. A city of millions, he'd simply encountered a startling likeness to his brother. Herbert died in Henry Bates's arms. He himself had seen the grave at Pará. Which meant that he had seen a real breathing man with the small boy, not an apparition. Scolding himself for playing a fool, he picked up the flowers and continued home. However, he could shake neither the persistent image nor the crackle of recognition that had penetrated him.

That night, he told Fanny. Mother and Thomas had both retired and it was just the two of them in his room, seated side by side at his work table. Her eyes filled with tears. "For all you believe, Alfred, can you not agree that there are matters which are inexplicable? Matters that warrant investigation, where you can bring your scientific logic to bear on phenomena that perplex?"

This time he agreed. Together they would attend a séance. For him, it was a matter of scientific investigation. And for that, he would bear an open mind.

*

A pale yellow spike of *Aceras anthropophorum*, the man orchid, stood inside a teardrop-shaped glass vase, forming the centrepiece upon the Mittens' sitting room console table. While his two botanist friends occupied themselves in the study, Wallace examined the orchid's flowers. Upon the central stalk, petals and stamens united into spherical heads from which dangled the slender humanlike limbs. He heard the soft hiss of slippers entering the room. More than one year of visits to the Mittens' household and he now recognized the approach of Annie Mitten.

"Would you not agree they're like so many useless men hanging about?" she said.

Wallace permitted himself a smile. "Perhaps like myself, the men find themselves suspended through no fault of their own, hoisted upon the stalk of societal rectitude, unable to move forward."

With the tip of her finger she gently tapped one of the flowers. "I should hardly think your situation parallel. These men are all alike."

She knew of his ambitions and his frustrations. He had yet to commence upon his Malay Archipelago narrative. The book would require unimpeded blocks of time with which he was presently not willing to part. And there was no pressing financial need. Proceeds of sale from his Asian collection meant steady income. Far better to ensure his name continued to circulate on a regular basis. However, the absence of a salaried position proved baffling at this point. After thirty-odd papers in three years, his abilities were apparent. He'd earned plaudits from all corners, with but one exception – yet how much influence could Newcastle exert?

Glancing between the orchid and her eyes, he said, "When met with resistance, all that remains is to persevere, to work harder."

"Work should not preclude pleasurable pursuits." Her cheeks flushed.

Observing her colour, Wallace wondered if perhaps he'd overburdened her by dwelling upon his dull topic. His sister Fanny frequently declared him a most taxing conversationalist. He also noticed how the pink blush upon Miss Mitten's cheeks had a comely effect. She was speaking to him.

"Pardon me, Miss Mitten. I hadn't … " He could not finish his thought, embarrassed now for having realized he'd been staring at her while she'd been talking.

Her eyes darted towards the vase. "I was merely saying that I had interrupted your contemplation of the orchid. Perhaps I should leave."

"No, please stay." Wallace was surprised at the insistency he heard in his own voice. "I would be interested to learn your thoughts. I find the orchid quite …"

"Inspirational?"

"Precisely. How did you know?"

"It is a design of such beauty and originality. I myself see in it the hand of God." She lowered her eyes. "However, I suspect you might ascribe a more scientific basis."

"I do not deny that in its beauty I see some advantage conferred, something that lends itself to survival. And I have also … You will think this is rubbish."

"No, I certainly do not. Please …"

Inchoate thoughts now crystallized, as though all they had been waiting for was Annie Mitten's questions. "This may sound foolish, but I've always felt something of a particular affinity to orchids. It is a feeling which predates memory, as if I have been guided to recognize in orchids a structure that is simple yet both highly modified and varied. Thus, and it seems to me by design, I find in them inspiration for how to live my own life."

"The desire to live one's own life simply, but with beauty and grace."

"Yes, yes, precisely."

His idea spontaneously expressed and laid bare, the moment felt as intimate to Wallace as any he had known. Before he knew it, his hand lay over hers. Dismayed, he was about to remove it, but she had already enfolded his hand with her own. As if by design.

CHAPTER TWENTY-TWO

Glasgow, September 12, 1876

When Wallace strode centre stage so that he might introduce that evening's featured speaker, he noticed he could not hear the slap of the floorboards beneath him. A deep rumble had filled the auditorium; more than a thousand crammed into Glasgow's Grand Hall. Members of the press were visible in the first rows, surrounded by venerable scientists. Latecomers filing in found places in the aisle or standing at the rear of the shoebox hall. The excited multitude combined with the gas chandeliers to build a swelter that had many daubing their foreheads and fanning themselves. No presentation at the British Association for Advancement of Science had garnered this level of interest since the legendary 1860 debate when hundreds (who, in the passing years and many re-tellings, apparently multiplied) witnessed Thomas Huxley trounce Bishop Samuel Wilberforce on the question of evolution versus creation, thus earning Huxley the moniker, 'Darwin's Bulldog'. As recently elected President of the Association's Biology Section, Wallace felt a rush of pride knowing he'd taken a direct role in generating such enthusiasm for a scientific topic. He had cast the deciding vote on the committee that approved Professor William Barrett's talk on mesmerism and spiritualist phenomena.

Wallace raised a hand to signal for silence. A thousand pairs of eyes and ears. A grand occasion. "Gentlemen, please. There will be opportunity for comments after the presentation."

When Wallace finished his introductory remarks, Professor Barrett came to the podium. The young professor was a slight man with trim beard contoured to the sharp angles of his face. In contrast to the prevailing dark fashions, he wore a suit of light grey cloth. Initially, his voice faltered. Mutters of unmistakable disapproval could be heard. But perhaps in answer to that challenge, his speech fortified and the hall's renowned acoustics volleyed his words. The horde then quietened and, when Barrett paused for breath, there was no sound beyond the hiss of gas lamps and creak of chairs.

Barrett first outlined his experiments and investigations into hypnotism, then proceeded to spiritualism. He cited arguments of sceptics and supporters alike. He detailed precautions he'd undertaken. He also described phenomena he'd discounted for lack of reliable indicia. There still remained, he argued, events for which no known scientific explanation could account. The professor concluded with a call for the formation of a committee comprised of reputable scientists. What was needed was a systematic, impartial and thorough investigation of spiritualistic phenomena. The public, which had heard so much about spiritualism and in whose minds there existed considerable confusion but also great interest, might therefore have proper guidance.

Amid the polite but restrained applause that greeted those remarks, Wallace arrived alongside Barrett. "Bravo, Professor!

I cannot recall an occasion when these vital topics have been treated in so thorough and scientific a manner."

Wallace summoned more applause from the audience. Then he held up his hands for silence, though it was hardly necessary for the approbation withered surprisingly fast. "This presentation will naturally excite a considerable amount of discussion, and perhaps some feeling. As this paper constitutes a record of facts, I ask that those persons who know nothing whatever of these facts kindly refrain from comment."

Some disgruntled mutterings were more than equalled by approving nods, Wallace observed. From the first row Sir William Crookes signalled for the floor.

In that dolorous tone known to all, the discoverer of thallium and inventor of the radiometer reminded the audience he had produced his own thorough report on spiritual phenomena two years earlier. This elicited groans from the uncouth quarter. Undaunted, Crookes iterated that his own rigorous experiments validated the existence of spiritual phenomena. Thus he respectfully disagreed with the Professor's excessive note of caution. The Association would do well to forge ahead and establish spiritualism as the newest branch of natural science.

Charles Ottley Groom-Napier sprang to his feet. Little choice for Wallace but to recognize the prominent geologist, fellow of the Royal Statistical Society and member of the Linnean Society – also the self-proclaimed Prince of Mantua and Montferrat and avowed descendant of King David. Groom-Napier launched into a long-winded and unintelligible history of his own spiritualist investigations.

Genuine unrest now gained foothold.

Concluding, Groom-Napier appealed to Wallace directly. "Mr. President, might I add that we British, as descendants of the ten lost tribes of Israel, have a duty – "

The gentleman never got to finish for all the outcries.

The audience's displeasure only deepened when, out of fairness, Wallace granted the floor to Reverend Thompson. The Reverend predictably denounced spiritualist phenomena, but made no reference to Barrett's paper. Audience members began to heckle.

"Please, everyone," Wallace pleaded, "let us keep to the facts presented."

"What facts?" someone shouted.

"I am a fact, am I not?" retorted Thompson. "Why can I not provide an opinion predicated on my life experiences?"

Laughter mixed with derisive comments compelled Wallace to stand yet again. "Please allow the speaker who has the floor to finish his comments – "

"Yes!" cried the Reverend. "Mr. President, I have more to say."

" – but I also ask speakers not to stray from the presentation in order to comment upon the remarks of other speakers."

"Well then," said Thompson. "I believe I have sufficiently made my point such that men of reasonable intelligence might agree."

With Thompson seated, hands shot up throughout the hall. Wallace tried to determine priority, settling upon a ginger-haired man whose fluttering handkerchief caught his attention. Scarcely had the man gotten to his feet when a voice broke out at the front of the hall.

"Enough already!"

"Point of order, Mr. Newcastle, please. The gentleman with the white handkerchief."

Undaunted, Newcastle carried on. "Our Association must not – "

Hoots and hisses flared from various elements, shouts of

support from others.

"Point of order, sir!" Wallace insisted.

"Fine, Mr. Wallace, but I can assure you of one thing … " Newcastle raised his walking stick and pointed it towards the stage. "One way or another, I shall make myself heard."

"And I can assure you, sir," said Wallace, "that I imagine no more chance at suppressing your views than you can imagine a medium's success at levitation."

To Wallace's satisfaction there ensued a storm of laughter. Though he was at too great a distance to confirm those nostrils flared, he suspected as much when Newcastle pounded his stick upon the floor.

"This is not some parlour game!" Newcastle exclaimed. "Many here among us have laboured for years to sway the public's respect and trust away from soothsayers and priests, and towards the scientific realm. Now you and your spiritualist friends wish to wrest control of this venerable institution in order to examine the illusions produced by the likes of that American charlatan recently descended upon our shores."

Someone called out, "Of whom do you speak?"

"Who else?" said Newcastle. "Henry Slade."

Wallace wished not to fan the flames, but slander could not go unchallenged. "I have met with Mr. Slade and can vouch for his integrity, sir."

"Then I'm afraid, Mr. Wallace," said Newcastle, "you too, are a practitioner of illusions. For you engage in the art of self-deception."

After that, no one could be heard. Cheers, catcalls and howls filled the air. Throughout the illustrious hall Wallace saw intelligent men knotted together, feet stamping, fingers pointing, arms gesticulating, notebooks waving. A reprehensible spectacle. Hundreds marched out. Barrett, who initially remained with Wallace and joined in his calls for order, abandoned the stage, scurrying towards the wing as if a mob might beset them – a mob of their fellow scientists, men whom Wallace had come to regard not only with the respect accorded one's peers, but in some cases with fraternal affection.

At the front of the auditorium, Sir William Crookes struggled into his coat. Five years earlier, Sir William's endorsement of spiritualist phenomena led to an anonymous scathing critique in the Quarterly Review that attracted much attention. The poison pen was widely attributed to Newcastle. Now, head bowed, the chemist's eyes were damp, doubtlessly in recognition of the opportunity lost.

Wallace too, put on his coat and prepared to take leave. Newcastle remained on the floor, presiding over his disciples in one aisle, chin angled like a mallet against Reverend Thompson who persisted in pleading some futile point. Wallace was sorry for his involvement. A debacle. Plodding off stage, a voice called after him. With the Grand Hall now half-empty, the words reverberated.

"Mark me well, Mr. Wallace, I shall be heard!"

Wallace raised himself, making a show of his straightened back, then marched off. He knew, however, that as much as he wished otherwise, that brash declaration would prove true.

He returned home to Dorking and presided over nothing more than the vegetable garden. He built a toy wooden horse for the children and completed an overdue essay. A week passed.

He was in his study fussing over the mantel clock. It never lost time at the old house, but the recent move to Dorking seemed to have unsettled it. With mixed success he'd taken apart and re-assembled other timepieces. Everything had its discernible function; the skill lay in the discerning. Spectacles perched at the tip of his nose, he had the movement cradled in his lap under a splash of window light, probing the strike mechanism with a sewing needle, when Annie cleared her throat.

"Dear?" she said from the doorway.

He waved her off.

"Yes, I can tell you're busy. And such an important bit of work, at that."

He nudged the spectacles back to where he could see her properly, though after ten years of marriage he could have painted that smile from memory. He pointed the sewing needle in Mrs. Wallace's direction. "Careful with your interruptions. I have in hand my lance."

"I suggest you lay your weapon down."

There was no playfulness in her voice.

He placed the clock-piece and needle on his desk. Annie handed him the newspaper, crisply folded to the letters page. A letter of Newcastle's had been printed in *The Times*. He wished to inform readers of the fraudulent abuses of one Henry Slade.

By that time, few Londoners had not heard of Dr. Henry Slade, as he titled himself. The American spiritualist had arrived in the city on July 13, 1876 amid dramatic magazine and newspaper reports. In America, many had travelled vast distances to visit the renowned medium in the hope of contacting deceased loved ones. Some were undoubtedly drawn by Slade's one thousand dollar reward to anyone proving his powers of telekinesis, levitation, partial materializations and other spiritualistic phenomena were produced by deception. The money had yet to be claimed. Reputedly, Slade's skills and extravagant bounty were not the only lure. Handsome, tall and charismatic, with luxuriant dark hair and handlebar moustache, his sittings held particular favour with many ladies among the high society.

Subsequent to his arrival in London that summer, Slade had conducted a steady flow of séances. He famously set few conditions on time of day, lighting or inspection of his premises. To the contrary, upon payment of twenty shillings, day or night, the attendee was brought into his room and matters commenced instantly, typically concluding within twenty minutes. The whole purpose of these séances, Newcastle thus informed *Times* readers, was the extraction of gold sovereigns in the most expedient manner.

The hallmark of Slade's fame was a form of phenomenon that, while soon replicated by other mediums, he claimed to have originated. During séances, a blank slate was held pressed to the underside of the table in such manner as to ensure he had no means of affecting its writing surface. A short time later, the scratching sounds of inscription upon the hidden slate would be heard. Slade remained seated motionless and in plain view throughout. The writing produced for the visitor constituted proof of spiritual communication more persuasive than table rappings, musical instruments that played themselves or murky disembodied voices commonly encountered with other mediums – any of which, for a nominal fee, he would also produce.

Attending a séance with his colleague, Professor Edwin Ray Lankester, Newcastle claimed to have snatched a purportedly clean slate out of the medium's hand and discovered the handwriting already upon it. Such fraud warranted the law's intercession, wrote Newcastle. But leaving aside the deprivation of one's hard-earned currency by a charlatan there was still another, much greater deceit that called for fullest censure:

The object of my letter is to stem the sea of delusion that has washed upon English shores. With more than three million adherents in the United States, the land where it first bred, and hundreds of thousands now in England, spiritualism is an epidemic. Yet few are prepared to fight it and, like a medical epidemic, it is left to men of science to soundly defeat this societal ill through education and prevention. Alas, were that so easy! At the recent meeting of the British Association for Advancement of Science, for the first time in the Association's history and over the strenuous objection of many of its most esteemed members, Professor Barrett of Dublin introduced the subject of spiritualism as a reputedly bona fide field of study. In permitting this corruption of our sciences with superstition, Section President Mr. A.R. Wallace degraded our nation's greatest bastion against falsehood and thus diminished its capacity to fight this dreadful plague. Now, the only defence against this scourge are the independent scientists prepared to valiantly oppose and bring to public light this ongoing fraud!

Sincerely,
R. Newcastle

Wallace looked up from the newspaper. Words catapulted through his mind, but his trembling voice found only one: "Degraded …?"

Annie stroked his hair.

He burrowed his face into the apex of her thighs. She smelled of dry grass and apples. And of Will and Violet. She cradled him. "*Ssshhh*, darling. *Ssshhh*."

He pulled away. The door stood wide open!

"They're both in the garden," Annie said. She drew him in again. He kissed her then unfastened her long, coiled hair. She unbuttoned his waistcoat. Chest heaving, his eyes sought out a venue, but every corner of his study was piled with books, papers and preserved specimens; the inner workings of the clock were arrayed upon the desk, delicately-carved armrests protruded from his narrow chair. He was contemplating the small area rug on the floor when she murmured, "Bedroom, darling."

Upstairs, after undressing, she joined him under the bed covers. Through the window which gave onto the yard, Violet's shriek floated in, quickly followed by both children's laughter. Annie caressed the side of his face. He did not respond. She nudged closer, the bedstead creaking

"It's all rather preposterous," he said, staring at the ceiling. "That any of my colleagues believe me misguided in my scientific pursuits."

"Those colleagues who don't truly know you are susceptible to misunderstanding."

"How? I speak plainly and accurately."

She traced a finger along his chest. "Yes, but form can be as important as substance. Sometimes direct talk is not what people wish. You also have an astounding single-mindedness of purpose. Once you seize upon an idea, you often rush headlong. That condition rarely permits a glance to the left or right."

"I fail to see how that pertains to their misunderstanding," he said. "If I am single-minded in my objectives, as you say, it is only with a view towards arriving at an opinion. However, once my position is formulated, I am quite receptive to dialogue. Indeed, it is at that point that differing views promote valuable insight. Do you see the wrong in any of it?"

Her breast had found its way into his palm.

"Not at all." She draped her thigh over his.

"Then there is no reason for their abusive attitude."

"None, darling." Her hand guided him.

"Single-minded, indeed," he said. "Perhaps I shall raise this further with Spruce."

"Certainly not," she said. "This, Mr. Wallace, you shall raise only with me."

"*Hmm?*" He wished to say more, for he had other thoughts. But then he felt her warmth, and his blood surged.

"Gentle, darling ... " She murmured in his ear. "Mmm?"

There was only her warmth. He nodded meekly, then he entered.

*

Upon Annie's advice, so as to ensure an even temperament, he waited until the next day to craft his response. *The Times* published his letter on September 19th:

> It is an object of scientists to probe the limits of nature with open mind. Many esteemed men at the Glasgow meeting embodied that ideal and showed considerable interest in the subject of which Mr. Newcastle complains. Likewise, several distinguished scientists and upstanding citizens have attended the séances of Dr. Slade with an open mind and witnessed indisputable phenomena not creditable to physical laws. I too experienced first-hand Dr. Slade's phenomena and hold no doubt as to their authenticity.
>
> Mr. Newcastle, on the other hand, went to Dr. Slade with the firm conviction that all he was going to see would be imposture, and he believes he saw imposture accordingly. In view of all the credible evidence and my own experience with Dr. Slade, I find it quite impossible to accept Mr. Newcastle's allegations.

It seemed to him the perfect response. Without bluster or ill-temper, he'd laid his reputation on the table of public record. Let Newcastle pursue the matter further, if he so wished. The public might then judge whose honesty and integrity could be trusted. For he had no doubt, and nothing to hide.

CHAPTER TWENTY-THREE

Dorking, Surrey, November 1, 1876

"How do I look?"

"Very dignified," Annie said. "And handsome."

Wallace gave a stern look to warn his wife off the compliments and stick to the descriptive.

"Just one more accoutrement shall finish you nicely."

"Another?" Wallace's shoulders sagged. She'd already tucked an elaborately folded silk handkerchief in the breast of his tweed jacket. It now protruded like a blossoming white iris. Mere frippery, though he could not deny its flair. He stepped towards the looking glass. Nothing amiss so far as he was concerned.

Annie was at the bedroom's dresser. For what, he couldn't imagine. She bent for the bottom drawer. He was watching the fabric of her tea gown shift along her hips when he understood what she was after.

"No Annie, please," he protested. "That would be too much. Truly, I won't wear it."

She was already approaching with the thing in her right

hand, blue eyes surveying the landscape of his chest. He extended his arms to forestall her. She kept coming however, lips stitched, the determination carved into her. His arms dropped in surrender. She lifted the ribbon from the case and as she hunted out the precise point for attachment the gold medallion hung like a mesmerist's coin.

A violent shriek rang out in the corridor, then feet pounded down the stairs.

"Will!" Annie shouted. "No running in the house! And leave your sister alone!" Back to the matter at hand, she must have caught his expression. Her voice employed the same firmness as with the children. "This is no time for modesty, Alfred. Quite the opposite."

"The lawyer shall be certain to raise all relevant accomplishments – "

Her glare stopped him.

"You elected to partake of this," she said.

"It is my duty."

"If so, then you must look after it properly."

"You mean, attend with pride, pomp and circumstance."

"You know as well as I do that you have held out your reputation for judgment. This, when we hardly have our feet back under us."

The rims of her eyes pooled and her mouth lost its tightness. He knew of what, and whom, she was thinking.

She brushed some lint off his shoulder, her hand lingering briefly, light as a butterfly. Then the walls of her face girded. She pinned the ribbon upon his lapel and turned him by the shoulders so he might gaze at himself. From the dormer a morning slant of light glinted off his spectacles. The medallion, however, hung lustreless. Indeed, what stood out was the white beard. Fifty-three years old, already. Father Christmas, Richard

Spruce now called him.

"You look very handsome."

"You'd already said as much without this … bric-a-brac. Its weight causes me to stoop."

He was joking, but there was no denying the forward cant to his neck, head incrementally sliding off the cambered surface of his shoulders. He straightened a fraction.

She kissed him on the lips. Then she pressed her cheek against his and whispered, "Darling, let's get your frock coat on, shall we?"

A short time later he was out the front door.

The autumn air was crisp and the sky fair, only one dark rope of cloud on the distant horizon. He paused beneath the front trellis. White clematis wove amid the woodwork like a starry constellation. He drank in their sweet almond scent, then he passed through the gate and onto the roadway.

As soon as he was concealed by the hawthorn hedge he removed the Royal Medal pinned to his lapel. Wallace traced his fingers over the engraving of Sir Isaac Newton, the man who epitomized scientific ideals, and remembered the award ceremony eight years ago. Of all those who'd advocated on his behalf in 1868 – and among leading men, only Ramsay Newcastle withheld his support – how many would still support him by the end of this day?

He slipped the medal into his pocket.

The road was quiet. Two houses down, beneath an ailing pear tree, Mrs. Ingram was instructing one of her servants on the placement of a ladder. She turned in his direction and he lifted his hat but did not slacken his pace, the sett stones clapping beneath his soles. One mile to the Dorking railway station, he was determined to make haste.

He observed that the dark braid of cloud in the distant

valley had now surmounted the green hills and rendered them a brooding tea-colour. To his right, on the dew-covered oval, industrious robins darted for food and at the other end of the pasture, amid a grazing flock, two or three sheep lifted their masticating muzzles to observe his transit. He breathed deeply, the air as invigorating as any pristine wilderness. But for his present concerns he might have considered himself a quietly contented country gentleman.

They'd moved to Dorking a mere four months ago. There was much to commend the change. Impressive Georgian homes surrounded their residence. The reasonable rent he'd negotiated gained them financial breathing space. Convenient rail access to London (only forty miles distant, he reminded those among the scientific community puzzled by his decision). But to Annie and Richard Spruce alone, he added that Daniel Defoe had resided in Dorking, Dickens wrote part of *The Pickwick Papers* – including a charming representation of the town – while lodging at The White Horse Inn, and the inestimable Thomas Robert Malthus had been born only two miles distant, in a country home called The Rookery, now a frequent destination of his own daily walk.

Approaching Dorking Station, Wallace steered clear of the sweepers purifying the roadway and stopped at the curb. A row of bushel baskets wafted a fresh orchard scent that proved irresistible. He selected his apple and the boy tending the fruit thrust out his blackened fingers. Wallace handed him the copper coin. The small hand withdrew inside a mottled coat sleeve. "Thank 'ee, sir," the boy mumbled, then wiped his nose upon the sleeve.

Wallace dropped the apple into his coat pocket. He marched to the wicket, then the platform, with the fruit bumping his thigh – distant reminder of jungle excursions when laden pockets jostled with every stride. At the news vendor's stall he parted with another coin.

The headlines for the day promised a world no better or worse than the day before. The Balkan crisis had heated up again, the Russians issuing the Turks an ultimatum to sign a truce with Serbia. The mills of the Mersey Seed Crushing Company in Liverpool had been destroyed by fire, three hundred now out of work, poor souls. A Philadelphia schooner went ashore on the rocks at Badger's Island near Portsmouth and remained in a dangerous position. Wagner's "Goetterdammerung" was hissed during its opening in Paris. And the weather forecast called for rain. Wallace recalled the fair skies outside his home. This nascent business of weather forecasting was not yet scientifically reliable, so far as he was concerned.

Along the train platform a fleet of blue-smocked men wheeled sack-laden hand-carts. The air swam with the musty-sweet odour of freshly-milled Gomshall corn. Newspaper folded under his arm, Wallace climbed inside the London-bound carriage. After an obligatory exchange of greetings with Mr. Paine (a tax assessor or real estate clerk or some such – they'd met at the Cahills' garden party Mrs. Wallace insisted on attending so they might meet their neighbours), he settled into an empty window seat. Opening *The Times,* he resumed his ritual of these past weeks. He immersed himself in the ongoing account of the trial that held him, as it did much of England, in morbid thrall – and in which he was to make his appearance this day: the prosecution of Dr. Henry Slade. When the train chuffed and slowly pulled out of the station, he barely noticed.

Henry Bates had undertaken to meet him in London and escort him to the Bow Street court house. His message sounded a note of anxiety – perhaps another complication in which he wished advice. They would consult en route. Notwithstanding its setbacks, their friendship was among his oldest. Four years of silence that began in the Amazon came to an end when Wallace wrote to express gratitude for the assistance rendered Herbert at his most dire time. The resulting correspondence was cool at first. However, once he'd departed for the Far East and initiated a flow of scientific ideas and theories, Henry followed suit with reports of his own work in South America. There ensued many enthusiastic accounts – adventures, discoveries and tribulations, an exchange rooted in the heaths and woods of Leicestershire.

Despite that shared history and the satisfying rejuvenation of their bond, each time Wallace opened one of Bates's letters, that hurried, almost agitated, cursive sent his mind's eye sailing back to that afternoon long ago, the earliest days of their joint enterprise amid the Amazon, and the incident that nearly destroyed their relationship.

There was a rustling among his fellow passengers – the conductor had entered the carriage. Wallace fished out his ticket and held it ready. They'd just passed Box Hill, its wooded slope overlooking the North Downs. To his right, the River Mole meandered beneath the escarpment as the valley wended towards Leatherhead. The whistle blasted once, twice, three times, as the train rumbled alongside a field of threshed oats. At the farthest end of the field, perched atop fence posts like a pair of crows, two farm boys waved their hats. He raised his own hat in answer, as did others. The boys laughed and shouted, their words inaudible over the rush of wind and clatter of trestles. Soon the only view was rolling grassland. Beneath a shadow of dark clouds, the fields remained verdant. He never tired of the countryside's beauty.

He had sometimes wondered what might have been had his Amazonian partnership with Bates not dissolved prematurely.

Whether his subsequent discoveries of natural selection and geographic distribution of species might never have occurred. Or conversely, whether working in tandem, having the benefit of each other's knowledgeable enthusiasm in regular discussion and debate, would only have accelerated the pace of his scientific breakthroughs. There was a peculiar alchemy to a relationship between kindred minds – over the years, he'd learned that much. And theirs was a friendship truly like the tide; rising and falling, forces unseen.

The tide at Waterloo Station was certainly full, Wallace observed. A sea of bodies in motion. Amid all that turbulence there stood one calm pool. Two Benedictine nuns, faces serenely attentive to the windows of his arriving train. With but one notable exception, men and women alike steered well clear, as though some terrible disease lurked in those black and white habits. That exception was Henry Bates. Under protection of the nuns' bulwark, with one finger working the skin beneath his wing-tipped collar, he scanned the carriage. Spotting him, Bates's face brightened and he waved his top hat furiously – breezy comfort to the sisters, no doubt. Wallace touched a finger to his own brim in acknowledgement.

It took several minutes to weave their way to one another.

"You come into the city far too infrequently," Bates said.

"Mrs. Wallace and I still await your visit. Dorking is but one hour away."

"I'm afraid the Royal Society keeps me rather busy," Bates said, "and the trifling amount of time left for my family and my collections is rather … Well, I'm sure you understand."

"Darwin insists you've now amassed the finest private collection of beetles in Europe."

"Awfully kind of him," said Bates, looking quite flattered.

"However, I suspect my collection compares poorly with the quality of your birds – Oh, my!" Bates's hands tightened round his umbrella. "Dreadfully sorry … I'd forgotten."

"Quite all right," said Wallace. "The money came in handy."

"I do try to ignore the gossip, but … In any event, I continue to keep my formidable ears open for opportunities on your behalf."

"I'm most grateful. No task too modest, I say."

Bates glanced at the station's clock. "I gather you are expected at the court house. So, shall we walk?"

They left the station and joined the funnel of pedestrians and vehicles streaming onto Waterloo Bridge. The wind was blowing gusts, men and women alike clutching their hats. On the bridge, wagons, cabs, carriages, omnibuses and livestock competed for space. Below, the steam packets were thick as pigeons in a park square.

Notwithstanding visits to London for various society meetings and an occasional social call, his migration into the countryside now made Wallace feel a stranger in the city. He imagined as more and more people came in search of work, the congestion – and his alienation – would only worsen. To think four million now lived there, when there had been but a million at the turn of the century.

A drover hollered, his flock impeded by a coach. Several sheep scrambled onto the footway, inspiring oaths and imprecations by embattled pedestrians pinned against the balustrade. The melee brought all traffic to a halt. Bates and he had a devil of a time squeezing through the narrow channel that still allowed headway. When they reached the other end of the bridge the wind dropped off. Then the rain fell. Bates opened his umbrella and, despite Wallace's protests, generously shared its cover. They'd been talking about their children. With the rain falling, Bates now raised the topic of the poor weather that autumn.

Enough was enough.

Wallace broke stride. Bates carried on a few more steps before he turned round.

"Did you drop something, old fellow?"

"See here, Bates. You and I have known each other some thirty years. This small talk is … irksome. Why not speak your mind?"

"All right." Bates extended the umbrella in his direction. "Please step under, or my spectacles will soon need a good wiping. As will yours, I imagine."

Wallace ducked under the umbrella and they walked.

Bates looked at him from the corners of his eyes. "With your recent hardship …"

"Say what you've come to say. I have a court appointment, Bates."

"Yes, quite right … as usual. What I meant to say was that when you published your essay on spiritualism so soon after your son … your terrible loss, many among us – "

"Whom do you mean by 'us'?"

"Our friends in the scientific community."

"Friends? Truly?"

"Right, then … your peers – no, your colleagues, shall we say? – We sympathized or, at least we understood."

They had reached Lancaster Place. Wallace unravelled the pretty iris Annie had so artfully folded and wiped his spectacles. Then he re-pocketed the handkerchief in tidy fashion, but without the same flair. He instantly regretted having used it.

"What did you and our colleagues understand?" Wallace asked.

"That with your recent grief, you were vulnerable to the

charlatans who prey upon those such as yourself – those who concoct miracles."

"Not miracles, Bates. Phenomena."

"My point is, we took account of the situation, as well as your extraordinary sacrifices and contributions in devotion to science, and remained largely silent about your affairs. And you restored our faith with your remarkable treatise on geographical distribution of animals – an incomparable book, truly. But then, well, first the debacle last month in Glasgow and, now, this trial in which you had no obligation to involve yourself … it's too much. Too much."

Wallace sank his hands into his pockets. "I shall never forget the kindness you extended Herbert in his final hours. Never. But what you say right now attacks my core beliefs."

"Beliefs? But where is the evidence to support them?"

"Have you not heard sceptics attack progressive thought before? Recall the vitriol that greeted Darwin's theory of natural selection?"

"Natural selection – your discovery – is science, based upon fact. What you have now involved yourself with – "

"Careful …"

"– is mere theatre … stage magic … superstition."

"Beyond the pale, Bates. You've gone beyond the pale."

"We are men of standing now, do you not see this? We are public figures, you and I. Myself, a boy who once swept the floors of a hosiery warehouse and you, who roamed about the countryside with rod and chain. With only the slightest idea of what awaited us outside England and barely the funds to book our passage abroad, we went and we did it. Not like Darwin, Lyell, Newcastle and that lot, but self-made. We contributed from the field! Not merely data, but ideas – new ideas. And now, when we are finally embraced by the very institution we have longed to serve, you … you elect to bring it into ridicule."

Chest heaving and tie askew, Bates's face was flushed, eyes large as chestnuts. Still a man of passion, Wallace observed.

When he stepped out from beneath the umbrella the rain beat upon Wallace's hat. He measured his words. "I do not endeavour to bring ridicule to you, myself or anyone else. But as any good scientist might, I strive to diminish our collective ignorance of the natural world. Those who wish to stifle legitimate investigation, who reject evidence out of some pre-existing prejudice … I consider such individuals to be opponents of science. They obstruct the ultimate goal: improvement of the human condition. Such men, great in reputation or otherwise, are of little concern to me."

Rain streamed from Wallace's hat. Combined with the moisture on his lenses, his old friend was obscured. He gave both his spectacles and his face a wipe. Bates's eyes were fixed upward, on the metal spokes of his umbrella. Deliberating upon what to say. Or biting his tongue.

No matter.

"Good bye, Henry."

Though he suspected that he and Henry Bates had just spoken for what would be the final time, Wallace bounded onto the roadway without a handshake or so much as a backwards glance.

CHAPTER TWENTY-FOUR
London, November 1, 1876

He tramped north on Wellington, the rain unrelenting. Foolish not to bring an umbrella, he realized, no matter how fine the weather in Dorking. The plush nap of his hat suffered terribly, as did his shirt collar. At Tavistock, the London Umbrella Company had a hiring station. He calculated carefully: three hours at four pence, nine for the full day, with a four shilling deposit. But only a few blocks remaining and, once he was inside, the rain might cease altogether for the balance of the day. Moreover, perfectly good umbrellas stood at home as a consequence of his poor judgment. He trudged on.

By the time he reached Bow Street, rain was battering the rooftops and lashing windowpanes. On the roadway, water sluiced between the stones and surged through the gutters, puddles forming in every fissure and cavity. Behind him, Wallace heard the charging clop of hooves. A brougham raced past and to avoid its splatter he pressed himself to the wall. At the back of the carriage the footman stood unflinching, straight as a ship's mast, water spouting from the corners of his hat.

Meantime his own hat, Wallace feared, was ruined. And from his dampened collar a chill seeped into his spine. Though he knew well it might also be raining at Dorking, he nonetheless pictured the sky of that early morning and, even as his mind admitted it was a school day, he imagined Violet and Will at play upon the lawn, their squeals entering his study while he nibbled at his biscuit and perused the Annals.

None of that would he enjoy.

The Henry Slade case. Within days of his letter's publication, Newcastle and Lankester hired a lawyer to prosecute Slade for fraud. The trial began mid-October. One week later, Wallace received a summons to appear as a witness for the defence. When he informed Annie of the summons, from across the dining table her brow had furrowed.

"Now, now," he said. "It will do tremendous good to speak openly."

"You do not see the worry in it?"

"Worry? For what possible reason?"

She said nothing.

He nested his cup in its saucer and planted his elbows on the linen, heedful of the smudge where he'd dropped the toast. "Whether the lawyers and judge be the wiliest men in London or complete dullards it will not change one jot of the truth."

"The newspaper reports have made it out to be a spectacle," Annie said. "More an entertainment than truth-seeking."

He too had read that the presiding magistrate permitted the prosecution to call the well-known stage conjurer John Maskelyne in order to demonstrate how the "tricks" of Dr. Slade might be performed. This despite the acknowledged fact Maskelyne had never even attended a séance! Naturally this cabaret elicited no lack of risible commentary from courtroom onlookers. While the ancient Bow Street court house tried only minor offences – summary matters of insufficient gravity for the Old Bailey – that hardly excused such twaddle. It was an affront to the justice and dignity of the accused. Even more worrisome, it demonstrated the magistrate's bias towards his own amusement at the price of a man's liberty.

"We can only trust," said Wallace, "that the obvious merit of the evidence called on behalf of Dr. Slade will prevail at the end of the day." He daubed the napkin then angled his beard towards her.

"Clean," she pronounced.

Satisfied, he pushed his chair from the table. The maid immediately appeared and began clearing his dishes. Instead of taking leave, he waited until her shoes thudded down the steps to the scullery. "You've not said much about it and I would like to know. Do my convictions – rather, does my prospective appearance on behalf of Henry Slade disturb you?"

Annie's lashes fluttered. "Whilst our sensitivity in spiritual matters has developed neither in the same manner nor to the same degree, that makes neither the less legitimate for their difference."

"Annie … "

"No, Alfred. We shan't speak of it more." She tucked her chin, the familiar pucker manifested. "Do what you must."

Now it was his own lips pursing, the wind driving rain against his face. Wallace spotted the Bow Street police station ahead, its famous lamps illuminated atop their wrought-iron pedestals. Blue-tinted orbs graced every other London police station, but not here, lest the Queen be reminded of the Blue Room where her husband had died while en route to the opera house. Everyone knew the loss for Her Majesty was profound – nearly fifteen years past yet still grieving – but how much greater the common good would that suffering be given some outward utility? Perhaps exercised towards ameliorating the suffering of those less fortunate?

Wallace crossed towards No. 4 Bow Street. He saw little to suggest the building enclosed a judicial forum. The sashes of its upper floor windows were rotted, the stonework blackened by soot, the paint everywhere blistered, and the banal stucco façade redeemed only by the Royal Arms. Newspapers reported a proper court house was soon to be constructed on the east side, with an adjoining police station. Not soon enough, surely.

He lined up with the horde at the bottom steps. Amid much shaking of umbrellas and stamping of boots, they filed into the foyer where he was directed to a bench in the public office. There he waited till well past ten o'clock. Finally, a white-haired bailiff with ears protruding like teacup handles called his name. The man's stiff comportment suggested a military background, thought Wallace, perhaps a Crimean War veteran.

Battleground experience might have explained why, after leading the way down a back passage, the bailiff remained unfazed upon opening the oak panelled door to the judicial chamber. The courtroom resounded like a raucous bazaar. Standing for want of chairs, the majority seemed idle onlookers, the sort who might otherwise find their entertainment in tawdry penny gaffs, public houses or perhaps the depravity of a dog fight – and the rumble they produced befitted any of those enterprises. Seated closer to the front were the well-heeled elite of Piccadilly and other genteel quarters.

As heads turned his way, voices fell off. The bailiff carved a path and he followed, lifting his chest under the scrutiny. A new commotion soon arose. Confined initially to those at the back of the room where he'd entered, it rippled forward, swelling steadily until it surrounded him.

Applause. He knew not what to make of it until it was conjoined by shouts.

"Set 'em straight, Mr. Wallace!"

"Our great calling needs you, sir!"

"We're all countin' on you Perfesser!"

"God bless you, Mr. Wallace!"

A booming voice from the front called for quiet, but nothing seemed to deter the cries and accolades. The bailiff paraded him toward a varnished wood rail that kept the public out of the business end of the courtroom. A gate swung open and they marched between the barristers' tables, all but two of which were filled with newspapermen. More reporters crowded a makeshift platform against the wall to his left. Along the wall to his right was the prisoners' dock from where Mr. Slade nodded his greetings. Straight ahead, on the elevated podium beneath the city's coat of arms, a magistrate leaned back in his chair and stared at the crown mouldings, or perhaps a stain in the ceiling plaster.

The clerk directed Wallace to the witness box and he was sworn in.

Annie continued to remind him how others interpreted much from body and facial gestures, superficial matters so far as he was concerned. Nonetheless, all eyes upon him, he tried to assert an erect posture. At the nearest barristers' table, Ignatius Munton rose. "If it please the court," said the defence lawyer. "I propose to question the witness."

"Yes, yes, Mr. Munton," said the magistrate. "Kindly do question the witness. That is the custom in a trial court."

A great roar shook the room. The magistrate, Frederick Flowers, looked pleased. He leaned back again and admired the coat of arms as if noticing it for the first time. Munton muttered some remark.

The opposing lawyer leapt to his feet. "Your worship, my friend has just made a comment casting this honourable court into disrepute."

"Mr. Lewis, I have one pair of ears and one set of eyes," said the grey-haired magistrate to the prosecuting lawyer. "And after presiding in this court for more than a dozen years, and this trial for what seems an equivalent time" – here he paused to allow the resulting gale of laughter to subside, while the reporters scribbled their pencils to nubs over this nonsense – "I should think there is little Mr. Munton might say that I have not heard a hundred-fold. So I would suggest the best way to curry favour with this honourable court," again he smiled and waited for the braying masses to relieve their mirth, "is for you to stop this jack-in-the-box routine you've adopted and allow – "

Laughter and hooting squelched the rest of his comment.

"Order!" the magistrate called. "Mr. Douglas, please!"

Wallace thought the clerk appeared quite put out as he laid down his issue of *Punch*, then contrived to adjust his periwig and smooth his waistcoat.

"Ladies and gentlemen! Order, please!" Douglas shouted.

While this was transpiring, looking out into the gallery Wallace recognized a half-dozen reputable mediums. Also familiar were certain ladies and a few society gentlemen. And of course, Newcastle and Lankester, a corpulent and ambitious zoologist seeking to make a name for himself under Newcastle's wing. Newcastle discreetly signalled someone. Wallace followed the direction of his gaze to a black-coated gentleman seated well off to the side. He had his collar up as if to fend winter's chill. The man's broad forehead was deeply creased, the beard as white as his own, but the countenance as famous as any in England.

It was common knowledge that, for reasons both of health as well as privacy, Charles Darwin seldom travelled anymore. Therefore his presence in court was wholly unexpected. Wallace doubted he was simply intrigued by the legal spectacle. And he knew him to be no friend of spiritualism. No matter. They'd disagreed before without any ill will or detriment to their relationship. Wallace supposed their enduring bond rested upon their fundamental adherence to the same side. The side of natural selection, as Mr. Darwin termed it. Darwinism, as he himself preferred it. For regardless of their shared credit in its discovery, he considered ownership of the theory to rest solely with Mr. Darwin.

Darwin was looking his way. Wallace supposed he'd been staring. He nodded and Darwin returned the gesture. There was little point in speculating upon Darwin's concern for the case beyond his friendship with Newcastle. So far as he knew, Darwin had no interest in Dr. Slade, or any other medium. Indeed, during their many conversations, he'd never said anything regarding spiritualism beyond, perhaps, the barest reference.

The magistrate, content that matters had sufficiently settled down, instructed Dr. Slade's lawyer to proceed. Munton nodded and directed himself at the witness box. Wallace noticed the barrister had the habit of teasing the tips of his moustache and this persisted now when he spoke.

"Sir, I should like to ask some questions as to your professional qualifications. You are the author of several scientific books – "

"I'm afraid that is not quite accurate."

"Please, I haven't yet finished my question, Mr. Wallace."

"I apologize, but only two of my books are scientific in the conventional sense. The one on Amazonian palms and the other on geographical distribution of animals. The remaining books were travel accounts of the Amazon and Far East and, more recently, spiritualism."

"Fine. Thank you for the clarification."

Wallace watched Munton shuffle some note papers on his dais, as though everything were now out of sequence. He hadn't wished to disrupt him, but the way the question had been framed sounded rather boastful.

"In addition to your books, you have also authored more than one hundred articles and essays that have been published in leading scientific journals ..."

"Yes."

"... and are a member or fellow of several scientific societies and organizations ..."

"Quite so."

"... and you are the co-discoverer, along with Charles Darwin, of the theory of evolution by natural selection."

"There I must correct you again."

Munton sighed.

He didn't wish to be obstinate, but this was a court of public record. A gloss upon the truth was as good as a falsehood.

"In my original essay on the subject, I did not call it evolution by natural selection. I wrote that organic change accrued by a process of adaptation to conditions over successive generations. The expression 'survival of the fittest'– coined by the famous philosopher Herbert Spencer – might equally describe the process. Natural selection was Mr. Darwin's term and credit must go to him. As for being the co-discoverer, I merely happened to stumble upon the idea at the same time as – "

"Mr. Munton," the magistrate interjected. "I was dearly hoping to see this witness's testimony conclude today and I fear that delving into the antecedents of modern scientific theory will sidetrack us. If it is your point that Professor Wallace is – "

"Pardon me, your worship," said Wallace. "But I do not claim the title of professor."

"No need to be modest here, sir," said Munton, a tight smile now beneath his moustache. "That you hold gainful employment with one of our prestigious institutions of learning is nothing to be shy about."

"I have marked examination papers at the Civil Engineering College. Is it that to which you refer?"

Laughter. The magistrate called for quiet, though his voice bore no conviction that his order would bring about the desired effect. Once again the clerk, Mr. Douglas, rose and called out for silence.

"Returning to your line of questioning, Mr. Munton," said Magistrate Flowers. "Is it your point that Mr. Wallace is a renowned and estimable man of science?"

"Yes," said Munton, "and that as such, he has highly developed skills of observation and analysis."

"Fine, then. Mr. Lewis …?"

The prosecuting lawyer stood.

"I take it you have no objection?"

"No, your worship." Lewis returned to his chair.

"There we are Mr. Munton, I take judicial notice of Mr. Wallace's scientific expertise. Now kindly move along to something more relevant."

In the prisoner's box, Slade closed his eyes and dropped his chin onto the ledge.

Munton's face sagged. He now worked his moustache with renewed zeal. "As one of England's most renowned scientific men, would you kindly inform the court of your opinion on spiritualistic matters?"

"In my view, it comprises a branch of anthropology."

"So you look upon spiritualism as an adjunct to the scientific realm?"

"Not adjunct, but integral. Spiritualism comprises one end of the scientific continuum."

"Yours is not a widely held view among our scientific elite, is it?"

"Most regrettably, many scientific thinkers preclude spiritualism's legitimate study. However one of our finest scientists, Sir John Herschel, once said: 'The perfect observer in any department of science will have his eyes open for occurrences in any branch of knowledge which, according to received theories, ought not to happen. For these are the facts which serve as clues to new discoveries and thus advance our understanding of the world.' So in my opinion, when intelligent rational people allege the occurrence of phenomena inexplicable under known laws, the answer is not to insist they are illusions or fraud, but to investigate. Utilizing a scientific approach, one must either verify or disprove the phenomena. If verified, they become fact."

Wallace caught Newcastle sitting amid the gallery shaking his head at this statement. How disappointing to see scientists of Newcastle's calibre oppose this most obvious iteration of common sense.

Munton had once again taken hold of his moustache, seeking by all appearances to tug its ends towards his ears. "Mr. Wallace, have you conducted any investigations into spiritualistic matters?"

"Yes, I began a methodical study in 1864. I have attended sittings with paid mediums. I also privately attended at the homes of acquaintances, and hosted sittings in my own home. On each occasion I carefully controlled the circumstances so as to ensure there could be no imposture or deceit. I also gathered data from many scientists and other men and women of good reputation who attended similar sittings under controlled conditions."

"And have you reached any conclusion?"

"I am satisfied as to the authenticity of spiritual phenomena."

"Bravo!" said someone in the gallery. A chorus of cheers and applause burst out.

"Enough, already!" Flowers shouted. "Let us have at least a modicum of respectability!"

Wallace could not have agreed more.

The rumpus abruptly died.

Munton's hands were clasped behind his back and he stood upon the balls of his feet. "You are familiar with the defendant Henry Slade, are you not?"

"I've attended three sittings with him."

"Kindly describe for us what happened on those occasions. In particular, I would ask you to tell us whether any measures were taken so as to determine the authenticity of Mr. Slade's services?"

"Services?"

Murmurs at the back of the room. Undoubtedly, thought Wallace, many others took equal umbrage at a comparison that conjured tailors, cab drivers and accountants.

"My apologies. Quite inadvertent," said Munton. "Did you take any steps to verify the authenticity of Mr. Slade's abilities, and if so, with what result?"

The magistrate had once again reclined in his chair, examining his manicure or such, whilst, in front, Mr. Douglas was immersed in his periodical. But everyone else was attentive, the room silent.

"On the afternoon of August 9th of this year, I attended

number three Upper Bedford Place in Russell Square and met for the first time with Dr. Slade. He escorted me to his parlour. It was brightly lit and at its centre stood a wood table and chairs."

"Mr. Wallace, please have a look at the table at the side of the room and see if you recognize it," said Munton. The lawyer then addressed the pack of reporters seated there. "Gentlemen, may I ask you to kindly vacate your table for a moment?"

Wallace had read in the papers that Slade's table had been the subject of some preposterous innuendo that it held concealed compartments or the like.

"Yes, that appears to be the same table."

The magistrate sighed. "Mr. Munton, we've been over this six ways from Sunday. The previous witnesses have all identified the table. I feel as intimate with it as if it were my own supper table. Try to maintain relevancy, sir."

Amid the guffaws, Munton said something inaudible and Lewis poised as if to stand then, with a dismissive wave and *P'shaw*, resigned himself to his seat.

A bloody carnival, thought Wallace. This, despite the fact a good man's reputation stood to be destroyed by bigotry and groundless accusations.

"Mr. Wallace, please tell the court what happened during the sitting with the defendant."

"Dr. Slade produced an ordinary double-sided school slate which I examined and thoroughly wiped clean. A small chalk pencil was set upon this slate which Dr. Slade then held with his right hand against the underside of the table. He pressed it tight against the woodwork with his fingers while the thumb remained atop the table. Dr. Slade explained he would try to summon the spirit of his wife, whom he referred to by her Christian name, Allison. She had died some dozen years earlier.

In order to summon her, he would first enter into a trance. He closed his eyes, keeping the fingers of his right hand beneath the table. His face slackened in a manner I'd witnessed in persons subjected to mesmerism, and I could tell he was in a trance state. Soon a sound of writing was heard, and in a few seconds the slate was produced with writing upon it."

"Upon which side of the slate was the message?"

"The message was on the upper side of the slate, that which had been pressed against the underside of the table."

"Do you recall the nature of the message?"

"Not clearly, this occurred nearly three months ago, however I believe it was something like, 'I am here to assist. Allie'."

Appreciative comments burbled among the throng. Munton cleared his throat.

"In the course of these proceedings we have heard allegations from Mr. Newcastle and Mr. Lankester that the defendant attempted to distract them through various movements, noises and even bodily contact. They testified that nonetheless, they witnessed contractions in Mr. Slade's right arm, which they believed to be proof he was writing the message beneath the table while the slate rested upon his knee."

Wallace fixed his gaze directly upon Newcastle. "There is not the least doubt in my mind that Dr. Slade could not have written this message."

"Kindly explain, Mr. Wallace."

"I observed Dr. Slade steadily. He may have shuddered once or twice, yet from my studies on the subject, such movements are almost universal among a medium entering into the trance state and quite involuntary. It posed no distraction. I would also stress that the message was produced in a matter of a few seconds, a feat counter-indicative of imposture. Three more messages of this kind were produced that afternoon and in no instance was there any movement of the type you say is alleged. To the contrary, on the final occasion, Dr. Slade permitted me to hold the slate under the table in the same manner as he'd done. In that instance, he placed both his hands on the table and I felt nothing transpire beneath the table but heard writing. Taking out the slate, a message had appeared to the effect that Allison was in communication with Bertie."

"Did you know to whom this referred?"

"I had a younger brother, Herbert. My sister and mother called him Bertie. But they were the only ones to use that pet name. Herbert died in 1851 and …"

"Yes?"

Wallace's throat tightened. He fought for composure, not wishing to make a spectacle of himself. "When my first son was born, we named him Herbert. I affectionately called him Bertie. Two and a half years ago Bertie …" His voice trembled, "…he succumbed to scarlet fever."

"Very sorry for your loss, sir," Munton said. "I only have a few more questions, so kindly bear with me. Prior to that visit with the defendant, when you found your son's name written on the slate, had you ever mentioned your son's passing, or even his name, to the defendant?"

"The loss of my son is something I discuss with no one but my wife. So the answer to your question is, No."

A chorus of gasps in the court. Newcastle wrote a note and passed it to Mr. Lewis.

"You mentioned earlier that you had paid Mr. Slade three visits?" asked Munton.

"After the prosecution of Dr. Slade commenced," said Wallace, "with heightened vigilance I returned twice more to ensure my testimony should be based on more than one set of observations. Each sitting proceeded in similar manner."

"Do you recall any of the written messages at these two later sittings?"

"On the final occasion, the slate was not out of my sight more than a second or two, and it was impossible for any human being to have written so rapidly. Yet the message was distinct, with the 'i' dotted and the 't' crossed. It read: 'Is this proof? I hope so.'"

CHAPTER TWENTY-FIVE
London, November 1, 1876

Mr. Lewis was a wiry bird-like man who might easily have remained inconspicuous outside the courtroom. However, he had great big scalloped eyebrows that almost knitted together and when he stood to begin his cross-examination Wallace noticed those two furry creatures greet each other. It made for a rather transfixing sight.

"Mr. Wallace, as a scientist, you pride yourself on rational clear-eyed judgment?"

"Certainly."

"Indeed, that is why your presence here is so valuable, we've been told. Your keen abilities as scientist ensure that the observations you offer are objective, devoid of the emotional interference to which so many of us are susceptible."

An uncomfortable iteration, Wallace thought, but decidedly true. "Yes."

Smugness crept into the lawyer's voice. "Yet you became involved in something known as the 'Flat Earth Challenge?'"

"I hardly see what that has to do with – "

"Just answer the question, witness," said Magistrate Flowers.

The most sordid episode, and they wished to rub his nose in it.

"You knew John Hampden, President of the Flat Earth Society, to be a most quarrelsome individual," said Lewis. "Yet in January 1870, you took up his public challenge to prove the earth round?"

"When Mr. Hampden selected the site for the Challenge – the old Bedford Canal in Norfolk, a straight six-mile channel – I viewed it as an opportunity to smite the religious despotism of the Flat Earthers. I'd worked as a surveyor. Proof of the curvature of an extended body of water was a comparatively simple matter."

Indeed it had been. On the morning of March 6, 1870 he'd stood on the canal's westernmost bridge, his telescope mounted atop the bridge's iron parapet. Overhead, one long reef of cloud travelled an otherwise unblemished sky. Visibility was excellent. When he'd peered into his telescope and adjusted the focus, he could not suppress a triumphant grin. Two markers, one six miles distant at the Old Bedford Bridge, another three miles away, had been fixed at the same height above the water as his telescope. When he'd bent to have a look, the middle marker appeared in the lens exactly as predicted, some five feet higher than the other two. Elegant and irrefutable proof of convexity.

"Simple matter, was it?" Lewis said.

"No right-minded man would have disputed the result."

"But Mr. Hampden did dispute it, now didn't he?"

"He did." Wallace had pocketed the reward, as was his right. But Hampden waged a tireless campaign. Newspapers, journals, scientific institutions, personages both familiar and unfamiliar, both inside Britain and continental, all received letters accusing Alfred Russel Wallace of thievery, dishonesty and cravenness. There was more. In June 1871 Annie received a letter:

If your infernal thief of a husband is brought home some day on a hurdle with every bone in his head smashed to a pulp, you will know the reason. Do tell him from me he is a lying infernal thief and, sure as his name is Wallace, he never dies in his bed.

Criminal charges, a restraining order and one week in prison failed to deter the madman. Wallace obtained a successful libel verdict, but Hampden's manoeuvrings meant his token settlement hadn't been achieved until a few months ago.

"Six years of grief. Hardly worth the trouble, would you agree?" Lewis now asked. "And you undertook it for what – five hundred pounds?"

How could a barrister like Lewis possibly understand? Despite his credentials, fixed employment continued to elude him. Worse, certain journals now exhibited reluctance to carry his articles. Annie speculated it had to do with his spiritualist writings. He did not see the connection: either his article stood on its own merit or it did not. Though it meant scientific and social isolation, he and Annie had already moved from London to lower costs. Then, upon advice of Rollins and Waddle, sympathetic Red Lions with greater sophistication than himself in fiscal matters, he sank his savings into a series of investments. Railways. Mines. Quarries. Each successively met with ruin. Debts still mounting, he feared he was no better with money than his father, so financially irresponsible he'd sent his children away one by one because he could not afford to house them. He, in contrast, would sell his Royal Medal, his collections, his blood if necessary, rather than inflict that separation upon his own family.

It was only the much delayed publication of his Malay Archipelago travel narrative that staved off bankruptcy. According to his publisher, it was the best-selling travel chronicles since Darwin's Beagle Journals. Critical success warmed him, but the royalties were more important; he no longer teetered on the precipice of financial disaster. The brink, however, remained within view. And thus the proposition that came to his attention in January 1870 had proven overpowering.

Notwithstanding the original five hundred pound reward he'd rightfully kept and a successful verdict of libel, he was out several hundred pounds in legal fees. Moreover, in remote outposts where he was not personally known, Hampden's missives damaged his reputation. Even among those who did know him there rumbled criticism that he'd brought it on himself with his money-grubbing. Newcastle had pointed to the fiasco in opposing Wallace's nomination for President of the Association's Biology section, no matter that it was unrelated to the post.

All that ceaseless aggravation and disappointment in the fruitless wait for justice? It left him with a bilious taste for the legal system.

A legal system to which poor Dr. Slade was now subjected.

"Would you not agree that this scientific episode in which you involved yourself proved, upon reflection, a grave error in judgment?" asked Lewis, when the flat earth debacle had been recounted for the court.

Wallace heard the question, but made no sense of it, his brain fogged.

"Pardon me, sir?"

"I am speaking of your involvement in Mr. Hampden's challenge. Not exactly a model of 'rational clear-eyed judgment', would you agree?"

Munton rose above the depleted pens, papers and tobacco pouch that lay scattered on the defence table. "Objection, your worship!"

"On what grounds?" asked Flowers. He had not quit his repose, reclined in his chair as though wounded, eyes examining the motto upon the city's coat of arms. *Domine dirige nos.*

Wallace recalled his Latin: Lord direct us.

"I should think," Munton said, "my friend's question was sarcastic, and thus abusive of the witness."

Flowers now swivelled round. "Why, Mr. Munton! What a *fine* bit of advocacy!" The magistrate glowered and his jaw set to work as if on some unpleasant piece of gristle. "Did you catch that, Mr. Munton? *That* was sarcasm. Now kindly sit down. I will allow the question."

Oh, the uproar. To Wallace's ears it sounded like a herd of braying donkeys. Even the medium's supporters guffawed and howled. In the prisoner's box, Dr. Slade, chin in his palm, eyes distant, sighed. Flowers pretended not to care about the laughter. But from the proximity of the witness box Wallace caught the glimmer of a smile.

"Now answer the question, Mr. Wallace."

Wallace squared his shoulders. "I would agree that, with the benefit of hindsight, my involvement with Mr. Hampden was highly regrettable."

Lewis's eyebrows converged. "In fact, while you have been held out to this honourable court as some cool-headed clear-eyed scientist, you not only exhibit considerable lapses in judgment, but you also inflate your own reputation."

"I don't understand."

"What I am suggesting, Mr. Wallace, is that you hold yourself out as expert on all manner of non-scientific learning.

You critique on any subject your whim dictates."

"That's not true."

From the floor Lewis lifted a stack of journals, newspapers and magazines and placed them on the table. Bookmarks were visibly affixed to each. The lawyer opened the first journal, the April 1873 issue of *Macmillan's Magazine*. "On the Church of England, you wrote thusly:"

> By its dogmatic theology and resistance to progress, the national church has become out of harmony both with the best and the least educated portion of the community.

"Part of your tract on the disestablishment and disendowment of the English Church, I believe?"

Wallace thought he heard a disapproving cluck or two within the room. A tiny minority. "I do recall advocating for creation of a national institution by which the moral and social advancement of the whole nation shall be permanently helped."

"Yes, no doubt. Some three years ago in the *Daily News*, you argued against free trade."

"With respect to coal, sir. We export far too much and have disfigured our countryside."

"I will not argue with you, Mr. Wallace, but this is an economic issue rather than a scientific one."

"Nor should I wish to argue with you Mr. Lewis, but it pains any lover of nature to travel through once fertile land and observe it thus scarred, characteristically diminishing the vegetable and animal life of the vicinity."

"You have also called for a land nationalization program."

"It is a pressing – "

"You claimed some kind of cyclical connection between clearing forests – our source for everything from household furniture to brooms to the floors we stand upon – and subsequent loss of topsoil?"

"It is a logical result. People must realize before it's too late."

"Not a jot of evidence to support you."

"Mr. Lewis," Flowers said, his voice weary. "That was hardly a question, now was it?"

"My apologies," said Lewis with an affable shrug. "Why don't we move along?" He opened the next magazine. "In the *Independent Review* you railed against British imperialism."

"I expressed my criticism, yes."

Lewis surveyed the remaining stack of items. "So many to choose from. But here is my favourite. Presumably influenced by your extensive experience with our legal system vis-à-vis Mr. Hampden. In the *Contemporary Review* you suggested improvements to the court system."

Flowers snapped alert. "He did?"

"I am sure his worship and the rest of us will be much edified by the following:"

It is in cases of civil wrong that individuals find the greatest difficulty (often amounting to an absolute impossibility) of obtaining justice. Voluminous and intricate enactments and precedents, and the tedious mode of procedure involve grievous delay and expense to every applicant for justice. The result is that it is often better for a man to put up with a palpable wrong than to endeavour to obtain redress.

Murmurs rose again. Wallace saw many nod their heads at this plain fact. From the magistrate came an audible sniff. Perhaps a sinus condition.

"And with your vast training in our legal system," said Lewis, "you proceed to expound upon how to reform the administration of justice."

"There is a wasteful – "

"– use of resources." Lewis pirouetted for the gallery of reporters, grinning.

"Our natural world does not reside in isolation," Wallace said. "One must take up issues."

"How nice it must be, sir," said Lewis, "to have the answers for all of our societal ills."

Another chorus of murmurs.

"Mr. Lewis," said the magistrate. "I take my lunch promptly at one o'clock, whether your questions are finished or not."

"Certainly, your worship. Let us then turn to matters more directly bearing upon this trial," said the barrister. He came around the table and approached the witness box. "Mr. Wallace, you are, without doubt, a prolific author. But all those theories and observations that appear in journals, magazines and periodicals are not written for the pure sake of science or the public good, are they? You earn money from these publications, correct?"

"The majority, yes."

"You have no employment nor independent means of income beyond your writing, do you? Other than marking papers, of course."

There were a few snickers, but they faded quickly, for there was a steel edge to the question. The room now silent, the strain in Wallace's voice was readily audible, even to his own ears. "It is true that I remain without a remunerative position."

"You recently sold to the British Museum your private collection of bird specimens – of which you had previously been heard to claim was perhaps the finest in the world?"

"Yes, I regret to say … " What could he say? That he had a household to run? Children and wife to feed and clothe? That the cost of tuition for better schools was unreasonable? Not to mention magazine subscriptions and membership dues and travel necessary to maintain his scientific standing.

"You face financial pressures, but stirring up controversy has made you famous, has it not? All this attention helps to sell more copies, thus lining your pockets quite nicely?"

Wallace straightened, lifting his chin to meet Lewis's gaze. "I admit to sometimes taking controversial positions, but I do this as a means of stoking debate, of promoting change when the status quo is unsatisfactory. I am not so desperate as to deliberately court controversy for the sake of income."

"No, your flat earth challenge hardly comes across as desperate."

Despite Annie's admonition, he slumped forward.

"All right, let us now cut the meat to the bone. Mr. Wallace, how many séances would you estimate you've attended?"

"Dozens. I have not made records of each one ..."

"No, of course not."

"... but I would hazard to guess fifty or sixty."

"Fifty or sixty?" Lewis's small chin lifted. "My, my, quite impressive."

"Scientific inquisitiveness demanded as much."

Magistrate Flowers leaned over. "Mr. Wallace, since your counsel appears unwilling to school you in the customs of witness testimony, let me inform you that you are only to speak when asked a question. Mr. Lewis's remark was neither a question nor a statement of law. It was mockery – which I will not tolerate! Are we clear Mr. Lewis?"

Lewis affected rapid bird-like nods.

"Continue, then."

The magistrate's armchair groaned as Flowers sank back.

Lewis rubbed his hands and cleared his throat. "You are aware that Mr. Newcastle and Mr. Lankester have exposed Mr.

Slade's imposture by – "

"Objection to the use of 'imposture', your worship," said Munton. "Mr. Lewis predicates his question on an unproven allegation."

"Very good, Mr. Munton," said Flowers. "Rephrase your question, Mr. Lewis."

"Sir, you have been informed that Mr. Newcastle and Mr. Lankester seized a purportedly clean slate from the defendant to prove it was not blank as he claimed." Lewis circled back to his table. "Did it ever occur to you sir, in any of those fifty or sixty sittings you have attended and in which you purport to exercise your utmost scientific scrutiny and vigilance, to likewise snatch up the allegedly blank slate, or sweep aside the curtain, or take such other similar measure that went beyond your powers of observation?"

Wallace bolted upright. "Certainly not! That would contravene the conditions of the séance. It would be …. dishonourable."

Newcastle clucked at Lankester. Wallace expected as much from the man by now. He also observed that while the gallery made no public display of indignation, their silence surely marked an understanding of the moral code to which he adhered.

Lewis twirled about, as if to ask the audience its opinion, though he directed his gaze at the crowd of reporters. "So, what could account for such a strong unswerving belief in spiritualism, I wonder? Shall we go from the bone to the marrow, Mr. Wallace?" Lewis had turned back round to face him, eyebrows now a singular forested ridge. "Let us talk of what drives your interest in spiritualism, shall we?"

Wallace tensed. In the ensuing silence, he heard the *whoosh* of air from women fanning themselves at the back of the court.

His palms were sweating. Spiritualists the world over were attacked at every turn as victims of delusion or fraud. Imagine the fodder were he to disclose how in his hallucinatory visions of a squiggly green image he saw his dead brother. This from an episode that represented a dark cavity in his life. By what right did it belong to the public domain? He'd never written a word about it, for hardly anything could be more personal. And what else? That he subsequently sought to replicate the feat and conjured up breathing trees? That this experience helped spawn his evolutionary theory? His entire body of research would be tarnished. And to no end. In his early ignorance he'd believed hallucinogens were the only portal to the spiritual world. Since then he'd learned there were many channels. And those gateways demanded ongoing study.

"I'm sorry, Mr. Lewis. What is your question?"

Flowers sat up. "Well done, witness. I was asking myself the same thing. Mr. Lewis, you seem to have little regard for this court's schedule. I trust you shall complete your questioning of this witness before my afternoon repast grows cold and no longer toothsome?"

Lewis tugged at his lower lip. "I ..."

"Counsel, you've performed admirably in your cross-examination and no doubt your clients will be quite pleased. But as you can see for yourself, some of the ladies at the back are rather weary from the close confines and all this standing about while you bluster. So let us try and finish expeditiously."

"Yes, your worship. I believe I can shorten my remaining questions." Lewis's finger skimmed down his writing pad until it reached its destination. "Mr. Wallace, it is your belief that we are all mere physical shells of an eternal spirit, a spirit that persists in some afterlife beyond our physical demise?"

"That is one way of expressing the idea."

"And those spirits are able to communicate with the living, as well as with other spirits?"

"We know that spirits communicate with each other, yes. As to communication with the living, it is unquestionable that some spirits contact or manifest themselves to those of us on earth who seek them out."

"Have you or have you not communicated with your deceased family members?"

"Sometimes."

"I imagine this gives you considerable reassurance, does it not?"

"I do not understand your question."

"The deaths of your brothers, your sisters, your father, and most recently your young son – the very notion that all these personal losses are not absolute, that your loved ones carry on, in a fashion, after their physical death, and that you may be able to communicate with them, I would suggest, grants you a measure of comfort. It is what sustains you and your belief."

Now, even the reporters who hadn't stopped scratching at their pads for a minute paused. And for the first time since Wallace had entered the witness box, Magistrate Flowers looked not at the back wall or the clock or the reporters or the lawyers, but straight at him, eyes mildly puzzled, as though he'd just materialized from thin air.

CHAPTER TWENTY-SIX
London, November 1, 1876

"Have to lock up the room, Mr. Wallace."

The Crimean War veteran approached. The courtroom had cleared.

Wallace stumbled down from the witness box. Expired air filled the room like bilge water. He plodded to the door where the bailiff waited, keys tinkling.

Expressionless, the man watched his approach. In a craggy voice, he said, "Lawyers and such as them always talk and talk. Trying to rub people's noses in it, if you know what I mean."

Wallace nodded weakly.

"But here's the burn – themselves, those men, they ain't much for actually doing things. You, you do things."

Wallace mumbled thanks – at least he thought he did – before the door closed behind him and the tumbler clicked. When he reached the foyer, he heard his name called.

Charles Darwin planted the tip of his umbrella into the carpet and heaved himself up from a bench. "Hope you don't mind my waiting for you."

They shook hands. Despite the demands of work and family, differences of opinion, the vagaries of health (Darwin's, primarily) and the not infrequent relocation of his own household – Darwin, he marvelled, had remained at Down House for some thirty-five years – their relationship remained cordial. Indeed, many times Wallace had found himself angling his neck at the Royal Geographical meeting, or a gathering of the Linnean, Entomological or Zoological Societies, hoping for a glimpse of that formidable cranium among the black-coated patrons of science. How delightful to make such a sighting and saunter over. Even when Darwin was steeped in serious conversation – his presence almost always attracted a sizable audience of inquisitors – he was warmly greeted. On a few occasions, Darwin even excused himself and together they'd found a private alcove where the nation's leading scientist then asked for his opinion on this, solicited his thoughts on that. All of it quite intoxicating.

But right now, at that particular moment, Wallace wished only to slip out of the court house, endure the solicitous or scandalized stares that would follow him to Waterloo station, then anonymously settle into a train carriage and allow himself to be rocked and swayed back to his wife and children.

Wallace said, "I had no idea you held such a strong interest in the case."

"As you are aware, Newcastle is a dear old friend and – "

A door swung open from a side vestibule and out rushed a white-gloved servant carrying a silver-domed serving plate.

"Excuse me, gentlemen," he said, scurrying past. The fellow disappeared through a door cut into the wood panelling on the opposite wall. The plate transmitted a savoury aroma and the lingering fragrance worked upon Wallace like a spell. The aroma of home.

Darwin waited until all indication of the servant's presence vanished. "I thought you should learn first-hand that I assisted Newcastle in his prosecution of Mr. Slade. That is, I helped fund the expense of it."

"Oh."

"Have I shocked you?"

"I would certainly say you got your money's worth with Mr. Lewis."

"I imagine it's been a difficult day for you."

"I have greater feeling now for those insect specimens I have pinned."

Darwin's eyes softened. "I would like to discuss it over lunch, if you would be so kind as to join me. Please, do me such favour."

Outside, they sheltered beneath the portico at the top of the steps. In the open, bullets of water strafed the pavement. Darwin put up his umbrella.

Wallace raised his coat collar.

"Where is your umbrella?"

"I thought to hire one earlier, but …"

"Surely your finances cannot be that bad."

For a moment, all that could be heard was the rain pelting down. Darwin's face flushed and he stared into his own beard as if he wished to conceal himself there.

"Oh, Wallace. I'm so deeply sorry for that comment. It was imprudent and – Why are you laughing?"

"Because it was precisely," replied Wallace, still chuckling, "precisely, what Richard Spruce would have said."

Darwin allowed a thin smile. "Given the inclement conditions, might I suggest the nearest establishment?"

"Certainly."

"Then we shall cross the road. If I may take your arm, my

umbrella might well fend the rain off both our heads and, in the process, I shall hopefully stay on my feet fording that torrent."

"A double benefit?"

"Exactly that."

They crossed to a four-storey building standing opposite. Moss crept among its stone crevices. Its sign intrigued them both: 'The Brown Bear, Russian Hotel and Public House for Gentlemen'.

It was a low place. Once inside, they saw that immediately. In the front room, a large contingent of coarse men and not a few vulgar women supped on their ales. Their terrible oaths alone made such a din that a proper conversation was out of the question. The publican, a lanky man with dark-rimmed eyes that seemed not to veer from the glass he was polishing, directed them to the back parlour.

Brown Bear, indeed. Stepping into the back room, Wallace felt they'd entered a cave. Drapes drawn, the lamps suspended from dark beams cast angled shadows and phantasms upon the plastered walls. There were eight or nine tables, their occupants engaged in discreet talk, speaking directly into an ear, or huddled forward.

A flash-house, he realized.

"You appear amused by the caste of our establishment," said Darwin.

For Darwin's sake, Wallace tried to dampen his enthusiasm. "I cannot say that I mind so much. Come, dear fellow, there's an empty table."

As they made their way, in the far corner chairs scraped and three men stood. Wallace recognized them as courtroom spectators.

"Pray sirs," said the stoutest man, bowing stiffly. The others, one wiping his moustache with the back of his hand – or his hand with his moustache – nodded and, at the first man's signal, bowed in kind. "Loads of room over 'ere, if you don't mind us bein' underway an' all." Upon their table were plates of boiled beef and potatoes in varying states of annihilation.

Darwin was quick to reply. "Thank you gentlemen for your kind invitation. However, Mr. Wallace and I must discuss some matters of business which necessitate privacy. Perhaps another day."

The large man jabbed an elbow into his neighbour's rib. "Private business, eh? Aye, the two of you'se won't be the only ones 'ere doin' that." He and his friends guffawed.

As they took their seats Darwin said, "You find that amusing ?"

"I most certainly do," said Wallace.

"It's a den of thieves!"

At the next table, the sawing of knives abruptly stopped. Two men exchanged whispers. Then, to Wallace's relief, they resumed their business – which in all fairness, he thought, may have been nothing more than the cuts of venison they assailed.

The keeper came over and Darwin ordered a brandy ("medicinal," he said, with no wink or smile). Wallace, in turn, asked for ale. For their meal, they each took the venison.

"I am surprised to learn you're eating meat again," Darwin said when the man left with their orders.

"If we British ever learn to grow and properly prepare a wholesome variety of vegetables, perhaps I shall once again enjoy a vegetarian regime. It seems a more sensible balance with nature. But, for vitality, I presently require some meat in my diet." Wallace chuckled. "My daughter Violet is highly grateful for the change. She remains only a nominal omnivore. I suspect you've never seen an eight-year-old sink her teeth into a shank of mutton or beef with such relish."

The corners of Darwin's eyes crinkled. "When my dear Annie was that age, she was a delicate eater. Working a single tine of her fork, she would pierce one pea at a time until she'd cleared the lot, the rest of the children urging her, 'Hurry, Annie, hurry,' for they'd finished long before and wished already to rise." He smiled and shook his head. "She had such a fastidious nature. Sometimes, when I returned from my afternoon stroll, she would gently scold my appearance – my hair had been tousled by the wind, you see? And she'd ask in utter earnestness, 'What if you were to have an important visitor?' She would sit me in the parlour and brush my hair, chiding me perhaps on the scuffs to my shoe leather or the state of my fingernails. 'There, father,' she'd say when finished. 'Even were the Queen to visit now, I should think you look quite presentable.' Then she would wrap her arms round my neck and kiss my cheek. When I finally returned to my study, the warmth of her still upon my skin, all my anxieties about this or that bit of research were thoroughly extinguished." Darwin spent a moment studying his interlocked fingers. "I suppose that is what the love of a child does. It purifies us of the adult world, makes us clean again."

Rain danced against the windows. At one of the tables, a party of men, all hushed tones, rose and left the room.

"For years after Annie's passing," said Darwin, "there were days I would return from my walk and expect to find her waiting inside, hairbrush in hand. I would – and I've never confessed this to anyone before – I would postpone opening the door, wishing to delay that raw moment when I would have to stand inside, confronting the irrevocable." A tremor passed through Darwin's cheek. He took out his handkerchief and blew his nose.

They sat in silence until their beverages arrived. Then

they toasted each other's health and the health of their families. Darwin asked after Richard Spruce and lamented his circumstances.

"An indomitable spirit, however," Wallace said of his friend.

"Would that we were all of equal resilience," Darwin agreed. He sipped his brandy.

There was a commotion at another table. A chair clattered to the floor and an unkempt man in shabby coat stood and pointed his finger inches from the nose of another. The seated gentleman, of finer cloth and well-oiled hair, raised his hands in surrender. Still no words exchanged, he slowly reached inside his waistcoat and produced an item – in the dimness it was difficult for Wallace to discern, perhaps a coin or a ring or such – whatever it was, it apparently allayed the first one, for he pocketed the thing and departed.

"A memorable lunch this shall be," Darwin said. "Though I must remark that the peculiar character of this place causes certain allusions, in my mind, to our own ancient affair."

"Not seriously?"

"Perhaps I am merely predisposed to such thoughts today. However it is also our unique history."

Their unique history. It seemed to eclipse all else – at least in Darwin's mind.

When their plates of venison, mashed potato and brussels sprouts arrived, Wallace tucked in, feeling as though he'd not eaten in ages. Darwin, after a few desultory forkfuls, largely abandoned his meal. He well attended to his brandy though.

"I rarely indulge," Darwin said after he'd set down the emptied glass. "But today, with the dreadful weather, the travel, and that inglorious spectacle inside the courtroom …"

"It was rather awful, wasn't it?"

Darwin nodded. "Magistrate Flowers is a sympathetic man

– he displays concern for the vulnerable in our society, or so I am informed – but the attention of the newspapers and the public gallery appears to have stirred some vaudevillian longing." He shook his head and sighed, air whistling from his nose. "How did it come to this, I ask you? Those first years following publication of our theory – "

"Your theory. Darwinism.

"No matter the name, I've always regarded it as very much our child. An embattled child, with two doting parents who, at least in the early years, shared the same vision for its future."

"A small united family?'

"Yes."

"With a bulldog by their side?"

The reference to Thomas Huxley, and perhaps memory of his successful debate in defence of natural selection, made Darwin smile. "Quite so."

"Well then, Newcastle must be the snapping little terrier who indiscriminately fastens onto the pant leg of both friend and foe – "

"Now, Wallace …"

"– until the garment is reduced to shreds and copiously drenched in blood."

Darwin shook his head. "You may disparage him, but I've been exceptionally fortunate to have Ramsay Newcastle's fellowship and support. Newcastle, Huxley and Sir Charles – whose passing last year caused me considerable upset – all stood as trusted advisors. Every man needs good counsel. At least that is the case if he intends to make his mark." With his fork, Darwin pushed one of the brussels sprouts to the other side of the plate, ploughing a watery green furrow through the potatoes. "I had always hoped … Rather, it would have given me immense satisfaction to fill such an advisory role for you.

I thought it the proper thing to do, a way of making amends."

"Dear heavens, surely that's well in the past. You owe me nothing."

"What would my place in history have been if you had not prompted me to action?"

"That cannot stand as sufficient reason for indebtedness. *Origin of Species* ultimately convinced many of the finest minds in this country, altering the public perception of our natural history. My essay would have persuaded no one."

"But we know your plans were more ambitious: 'With the mechanism deduced, my notebook finally has all the ingredients for a thorough treatment of the subject.' You recall writing those words? They were in the letter that accompanied your essay. I do confess that upon reading your letter and essay on that long ago morning, my only immediate concern was how I might honourably retain my priority on the topic. That was where my advisors stood me well. Newcastle saw the essay's importance, but emphasized it would be the book, not a presentation at a hastily convened scientific meeting mid-summer, or publication in a comparatively obscure publication, that would become the legacy. If natural selection theory was to prevail over entrenched creationist beliefs, it required credibility within both the scientific and greater communities. He regarded you as someone whose efforts at a full volume on the theory would lack the weight of authority mine might offer. Sir Charles concurred. And that thought stabbed at my vanity, I confess. Yet my guilt stems not merely from wishing to supersede you, but for standing upon your shoulders."

"Dear fellow, that can hardly be the case."

"I was a man gripped by timidity, frightened of future public reaction to a revolutionary idea. The book on which I worked had already absorbed twenty years of my life. More than a thousand pages of meticulous notes, with perhaps yet another thousand still to be written. I'd determined that nothing short of the most exhaustive armour-clad proof would suffice if I wished to attach my name to the idea. Then came your essay. It formulated much the same theory in succinct, clear and persuasive fashion, to be sure. But what struck me foremost was its exuberance. How it gloried in the idea without any of the doubts and misgivings I had long endured. I was uplifted by your confidence. It meant I was right. That we were both right."

"If that is the case, then I am gladdened even more."

"Do you now see, Wallace? Your work deserved greater attention!"

At the next table, an uncouth drunkard slurred, "Aye, you deserved greater attention, you did!" His partner, elbowed him in the ribs and they sniggered softly.

Darwin curled his lower lip, but lowered his voice. "Your contribution was essential to my success. Your essay inspired a clarity of vision that had altogether been precluded by my own cowardice. I undertook preparation of a new manuscript that distilled my original planned publication to its essence, determined that my book should be first to the printer. In the interim, your paper went before the Linnean Society at the same time as my own materials. This discharged my duty of fair dealing – anything less would have been dishonourable – but concomitantly, it obviated the possibility that my forthcoming book would be seen as merely an expansion of your idea."

Darwin hoisted the brandy glass to his lips, forgetting it was empty. Through the compound lens of the tumbler his wall-eyed visage blinked rapidly, then he set the glass down and propped his elbows upon the scarred wood.

"While my actions were quite defensible within moral

bounds – I was the beneficiary of my friends' good deeds and neither stole from nor deceived anyone – nonetheless they have remained a strain on my conscience. I have since sought to share originality in the idea, but you have consistently deflected credit."

"Oh, now really – "

"Please, allow me to finish by telling you that it was for these reasons I had always hoped to act as something of a wise counsel to you, even when our views began diverging. So long as we retained our mutual goal, that natural selection should usher in a world where science and reason would displace superstition and prejudice, I believed I might serve you well."

Darwin sniffed. "Trouble was, I couldn't keep apace. You opposed my theory of sexual selection as inconsistent with evolutionary principles. But when I offered concessions you were busily advocating that man evolved through natural selection. And before I could give that matter the thorough examination it required for public exposition, you disavowed the operation of natural selection upon the human mind, advocating an intelligent design in our mental development – "

"In the development of our souls."

"You skipped from one subject to another, venturing further and further afield – your spiritual writing, your political opinions, cultural commentary, etcetera – so that, not only could I not keep pace, but I saw you tugging our grand idea in the wrong direction altogether. You made it impossible to work in concert."

"I never sought to rebuff you – I cherish our friendship. However when facts support a certain truth, I see a ..." Wallace stole a glance towards the thieves at the neighbouring table.

"Reluctant to say it aloud? Allow me: you see a moral imperative."

Wallace nodded.

"Perhaps, then, you regard myself and others lacking that same moral imperative?"

Wallace hesitated before speaking. "From time to time I have observed, shall I say, a preoccupation with extraneous matters that impede the growth of knowledge."

"Can you understand then why some perceive a certain, shall we say, hubris, in your accomplishments?"

"Is that a sentiment in which you share?" Wallace asked.

"No, I do not share that view. However, I do notice that when it comes to ideas, you hastily pick up the first sword that suits you, plunge into the thickest part of the fray, and revel in the parry and thrust – regardless of who lies wounded. Among some, that tends to create a negative impression."

Wallace sought to suppress the foul mood that now crept upon him, lest it seep into his voice. "Beyond the matter of personal conviction, when I enter the fray and wield my sword on behalf of an idea, as you have described it, it is also how I make my living. A point Mr. Lewis did not fail to mark."

"But this paroxysm of superstitious belief …" Darwin took hold of the table as if to prevent it, or himself, from shaking. "I apologize for that remark."

"There is no need," Wallace said. "Candour in pursuit of truth is laudable."

Darwin slowly shook his head, perhaps regretting that it was he who had invited the frank discourse. "All right, then let me say this. With the presentation of Professor Barrett's paper at the British Association meeting and now your testimony on behalf of that blatant …" – his breath came heavy now – "that … *charlatan* Slade, you crossed a bridge and entered a hinterland. Ill-content to travel your theistic road merely with like-minded followers, you seek to take the rest of us with you.

And therefore, while I maintain for you a cordial, even fond, predisposition, and as much as I detest crowds, I came today to show you that Newcastle's fight is equally mine, perhaps more. No matter my decrepitude, you cannot expect me to allow my historical legacy to be undermined. Spiritualism and the sciences shall not – cannot – be integrated!"

Wallace leaned forward. Finally, the heart of the matter. "Allow us then to set aside our personal attachments and consider this as men of reason."

Darwin folded his hands together and cleared his throat, then nodded for him to continue.

"Less than twenty years ago you and I uncovered one of the most fundamental principles operating upon our natural world. Would it not be reckless then, to suggest after millennia of investigations have only so recently yielded such a profound discovery, that science has suddenly exhausted its stock of mysteries? That we now know everything about the world order?"

Though silent, that formidable countenance assented to the incontrovertible.

"Let us also consider how laws of nature are often derived from observed facts. Sometimes, those facts and the laws they heralded are initially declaimed as heretical yet historically upheld. Copernicus and Galileo, to cite but two examples. Currently, there are dozens of honest and intelligent men, including several reputable scientists, who attest to scrupulous observation"– already Darwin was shaking his head, blinking hard – "of supernatural phenomena. Ergo, such phenomena, as creditable observed facts, suggest a hitherto unknown law of nature. A law that extends our knowledge of the natural world in a manner similar to when natural selection imparted new insight for creationists. Hence the study of spiritualism no more embarks upon theism than your own assay of molluscs."

Darwin slammed his fist, rattling the plates and cutlery. "I beg to differ!"

In short order, the publican wandered over, bringing with him the smell of fried fish. "Can't say I thought it'd be the two of you upsetting the peace of me other patrons."

"A minor difference in point of view is all," said Darwin.

The man snorted. "Aye, that's usually how it starts." He glanced from one to the other, satisfying himself, then cleared the plates. "Would you be wanting another brandy, sir? Or another ale for the gentleman?"

Darwin, head bowed, said no.

Not half finished his pint, Wallace too declined.

"Right, then. I suppose I'm safe to leave you two on the understanding this here is a quiet room."

The shudder of floorboards accompanied the man's departure.

"Dear fellow, how terrible of me," Wallace said. "I had no inkling that I might upset you to such a degree."

A tremor ran beneath the great scientist's left eye and his hands fled to the underside of the table. "I apologize for my outburst. As you may have already ascertained, I lack a certain tolerance for social involvement." Darwin's blue-grey eyes again latched onto Wallace, but softly, perhaps with sadness. "To re-coin the earlier analogy, we remain two parents of a precocious and beautiful child. We each clasp her by the hand and wish to lead her safely into adulthood. Instead, I fear she will be torn asunder."

Wallace gently asked, "You wish for me to let go?"

"We speak of my life's work. You, you have many fields of study, many causes, many prescriptions."

"Each one integral to evolutionary theory."

The great man was once again whistling through his nose. "How? Precisely how is resolution of the Irish Question, or the rights of tenant farmers, or the rights of women, related to natural selection?"

Wallace shifted onto the front edge of his seat. "A fine enquiry, so let us consider certain facts. Since that ancient epoch in which our species first descended from their trees to achieve bipedal form, the physical anatomy of the human brain has not varied to any significant degree. Think about that! Even in the most uncivilized society – those Fuegians you long ago encountered – you will find a brain without physical distinction to our own. Thus evolution by natural selection has had no effect upon physical development of the human mind. Why is that?"

"I utterly fail to see how your question answers mine."

"Please, bear with me."

Silence, albeit that Darwin's chest heaved rather hard.

"Consider further," Wallace said, "that of all the species populating this planet, humans alone are endowed with the gift of consciousness. That self-awareness provides opportunity not merely for survival, but for qualitative improvement in our own life and that of others. So, while natural selection has ceased to operate on the physical aspect of the human mind, judicious use of our mental faculties can foster other forms of organic change. This, *this*, suggests the next stage of our evolution occurs not at the level of the anatomical but the mental. It also explains human development where survival of the fittest fails. After all, what adaptive purpose is served by a musical talent, or the innate ability to draw, or to write great literature, or perform higher mathematics, or even to attain an eye for beauty? There is no Malthusian – no Darwinian – purpose."

"That proves nothing."

"But the implications are dramatic: Dickens' literary excellence produces the most moving depictions of mankind's cruel indifference to the plight of the poor and unfortunate. He thus helps instil compassion and commends social, economic and political change. Brahms' cello sonata expresses a range of human emotion that promotes introspection among even the cynical. Rembrandt's paintings of cripples, prostitutes, Jews and beggars advances democratic and anti-authoritarian impulses. How do we account for these?"

Darwin did not answer. Wallace noticed that conversations elsewhere had snuffed like candle flames.

"Peeler," someone hissed.

All eyes now trained in one direction. Wallace followed their collective interest to a policeman who stood rooted at the doorway as if further ingress at such a den of iniquity would taint him. He squinted into the room's shadowed corners while one set of fingers conspicuously tapped his truncheon. As though any of these slippery fellows posed a physical menace! When the policeman's gaze fell upon himself and Darwin his eyes widened. He tipped the brim of his helmet (what could he imagine their presence might signify?) then continued his sweep of the premises. Apparently contented that whoever he was seeking was not present, that blue tunic disappeared the way it first came.

Around them, voices flickered again.

Wallace made sure he once again had Darwin's attention. "What I was saying, dear sir, is that humans enjoy the distinct ability to aid their fellow men. This facility coexists with irrefutable evidence of spiritual phenomena. Spirits have influence in the earthly sphere. If we are receptive, they can guide us, direct us on how to help others. When all of mankind has been uplifted, when it is spared the pain and afflictions which prevail to this day – not only nature's harsh events, such as plagues and storms and famines, but the oppression of the weak by the powerful – we will not only overcome our physical limitations, we will have fully developed our intellectual powers and ennobled our spiritual being. In so doing, our own evolution is perfected. How is this anything other than the most desirable aim? The most intelligent design? It completes evolutionary theory. It is the very purpose for all of the material universe. As such it not only belongs amongst the natural sciences, but ranks at its highest echelon. You ask why I involve myself in myriad causes? I answer that it is our life's purpose."

It was a few moments before Darwin spoke. His tone was not unkindly. "After losing my precious Annie, then Charles Junior, an afflicted child who brought no harm to anyone or anything, Mrs. Darwin and I despaired and we too sought a way to cope through the pain. The grief-stricken are quite vulnerable. So when the possibility that a beloved might not be forever lost is offered to us, who wouldn't find temptation? And how much more so when others in the family subscribe? My wife's own brother, Eras, is an avowed spiritualist. Thus I refrain from judgment on your choices. However," his voice hardened, "that makes the offence of Slade and his ilk all the more egregious. They feed pandemonium by fraud and it gives false hope."

"It is only a false hope if proven such after an objective investigation. I do not ask you to subscribe to my belief, nor did I solicit the Association's attention with such an intent. I merely ask you to concede there exists an alternate theory supported by credible observations. I ask you to investigate that theory with an open mind."

"Your personal belief needn't move you to advocate the

idea before the entire country! By lending your name to its cause, you offer this movement an air of legitimacy. Worse, you insulate it under the reputable cloak of science and in the same stroke stain your good name in the annals."

"Scientific ideas must circulate freely if they are to promote discussion and knowledge. And when I enter into that public realm, I cannot see how in all decency I might discard the truth any more than I might omit my shirt and trousers."

He thought Darwin would surely concede his point. Instead, the scientist sank his head into his hands and looked as if he might be ill. A moment passed, then the elder statesman complained that the day had taken its toll. He slowly rose from the table.

Wallace also stood. "I gather I have contributed to your decline this day?"

The slightest shade of a smile appeared on Darwin's lips. "No, I should think this is something I have truly brought on myself."

With that, he bade Wallace goodbye.

CHAPTER TWENTY-SEVEN
London November 1, 1876

A surging black pall obscured his view, the train's progress now marked only by the trestles' liturgy: *thick fog … thick fog … thick fog*. Wallace wondered if the dark scarf of smoke resulted from too much coal in the firebox, or perhaps excessive draft in the boiler tubes. Whatever its cause, he hoped the fireman would rectify it shortly – the gloom hardly helped his mood.

Before the window had shrouded, they'd groaned out of Sutton station, passing New Town, where he saw the future of the English countryside writ in the banality of ever-expanding suburban houses, and then the train entered a broad valley. Bloated loamy clouds insinuated themselves atop the valley like angry fists and an ashen drizzle fell upon the landscape. They passed trampled cornfields, forlorn yards of sinewy hop vines and rows of barren cherry trees in witchy black orchards. Then the glass went smoky dark.

The train would be in Dorking within the half-hour, but it was not soon enough for him. He felt trodden down after his lunch with Darwin. As intelligent a companion as one might ever hope, yet he sifted through everything for scientific cause and effect. As though solace for grief or disappointment might project itself in some conjurer's tricks. As if certain things don't exist in their own right. Wallace's hands stumbled into his coat pockets and there, like an old crust of bread, he came upon the Royal Medal. Perhaps Annie had been right, that he ought to have worn it in court. But would it have deflected any of the damage this day? Unlikely. Indeed, he recalled that the committee recommending him for the award had made a point of noting it was principally for his work in biogeography.

It seemed the great men of science were forever impressed by clear boundaries. Well, boundaries weren't mapped unless someone went into the field and obtained data. If he had proposed his oceanic divide without evidence they would have made him a laughing stock. Yet from their armchairs they tell him of what folly he engages when it comes to spiritual phenomena. It made no more sense coming from Mr. Darwin's mouth than when others had tried to explain it.

Wallace stared out the train window. The locomotive's funnel of steam trailed white once more. In the far distance were the Surrey Hills and Dorking, where he and Annie had made a fresh start. Their small tribe strong and healthy. No matter the Slade affair. No matter anything. He knew Henry Slade would be convicted at the end of his trial. That certainty had been betrayed by all the courtroom antics. Betrayed by predisposition. What the magistrate failed to see in his rush to deliberate upon facts and law, and what Darwin failed to see in his determined quest for cause and effect, was that the truth sometimes resided elsewhere. Eyes pressed firmly to their microscopes or to their magnifying glasses, or their telescopes, they failed to see the natural world in all its beauty. Sometimes indistinct, sometimes merely promised in a glimmer, this beauty conferred precious counterweight to so many ills. And he thought himself ever blessed; he'd savoured more than his fair share of beauty.

Slowly they drew towards the Surrey Hills and he felt his emotions lift like the resolving grey clouds over the valley. As the carriage rattled and swayed, bearing him ever closer to home, he recalled the sublimity of all those glorious birds of paradise. The conical horns of volcanic tuff he'd once seen rising starkly from a tropical cobalt sea. He remembered the durian's velvet custard on his tongue. The yeasty warm breaths of his sleeping children when he bent his face close to theirs. The pink button of Annie's pursed lips. And, finally, there were the rustling waters of the Rio Uaupés, scrubbing away all sound from the viscous air inside a thatch hut, while his feverish eyes beheld a shimmering green silhouette, one that canted and wove, its shadowed essence pulsing, brimming with the certainty of life.

The train was passing grasslands, glistening stalks flattened by rain, and Wallace opened the window, eager for some air. At that moment the tracks bent left. The train's curling motion caught him off guard and he landed heavily in his seat. Glancing up again, he saw inside the window a butterfly, its fluttering violet wings luminous as they caught the light. A common blue. Strange, he thought, it was well past their season. The butterfly landed atop the seat back opposite and perched as if examining him, as though he were the one defying odds. A hardy specimen. Wallace wondered then if perhaps he'd been too hasty in making his identification, judging by size and colour without taking account of the individual. Might there be some unique adaptation he'd missed? He leaned forward for a closer look, but the next instant the butterfly rose, and in a flight more graceful than he could allow, it sailed out the open window and was instantly gone from view.

Wallace settled back into his seat, smiling. A discovery for another day, then.

Author's Note:

In writing about Alfred Wallace I've tried to remain heedful of historical fact while approaching the story imaginatively. To serve the story better, I've occasionally departed from the strict chronology of events in the historical record. I've also woven into the narrative several letters that are genuine, albeit edited. Characters other than minor ones are real with the exception of Ramsay Newcastle which is based on Joseph Hooker Jr. who took a rather adversarial position against Wallace. But given the fact that Hooker played no direct role in the Henry Slade case, I thought it fairer to create the composite character of Newcastle.

Darwin did financially support the prosecution of Slade, but there's no evidence that he met with Wallace. Despite Wallace's prolific writings, he wrote very little about either his brush with death in the Amazon in 1852, or his arrival at a modern theory of evolution in the Spice Islands in 1858, each of which was accompanied by fever.

Acknowledgements:

I am particularly grateful to Alan Sirulnikoff and Dominik Loncar for their unwavering faith and support, and to David Jones, Al Maclachlan, Rick Madonik, Sylvia Romig and Steve Whibley for so generously sharing their thoughts. In researching this story, I have benefited from a multitude of resource materials and highly recommend:

www. people.wku.edu/charles.smith/home.htm
www. wallacefund.info and www. wallaceletters.info

Ross A. Slotten's *The Heretic in Darwin's Court* (Columbia, 2004)
Wallace's autobiography *My Life: A Record of Opinions and Events and The Malay Archipelago* as well as his other books, essays, articles and letters.

For more great reading go to:

www.aurorametro.com

More historical fiction:

The Physician of Sanlucar by Jonathan Falla
978-1-906582-38-8

Kipling and Trix by Mary Hamer
978-1-906582-34-0

Pomegranate Sky by Louise Soraya Black
978-1-906582-10-4

The River's Song by Suchen Christine Lim
978-1-906582-98-2

Leipzig by Fiona Rintoul
978-1-906582-97-5

Liberty Bazaar by David Chadwick
978-1-906582-92-0

Tracks, Racing the Sun by Sandro Martini
978-1-906582-43-2